TJ GREEN

WOLFSHOT

STORM MOON SHIFTERS (BOOK 3)

Wolfshot

Mountolive Publishing

PO Box 28, Vila do Bispo CTT, 8651-909, Portugal

Copyright © 2025 TJ Green

All rights reserved

ISBN eBook: 978-1-991313-20-1

ISBN Paperback: 978-1-991313-21-8

ISBN Hardback: 978-1-991313-22-5

Cover design by Fiona Jayde Media

Editing by Missed Period Editing

This is a work of fiction. Names, characters, businesses, places, events, locales, and incidents are either the products of the author's imagination or used in a fictitious manner. Any resemblance to actual persons, living or dead, or actual events is purely coincidental.

No portion of this book may be reproduced in any form without written permission from the publisher or author, except as permitted by U.S. copyright law.

Contents

One	1
Two	11
Three	18
Four	28
Five	39
Six	48
Seven	58
Eight	67
Nine	78
Ten	85
Eleven	92
Twelve	98
Thirteen	107
Fourteen	117
Fifteen	129
Sixteen	135
Seventeen	145
Eighteen	155

Nineteen	162
Twenty	173
Twenty-One	181
Twenty-Two	187
Twenty-Three	196
Twenty-Four	204
Twenty-Five	213
Twenty-Six	220
Twenty-Seven	228
Twenty-Eight	236
Twenty-Nine	242
Thirty	250
Thirty-One	265
Thirty-Two	276
Thirty-Three	285
Thirty-Four	293
Thirty-Five	302
Thirty-Six	311
Thirty-Seven	323
Author's Note	335
About the Author	337
Other Books by TJ Green	339

One

Maverick Hale sipped his whiskey, his attention fixed on the large, centuries-old tapestry that hung on the wall of his flat above Storm Moon.

It was in excellent condition despite its age, with only a few areas where the silk thread had worn thin, or the colour had faded. It was a map of Medieval Europe, and many countries bore little resemblance to their current iteration. Images of mythical creatures were scattered across the landscape, as were castles and rivers, settlements and lakes, with the borders marked in red silk. He found it hypnotic, and ever since he'd bought it from the shifter auction, he had spent a lot of time lost in the details. Particularly the wolf heads stitched in gold thread that marked safehouses for shifters across the region. *Or so he had been told.* It was the main selling point for the item. He wondered if such sanctuaries still existed, and if so, what state would they be in, or what secrets might they reveal.

A knock at the door drew his attention, and with a shock, he realised the room was now dark, the sole light coming from the angled light fitting that illuminated the tapestry.

"Come in!" he called, turning on a lamp on the side table.

Arlo, the pack second, and manager of Storm Moon entered, dreadlocks swinging and a bounce in his step. "I see you're still obsessing over that." He nodded to the tapestry as he crossed to his side. "Planning a trip to find them?"

"I must admit, the thought had crossed my mind. It would take months, though. Years, actually." His attention returned to the tapestry. "There are roughly two dozen across France, Germany, Spain, Portugal, the Netherlands, and Scandinavia."

"And further. Eastern Europe, too." Arlo frowned, leaning in. "Istanbul, by the look of it." He shook his head, a trace of wonder in his expression. Maverick knew he loved history, particularly shifter history. "All those old empires, vanished. The map is nowhere near detailed enough, Mav. You would need more specific directions. I wonder if there's an accompanying document that goes with it. Or was. You'd think if it existed, it would have been at that auction."

Maverick sighed as Arlo voiced his own thoughts. "True. I should just consider it an object of beauty and leave it at that. Just like the other lots I bought."

The shifter auction at Burton and Knight had taken place a month earlier, in March, and had attracted a huge crowd of enthusiasts. He hadn't been intending to go, but in the end, curiosity had got the better of him, and he went with Harlan, the American occult collector who worked for The Orphic Guild, and Morgana, one of the witches who lived at Moonfell. Only Harlan had been to an auction before, and he helped them navigate the nuances and complexities. Morgana had bought a variety of documents—for their library, she had explained, as if she had needed to justify her interest. Maverick, however, had only bought one document, a hand-drawn map of wolf-shifter pack territories and sacred sites in the 1500s, encompassing the UK and Europe. He thought it complemented the tapestry well.

His other purchases had been a collection of wolf head amulets, an engraved wolf mask inlaid with moonstones said to aid transformation, and a few other objects.

There were lots he had been interested in that he couldn't afford, and others he would have dearly liked but went to unknown bidders. Harlan had been purchasing on behalf of several of his clients who he refused to name. The whole event had been fascinating, the sheer volume of objects overwhelming, and it had renewed Maverick's interest in his own history. He wasn't just a wolf-shifter and the pack alpha. He was part of something bigger that had been passed down through generations, and maybe across borders from the Otherworld. For a moment, he felt lost in the sheer volume of all that had gone before, and suddenly knew how collectors developed obsessions. He was developing one with shifter art.

"You've gone blank on me again," Arlo said, a trace of amusement in his voice.

"Sorry." Maverick dragged himself back to the present and turned to Arlo. "Everything okay downstairs?"

It was Thursday evening, one of their busiest nights. A band was booked for the club, a local group that promised to draw a big crowd.

"Yeah, all good. We should make a lot of money tonight. But Hal hasn't turned up. He's normally always on time, and as yet, he's a no-show. He's not answering his phone, either. I asked Hunter to go and check on him."

Maverick frowned. "We promoted him, right?"

"A couple of months ago, while we were dealing with Owen. He works the club's entrance now. He's good at it, too."

"I agree. He's management material." Hal had dark, shoulder-length hair that he tied in a top knot, and always wore a good suit. He handled the difficult customers well, and never let them abuse the two women who manned the ticket booth and cloakroom. He was also the oldest son of one of the shifter families who had been members of the Storm Moon Pack for years. "Perhaps he's been held up in traffic. Or maybe he was out last night, and had a skinful."

Even as Maverick was saying it, though, he thought it unlikely, and so did Arlo, from the look on his face. "He uses the Tube, and he's not a drinker. Plus, it takes a lot to get us drunk, as you well know."

"Who does he hang out with?"

"A few of the staff, but he worked last night and apparently went straight home. It's not far. Edge of Tooting."

A trace of worry gripped Maverick, but he shook it off. "I'm sure there's an easy explanation."

"Let's hope so. I just thought I'd keep you informed, anyway."

"Did Hunter go alone?"

"No. He went with Tommy."

Hunter and Tommy were from Cumbria, and had joined the Storm Moon Pack together, both looking for a change. Hunter needed a distraction after splitting up with a witch who lived in Cornwall, and Tommy... Well, Tommy liked to party, and London offered that. Both were proving to be excellent additions to the pack, and both were good fighters, especially Tommy, who was as enormous and hairy as a bear.

Pleased with the choice, Maverick nodded. "Good. Although, if anyone attacked Hal, I'd be surprised. Everyone knows he's a member of our pack. They attack him, they attack us. Maybe it's something else. Girl trouble?"

"Not as far as I know. He seemed like his usual self last night." Arlo was already turning away, his long stride taking him across Maverick's luxurious flat to the door. "I need to get back downstairs, but I'll keep you informed."

Hunter lifted his head and sniffed the corridor outside of Hal's flat. The rich scent of spices was coming from a flat down the hall, and incense drifted from another, but Hal's flat gave nothing away.

He knocked on the door and raised his voice. "Hey, Hal! It's Hunter and Tommy. You okay?"

Tommy pressed his ear to the door and shook his head. "Can't hear a thing."

Hunter dropped to the ground and tried to peer under the door, but it was fitted well, leaving no clue as to what lay beyond. On his feet again, he said, "This place is nice. I don't get dodgy vibes. You?"

Tommy shook his head and brushed his hair off his face. "No. Well painted. Smells good. Friendly. Nice area, too." He stepped back, assessing the door. "Want me to smash it so we can get in?"

"Fuck, no!" Hunter loved Tommy like a brother, but sometimes he wondered what he was thinking. "He wouldn't thank us for that, and the neighbours would call the police. Besides, don't you listen to me? I have these!" He fished the lockpicks from his pocket and swung them in front of Tommy's face. "Domino taught me how to use them."

Domino was the head of security for Storm Moon, and a woman with many skills. And she was seriously hot.

Tommy smirked. "Private lessons. Is that the only thing she taught you?"

"I'm not telling."

Hunter and Domino flirted a lot, but so far, that was all. *For now.* The other night, though, as she'd shown him how to use the lockpicks on Arlo's office door, they had leaned in, heads close. He was inches away from kissing her when Jax, another shifter on the security team, had appeared behind them, and they had eased apart, Jax smirking.

Making sure the hallway remained empty, Hunter tried various picks, glad he'd spent so much time practicing what was a very fiddly job, and eventually the lock released. He eased the door open. The flat was in darkness, so he fumbled for the light, flicked it on, and slipped inside.

The apartment was nicely furnished, but reasonably plain, and very small. Within a minute they had searched the whole place, and there was no sign of Hal. The bed was made, the rooms were clean, and there was only a mug in the sink.

"At least," Tommy said, heading to the curtained windows, "there's no sign of a fight. Why are the curtains drawn, though? If he went out today and was held up somewhere, the curtains would be open, right? Unless he likes to live in the dark."

"Unless he didn't come home after the club last night," Hunter pointed out, worry knotting in his gut. "This place smells stale. Unused."

"Which means what?" Tommy scowled. "Is he injured somewhere? Dead?"

Hunter glared at him. "Don't even suggest that."

"I don't fucking like the idea! I like Hal. He's a great bloke. But why else would he not be here? Even if he found a girl to go home with, he'd still be at work. He's focussed. He doesn't get distracted over women like someone I know."

"Neither do I, you wanker. And Domino is not some girl, so shut up!"

"Tetchy!"

Hunter ignored him, focussing on the room. "Let's check the wardrobe. Maybe he had to leave quickly."

"His parents are in the pack!"

"Maybe he got into trouble and kept it from everyone. Maybe someone threatened him last night," Hunter reasoned. "Sometimes people have secrets, Tommy. Unlike you, who is an open pamphlet."

Tommy flipped him the bird.

Hal's bedroom had a built-in wardrobe, and it was filled with a handful of suits and more casual clothing. His toiletries were in the bathroom, and an overnight bag and suitcase were at the bottom of the wardrobe.

Hunter knew this was bad news. Hal was missing, and they had no idea where he was. "Let's trace his route home. He'd have taken the Tube and used the main road, but there's a small park close by. Maybe he wanted to stretch his wolf. No harm in checking, right?"

Tommy nodded, still studying the flat, and from the grim look on his face, Hunter knew he was worried too.

Arlo was relieved to see Hunter and Tommy walking across Storm Moon club's dance floor, shouldering their way through the crowd, oblivious to the dancing. Dionysus, their resident DJ, was playing a set before the band started. The pair had been gone for a few hours, and he'd started to have fears for their safety, too. However, Hal wasn't with them.

"They're back, Dom."

Domino, a slim and muscular woman in her thirties with long, chestnut brown hair, looked up from the computer. "With Hal?"

"No."

By the time she'd walked around the desk, Tommy and Hunter had entered the office, both looking frustrated and wary. Hunter's eyes skimmed to Domino, but there was no hint of his usual flirting in them, and his gaze landed on Arlo. "He's not there. We think he didn't go home last night." He ran through what they had found, Tommy adding details.

Arlo sank onto the sofa in the corner while he listened, and the others joined him in the seating area, all four leaning together over the table in the centre. "No sign of a struggle?" Arlo asked.

Hunter shook his head. "It was clean and tidy, much as I'd expect from Hal. We decided to check what we think would be his route home, too. We even thought he might have gone for a run in the closest park. Didn't find a damn thing, other than a faint scent of him." Hunter sighed. "Days old, I estimate."

"Any blood?" Domino asked.

"No. Not his, anyway."

Arlo had experienced a creeping dread ever since Hal had failed to arrive at work, a feeling he'd distanced himself from as he tried to be rational and not leap to conclusions. Hal was a young, fit wolf-shifter who would not be easily hurt. He was clever, and he could fight in his human body as well as in his wolf. Now, however, his fears came flooding back. "This is bad. Very bad. Do you think he's been kidnapped?"

Domino snorted. "Why kidnap him? He doesn't have loads of money, nor does his family. He's not an influential shifter with political affiliations, and no dark secrets either, I'm sure." She focussed her intense stare on Arlo. "Have you checked with his parents?"

"Of course. I called them earlier to make sure he wasn't with them, before I asked Hunter and Tommy to look for him. Kept it light, obviously, and when his mum said he wasn't, I suggested he was probably just running late."

"Was she worried?"

"No, just puzzled. She was at the unit with his dad." His parents ran a service garage that repaired cars, and Hal's younger brother had started working there. "Said he didn't often go there. They always caught up at home. She sounded busy. I told her not to worry and I'd chase it up." He flopped back against the cushions. "Bollocks. Now I need to call her again and she's going to be worried sick."

"Let me." Domino was on her feet and striding to the desk. "Maybe his brother has heard from him. Even his sister."

"His sister is fourteen. I doubt she'll know anything." Arlo checked the time. It was close to nine, and Hal should have been there at five. "I don't like this at all."

"Me neither, mate." Hunter frowned. "You want us to go back out? We could have missed something."

Arlo shook his head. He was half listening to Domino's phone call, so he already knew the bad news before she rejoined them. He pre-empted her. "He's not there."

"No, and now they're worried, too. I asked her to call other family, old friends. Fuck." Arlo didn't need to tell Domino anything, as she was already phoning again. "Time to tell Maverick and make a plan."

Two

Maverick assembled his senior staff as soon as Domino called him, and they crowded into the Security Office that overlooked Storm Moon's dance floor.

Along with Domino and Arlo, Vlad, the broad-shouldered blond giant from Denmark who was the club's Deputy Manager, had joined them. He leaned against the one-way window, part watching the floor below, part watching the office. Grey, the shaven-haired Deputy Head of Security had been watching the crowd by the bar in the main room, but now he scanned the camera feeds in the corner while he listened. Tommy and Hunter remained, eager to help.

Maverick had also summoned Jet, the petite woman who was employed as one of the bar staff but acted as the pack's spy, and after gathering as much information as possible from the others, he turned to her. As usual, she was dressed entirely in black, and her short sleeves displayed her tattooed arms. She perched on the edge of the desk, legs crossed, high-heeled ankle boots and short skirt showing off her shapely legs.

"Please tell me," he said, turning to her, "that you have heard something from the punters."

"Just the usual, and I've been sure to know about new arrivals in the community, or any feuds that have sprung up." She shrugged. "I always do. There are the usual rumblings about the North London Pack. Castor's pack is growing. A few lone wolves have joined and have jobs in his pool hall. He's been involved with moving stolen goods—again. However, none of that involves Hal. There are rumours that a few bird-shifters have arrived from Europe, but they haven't been here yet. Therians are doing their usual dodgy things, such as trading on the occult black market. And of course, there are a variety of magical practitioners, but again, nothing unusual. Plus, we have had new customers, but we always do." Her booted foot kicked the table as she adjusted her position. "The staff know that Hal hasn't arrived. It's unsettling everyone, because they all know it's unlike him."

"Did you speak to him last night?"

"Sure. He seemed fine. Winked as he left, and said 'See you tomorrow.' We had a good night. No issues with the customers. No drunks that had to be thrown out. There must be a rational explanation, right?"

Maverick walked to the window to stare at the dance floor below as he gathered his thoughts, aware that everyone was watching, and no doubt debating a dozen courses of action, just like he was. He wanted to see Hal saunter in, but knew that wouldn't happen. He was in trouble, and already Maverick's wolf was rising. *If he was dead...* Maverick pushed that thought away. If someone had something to prove, a bone to pick with Maverick or his pack, Hal's body would have been left as a warning, just like before. This was something different.

"All right," he said, coming to a decision. "We will all question the staff tonight—human and shifter—asking what they know about Hal, or what he's been up to. Or anyone who might have any issues with him. Anything unusual. The slightest thing! Then we search Hal's route home again, and we have a pack meeting tomorrow—if we haven't found him, of course. He'll have friends outside of the pack, too. He could be with them. I'll talk to his parents, follow up on Domino's call." He could envision that conversation now. *It was going to be a nightmare.*

"Are you sure?" Domino asked. "He's on my staff."

"It's my responsibility. I'm the alpha."

"And if he's still missing tomorrow?" Grey asked, arms folded. "What then?"

"We put the word out that he's missing," Arlo said, "to the entire paranormal community, and we tell them that if a single hair on his head is damaged, they answer to us."

Tommy grunted. "Don't wait for tomorrow. Send the word out now. We have a full house. Tell the security team and other staff to put pressure on the paranormal community now. Spook enough people so that if someone has got him for some weird fucking reason, they'll release him quickly. No offense, Jet," he turned to her apologetically, "but your style is low key, as it should be. The time for that has passed."

Maverick nodded his agreement. "I like that idea. I want news, and I want it quickly. We have hours left before closing. Let's stir up some shit."

"If he walks in, looking just dandy," Grey pointed out, "we will all look like worried grannies. He's a few hours late. Boys will be boys."

But Maverick's gut told him it was more than that. Maybe it was his alpha super-sense, or just plain intuition. He didn't have a direct connection to any pack member, like a psychic link, but he had good instincts. "I don't care. We'll look like a protective pack, and it will be a good reminder to our members to turn up on time, unless they want me breathing down their necks. Plus, the wider community will know not to fuck with us." He checked the time. "Tommy, Hunter, sweep the immediate surroundings, then the common and the park. We'll meet at midnight in here. Don't be l ate."

By midnight, as Domino had suspected, they still knew nothing, despite questioning customers and staff. It was as if Hal had vanished into thin air.

"Let's use Jake," she suggested to the gathered group once they were all back in the office again. "The therian we have a deal with."

The band had stopped playing, and Dionysus, the DJ, had taken over again. But he was winding down, and the crowd was thinning, which gave Domino the mental space to distance herself from the situation and approach it objectively.

"That shifty bastard?" Vlad rolled his eyes. "Why him?"

"Because he'll know shifters that we won't! And he owes us. Plus, he helped save my life. He might help us find Hal." She refused to say *save*, because that suggested he needed saving, and it wasn't something she was prepared to admit yet.

Jake was a therian-shifter who had been involved in the business with Pûcas and the therians when Kane had been murdered. They'd had to sedate him to capture him, and in the course of catching him, she had ended up being captured by therians herself. He'd eventually told them the place to look for Domino, and she'd met him a couple of times since. They had all presumed he would end up hanging out at Storm Moon a lot, but apart from the occasional visit, he'd kept to his old haunts.

"We have his number," she added, when everyone looked sceptical, "and no one is offering me any better suggestions."

"I've got one," Arlo said, eyes widening. "We ask the witches to help. We have items belonging to Hal here. He left a hat in the staff room. They can use a spell to search for him."

"It's after midnight," Grey pointed out. "It's a bit late to be rattling them up."

"They keep late hours like we do." Arlo looked pointedly at Maverick. "We shouldn't delay."

Arlo meant, of course, the Moonfell witches who lived in the Gothic mansion on the edge of Richmond Park. It was a magical place, steeped in secrets and history, and they were now firm friends. Almost part of the pack. Plus, Arlo still loved Odette, the youngest resident witch, even though he wouldn't admit it. Probably even to himself. The pack's connection with them had grown even deeper when Morgana started seeing Monroe, one of the security team members who was currently in the club, ensuring that everyone was leaving.

Maverick was considering their suggestions as he sipped his rum and Coke, perched on the edge of the desk. Domino knew him well enough to know that he may look calm, but he was furious at the situation. "The witches are a good idea, but let's save that for tomorrow. As desperate as we are to find Hal, it's not fair to disturb them at this hour. Besides, I really want to explore all options first." He turned to Domino. "Call Jake and ask him to come here. Or we'll go to him."

Domino turned away to make the call, but the phone kept ringing, and when he didn't answer, she gave up. "No answer," she explained, facing the others. "We have an address, so we could try him now?"

She expected Maverick to leap to his feet and lead the hunt, but instead he shook his head. "No, not tonight. We don't know if he's just out or in trouble, and I want more information before we go charging in. Something feels off. *Very off.* This calls for caution." He stood and paced to the screens showing the feed from the security cameras, watching the club empty and the staff start to clear glasses and tidy up. He finally turned around to study them. "We've been questioning people for hours, and it's been a long day. I'm worried about Hal, of course, but we'll leave it for tonight and start fresh tomorrow. And that means a pack meeting. Let's call it for midday, Arlo." Arlo nodded. It was part of his role to organise pack events. "With luck, we'll hear from Hal before then, and we'll laugh it off. I'll shout a lot, of course, for worrying the shit out of us. But no hunting tonight, unless a few of you go together."

There were a flurry of nods around the room, all of them unsettled.

Domino still wanted to pursue finding Jake now, but she accepted her alpha's decision. He was right. They didn't know much at all, and the whole thing was odd. Charging out at night might leave more of them in trouble. "I'd like to find Jake tomorrow afternoon, if Hal still hasn't turned up. I'll take someone with me."

"Me!" Hunter said. "I want to help. I can't sit around all day doing nothing."

Plus, Domino knew he wanted to spend time with her, too. If she was honest, she wanted to spend time with him. She'd been resisting a date, but this was work, right? She nodded. "Thanks. Two of us should be enough."

"Which means," Grey said, turning to Arlo, "you should visit the witches."

"And maybe," Maverick said, eyes on Grey, "we call Maggie. But let's not rattle that particular cage just yet."

Grey just laughed.

Maggie Milne, DI with the Paranormal Policing Unit, was a good friend who was getting friendlier by the minute with Grey. They had a spark. Chemistry. But calling in Maggie would make things more official, so Domino could understand why he'd want to hold off.

Domino took that as her cue to address her team. "All right. Let's finish up here and head home. Tomorrow will be a long day."

Three

Maverick knew it would be a difficult pack meeting, but it was worse than he'd imagined.

They had gathered in the bar at Storm Moon, which was closed until that evening, and was a common place for the pack to meet. The windows, normally shut and sealed with heavy wooden shutters, had been opened to let in a fresh spring breeze, but it didn't lighten the mood. Instead, the weak sunshine illuminated a very worried group of friends and families. They had asked lots of questions, and unfortunately, he couldn't answer many of them. Worse was that Hal's mother had been tearful, and his father angry. And no one could tell him anything useful.

"I suggest," Maverick said, finishing up, "that you travel together at all times, especially at night. No lone trips. No bravado. You hear anything, and you bring it to me. We have other options that we're exploring today, and I will keep you all updated."

"If we can't find him?" Barratt asked. The old alpha was always willing to unsettle rather than reassure.

"We will." Maverick's tone brooked no further argument, wishing he'd just shut the fuck up for once or leave the pack. He'd willingly ceded the alpha position, but he couldn't stop interfering.

He watched the pack leave, examining them for expressions of guilt or secrets, but saw nothing to give him any concern. He shouldn't distrust his own pack, but feuds happened, and he had to be realistic. Only the security team remained. They were mainly male, but a few females were on the team, too. Cecile and Fran, both very capable fighters and trackers. And Domino, of course, the head of the team.

Before Maverick could address them with the day's plans, a shout from the front door that led to the street summoned his attention. John, who regularly manned the door in the evening, had been locking up after the pack left, but now he called Maverick over. "You have a visitor. I think you'll want to see him. I'm just not sure if you want him in here."

"Who?"

"Castor Pollux."

Maverick groaned on hearing the alpha of the North London Pack was on his doorstep. "You're kidding me. Who with?" He had a vision of him bringing an entourage of his heavies.

"Just him, surprisingly. Do you want me to let him in?"

"No, I'll take him to my flat. Tell him I'll be with him in a minute." Maverick called Arlo over. "Castor's here, so I'll leave you and Domino to organise a search. You know my thoughts on it. Ask the local businesses as well—all of them. But in twos."

Arlo nodded. "I'll head to Moonfell, while Domino and Hunter find Jake. Sure you don't want me with you and Castor? Or one of the team?"

"He came alone."

Arlo raised an eyebrow. "Really?"

"Really. I don't know whether to think it's good or bad. I guess I'll soon find out. Better not keep him waiting. You know how twitchy he gets."

Knowing he'd left everything in good hands, Maverick stepped outside with a nod of thanks to John, and found Castor leaning against the wall of the building, observing his surroundings through narrowed eyes. He was tall and lean, with high cheekbones made even more prominent by the fact that Castor's dark, shoulder-length hair was pulled up on the top of his head in a knot, the sides shaved. The last time he'd seen Castor, there'd been a huge fight in his pool hall—not instigated by Maverick's pack. Many things had been broken, including bones, but they had parted on relatively good terms. He still didn't like him, though.

He stuck his hand out, determined to be pleasant. "Castor. Good to see you. I think."

Castor smirked as he gave his hand a firm shake. "Same." He nodded at the departing pack. "You had a meeting. Trouble?"

"Possibly," he said warily. "I presume you have issues, too, or you wouldn't be here. Let's not talk on the street, though. Come up to my flat."

"You got things to hide in your bar?"

"Just meeting number two." He led the way around the building and through his flat's entrance, and then up the stairs to the first floor. "I'm surprised you're alone."

"I needed to clear my head. Think. I can't do that with Hammer gobbing off in my ear."

"Ah, Hammer. Always a delight." Hammer was Castor's second-in-command, and he was a brute.

"But he's good at what he does."

"So is Domino, and she's a lot better looking, too."

"Can't argue with that."

It had been chilly outside, the April weather asserting itself and promising rain after what had been a sunny morning. Fortunately, Maverick's flat was warm. "Leave your jacket on the chair, Castor. You want coffee or beer? Or something stronger?"

"Beer is just fine." Castor wore a boxy leather jacket, and he slipped it off and threw it over the closest chair as Maverick suggested. "Nice place this, Maverick. No expense spared, I see."

"It's my home. I like comfort." Maverick went into the kitchen at the rear of the open plan space, watching Castor take it all in. The long velvet sofa and armchairs, the rich colours, the art. "I know you make a lot of money, so I'm sure it's like your place."

Castor rolled his eyes and sat on the barstool on the other side of Maverick's breakfast bar. "Not exactly. I run towards black leather myself. It's a bit more manly."

"I don't need acres of black leather to prove my manliness, but let's not insult each other just yet. There's time for that." After opening two beers, Maverick passed him one and leaned on the counter. "So, what can I do for you?"

Castor sipped his beer, staring at Maverick as he did, as if deciding whether this was really a good idea. Maverick waited, impassive, and when he lowered the bottle, Castor said, "I think I have a spy in my pack."

"A what?" Maverick's hand remained in the air, beer part way to his mouth. "I hope you don't think I have anything to do with it."

"No. That's why I'm here. I don't know who to trust, and you know that for me to admit that is hard. Very fucking hard."

Maverick walked around the counter and sat on another stool. "I don't understand. Is this some sort of test?"

"No, you dick. I'm serious. Something is stirring around my neck of the woods. I can smell it. It's bad. Dark."

"*You're* bad and dark. You run rackets. Extort money."

"I knew this was a bad idea." Castor made to stand, but Maverick shooed him back to his seat.

"Sorry, but that's the truth. However, I'm listening. Go on."

"I can't put my finger on it, that's the trouble. Normally, I can sniff things down and root them out. I'm belligerent. Persistent. It's why I'm where I am. You know this, because you do it, too. Maybe in a different way to me—"

"Definitely in a different way to you." Maverick might be an alpha, but he was nothing like Castor, who had few boundaries. "Why do you think you have a spy?"

"The pack, some of them, feel different. An air of unease has crept in. They've always fought, we're that type of pack, but…" he shook his head again. "It's just odd."

"I heard you had a few new pack members join you. Lone wolves."

"A month or two ago. They seem solid enough, so I don't think it's them. It's the older members who seem off."

"Even Hammer?" Maverick couldn't keep the incredulity out of his voice. "He's been with you forever."

"Hammer hasn't done anything wrong, but I have this unease that I can't ignore." He shrugged, thoughtful. "He's more distant. It's slight, but I've noticed it. The thing is, no one has challenged me to be the alpha. I've been expecting it. I've been training harder than I have in a long time, and as yet, they're all still listening to me and doing what I ask. It's there, though, Maverick." He stared at him directly, his dark brown eyes almost black. The hard eyes of a brutal wolf. "I would imagine you'd like that, though. For me to go."

"No, not at all. Better the devil you know, and I'd rather deal with you than Hammer." Maverick rubbed his stubbled face, knowing that many of Castor's pack would be far worse than him. He was too tired and had too many of his own problems for this. "Are you asking for my help with something?"

Castor didn't answer his question. "You had a pack meeting just now. Are you feeling challenged? Are things amiss here? I want to know if it's just my pack."

Maverick knew Castor was being honest. This was no weird trap. Besides, a trap to do what? He hadn't asked him for any favours. *Yet. Unless this was a long game...* But Castor might have answers to their issue. "No one is challenging me, and the pack feels fine, apart from one thing. One of my shifters has vanished." He explained succinctly what had happened. "Has that happened to you?"

Castor shook his head. "No. Not that I know of, anyway. My staff are all still at work, but like you, many of my pack have jobs elsewhere. I don't keep daily tabs on them. And before you ask, your missing member has nothing to do with me. Worrying, though. Maybe he had stuff going on you don't know about."

"Maybe. My mate, Kane, did. He was keeping huge secrets that I knew nothing about." Maverick considered himself a good judge of character, so to find that out had shaken his faith in himself. "We are going to find Jake today, regardless. The therian-shifter who knew your club members. You remember, the two shifters who caused the fight in your bar when they tried to run."

"Those!" Castor's mouth twisted. "One has left London—supposedly. The other is very lucky he's still in the pack. He's only there so that I can keep an eye on his sorry ass. That would be Jake, right?"

"Right."

"He's not one of my contacts, so I have no idea where he is." Castor shuffled, eyes darting about the room before settling on Maverick again. "I want to know if you've heard any rumours of another club. An *underground* club."

"Like a nightclub?"

"No. Something else. I think... Fuck." Castor started pacing, a grace to his long strides. He was a formidable fighter. A formidable wolf. All his energy was bundled up tightly, and Maverick had seen it explode. Now, it looked like his wolf wanted out. He steeled himself. But when Castor turned to face him, he was fully in control. "Some kind of fight club."

"Like the film?" Maverick laughed, and then stopped. "Are you serious?"

"No, I don't think it's like the film, but some kind of challenge."

Maverick was bewildered and then worried. "Okay, you need to start making more sense. What exactly have you heard?"

"I overheard a conversation I shouldn't have. A couple of my younger pack members, both full of swagger, were talking quietly in my office and didn't know I was outside. I'd been out and wasn't due back for hours." He shrugged. "Cancelled meeting. Their voices were low, and it was late. A light was on, so I approached very quietly because they shouldn't have been in there and they bloody knew it. It was after closing, by the way, and some staff were behind the bar area, clearing up in the back. No one had seen me enter. I was about to burst in, when I suddenly knew I shouldn't. They were too furtive. I listened, and heard them say something about the place being too important. That to reveal it too soon would be bad. That this was the chance for something new, and that challenge was the wolf way. I think that was it, anyway. And then they stopped talking as if they suspected I was there—which I think is paranoid of me. I was very quiet. I retreated, exited, and then entered again with a bang of the door. By the time I was inside, they were out of my office, the clean-up crew had exited the kitchen, and everything looked normal. So I pretended it was." Castor levelled his gaze at Maverick. "Very un-alpha like behaviour, but you have to know when to confront and when not to, right?"

"Totally. Do you think they knew you heard them?"

He shook his head, looking thoughtful. "No. They acted just like normal."

"And that was all you heard? Just those two?"

"Yeah, but now that I know, I'm watching them. Discreetly, of course. They're tight with another few shifters. All long-standing members. And they all look like they're hiding something."

"What about Hammer? Does he know?"

"I decided to keep my own counsel. Until now. The only reason I'm here is that I know you have no interest in my pack at all, and I need your perspective. Am I being paranoid?"

Maverick considered his story. It sounded fantastical, but he'd experienced the realities of ignoring his instincts only too recently. "No, you're not, and you're wise not to tell Hammer. He's been around a long time, and he would know how to behave around you. But why wouldn't he tell you if he knew something? He's been with you forever!"

"Maybe there's a better option."

Maverick repeated the words Castor had overheard. "'Challenge is the way of the wolf. The place is too important.'"

"That's not the exact words," Castor warned him. "They were almost whispering, but I definitely heard the word 'challenge' loud and clear."

"Hence a fight club. Shit." Maverick placed his half empty beer on the counter. "No wonder you're worried. Logically, if someone has got this weird, underground thing set up, they wouldn't want alphas. We have too much power."

"Doesn't fucking feel like it right now. I feel like I have no power at all. I pride myself on my knowledge, Maverick. Knowledge means power in my world. I am being kept deliberately in the dark."

"Not by everyone, I'm sure. Probably just the handful you suspect." He considered his own pack. "I'm pretty certain my pack are clean. For now, at least. Unfortunately, I'm even more worried about Hal. Say it does exist…are they recruiting?"

"By force? Doesn't sound like a good thing."

"No, it doesn't, but maybe…" Maverick trailed off, trying to follow his thoughts to a logical conclusion. "We don't know enough yet. It could be a bunch of misfits fighting in a cellar, or a sacred site. Or even just a bloody warehouse. Hal's disappearance could be utterly unrelated."

Castor snorted. "Yeah, right."

Maverick laughed. "Yes, my witch friends do not believe in coincidences, either. Have you got a plan?"

"Besides acting like I know nothing, but being as watchful as possible? No. Have you?"

"Nothing concrete yet, but I trust that we'll find out more today, and then we can reconsider our strategy." Another thought struck him. "Does your pack know you're here?"

"No, and it will stay that way. I took a very roundabout route to get here today. I'll do the same on the way back. All public transport—which I despise, by the way."

"Sensible, though. I'll limit your information to just a select few, too. My inner team. *I think*." Maverick rubbed his temples, feeling them tightening with tension as he decided who to include and who not to. "Thank you, Castor. I appreciate your trust. As soon as I know something, I'll tell you." He already had Castor's number, as he had for all the current alphas.

"Only use my personal number," Castor warned as he stood to leave. "And don't leave messages. I'll come to you."

With that, he finished his beer, grabbed his jacket and left, leaving Maverick wondering just what he was getting into.

Four

Arlo cruised along Moonfell's drive with the windows down, taking in the fresh spring scents of the flowers in the borders made more intense by rain. The banks of daffodils and narcissi, crocuses, pansies, primroses, and tulips all reached towards the light, as did the unfurling, bright green leaves on some of the trees and shrubs.

Entering Moonfell's grounds sometimes felt like passing into an enchanted land. All sounds of the outside world, such as the traffic on the road, vanished, replaced by the chorus of birds and the drone of bees. Honeybees that had their own magic. He longed to slip into his wolf and charge around the grounds for the sheer fun of it, but first he had a job to do, and thoughts of Hal banished his good mood.

He parked at the front of the house, utilising the turning circle by the broad steps that led to the entrance. As he exited the car with his backpack, he saw a figure with white hair crouched in the border under one of the windows, a large trug next to her, and an array of gardening tools. Hearing his arrival, Birdie stood, turned, and waved. He waved back, heading immediately to shelter in the large porch, and wondering why Birdie was gardening in the rain. However, as she approached, her trug full of weeds, he realised she was perfectly dry, walking under an invisible umbrella.

"That's a neat trick, Birdie."

"Quite deplorable, really. I should enjoy the rain like the garden does, but I was right in the middle of weeding when it started, and really wanted to finish that patch." She shook her fist at the sky—her tiny fist on her birdlike arm, her small frame barely up to Arlo's chest. "Can you hear me, weather gods? You'll have to do more than that to stop me!" Then she grinned broadly at him. "Plus, the damp makes my arthritis play up, and we can't have that."

"I thought the Goddess got rid of that when she gave you twenty years back."

"She improved it. It still plays up at times." She pushed the front door open, dumping the trug on the porch and wiping her muddy boots on the mat. "Enjoy your youth, Arlo. Age creeps up on you, and the next thing you know, your joints are aching, you can't stay up all night partying anymore, and things sag." She reached up and pinched his cheek, eyes sparkling with amusement. "You're such a handsome boy. You'll age well, I can tell."

Arlo laughed, remembering how playful Birdie could be sometimes. "You've got a spring in your step today."

"Beltane is looming. It always puts fire in my belly. Used to put it in my loins, too." She threw her head back, laughing at her own cheekiness. "The parties we had at Beltane... Anyway, enough of that. I can see you blushing."

"You wish I was. It takes more than that to make me blush." Although, he had to admit that the thought of Birdie prancing around a Beltane fire in her youth was quite entertaining. And now she was grandmother to Odette, the woman he would totally love to see prancing around a Beltane bonfire. *Naked, preferably.*

Birdie smirked, as if knowing exactly what he was thinking, and once again he wondered just how much the Moonfell witches with their perceptive ways could see. Odette, the youngest—and to his eyes, the prettiest—was extremely uncanny. Her ability to see to the truth of things, to paint what could not be seen, and her odd connection to the moon gates made him wonder if she could see that he still loved her. He both hoped she could and couldn't. He didn't want her pity.

"Come on," Birdie said, setting off at a fast trot down the dramatic hallway with its huge curving staircase, colourful rugs, and beautiful wallpaper, "I need a cup of tea and a slice of cake. Then you can tell us all about your missing boy."

"He's not a boy. He's a man." He stared through open doorways as they walked, as usual fascinated by the house. He knew it reasonably well, and yet every time he was here he saw something new. It was as if the house chose to unveil itself to him, little by little. A painting he had never seen before, or a weird occult statue. And always the pervasive scent of incense and wood. He struggled to focus on the issue at hand. "Something's very wrong, Birdie. I know it. Maverick has found out a bit more since we last spoke."

The mysterious club. Like Maverick, he wondered if Castor Pollux was playing tricks, but for what purpose? Perhaps Odette needed to meet him, although the thought of Castor's hard, black eyes appraising Odette made his wolf flex in anger.

Birdie turned to him, stopping at the closed kitchen door, jazz music drifting from the other side. "Take a breath, Arlo. Your wolf can exercise afterwards."

"He's fine. I'm fine. I'm just thinking about something."

"Boys," she muttered, pushing open the door and ushering him into the kitchen. Then she headed to the sink to wash her hands.

He paused just inside the door, as always wowed by the scale of the great Gothic kitchen, with its enormous arched windows, black tiles, and dark cabinets, and the plants hanging in corners. It wasn't his home, or ever had been, and yet he always felt like he was coming home when he stepped inside. *Magic, perhaps.*

Morgana was standing at the six-burner hob top, stirring a large pot of something fragrant, foot tapping as she hummed along to jazz music he didn't recognise. Steam rose in pinks and purples, carrying the scent of summer. *A potion.* Dressed in black, as usual, she looked up and smiled. "There you are. We thought you'd be here earlier."

"I was held up by a meeting." He crossed the room, putting his pack on the kitchen table that was in the dining half of the room, close to the fireplace and small sofa. "A tricky one."

"Your missing shifter. Is it causing trouble?" She watched him, setting her spoon to stirring on its own, a strangely mesmerising action that Arlo had trouble ignoring.

"The pack is worried, of course, and we have told them to travel only in pairs. It seems both over the top and inadequate. The whole thing is just weird."

"It's lucky we like weird, then," Morgana said, putting the kettle on to boil. "Tea?"

"Whatever's going. Thank you."

He moved to the window to see the kitchen garden beyond, but the rain was falling heavier now, blurring out the garden as it streamed down the windows. A gust of wind threw it against the glass with a clatter.

"I think," Birdie said, taking off her layers of cardigans and slipping out of her boots, "that you timed that well. This is settling in for the afternoon. Now, what have you brought us?"

"Hal's hat. He left it in the staff room. Is that okay?"

"Perfect. It may even have a stray strand of hair in it. Now, tell me of Maverick's news." She sat at the table, and Arlo joined her, pulling his pack towards him. He was about to speak when Birdie held up a finger. "Actually, Odette is on her way, so sit tight on that news. She's very keen to help."

He nodded and passed her Hal's hat, a dark grey woollen beanie. "Have a look at that, then, while we wait." He ran his hand through his hair, self-conscious about his appearance. *Idiot. As if it mattered.*

Morgana placed a tray down, containing a mix of mugs and cups next to an earthenware teapot, and a plate with a partially consumed walnut coffee cake topped with buttercream icing. She sat next to Arlo. "Slice?"

"A large one, please."

She smiled. "So good to have men about the house again. I like being able to cook more. Not long now until Lam and Como will be here all the time."

She didn't mention Monroe, who he knew Morgana had gone on a few dates with. According to Monroe, they had gone well, but he hadn't shared details. He decided to respect her privacy. "Are they coming for Beltane?" He knew the witches would celebrate it, as they did all the pagan seasonal celebrations.

"No, unfortunately. They have exams, so both are very busy. We'll have a big summer solstice celebration instead. A proper party, with a bonfire and a ritual. We'll invite the whole family."

"Not all will turn up," Birdie said, a trace of regret crossing her features. "The boys, of course, Ellington and Armstrong. Horty won't miss it. She'll be here for Beltane, too. Maybe Anton and his children. Perhaps Simone, too."

Arlo was familiar with some of the family, but not all. Armstrong was Morgana's father, and Ellington was Odette's. He knew that Horty was Birdie's rambunctious sister. "Sorry, who are Anton and Simone?"

"Anton is Horty's son, and Simone is my middle child."

Morgana rolled her eyes. "Aunt Simone is a little bit like Jemima, Como's mother."

"Horty's daughter," he clarified.

"Yes. She isn't a big fan of Moonfell. Anton likes it, though. He has two lovely children, and his wife is great. They live in Wales, though, so not close."

"Closer than Italy," Birdie pointed out. "Which is fortunate, or Horty would be most put out."

Arlo tried to file the names away, constructing a family tree in his head. "And Simone lives where?"

"Kent," Morgana answered. "Phoebe, my cousin, lives in London with her son, Samuel. Her husband does something flash in banking." She slid a plate with his slice of cake across the table. "I hate the corporate world."

"But she's a witch? Well, all of them?" he asked.

Birdie huffed. "Simone neglects her magic, and Phoebe is in denial. We'll see how long that lasts now that she's nearing menopause."

Arlo blinked, thinking he was hearing things. "Menopause? What does that have to do with anything?"

"It's a time of awakening, that's what." Odette spoke from behind him, approaching so quietly that Arlo almost spilled his tea. "And Phoebe is rapidly approaching it."

"Bloody hell, Odette! You nearly gave me a heart attack."

She slid into a chair, a mischievous smile quirking her lips, her soft curls framing her face that bore only the faintest trace of makeup. "Didn't your wolf hear me?"

"No! You crept up—deliberately." The door to the back stairs was in the corner of the room, far less grand than the sweeping ones at the front of the house, and she'd entered that way. "It's freaky how you can hide yourself from my wolf."

"Just magic." She reached for a slice of cake. "Excellent. Thanks, Morgana."

He recalled what she'd said. "Why is menopause a time of awakening?"

Birdie answered first. "It's just like when we're teenagers. Hormones are changing. Magic sparks up. As it is for your wolf, it's when you start shifting and mastering it. For women, though, that huge menopausal shift will either awaken latent magic or force you to confront what you have buried. Silly girl." She tutted and sipped her tea. "You cannot deny Moonfell magic. Even Simone keeps it ticking along. We were talking about our solstice party, Odette."

"I can't wait for that, although I love Beltane, too. My sister, Giselle, practices witchcraft," Odette told Arlo. "She's not silly enough to deny her gift. Neither is Merlin," she said, referring to Morgana's brother. "I bet his kids, Ellen and Marion, are firing up their magic right now!"

"They're teenagers," Morgana added for Arlo's clarification. "Yes. A solstice party will be wonderful. We must start planning now. Anyway, enough of our family drama. You need help finding Hal. Tell us Maverick's latest news."

Arlo relayed Maverick's conversation with Castor. "Obviously, we have to consider that it's Castor who told us, and he's a slippery bastard at the best of times, but Maverick thinks he's been truthful."

"Have I met him?" Odette asked, breaking off pieces of cake to eat with her fingers. "I feel sure I would remember him."

"No, you haven't. I don't think any of you have. We prefer to have little to do with him and his pack, because we don't like anything about them. Fortunately, they keep to their own patch. For Castor to ask for Maverick's help is odd." Unlike Odette, he forked up a huge mouthful of cake and ate it with relish. "Wow. That's awesome. Anyway, I genuinely don't know what to think. And no," he said, forestalling Odette's offer, "I don't want you to meet him, even to see if he's a lying shit."

She smirked. "You don't think I can handle a big bad wolf?"

"I know you can. It's just…I don't like the idea."

"Is he devastatingly handsome? Will I swoon over him?"

He knew he was being teased. "He leers at women. He's a troll."

"I don't need protecting. I could always hex him. Just a little. Give him a rash somewhere unpleasant, perhaps."

He laughed. "That sounds like a great idea."

"So let me meet him."

"We'll see. If me or Mav have doubts, or something dodgy happens, you're in."

She turned towards her two coven members and rolled her eyes. "I would have thought things are dodgy enough already."

"Now now," Birdie said, shooting a warning glance at her granddaughter. "Let Arlo and Maverick handle this as they see fit. At least, Arlo, you brought us Hal's hat." She turned it inside out, extracting a strand of dark hair. "His, I presume?"

"I guess so. You've met him, I think. Wears his hair in a top knot."

Morgana nodded as she took the hat from Birdie. "Nice man. I remember him. A traditional finding spell, Birdie, or something different?"

"No reason not to try the usual way first. But you didn't find anything suspicious when you looked for him?" She directed this at Arlo.

"No. Hunter searched last night, with Tommy. Checked his route home. No scent of blood. No sign of a fight at his flat. They didn't think he even made it home. He could have gone for a run over the common or the park before he went home, but it was already late, so I doubt it."

"He went willingly, then," Odette said. "That is the only thing that could have happened. Unless someone executed a kidnapping by tranquilising him, as you did Jake. But you can't do that on the main road in Wimbledon."

"Plus, there was nothing quiet about that!" Arlo reminded her. "It was a bloody nightmare."

"Let's think about this underground club idea of Castor's," Birdie said. "That sounds both interesting and dangerous."

"He overheard something," Arlo stressed, "and wasn't sure how well, either. He admitted that."

Birdie narrowed her sharp blue eyes at him. "But he heard enough to send him to Maverick. He feels unsafe in his own place. His own pack. This Castor sounds brave to me. That's quite something to admit, especially to another alpha. He could be killed for that."

"He trusts Maverick."

"With good reason. He's a good man, but even so…" Birdie leaned forward, and Arlo found himself caught up in her intense stare. "You might not like him, but it's brave. Even you must see that. Gutsy."

"Yeah, he's gutsy all right."

"Are you sure none of your pack seems different? Wary? Overconfident, perhaps? If Castor is right, why would your wolves be excluded?"

"Distance. We're a long way from his territory."

"But this is London. It's easy to get around. If they got to Hal—whoever *they* are…"

Her words hung in the air, and Arlo found himself thinking of his pack at the meeting. Re-examining every face in the light of new knowledge. *Did any of them look odd? They were worried, but who wouldn't be?* "No." He said it with conviction. "I'm sure they're clean. But I have to be honest, Maverick isn't telling everyone about what Castor heard."

"Sensible." Birdie stood up. "I'm going to try the spell now, upstairs in the library. You stay here," she said to the others in general. "No need for us all to go. I'll call if there's anything to see."

"She doesn't think she'll find anything, does she?" Arlo said gloomily after she'd left.

"Not necessarily." Odette shrugged. "Sometimes, it's easier to work spells without an audience."

A bell sounded from the other side of the kitchen, and Morgana stood up. "My potion is finished. Bottling time."

She bustled over, a swing to her hips as she danced to the jazz music, and Arlo realised he could happily stay there all day. It was such a relaxing place to be. Except that he couldn't, because there was too much to do, and he would outstay his welcome. His gaze drifted to the windows again.

"Your wolf needs to run, Arlo," Odette said, smiling gently. "Go on. Head outside. Something may come to you out there. I know the weather won't bother you. The garden loves the rain, so it may lead you in a merry dance. You'll like that, too."

"A merry dance?"

"With the paths. You know how they tease." He was torn. He did want to run, but Odette was here. She smiled again, as if she knew his thoughts. "I am going to find my crystal ball and see what it tells me. It will take time, and it might tell me nothing, but it seems like a good idea, so my gut tells me I would be unwise to ignore it."

"Your intuition."

"Exactly."

He stood and stretched. *Yes, letting his wolf out in the day in Moonfell was just what he needed.*

Five

Hunter stood on the corner of the road where Jake lived, scanning his surroundings.

So far, it was a normal suburban street, full of normal suburban houses. Nothing felt off or looked odd. Although, what he expected something strange to look like he had no idea. Images from film noirs, of men in trench coats and low-brimmed fedoras leaning against lamp posts.

"So far so good," he said to Domino.

"He's still not answering," she said, checking her phone. "I'll text him that we're here and remind him of his damn obligations."

"What if he's disappeared, too? Maybe kidnapped."

"He's a therian, not a wolf."

"We don't know what's going on yet. The club—if it exists—could want anyone. Sounds bloody freaky to me," he said, pulling the collar of his leather jacket around his neck as it started to drizzle. "What number?"

Domino led the way up the street. The houses were large, three-storied, all looking reasonably well maintained. "Twelve. This isn't the type of place I expected Jake to live."

"You were imagining some rundown back alley?"

"Something like that."

"Me too, but he's probably got a legitimate job, as well as making dodgy deals." He stopped in front of house number twelve, taking in the well-tended front garden and a list of names next to the front door. "Three flats. Seeing as he isn't answering his phone, let's try the old-fashioned way. You hang back. See if a curtain twitches."

Hunter rang the bell for Jake's flat that was on the top floor. When no one answered, and Domino shook her head to indicate she hadn't seen any movement, he tried the others, starting on the ground floor. Within seconds he heard a door opening inside, and then the front door flew open.

"Yes?" a harried-looking woman asked him. She was young, her blonde hair dishevelled. "I hope you're not selling anything."

Hunter gave his slow, easy smile, designed to disarm and charm. "No, just looking for Jake who lives on the top floor."

"Jake?" She rolled her eyes, and then scanned him from head to toe. Her demeanour softened. "What's he done now?"

"Nothing. We just need to talk to him, but he's not answering his phone. Is he okay?"

"As far as I know, but he's elusive sometimes. Likes to think he's James Bond. Idiot."

"Is he home?"

She checked her watch. "He'll be at the pub now. The Laughing Cow, two streets down. New job. He can't afford to mess it up."

Hunter leaned against the frame. "Sounds like you know him well."

"Not really. We chat sometimes. We both keep odd hours." She didn't elaborate, but Hunter couldn't detect anything paranormal about her, so he didn't ask.

"Thanks. We'll head to the pub, then. If we miss him for some reason, tell him Hunter and Domino came by, just for a chat."

Her gaze slid over his shoulder to where Domino waited on the street. "All right. Will do."

"Thanks." He grinned again, just to be memorable, and sauntered back to Domino. "The Laughing Cow is where we'll find him."

"Charmed her, did you?" she asked, amused.

"Of course. I suggest one of us watches the back entrance, and the other goes through the front door. Just in case."

"He better not run," Domino said as they headed to the pub. "Although, why would he? We left things on good terms, so why not answer now?"

"You tranquillised him and chained him up. Even if you did apologise, it would piss me off."

"We let him go with zero consequences!"

Hunter laughed. "Yes, great memories for him, I'm sure."

"He nearly killed us. I was kidnapped!" She was getting more belligerent by the minute. "I'll head in the front, you wait at the back."

"And if he shifts?"

"It's daylight. Of course he won't."

"You're steaming mad. I can see it in your eyes. Your wolf is snarling back there. It's very sexy." His eyes lingered on her lips for a moment, just to remind her of what he was thinking about. "But not great for looking friendly in a pub. You wait at the back, and I'll go in the front. That way, if he runs, you can hit him hard. Besides, he doesn't know me." Hunter hadn't been part of the pack at that point.

Domino huffed, looked as if she was about to protest, and then gave in. "Fine."

The Laughing Cow was a large, red brick building on the corner of the road, an alley running down the back to the rear door. Hunter waited until Domino was in position, and then headed inside, just as the rain started falling more heavily. *Something else to annoy Domino.*

The entrance hall had two doors. The left one led to a bar and the other to the lounge area, and Hunter could see both were busy late on Friday afternoon. The lounge was traditionally decorated with wooden tables, chairs, and a few booths, and a woman was serving behind the bar in there. He headed to the bar area which had a pool table, and although he had a description of Jake, he knew who he was immediately. He could scent his therian magic. He was of average height and bulky of build, cleanshaven, with short, brown hair. Fortunately, there were no other therians or shifters of any kind around. It was a family pub for the local area. Hunter knew that Jake would detect his wolf, so he didn't loiter.

He leaned on the bar. "Pint of the local please, mate, and a glass of red wine." Domino would want a drink. Jake eyed him warily, but pulled the pint as Hunter extracted his wallet. "Jake, isn't it? Just need to chat, nothing sinister. I'm from Storm Moon."

Jake froze, eyes darting everywhere.

"Seriously," Hunter said, ready to bolt after him, "I just want to chat."

"Who's the wine for?"

"Domino, and she's right outside the back door, so don't even think about it. Besides, this is a new job. You want to keep it, right?"

Jake leaned in and lowered his voice. "I do not want trouble here."

"If you'd have answered your phone, we wouldn't be here at all, you idiot. But no, there'll be no trouble. We just want a drink, and to ask you a few questions." Their eyes met, each assessing the other, and Hunter shoved his wolf way back. "Please. It's important, or we wouldn't be here. And I'm seriously in need of a pint."

Jake scanned the customers who were all too busy talking to mind them, and nodded. "Fine, but it needs to be quick."

Hunter texted Domino and settled on a barstool, pulling another next to him. When she entered, hair damp from the rain, she scowled at Jake, took a drink of her wine, and sat. "Jake. Glad to see you here. When you didn't answer, I assumed the worst."

"I'm trying," he said, keeping his voice low, "to leave some of that crap behind me. The old me."

"I can see. You've lost weight. Cleaned up." Domino settled, shoulders dropping as she relaxed. "Good for you. All that wheeler-dealing not working anymore?"

"To be honest, being involved in a kidnapping was a step too far for me. I'm glad that wanker and his bloody cronies are dead. It gave me space to think and move on. Did he really die in that hillside collapse in Wales? I heard the rumours."

Hunter gave a short laugh. "No rumour. It was an ugly end."

"And," Domino added, "you probably heard that we killed the rest of them in Brixton."

"Of course. That made waves. Big waves." His eyes narrowed. "Gave Storm Moon a rep. And that bloody DI Milne."

"Good." Domino was abrupt. "Has Hunter explained why we're here?"

"He just said you wanted to chat. About nothing good, I'm sure." He stared at Hunter. "I haven't met you before."

"New pack member. But I was caught up in that business, same as you. And now there are rumours of a new problem. An underground club."

"I said I've moved on from that life."

"But you're not deaf," Domino said. "And no one moves on that quickly. You still have friends in that world. For fuck's sake, you're a therian. It's what you do."

He looked affronted. "We're not all dodgy."

"Oh, come on!"

A man came to the bar and Jake made to move away. "Let me serve him, and I'll tell you what I know. It isn't much!"

"At least we found him," Hunter said to Domino when they were alone. "He's not what I expected."

"He was a slob before. Maybe that business with the Pûcas did him a favour."

Domino's perfume drifted to him, and despite her damp hair, she looked good. He wanted to kiss her. "When we've finished here, why don't we stop for dinner somewhere? A curry, perhaps. Just us two."

"But we should get back..."

"To do what? We're gathering information. We'll phone Maverick, let him know what we've found, and tell him we're starving. That's not a lie. I am! Besides, we're not at school, and you're head of security. We're allowed to eat. Plus, I never get to see you alone."

She smiled at him. "This is alone."

"And I like it. If *you* didn't like the idea, you would have said no to me accompanying you, and yet, here we are."

"We are working together."

He eased away from her, defeated. There was patience, and then there was being an idiot. "Okay. I accept being rejected. I'll move on, and not pester you again."

She blinked, seeming shocked. "Hunter, it's just that—"

He interrupted her. "We're pack, you're my boss, it would be weird. I'll move on. No hard feelings. I mean, you flirted with me —*a lot*—but we all flirt. That's okay. Now I know." Except he was annoyed with himself for thinking they would get together. He'd obviously misread the signals. Or read too much into them. *She'd flirted. So be it.*

He turned away, ego bruised, but still determined to make the friendship work. He loved being in the Storm Moon Pack, and loved his job. Domino had made her choice and her feelings clear. He would not be *that* guy. The twat who couldn't take rejection. He focussed on Jake when he turned back to them, aware that Domino had turned away, too. "Spill then, Jake. We have places to be."

Jake wiped the bar down as he talked. "You mentioned a club."

"An underground one. Rumours of one, at least."

"Well, that's all I've heard, too. A few of my friends have been talking about some kind of challenge club for wolf-shifters."

Domino leaned in. "Where is it?"

"No one knows that! It's just a rumour. We don't even know who started the rumour. There are just whispers about an old temple that demands tribute, and there's a club to do it."

"A temple?" Hunter couldn't keep the incredulity from his tone. "You're fucking kidding."

"No." He studied them. "You've obviously heard something yourselves, so why come to me?"

"Because," Domino explained, "we heard less than you. And a shifter has gone missing from our pack. Vanished on his way home last night. He's solid. Reliable. We want answers. Tell me about this so-called temple."

Jake pulled at his ear, face scrunched, clearly weighing up his options. "Someone, I don't know who, has supposedly woken up an old god, and like all gods, he needs blood."

Hunter groaned. "Fucking blood sacrifices. Are you shitting us?"

"No. I thought my mate was having me on, but he swears it's true."

"We'll speak to him, then."

"No, you won't." Jake shrugged. "You won't learn any more, because he doesn't know. If he did, he'd have told me—because trust me, I asked a lot of questions, just like you. He didn't know. But he said, because he was sceptical too, that if it was true, it would shake up the wolf-shifters, and he thought it was hilarious. He said, 'They'll have more to answer to than just bloody alphas, mate!' And then he laughed. So that's all I know. I don't know where it is, or who the damn god is, or who resurrected the bastard. For all I know, someone got pissed and started a rumour for the hell of it." He eyed another customer at the end of the bar. "Gotta go. Happy?"

"Not really," Domino said, "but thanks. And will you please just answer your phone next time we call?"

He grinned. "I'll think about it. Nice to see you though, Dom. And good luck. I think you'll need it."

Hunter sipped his pint, not sure what the hell to think, except *fuck*.

Domino nudged him. "Come on."

"Can't I finish my pint first, after hearing *that*?"

She downed her wine. "Okay, but I want to apologise, and I'd like to do that over a curry. Then we need to discuss this conversation."

He rolled his eyes. "You don't have to massage my ego. Plus, Maverick needs to hear this."

"He will, but I think you'd like to hear what I have to say."

"We can talk in the car."

"So you don't want a curry?"

"I want a date-curry, not a curry-curry."

She giggled. "What the hell are you like?"

"I'm a horny man who's been patient, and I finally get the message. I'll survive."

Then she did the unexpected. She cupped his face, leaned in, and kissed him, full of promise for more. "I'm sorry. I like you. Really like you. And I want a date-curry, please."

He grabbed his jacket, pint forgotten. "All right. Now you're talking."

Six

Maverick ended the call with Domino and sat in silence, trying to absorb the news.

An old god had been awoken and demanded blood. That sounded insane.

"It's bad, isn't it?" Grey asked him from the corner of the security office. He'd been turning on the video screens and checking the security camera feeds, ready for a busy Friday night, but now he wheeled his chair across the floor to the desk. "Go on."

"It's *very* bad. I'd think someone is having us on, but with Hal missing, that would be stupid of me." He buried his face in his hands, wishing it would all go away, and then looked up, resigned. "According to Jake, someone found an old temple, and has rattled awake an ancient god who now wants blood sacrifices from wolf-shifters. I don't know who this damn god is, or who the bloody idiot is who decided to wake an old god, but there we go."

Grey sat for a moment in silence, studying Maverick, and then slumped back in his chair. "Okay. That is weird and downright disturbing. Being logical, if a god wants wolf-shifter blood, is that because it's a God of Wolves? Or maybe whatever or whoever the god is, is an enemy of wolves? Does that make sense?"

"Nothing about this makes sense."

"But you know what I mean."

Maverick tried to calm his thoughts after the initial shock. "I do, but I have no idea. We need to be logical. Honestly though, I don't know any wolf gods. I certainly don't worship any. I don't think anyone does."

"But an old one? Surely you used to have them? Cultures do, and then things change. Think about all that stuff that was sold at the auction. I mean, look at the amazing tapestry map you bought...the documents." He shrugged. "I've got to admit that I didn't know you had anywhere near that amount of shifter history, or that it would be so varied. I talked to Morgana about it. Your history is far more interesting than I thought."

"Cheers!" he said dryly.

"I don't mean it in an insulting way." Grey shuffled in his seat as he warmed to the subject. "I gather that there were objects on sale that went back hundreds of years. Magical objects that are related to shifter magic specifically. She also told me that there were hugely influential packs across Europe, many of whom had connections to royalty, of which there were lots of related documents. Plus, Morgana said there were details of pack rituals, too. Did you know about any of that?"

"No. Lots of it was news to me. As the alpha, I have made it my business to know some of our history, but even I was surprised at what was there." The auction had acted like a shot of adrenalin for Maverick. As he'd studied the lots, a sense of pride grew at what had gone before. He suddenly saw his place and his pack's place in the long history of their race. Because he had grown up in a small, rural pack, they hadn't spoken of the bigger packs or politics. "I felt like an idiot for being so ignorant, if I'm honest. I wish I'd had the money to buy more."

"You shouldn't feel bad about it. The people who'd collected all of that, and who bought it, are active collectors. Obsessives. That's why Harlan makes so much money. You have other things on your mind. But do you think the club and the temple came from something someone bought there? Or is it just random?"

Maverick huffed, furious with himself. "I didn't even consider that."

"You had a list of the lots, right? We can look at it. See if anything strikes us. Hell, I'd like to look anyway."

"It's upstairs, so I can get it soon." Grey was always helpful, and his mood started to lift. "Thank you. That's good thinking. Okay. Let's be logical. Someone somehow found an old temple. It could be underground. They found a Mithraic temple in London a couple of years ago."

"I know. I went and saw it. Very cool."

"Exactly, so it's possible. Construction is happening all over the city. Maybe they triggered something."

"Like rubbing a bottle and releasing a genie."

"Let's not bring Djinn into this. Maybe they cut themselves, spilled blood in the wrong place, and awoke something."

"Or," Grey suggested, "it was in a family home all along, and someone decided to activate it. But the god needed more blood. Shifter blood. So they set up a secret club."

"A family home with a temple?"

"There are bloody big houses in London, and lots of rich people. It's possible. Maybe even just hearing about the shifter auction prompted them to use it."

Maverick relented. "Okay, we'll consider it. But would it be a shifter family? There are shifters who don't belong to packs.

Castor and I run the two biggest packs, but there are smaller ones. Family ones. They usually just want to keep their head down."

"But what if someone had an experience that changed them, and they decided to get all religious?"

"This is just mad speculation."

"We need to keep an open mind, and therefore we need to think of various scenarios, Maverick. It will give us leads to follow up. Hal is missing. We must consider everything."

"I can see that you've been dating Maggie. You're picking up her lingo."

Grey grinned. "One night out together does not equal *dating*. But I was in the Forces, and that teaches you to be analytical. Strategic. Someone has set these events in motion. Sounds like it's close to where Castor is, but they are clearly branching out. We need places to start looking. Tell me about this challenge business again."

Maverick stood and walked to the fridge, pulling out two bottles of beer. "Want one?"

"Sure."

Maverick uncapped them and handed Grey one, then walked to the one-way glass window, watching the club being prepped for customers. Monroe, Vlad, Jax, Cecile, and Xavier were together, talking earnestly by the stage. All looked worried. Tonight it was Monroe on the club door. One of their biggest shifters. *What if any of them were abducted?* It just didn't seem possible.

He sighed. "'Challenge is the way of the wolf.' That's what Castor said he overheard, or something close. And that the place was too important, but for what, I don't know. For info to leak on it too soon? For a change in our society? It's all so vague."

Grey joined him at the window. "Okay. Wolves like fighting. It's in your nature. Challenge isn't sacrifice. Not in the traditional sense."

"Shit! Of course. But in a challenge, you normally spill blood."

"Exactly, from the victor and the vanquished. I've never been in a fight where I haven't spilled some blood. Not necessarily a fight to the death."

"Bollocks. So it could be like a fight club!"

"Maybe. But doesn't that sound better than Hal being laid out on a slab and the blood drained out of him? Bearing in mind this is pure speculation."

"Hal wouldn't give a crap about a fight club. It still means he was kidnapped." Maverick looked down at the group gathered below. "Okay. Let's call the security team together, tell them what we have so far. See if they have any suggestions. With luck, Arlo will be back soon." He checked his watch. "Where the hell is he? He's been gone for hours!"

"He's at Moonfell. What do you think he's doing?"

"Not shagging Odette, I hope."

Grey laughed. "Give it time. No, he'll be in the garden while they do their witchy thing. I'll message him. Tell him to get a bloody move on."

"He can't answer his phone as a wolf."

"For when he shifts back!"

Maverick smirked at Grey's irritation, but watching his security team again, his smile faded. If anyone was going to be kidnapped next, he wanted it to be him, because if they wanted a challenge, he would give them one.

Arlo was soaking wet when he shifted back to human in Moonfell's garden and entered the glass house that held the witches' vast collection of herbs and poisonous plants.

The rain drummed on the glass as he towelled himself off, the scent of soil and verdant greenery wrapping around him, his olfactory senses already overloaded from his time in the garden. Odette had been right. The garden had teased him, closing off paths, leading him in circles, finally herding him to the orchard and the beehives. Their calm, steady droning had soothed his nerves, and the branches had offered shelter from the rain.

He knew, however, that he couldn't linger, and he returned to the main garden by way of the long, yew hedge, pausing for a while under the moon gate. Arlo wished he could see glimpses of the past through there, like Odette sometimes did, but he contented himself by enjoying the garden as it was, with its huge topiary animals that seemed to act as guardians of the place. In fact, he had never considered them as such before, he realised, as he pulled on his jeans. He absently patted his dreadlocks dry as he stared out of the windows at the garden again. The garden was much barer than in the summer months, of course, with only the bones of the splendour on show. The perennials had only just started to bloom, and the topiary figures were more obvious. He could see the head of the dragon, the unicorn's horn rising in a spiral by the far wall, and the sleek cat trimmed to look like it was racing across the top of the hedge.

"Enjoy your run?" Morgana called out from behind him.

He spun around, annoyed with himself for being caught unawares. "Bloody hell! How did you mask your approach from me? I'm a shifter, but I couldn't even scent you."

"Sorry, Arlo. I'm catching on to Odette's teasing ways. Just a little spell, of course." She crossed to his side, looking out at the garden as he had been. "Something caught your eye?"

"Yes, the topiary figures. It struck me that they're like guardians of this place, and it's weird because I've never thought that before. And yes, I loved my run, thanks."

"Good." She smiled, eyes turning mischievous. "If you're sensing that they're guardians, then that's because they are. And the fact that you thought that means they have let you see it. The garden likes you. Isn't that good news?"

"Seriously? They have a true role here, like sentient beings?"

"I wouldn't put it quite like that. Or," she tapped her lips with a finger, eyes still on the garden, "maybe I should. Isn't it fun to have secrets slowly unfolding? Come on, Arlo. We have news."

He hurriedly pulled his t-shirt on and thrust his feet into socks and then his boots. "Great!"

"Not that great. But come and hear it from the others."

Odette and Birdie were sitting at the kitchen table again and he sat next to them, noting their preoccupied expressions. "Not good news, then."

"Not from me," Birdie confessed as she passed Hal's hat to him. "The spells—I used a few—could not pinpoint Hal's location. They indicated he was north of the Thames, but that's all. He is still alive, though, so that's good."

A knot he didn't even know he had in his stomach loosened at that news. "Thanks. I hadn't even wanted to entertain the possibility that he wasn't. Are you sure he is?"

"I used a pendulum and asked. It said yes, so he is."

"Oh!" Arlo had read about using pendulums, so he just nodded. "Cool. What does the rest mean, though?"

"That I couldn't pinpoint his location? That the place is warded. Or he is. The place is, I suspect. I have no idea who this old god is, but he will have power. Or she, of course."

"Damn it. I suppose I should have expected that." Odette was waiting patiently, and he turned to her. "What about you? Seen anything?"

"Of sorts." She was calm, considered, and her dark eyes seemed larger than normal. "I felt him. It is a male god—or something masculine, with godlike power. I don't know his name, or where he came from, but he feeds on chaos and blood. His presence is like a shadow. He's growing in strength, too."

Arlo was momentarily stunned. "You *felt* him? How?"

"Through my crystal ball. Sometimes I feel like I actually fall into it when I'm searching. It's like I'm swimming in darkness." She sounded spaced out, like she'd been drugged. Maybe that's why she was sitting so quietly. She was dealing with aftereffects. "His pull was like the tide. Powerful. Dark. He has been sleeping for a long time. I even sensed his glee at being awake again." She shuddered and shivered, as if still feeling him. "He will be hard to deal with. He's not used to being refused anything."

Birdie snorted. "Like any god, then."

"Even your Goddess?" Arlo asked.

"Yes, although She is better than most."

Arlo tried to focus on practicalities. "How do we defeat this thing? Once we find it, obviously."

"Well," Odette said, seeming to shake off her torpor, "it seems he was asleep before, so there must have been a way to do it. If it was done once, we can do it again."

"You're suggesting he was trapped somehow. Or bound."

She shrugged. "Perhaps. Sorry I can't be more specific right now. With new information, I might be able to find out more. But, I am wary of alerting him to us. To you. For now, he operates in the dark with a chosen few. Best not to rattle him. Yet."

"You make it sound like he's planning something."

"He might be. It sounds like some of Castor's pack are. Something has been set in motion." Her hands closed over his. Soft, warm, and small. "Nothing good. Promise me you'll be careful."

"Of course."

And then her eyes darkened again, her voice shifting to a harsh whisper. "*He wakes beneath the city stone, where the Wolf-God made his ancient throne. Blood will flow and packs will fall, when battle-hunger claims them all. The old one rises, fierce and bold, to claim what was his prize of old.*"

Arlo shivered as the words wrapped around him with a strange, sinuous power, and he gripped her hands, focussing only on her—although he felt Morgana and Birdie lean in. "Odette! Are you all right?"

She took a deep breath, eyes clearing as they focussed on him again. "Sorry. Did you say something?"

Birdie placed her hands over both of theirs. "A prophecy!"

"A fucking what now?" Arlo was not ashamed to admit he was scared, Odette's words seeming to ooze into his blood, his thoughts.

Birdie was staring at Morgana, not him. "Write it down, Morgana. We must think on this. Arlo, in the meantime, go back to your pack, and tell Maverick everything. Be careful who you trust. This will get far worse."

Seven

When Domino arrived back at Storm Moon, her mood was good, despite the circumstances.

She and Hunter had eaten a great meal. A date meal. They had flirted and teased and she had enjoyed it immensely. Afterwards, they had kissed like horny teenagers in the car, and her libido had roared to life. All her pent-up desire for him had released like a volcano, and even though she knew she'd bottled it up, her response to him was still a shock. Now, all she wanted to do was get naked with him. But that would have to wait. Reluctantly, they had dragged themselves back to Storm Moon, the feel of his lips on hers, and the way they blazed fire along her collar bones and her neck still at the forefront of her thoughts.

But when she entered the security office at Storm Moon, filled with a large portion of the team all talking loudly, those thoughts were shoved roughly aside.

"Bloody hell," Hunter said, voice low as they entered, "I think we've missed something."

"I hope no one else has gone missing," she said, threading through the group to join Maverick and Arlo who stood by the desk, Hunter at her side. "Guys, what's going on?"

Maverick frowned as he turned to her. Already, a golden light kindled deep in his eyes, a sign of his agitation. "Odette has made some weird fucking prophecy today. It made us sound like we're all bloody doomed!"

Arlo shrugged, as if to apologise. "It was the freakiest thing I've ever heard. Odette looked like she was possessed." He nodded to the security team, all in heated debate. "We're trying to work out what it means."

"Go on, then," Hunter said. "Tell us."

Arlo fished a piece of paper out of his pocket and read, "'*He wakes beneath the city stone, where the Wolf-God made His ancient throne. Blood will flow and packs will fall, when battle-hunger claims them all. The old one rises, fierce and bold, to claim what was His prize of old.*' I'll be able to quote that without reading it soon."

Domino shuddered. "Okay, that's creepy. What god?"

"We have no idea."

Maverick snorted. "We've had a few suggestions, though. Vlad reckons it's some old Norse god. Fenris or Fenrir, son of Loki. Not sure what he'd be doing under London, however."

"He'd have come with the Vikings," Hunter said confidently. "I've heard of him."

Everyone has heard of Fenrir, Domino thought, but no one she knew in the shifter world ever really gave him a second thought anymore. "I suppose we shouldn't discount him," she admitted, "but I don't see it. Any other options?"

"I suggested," Arlo said, glancing at Maverick, "that we call Harlan. He's good at that sort of thing. But Grey has also made a good suggestion. He said we need to examine the list of lots from that auction, see if anything there might be responsible for this."

She nodded. "That's a great idea. You still have it then, Maverick?"

"Yes. I was going upstairs to look at it, before Arlo rocked up with the latest news. I'm hoping the Moonfell witches can narrow things down for us—location-wise, that is."

"They'll try," Arlo said, sitting on the corner of the desk, "but Birdie says the place itself—the temple or the club or whatever the hell it is—is warded. The good news is, she is convinced that Hal is alive, and that he's north of the river."

"Which backs up Castor's news," Domino said, thinking through the implications. "That narrows things down a little."

"Not enough, though. We need more specifics for an effective search. What about Jake?" Maverick asked. "Did you trust him?"

"Yes," Domino nodded, looking to Hunter for confirmation. "He seemed legit. He looked better. More together. Said he's trying to walk away from his old life, and I believe it."

"Me, too," Hunter confirmed. "He didn't really want to get involved, and I don't blame him. We asked to speak to his mate who he got the news off, but he said it was pointless. That he couldn't tell us any more."

Looking weary, Maverick rubbed his face. "At least we can confirm that Castor isn't lying, and that what he heard seems legit. I should call him. Let him know. As odd as this seems, I think we need to work with Castor. And I know," he held a hand up to forestall any objections, "he's still untrustworthy, but he seemed genuinely worried to me. To not trust anyone in your pack..." he trailed off, looking pointedly at the security team.

Domino met Arlo's eyes and saw her own worry mirrored in his. "Maverick," she said, her tone sure and forceful, "you can trust us. I've heard no whispers from anyone here."

"Me neither," Hunter put in. "Nor has Tommy. We're good here."

"Plus," Arlo pointed out, "the North London Pack fosters competition, and that fosters resentment. We don't work like that. It will be harder to get a foot in here."

"For now," Maverick said, his attention returning to them. "But if there's magic involved, or some kind of super-alpha control, then it doesn't matter how loyal someone is. They'll have no choice. Hal was taken, I really believe that."

Before Domino could reply, Grey joined them, running his hand over his shaved head as he eyed them all. "I've split security into teams of two, just in case. It's hard to know if whoever's behind this will target the club, but if we're taking precautions with the pack, we treat the security team the same. They're not spread out as much, but we'll manage. Plus, it's Friday, so we have a lot of the team on. Cecile is with Monroe on the club door, and Jax is with John on the front door. Fran and Tommy will be by the stage exit. The band will be here soon. I wish it was just a DJ night. Then we wouldn't have three bloody exits to worry about."

"How are they dealing with it?" Domino asked, watching them stride outside. The bar was already open upstairs, and the club would be opening very soon.

"Unsettled and pissed off. Worried about Hal. Nothing new there. They want to hunt. Do something useful."

"They will," Maverick said. "But we need more to go on first. I'll bring that list of lots down and read it in here. I want to be around in case there's trouble."

"Where do you want me?" Hunter asked, glancing between Grey and Domino.

"Your call, Grey," Domino said. "You've organised the rest."

"With Xavier, patrolling the club. Anything unusual, tell us. I'll be monitoring the cameras."

"I'll be upstairs, then," Arlo said, "in the main bar. I'll patrol, liaise with Vlad. We'll work it between us. No Mads tonight?"

Grey shook his head. "No, or Rory. Night off. Jet is down there already. She knows what to do."

Domino was pleased with the arrangements. It was what she'd have sorted herself. "I'll patrol, then. Either with Vlad or Arlo."

"Never alone," Maverick reiterated, fixing her with his alpha stare.

"But surely we won't be snatched from the club, surrounded by people?"

"We have no idea what's going on. We stick together. Same goes for you, Arlo. If one of you is alone, you remain in the bar, by the bar staff. Understood? Be wary of distractions or traps. I will go through my list of lots, and then join you."

Morgana and her two coven members sat at the kitchen table for a long while after Arlo had gone, discussing how best to help the shifters.

Morgana had been out recently with Monroe, sharing some wonderful meals that left her glowing after he treated her like a queen, and she was determined that he would not end up vanishing like Hal into some Shifter Temple of Doom. They had kissed, a lot, on the long sofa in her east-facing living room, stretched out in passionate abandon, but that was as far as it had gone, and that was down to Monroe being a gentleman, and she being stupidly nervous about getting naked with the large, sexy shifter and being found inadequate. She was trim and fit, but she did not have a typical shifter physique, and that's what worried her. *Next time*, she promised herself. *Next time she would invite him up to her bedroom and have wild sex that made her feel like a goddess, never mind a queen.* Plus, she liked him more than she expected to, and couldn't bear the thought of him being hurt in all of this crazy business, or of their relationship ending before it had even properly begun.

"You're daydreaming again," Birdie said. "You have the 'dreamy with Monroe' face on."

"I do not!"

"You so have, and I don't blame you. He's got muscles on muscles." Birdie's fingers drummed on the old wooden table. "This is a fine pickle we're in. I need a good, stiff G & T. It helps me think."

"In that case, get me one. I need to think, too," Morgana said sarcastically. "Odette?" The colour had returned to her cousin's cheeks after her Otherworldly announcement. "One for you?"

"No. I can't face it. Tea for me. Something restorative."

"I'll get it," Birdie said, rising to her feet.

Morgana realised they were almost in the dark, and with a flick of her fingers, candles ignited around the room, and the lamp by the fire turned on, casting a soft glow. The drumming rain had made the kitchen a meditative space, and now she felt as if she were waking from a trance. It was as if Odette's prophecy, for want of a better word, had cast a spell over them all.

"If we can't find Hal, and there are no other spells to help us find him right now, then we must look at other options. Maybe we should visit Castor's pool hall," Morgana suggested.

"And do what?" Birdie asked, passing her the glass of gin and tonic. "I'm terrible at pool."

"Not to *play*! To see what energy or magic we can detect in the area. Maybe we can devise a tracking spell that we use there." Morgana mulled on her idea while sipping her drink that was decidedly heavy on the gin. *Maybe Birdie was right*. It *was* helping her think. "Sort of like a compass."

Birdie narrowed her eyes. "Intriguing. How would that work?"

"I don't know yet. It's just an idea. There are old compasses upstairs, though, and other odds and sods that our ancestors used for travel that I haven't looked at properly in years. Maybe I could spell a compass to specifically find shifters. And there's that display on the second floor, from one of our ancestors who travelled through India years ago. What was his name?"

Odette rolled her eyes. "We have hundreds of ancestors who have trekked all over the place."

"But he was more of an explorer," Morgana said, annoyed with herself for forgetting his name. "I was looking at his things only the other day. I'll go up, post-gin, and look again."

"Is this part of your room move?" Birdie asked, looking slightly put out.

"Yes. I know where I'm going, I told you. It's a lovely room looking west, so I have a sunset."

"I know. I shall miss you on the first floor."

"Good grief, Birdie. I only sleep there. You see me all the time!"

"I suppose."

Morgana decided to move on from this touchy topic, which really shouldn't be an issue at all. Birdie was getting stuck in her ways, but maybe that was age. "Odette, tell us again about this Wolf-God. That was the name you mentioned."

"I can't." Odette stirred her tea, the fragrant herbs drifting on the steam. "I didn't even know I said it."

"But it must have left you with an impression," Morgana said. "Even if only fleeting."

Odette eyed her regretfully. "No. It genuinely was an *absence*. I was talking to Arlo, quite *compos mentis*, and then you were all looking at me like I'd gone mad."

"Maybe," Birdie suggested, "the fact you were holding Arlo's hand triggered it. You were in direct touch with a wolf-shifter."

"Perhaps. I just wanted to reassure him. Warn him. I guess," she hesitated, staring into her tea, "we still have a connection. I sense things from him."

Odette looked a little lost, which was most unlike her, and Morgana wanted to comfort her younger cousin. "I suspect you always will, and perhaps that's a good thing, if it triggered your warning. Odd though it was for you."

Odette flashed a brief smile. "Yes. I only remember the feeling I had when I looked in the crystal ball. The feeling of diving in and being on the edge of this...consciousness. It's old. Very old. And it felt rooted in our earth."

"A native god, then?" Birdie asked.

"Perhaps."

"One that likes blood and battle," Morgana suggested. "Challenge. Archaic notions of glory."

"It sounds almost gladiatorial," Birdie mused.

"We need to know more," Morgana said, frustrated that so much remained vague. "Much more. Of course, our other option is that we capture one of Castor's pack members ourselves. One of the ones he overheard, and we spell him to reveal all. Or Odette tries to read him." Then she frowned. "Although, it would probably give too much away, and maybe endanger Hal."

Birdie nodded. "I agree. We'll save that option."

Morgana drained her glass, suddenly restless. "I'm going up to search that room with all the travel gear. I can't rest until I have."

"To eventually spell a compass?" Birdie asked.

"Or something of the sort. A Wayfinder." She had half-risen to her feet, but now she sat again, focussing not on her coven, but on something she had read. "By the Goddess! That's exactly what we need. A Wayfinder. One of our grimoires mentioned one in regard to finding covens. That was years back. Fifteenth and sixteenth century, when covens were hidden."

"And before!" Birdie said.

Odette huffed. "And since."

Morgana ploughed on. "They were a way for witches to find support. Safe places. Surely, wolves would have had similar objects. Maverick bought that tapestry with all the safe places for packs marked in gold thread. There would have been other ways to find them. We can make a Wayfinder to find an old temple. It will be full of shifter magic."

"What about what you bought from the auction?" Odette asked.

"They were documents pertaining to powerful shifter families. I've yet to study them properly," she confessed.

Birdie finished her drink, too. "Well, you've sold me. Let's go and look at what we've got, and more importantly, what we can craft."

Eight

Grey finished checking the security feeds, happy that the club was running smoothly and there weren't any issues.

He could see the security team patrolling in pairs, and although he had studied the customers until his head ached, he couldn't see any suspicious behaviour. The three sets of shifters on the doors were handling things fine, so needing a break, he spun on his chair and saw Maverick sitting quietly on the sofa in the seating area, studying the glossy brochure of lots. A notepad was next to him, covered in scribbles.

"Any success, Maverick?"

"Depends what you mean by success." He stretched, placed the guide on the table, and rolled his shoulders. "There are so many interesting pieces, lots of which I'd forgotten about. I'm annoyed that so many of these objects have gone to non-shifters."

"Maybe. You don't know."

"I guess not, but I suspect. There were other shifters in that auction, I could tell by their scent, but they were outnumbered by humans." He sighed as he glanced at the brochure again. "We gave each other those half-nods of acknowledgement. The sort of 'I know what you are' look. That was all, though. We respected each other's privacy."

"Beer? Coffee?" Grey asked, trying to decide what he wanted before he sat down to talk to Maverick.

"Beer. It's too late for coffee. Shifter metabolism copes well with many things, but coffee will still keep me up, and I don't want to be groggy tomorrow."

"I'll join you." Grabbing two beers from the fridge, Grey handed one to Maverick and sat opposite him. "The shifters you detected. Not all were wolf-shifters, I guess?"

"No. Some were, but none that I knew. Others were bird-shifters, and there were therians, too. And a bear-shifter! You don't see many of those in town." He laughed.

"Are bird-shifters the next common shifter group in London?"

"Maybe more so than us. *Maybe*." He sipped his beer. "They have a different energy. Lighter. Faster. And they don't have a pack mentality, either. They call themselves clans."

"Really? Why?"

"Historic, but other than that, I don't know."

Grey didn't know much about bird-shifters, but why would he? Now, however, he was curious. "You guys keep to yourselves, though?"

"Pretty much. They do their thing, we do ours. We're just different paranormal groups in London."

"Are they territorial?"

"Hell yes. Amongst themselves, of course. Birds have hunting grounds, too. They fight as well, but not like us."

"Unless the bird is a predator? Like a raptor or an owl."

"Fair point."

"Were there bird-shifter lots there, too?"

"Yes. Many, many different objects. It was bewildering. I sort of glazed over if it wasn't of interest to me." He grunted. "Another thing I'm annoyed with myself over."

"You couldn't have known this would happen." Grey picked up the colourful book and flicked through the pages, impressed at the full-colour images that captured the objects, and the sheer variety of them. "Wow. Drinking horns, silver daggers with runes, ceremonial cloaks." Grey read a description. "This says that this is a Greek silver mirror that shows a shifter's true form. This suggests these are real, magical items. Did you test it?"

"No, I bloody didn't."

Grey kept skimming, drawn more and more into the objects that had been sold, his mind flooding with images of exotic places, temples, and palaces, all filled with intrigue. "I am generally not a fanciful man, Maverick, but some of these things are amazing. Anything on shifter gods?"

"Towards the back. Mainly art—sculptures and paintings."

Grey murmured to himself as he searched. "Bastet, Zeus—of course—Loki, Ceridwen... Merlin!"

"Not a god, but he shapeshifted—supposedly. A stag, hawk, wolf, salmon, and he changed his age, too." Maverick nodded at the book. "There's also a small section on Taliesin. He was linked with Ceridwen."

"Do you even need Harlan? It sounds like you know a lot yourself."

"Not like he does—or so I assume. Nor do I have the books he'll have access to."

"Or the witches, maybe, in that vast library of theirs." Grey's interest in shifters, despite the fact he worked for them, was mild. He accepted what they were and that there was a paranormal society, but that was it. He had never questioned their past or lineage, beyond what they had experienced with the Bone Crown. That had fired up a brief interest before vanishing again. But now, he looked at Maverick in a whole different light. "This is vast, right? Shifters occur across all cultures, and have done for centuries."

"Pretty much."

"And now one of the old gods has returned." Grey tapped the book. "Anything in here that could have woken it? Him?" he corrected himself, remembering what Odette had told Arlo. "Or that can help us?"

"If we don't have it, it doesn't matter what's in there that can help us. But as far as waking a god, there is nothing in there that could do that. Unless something has hidden qualities."

Grey had gut instincts, and he trusted them. "This is something else, Maverick. I feel it. Twenty-four hours since Hal vanished, and no sign of him. I don't like it. It's slick. Pre-planned. Who the fuck is behind it?"

"I don't know, but I need to get in there and bring it down from within."

"With a team, preferably."

"If I get in there, I'll send word. Somehow." Maverick's anger was growing, and although he was not a reckless alpha, Grey knew that his patience was being tested.

Grey ignored his comment—for now. "It's unlikely we'll find out more tonight. Have you got plans for tomorrow?"

"Nothing specific yet. Other than speaking to Harlan."

"And Maggie?"

Maverick massaged his temple. "I suppose I should call her."

"Others may have gone missing. You should." Grey knew that packs liked to manage their own business, but this was different. "If she has leads, you'll kick yourself for waiting."

"Yeah. Okay. First thing tomorrow." Maverick pushed to his feet, distracted and irritable. "I'll patrol the club."

"With someone," Grey reminded him.

"I want to be taken." Maverick's eyes bore into his, a feral gleam kindling in them, challenging him to disagree.

Grey could normally handle a challenge, but Maverick was no ordinary man—or shifter. When he decided to exert his dominance, not many could withstand him. Grey tried to hold his stare, but then relented, dropping his eyes to the table. He still spoke his mind. "Not yet. We need to be able to find you."

"It can't come soon enough for me."

"You need to think of your pack."

"I *am*." Maverick's wolf was simmering, his voice harsh and guttural. He had gone from frustration to aggression in seconds.

Grey took a second to wonder if it was wise to question the alpha in this mood, but did it anyway. If the deputy head of the security team couldn't do it, who could? He looked up at Maverick again, startled by the wild look in his eyes. "And the chaos that would follow? For Arlo and Domino? For everyone else?"

Maverick didn't answer. Instead, he strode out of the room, the door banging behind him, and Grey heaved a sigh. *Great.* He'd pissed off the alpha. And worse, an alpha that had now decided he wanted to be taken.

Bollocks.

Hunter wasn't sure if he enjoyed the distraction of patrolling the club or not.

The customers were in a great mood, and the place was buzzing. The band was good, and the DJ set after that kept everyone on the dance floor. And yet, their collective mood couldn't lift his own. The shifters were wary and tense, especially the security team. He and Xavier patrolled together, examining every interaction, every unknown face with suspicion.

"This is insane," Xavier finally said as they drew close to the bar at the back of the room. "How do we distinguish a potential attack on us? On our pack?"

Xavier was French, in his late twenties like his cousin, Cecile. Both were tall and long-limbed, but Xavier was dark haired, whereas Cecile was a honey-blonde. Xavier had been attacked by the demon weeks before, and had taken a long time to recover from his injuries. It was thanks to Morgana's skills that he had survived. His deep claw wounds had healed, but had left scars. Probably mental ones, too.

"We can't, not really," Hunter confessed. "We can only look for odd behaviour, and surely it will come from unknown shifters."

"Not necessarily, if we're to believe what Castor said. One of us could be part of it." His eyes were fixed on the crowd as he said it, his lips tight, and Hunter understood his unease.

"I know, but it's unlikely. I trust our pack. Don't you?"

"Most of the time, but after Hal?" Xavier shook his head. "I'm not so sure. As for unknown shifters, there are always so many here. And you." He turned to him. "You're new. What have you got to lose?"

Hunter tried to contain his shock. "Everything! I love this pack. It's my home, and I am loyal to everyone here. Especially Maverick." He squared up to him, feeling his wolf rise. "I watched over you while you were injured. Helped fish you out of the fucking river. You think I'd betray you now?"

Xavier studied him, the beat of the music thundering in Hunter's blood as he withstood his scrutiny. "No."

Hunter released a breath, wondering for a moment if he'd end up fighting Xavier. Tensions were escalating already. "Good, because I fucking wouldn't." He forced himself to calm down, turning to the crowd instead. "Most people here just want a good time. I'm hoping that the witches' wards on this place keeps us safe."

Xavier shrugged. "But it's as they say. In a paranormal club, it's hard to ward against many things."

Hunter felt for the amulet that he'd tucked under his shirt that morning. It had been a gift from Briar, his ex-girlfriend. She was a witch from White Haven. It was a silver and copper amulet, spelled with protection, the head of a wolf engraved on it, with two small moonstones for eyes. It had been made by El, another witch, a jewellery maker with her own shop. Powerful spells had been woven into it from her magic, as well as Briar's. Protection, clarity, the ability to withstand hexes... Enough to keep him protected from general ill intent. He didn't often wear it lately. It reminded him too much of Briar, and it felt weird, considering how he felt about Domino now. However, with circumstances as they were, he'd decided to wear it. It was warm under his fingers from the heat of his body, and just touching it made him feel stronger.

"If we stick together," he said to Xavier, "we'll be okay."

"What do you think Hal will be doing? What tests or tribute are you expected to give to a god?" Xavier's dark, speculative look was back.

"I don't know. If it's a challenge, then he would have to fight other wolves, I suspect. Maybe therians." Hunter had been in his fair share of fights, some of them very bloody. It was one such altercation—a beating more than a fight that had left him half-dead—that had sent his family running to Cornwall. "Not enough to kill him, hopefully. Enough to entertain. Hard to know what else it could be."

"If they take me," Xavier's voice dropped, "I don't know if I'm strong enough to fight for long. I'm still not recovered. Not fully."

That was quite an admission from a wolf, and maybe he said it to make up for accusing him.

"You're still stronger than most," Hunter reassured him. "If Domino didn't think you were fit enough to be back on the team, you wouldn't be. I trust you'll have my back if I need you, and that you can fight, if the worst happens." Xavier just nodded, and Hunter looked back over the crowd again. It was thinning now. *Almost closing time.* "Come on. One last round before we close."

As Dionysus completed his set, they circled the room, encouraging everyone to leave, watching as conversations ebbed, drinks were finished or abandoned, and they all flowed towards the exits. The sound of chatter and laughter was loud, replacing the music that had finished. The club was hot, the floor sticky from spilled beer, and the scent of perfume, aftershave, and sweat hung on the air. But no one loitered.

Hunter relaxed as the last of the customers left, feeling the atmosphere change as it always did at this time of night. "I'll check the toilets, Xav. Just to make sure."

Leaving Xavier doing a final sweep of the small lounges, he knocked on the door of the women's toilets, shouting before he headed inside. After ensuring it was empty, he checked the men's too, watching a man leave as he entered.

And that was when he saw the small, silver coin on the sink, glittering under the light. Planning to add it to the staff tip jar, he picked it up and immediately realised his mistake. It hummed with magic, imperceptible before he handled it. His fingers buzzed, and a tingle ran up his arm and radiated across his body. An image filled his mind of a huge bronze door, heavy with patina, a snarling wolf rearing out of it in bold relief, and a location, perfectly clear.

The Hall of the Wey Wolf.

He knew its name. It was implanted, like the image and the location. He could see its shadowed rooms. Its rich reliefs and engravings. He felt its pull even as he stood there, seeing his own dark eyes wide with shock in the mirror over the sink.

Shit. After all the care they had taken that night. He tried to drop the coin and couldn't, and instead lifted it to see it properly. Not a coin, as he'd first suspected. *A token.* It was battered, the surface scratched, and when he twisted it, the figures engraved in the centre, two fighting wolves, seemed to move. Runes ringed its edge that he instinctively understood. *Welcome, brother.* On the back was a compass rose with wolf heads at the cardinal points.

And the call. He felt it. Knew he couldn't resist. The longer he stood there, gazing at his own reflection in the mirror, the more it gripped him. He had to go. He had been summoned. A challenge must be accepted, as the Wey Wolf demanded.

Fighting to control his mind, Hunter fumbled for his amulet and gripped it tightly with his other hand. *I need to put the token down.* If he could, he might save himself, and then they could rescue Hal.

But as much as one part of his mind wanted one thing, the other was desperate to find the Hall of the Wey Wolf. It was blazing like fire in his brain. A call he couldn't resist, no matter how much he gripped his amulet. He thought of Domino, of the pack. Of his alpha's commanding stare. If Maverick was outside now, he could stop him. They could tie him up.

However, even as the rational part of his mind suggested solutions, he knew that to keep him back would kill him. He had to go.

But the token.

His palm had clenched around it, and he forced it open again, uttering blessings to Briar and to El. He felt their cool, strong magic like a balm to his fiery desires. He had to give the token to someone. Hunter headed out the door and into the corridor, making his way to the main room, forcefully slowing his steps, hoping he could avoid shifters. The temptation to take another with him was strong.

And then he saw Jet. Small, human Jet, who would not be cursed by the token—he hoped. Who would know what to do with it. She finished her conversation with one of the bar staff, laughing as she walked away, and he stepped in front of her.

"Hunter! Are you all right?" Then she really looked at him, and her smile vanished. "What's happened?"

Hunter found he couldn't form sentences. Could barely open his mouth. However, calling on the witches' magic and still gripping their amulet, he summoned his last bit of free will. He thrust his hand at her, palm open. "Take this. Do not let a shifter touch it. I must go."

Her face drained of colour as she stared at it. "Hunter?"

"Take it. And don't stop me. *I must go. I know where it is.*"

She grabbed it, palming it like a magician, and he wondered if the call would cease, but it didn't. The pain of losing it almost caused him to roar.

Understanding flashed in her eyes. "Tell me where."

But he couldn't say the words. It was like his mouth had sealed shut, and he shook his head. "I can't. Don't stop me!" He turned away, and with relief, saw that the exit was open. And then he ran.

Nine

Maverick was at the entrance to the club, at the bottom of the stairs where the ticket booth sat and coats were stored, talking to Monroe and Cecile about the evening, relieved that the night had gone well.

He'd calmed down after his argument with Grey, and he vowed to apologise to him later. His anger and frustration had got the better of him, and that wasn't acceptable. *Especially as the alpha.* Grey was right; his place was here, but even so, he still wanted to find the club. Get in it and tear it down. He saw Hunter head past the door, almost running towards the exit to the carpark, situated to the side of the stage.

The oddness of it struck him, but no one was shouting. Then he heard running feet, and Jet exploded through the doorway and thumped into Maverick's chest. "There you are! Hunter has been bewitched. Cursed! He's going somewhere. I think he's been summoned." She was racing. Gabbling. "Someone has to follow him. But not stop him! He insisted on that."

Maverick pushed past her, running into the main club with Cecile and Monroe on his tail, and Xavier joined them. He tore off his shirt, ready to shift, the other wolves doing the same. Jet raced after them, shouting, "Not you, Maverick! I have to show you something."

All of them paused on the threshold to the carpark, Tommy already halfway up the steps, shouting, "Hunter! Where you going, mate?"

Maverick rounded on Jet. "Make this quick. Why not stop him?"

"He just said he *had* to go. He was tormented. I could see it! But not you. *I need you*!" Jet had never asked him for anything. Until now.

He turned to the others. "Go. Follow him, but keep your distance!"

In seconds, the wolves had stripped, shifted, and ran.

"What the fuck is going on, Jet?" They were alone in the narrow passage that led to the open emergency exit door, the night air cool on his skin, and it helped to clear his thoughts. "Tell me."

"I have to show you something, but you have to promise me not to touch it. In fact, where's Grey?" She spun around, searching for him, and Maverick saw the bar staff, all human, watching them as they cleared glasses. And he was just standing there, half naked. *Fuck.*

Dionysus, still in his DJ's pulpit, called down, "Everything all right down there?"

"Fine!" The last thing he needed was their perpetually stoned DJ getting involved. He pulled his t-shirt on. "Why Grey?"

"He's human." She stared at him, weighing him up. "I think it will be safest. I don't know enough about what I have."

"You don't trust me?"

"I don't trust what Hunter gave me, with very good reason. He explicitly told me not to give it to a shifter. That was all he could manage before he raced off."

Maverick placed his hand on the small of her back, ushering her forward. "The security office, then."

They were halfway there when Grey came running, but Maverick shooed him back. "To the office."

"What's happening with Hunter?"

"Office. *Now*."

Maverick's wolf was rising again, and he thrust it back. *Not now*. Even though the cool air was calling him, and he longed to race with his pack. As soon as they were in the office, he slammed the door shut.

"Show me."

"What the fuck is going on?" Grey asked, staring between them.

Jet took a breath to gather herself. "I think Hunter has been cursed or bewitched or something. He gave me a coin. It cost him a great deal to give it to me, I could tell. He struggled to get every word out. He stressed that a shifter could not touch it. But I don't know how powerful it is just to look at. Can you feel anything on me, Maverick? And don't lie!"

Both humans studied him, and he closed his eyes. "Let me see." Maverick inhaled, leaning closer to Jet. Scenting her perfume, the rum and Coke on her breath, the faint smell of her deodorant. Her energy. He heard her heart beating, quicker than normal, but he sensed nothing remotely magical. "No." He opened his eyes again.

Jet glanced nervously at Grey, then took a step back. "Keep your distance." She reached into a pocket, extracted something and opened her palm. "He gave me this."

A dull, silver coin lay on her hand. Too big to actually be a regular coin. And it was old. Battered. He waited, trying to ascertain any magic. "I can't feel a thing. Are you sure it's magical?"

"Very sure. I will never forget Hunter's face. He was in pain. It was killing him to hand it over. He fought to do it."

"Have you looked at it properly?"

"No. I stuck it straight in my pocket. I can't feel anything from it. No tingling or anything. It's just warm. Probably body heat."

Maverick leaned closer and his anticipation rose. "He's left us a clue. Is that a wolf on it?"

"Let me examine it," Grey said. "You happy if I pick it up, Jet?"

"Yes, if you are."

Grey picked it up between finger and thumb, gripping the edges so they could all see the image in the centre, and he held it under the desk light. "Feels okay to me. I think it's a token. Something you'd present to someone to prove you belong. It's very worn. Runes around the edge. Two fighting wolves in the middle." He twisted it so the light played over its surface, and Maverick caught his breath.

"It's moving. The image, I mean."

Grey narrowed his eyes at Maverick, and then the coin. "I can't see that."

"Nor me," Jet said, leaning in close. She placed a hand on Maverick's chest. "Not too close for you."

Maverick nodded and stepped back, shoving his hands in his jeans' pockets. "I can definitely see it move slightly, and the longer I stare at it, the more I want to touch it. What's on the back?" Grey flipped it, revealing a compass rose, four snarling wolf heads on each point. A faint image seemed engraved behind it. "Is that a hall or a room behind the compass? Can you see it? It's faint."

"Just about." Grey twisted it under the light again. "Yeah, it's faded, but some type of hall, surely. There are columns."

"Like a temple," Jet suggested.

"That's it. The place where Hal and Hunter have gone." Maverick slammed his hand on to the desk. "I should have followed."

"No." Grey shook his head vigorously. "Jet did the right thing by keeping you here. We need to take this to the witches to unlock its magic."

Jet's jaw clenched and flexed with worry. "What about the wolves following him?"

"They better have sense enough to wait, or we'll have lost half the security team," Grey said. "Was Domino one of them?"

"Not from down here. She's still upstairs, as far as I know." Maverick turned to Jet, tearing his eyes off the token. "Tell me exactly how he behaved."

"He came out of the side passage, where the lounges and toilets are, and intercepted me. I knew something was wrong immediately. He looked so worked up. So utterly unlike Hunter. He was struggling to control himself, to speak. I think he just wanted to run. It really hurt him to give me the token. He insisted you not stop him. It's as if he thought he'd be in danger if you did. He also said he knew where it was, but when I asked him to tell me, he couldn't. He was also gripping something with his other hand." She demonstrated with her own hand. "I didn't see what it was, but it was on a chain."

"That's good! Well spotted. We'll ask Tommy."

"If he comes back," Grey warned. "You know how Tommy gets."

Maverick's thoughts raced, trying to decide what to do first. If his wolves returned knowing where Hunter had gone, it was tempting to head there right now, but that would be foolish. If he joined the challenge, he wanted the odds stacked in his favour. Now was not the time. *But if the shifters chasing him didn't come back...* He didn't even want to finish that thought.

"I need a drink. A strong one." He crossed to the bar. "I'm having rum. Neat. Anyone else?"

"With Coke for me," Jet said, crossing to the window to look down on the club. "I'll come back for it after I've closed the doors. In fact, we should let the staff upstairs know what's happening. Domino needs to know about Hunter." She hesitated. "You know they have a *thing* going?"

Maverick nodded. Anyone would be blind not to see that. "I know."

Grey pocketed the token. "Let me fill her in, and I'll take this with me. You two stay here. Talk things through. Then we'll decide whether we call the witches tonight or tomorrow. We also need to see if Xavier saw anything. He was with Hunter—or should have been."

Maverick poured a generous shot of rum for all three of them, knowing Grey would take it neat. He wanted to rouse the witches and unlock the token's secrets, but it wasn't like he'd be raiding the so-called club right now. "Yes, he should have. We need to walk through Hunter's movements, find out where he found the coin. Some bastard left it behind, which means someone from that damn club was here." He knocked the first rum back so quickly it burned, and immediately poured another. "In my own damn club. Fuck." He stared at Grey. "What if anyone else has gone?"

Grey went to the door. "If we're compromised, you are at risk, and we cannot lose you. Stay put with Jet. I'm locking things down."

Ten

Grey now suspected that whoever was behind this unknown club was human. They would have to be to handle the token. Unless someone who was already a member could handle it.

He had so many questions, so many ideas, and he needed to explore them rationally. *But not yet.* First, he needed to lock up and make sure there were no other tokens lying around. The trouble was that tokens could have been left anywhere. Under the sofas in the lounge area, tucked down cushions, or even dropped on the floor.

After making a thorough check of the toilets, he decided to recruit the human bar staff and the girls on the ticket counter to search for them. He called them together in the middle of the empty club that always felt huge once the place was closed, and showed them the token. He fielded questions as best he could, told them to abandon the glasses cleanup, and to search the entire floor, bringing him any suspicious objects, whether they looked like the token or not.

"A guy tried to pass something like this when he paid for a drink," Miles said, taking it from Grey, his expression thoughtful. His head was part shaved with a short mohawk, and Grey had long suspected he knew more about the shifters than he was letting on. "I handed it back. He was very apologetic."

"Really? What did he look like?"

"Average height, maybe five-ten." He shrugged. "We were busy. I didn't notice details. What's the deal with it? It has wolves on it."

"Just some type of private party invite. Like a game," Grey said, thinking quickly. "Just find as many as you can, and give them only to me. No one else. Whoever finds one gets a bonus in their pay."

"Is there a problem?" Jade asked. "I saw the security team take off."

"They have a few things they're following up. Just focus on this for now."

He retrieved the token, and left them discussing it between them, no doubt wondering what the hell was going on, but they split up pretty quickly to search. The added incentive helped. He ensured the back door was locked, and that behind the stage was clear, and then headed upstairs. The ground floor bar was just as quiet, and Arlo sat in the corner booth talking to Vlad and Domino. Reassured by the calm atmosphere, he indicated to Arlo that he would join him in two minutes, ensured the entrance door was locked, and searched the toilets. It didn't take him long to spot another token. It was on the floor, half behind the bin in the men's toilets, like it had fallen out of someone's pocket.

He picked it up carefully, as if it might bite, and held it up to the light. It was exactly the same as the one Jet had given him, just maybe slightly less battered. *Thank the Gods he'd found it first.* Pocketing it, he completed a sweep of the bar, deciding to recruit the bar staff as he had downstairs.

First, he needed to speak to the shifters. He wasn't looking forward to breaking the news to any of them, especially Domino. Normally, he felt he had an equal relationship with the wolves. Yes, they were stronger, quicker, intimidating when they chose to be, and sometimes when they didn't. They had a presence that was hard to ignore. However, Grey was ex-Services and trained in combat, so he knew he could hold his own. Now, though, he felt protective of them. They were his friends. His family. And they were all at risk. Vulnerable because some crazy had awakened an old god that could have repercussions for all of them.

He'd seen Hunter's behaviour when he'd been shutting down the security cameras in the office, and knew something was wrong from his body language. *Of course!* Grey mentally slapped himself. He could hopefully track Hunter's movements on the feeds. That was his next job. With luck, he could also search for the man who tried to pass the token off to the bar staff.

Arlo was still sitting in the corner booth by the bar, half an eye on the cleanup while he talked to Vlad and Domino, but as Grey approached, his eyes narrowed. "What's wrong?"

Grey looked at Domino, and then back to Arlo. "Hunter is gone. Just be calm while I explain." He ran through the events, and when Domino shot to her feet, face ashen, Arlo pulled her down again.

"There's nothing you can do," Grey told her. "Not yet."

"He could be hurt. Killed!"

"And if we all go after him and are taken?" Arlo asked her. "The pack will fragment. We wait. Grey is right. So is Maverick." Arlo shook his head, clearly reining in his own urge to hunt from the way he gripped his glass. His knuckles were white.

"You may want to ease your grip on the glass, Arlo," Grey recommended.

"Yeah, sorry. Show us the tokens, please."

Grey studied their pensive faces. Their wolves were rising, the golden glow kindling at the back of their eyes. "No. Not now. I'll take photos for you. Right now, I want to search this floor, and I'll use the human bar staff to do it, like I did downstairs. Just to make sure there are no other hidden surprises. There could be other tokens, or even something different but equally dangerous to you."

"I think we should know what to look out for," Vlad pointed out.

"Like I said. *Photos*. I'll head to one of the offices to do it. You didn't see Hunter and the effect it had on him. Or on Jet, just by seeing him like that."

Vlad exchanged a worried glance with the others. "That bad?"

"Doesn't it sound it?"

Arlo nodded. "Someone was here then. We were targeted, and they were happy to take any shifter."

"Looks that way." Grey glanced around him. "Where are John and Jax?"

"Staff room."

"I suggest you take them downstairs with you to the security office and wait there while we search." He looked at Domino, and his hand closed over hers where it was clenched on the table. "Hunter is strong. We'll work out what he was holding in his other hand, and where he was going, and then we'll find him and Hal. Promise me, all of you, no heroics tonight. No searching alone. And no touching anything!"

After exchanging reluctant expressions, they all nodded, and Vlad said, "We promise."

"Good. Get down there, and I'll be with you soon."

Hunter had one objective in mind, and that was to reach the Hall of the Wey Wolf. It was in north London, across the river, and it would take a while to get there.

The urge to find it wasn't making him shift, so he still had free will about that. *But which way was best?* Some of his pack were behind him, keeping their distance, but tracking him. He was at war within himself. He should shake them off, disguise his path—the spell was telling him that—but he wanted them to know where he was going, and Briar's amulet was allowing him to remain clear-headed on that fact.

Wolves couldn't follow him on the Tube, other public transport, or in a taxi, and right now, with the desire to get to the hall growing with every step he took, getting there fast was winning out. Travelling in his wolf would take far too long. He was heading to the Tube when a black cab passed him, and almost without thinking about it, he stuck his hand out, hailed him, and jumped in. He couldn't say the full address; the token's magic forbade it. In fact, he wasn't even sure he knew the address, but he knew where it was, so he told the cab driver the general area. Safely on his way, he looked out the back window, seeing the shadows of wolves come to a halt, and knew he was on his own now. He just hoped that the token could be decoded.

The farther they travelled, the more the hall became clearer in his mind. He saw torches, old fashioned ones, held in wall sconces, their flames making grotesque shadows. He saw runes carved in walls, reliefs of wolves, sturdy columns, and twisty passages, and smelled blood and fear. And with every mile, two eyes blazing with fire intensified in his head.

When the cab finally stopped, he paid his fare almost mechanically, stumbling onto the road. For ten minutes he crossed roads and skirted back alleys, finally making his way to a Victorian house that was in the process of being renovated, on a street not far from Finsbury Park. It was at the end of the road, and he knew he had to go to a side entrance. A skip was on the front, half full of rubble, and the place looked empty, but it called him. He ran down the narrow side-passage and banged on the door, and while he waited, he noticed the brass door knocker was a wolf's head.

In seconds a man answered, slightly shorter than Hunter, a half-smile on his face as his eyes swept over him. Behind him, Hunter made out a hallway, dimly lit, in a state of renovation, too—half-wallpapered walls, paint splashed floor. A general air of decay. The acrid scent of cigarette smoke drifted from a room at the end of the hall, along with the low hum of voices.

"You're new," the man said, still amused. Cocky, even. "You must have something for me."

"You invited me. I'm here. Let me in."

"The token." The man held his hand out. "I need it. It's your passage to the club."

"I haven't got it." Hunter's eyes blazed, he knew they did, and his wolf was simmering, but he had enough control not to tell the man what he'd done with the token. His charmed amulet was safely out of view.

The man faltered, doubt in his eyes. "You must have. It's impossible not to have it."

Hunter grabbed him around the throat, lifted him bodily off the floor, and slammed him into the wall. "Well I haven't got it, and unless you want me to tear you limb from fucking limb as my first blood sacrifice, you *will* let me in." The pain and urgency of needing to be here was fading now, replaced by cold, hard anger that this man would dare refuse him.

A shout came from the other room, and another man emerged, his features indistinct in the dark. "Problem, Barry?"

Hunter kept Barry pinned in position, the rational part of his brain wondering why they weren't used to dealing with snarling shifters when they were running a club for them. The other half didn't care. "Little Barry here seems to think I need my token, but seeing as it led me here, it's done its job. Would you like me to spill his blood right now to prove myself?"

"No! Just let him go. We'll address the missing token later."

Barry clawed at Hunter's hand, and he squeaked out, "Yes, later. Follow me."

Hunter dropped him, and Barry stumbled to stay upright. He looked as if he might speak again, but then clearly thought better of it, and Hunter followed him down the corridor to another door while the other man retreated. *Coward*. Inside, steps led down, and damp air met him, along with the scent of wolf.

He was in.

Eleven

The atmosphere in the security office was tense, but if anything, Domino was relieved. Discussing the events of the night with her team gave her purpose, and helped distract her from worrying about Hunter. Plus, at least Hal wouldn't be alone now.

After hearing Jet's account firsthand, she pulled up the security videos. Maverick, Arlo, Vlad, John, Jax, and Jet all crowded behind her. Knowing the area and time they needed made it easy, and they replayed the feed from the camera that recorded the passageway and the entrance to the toilets.

"There," Jet said, as they watched Hunter exit the female toilets and enter the men's. "He looks fine. Calm, normal. But when he comes out, look at his hands."

"He's holding the token," Arlo said, nodding. "And something in his other hand. Any idea what it is, Dom?"

"No. He doesn't usually wear jewellery." She frowned as she considered the curry earlier. It seemed like years ago, not just hours. "I noticed a chain under his t-shirt, but didn't think twice about it. We were busy."

"The guy," Vlad prompted her. "Coming out of the toilets. Let's have a look at him."

Domino replayed the digital feed, pausing to examine the man who had left the toilets before Hunter. "He's the last one out. Anyone recognise him?"

"No," Vlad said. "I was behind the bar upstairs for much of tonight. He didn't loiter there. I'm good with faces."

"He's not a regular," Jet confirmed. "I'd know him."

"I remember him entering," John confirmed. "Arrived on his own, but nothing new there. He didn't speak, just headed inside. You notice anything, Jax?"

"Nothing more than you."

Domino studied his frozen image. Average height, short beard, nondescript dark hair. He wore a shirt with jeans rather than a t-shirt. "We don't know he left the token," she said, "but we must consider him. I'll print his picture."

"I take it," Arlo asked Jet while she readied the image, "you haven't heard anything about an unusual club while doing your rounds tonight?"

Jet shook her head. "No, I was just telling Maverick. A few did comment, however, that the North London Pack were having issues. They didn't elaborate. Just said a few pack members were unsettled. No specifics. When I asked if there were issues with Castor, they said they had no idea."

"Who is 'they?'" Maverick pressed.

"A couple of shifters who aren't in the pack, but know some who are. They didn't elaborate. I was wary of pressing them too much."

Domino took the image off the printer and tacked it onto their notice board, and then returned to the video, watching the man exit the club without doing anything else. Then she focussed on Hunter, but it was hard to see him properly as the camera offered only a side view. Jet was right. He looked agitated. All her fears for him came rushing back when the team who were following him returned, slamming into the office, followed by Grey, who had let them in.

"You lost him, didn't you?" she asked them, too anxious to be anything other than blunt.

"He jumped into a bloody taxi!" Tommy was furious, and his hair was a tangled mess as he pulled his jeans on. "A fucking *taxi*! How the hell could we follow him?"

Jet intervened, half Tommy's size. "He's not in control. The curse, or whatever it is, is strong."

The office was suddenly crowded with the arrival of Fran, Cecile, Monroe, Xavier, and Tommy, all hot after their chase, and tension was rising again.

"Well, I'm in the fucking dark," Tommy snarled, "so someone needs to tell me what the fuck is happening!"

Domino listened while Jet and Maverick went through it all again, trying to make sense of it. "At least," she said, when they had finished, "we know what happened to Hal. Someone gave him a token too, or slipped one in his pocket. Again, that could have happened here, or outside. Maverick, you need to share Castor's news, too." Maverick just glared at her. "You do, and you know you do, or everyone only has half a story."

The team listened, incredulous, as Maverick updated them on his meeting with Castor. Domino had expected a belligerent response, but instead there was only an uneasy silence.

"Well, I," Grey began, heading to the monitors, "am going to look at the feed from the camera by the toilets."

"Already done." Domino pointed at the image she'd printed, glad to change the conversation. "Recognise him?"

Grey pulled it down off the wall. "Give me a minute." He left the office, and she listened to Monroe relate their chase while she wondered what he was up to.

"Maybe," Arlo said, "Maggie can track down the cabbie. Find out where he went."

"Great idea. Spot the registration?"

Cecile reeled it off. "I want in on this hunt. None of this male bullshit about leaving the females out of it."

"Have I ever left you out of anything?" Maverick looked affronted.

"Just saying. I like Hunter and Hal. I want to help. This token business is shit. Underhand. And a damn fight club? Distinctly male bullshit."

Grey re-entered the office, waving the photo, a broad smile on his face. "This is the guy who tried to pass off a token as change to the bar staff. It's definitely him. We have our guy."

Tommy took it from his hand. "Let me see him. I'll rip his fucking head off. Show me the tokens, Grey. I'll find him tonight."

Grey folded his arms, defiant. "No, you will not. The tokens are going to the witches."

Tommy stepped forward, as menacing as a wild bear. "Grey, do not stand—"

Grey stopped him with considerable balls, Domino thought. "Do not say another word, Tommy. You shifters are all riled up and angry. I get it. We are missing two of our own, and he's your best mate. I feel it just as much as you. But I am telling you now, you will have to rip me apart to get these tokens, and I'll give you a damn good fight doing it."

Maverick stepped in. "Stand down, Tommy. We do this right, and we do this together. And we do it soon."

"Tommy," Jet said, cutting in. "Hunter was holding something in his other hand tonight. Something that was on a chain around his neck. Do you know what it was? He was gripping it as tightly as the token."

Tommy cocked his head, confused, and then his expression cleared. "Aye, I know. It was that witch's amulet. A present from his old girlfriend, Briar. He didn't often wear it, but he put it on this morning after Hal vanished. Said it might help, and that he'd be a fool to ignore it."

Domino felt as if someone had thrown a glass of cold water over her. *He was wearing something from an old girlfriend?* And then rational thought kicked in. *That was a good thing, obviously. Anything that would keep him safe was good.* "She was a powerful witch, I understand?"

Tommy nodded. "An earth witch. I met her once or twice. Little thing. Gentle." He turned to Jet again. "He was holding it?"

"Gripped in his fist. I'm sure it was helping him resist the token, if only for a short while."

Tommy smiled for the first time that night. Shoulders dropping as his anger subsided. "That's one positive thing, if he can hang on to it. I don't feel he's so alone now."

Domino shoved her irrational jealousy aside, buoyed by Tommy's mood. "Great, let's hope it continues to give him strength."

Maverick nodded with approval, too. "Grey, thanks for your help tonight, but head home now and go see the witches first thing. It's not like they can do anything tonight. Make sure to tell them about his amulet. You happy having those tokens at home overnight?"

"Of course." Grey grabbed his jacket. "I'll take you home, Jet."

Jet nodded. "My jacket is upstairs. I'll get it."

Grey followed her out the door, but his eyes met Domino's briefly. "See you tomorrow. Go home, rest. All of you."

"He's a cheeky fucker," Tommy complained once the door was closed.

"And he's right," Maverick said, before Domino could leap to the defence of her deputy. "He's keeping a clearer head than any of us. All of you, grab a drink, take a seat, and let's debrief before you go home. Then we tackle this with fresh eyes tomorrow."

But Domino knew she wouldn't sleep. *Not until this was over.*

Twelve

Hunter followed Barry down to a long, low-roofed cellar, where one wall was partly knocked through to create a rough-edged doorway. One thing he knew for sure, thanks to the token's implanted memories, was that beyond it was a passageway that led to the Hall of the Wey Wolf.

He presumed that during the course of renovating the cellar, they had discovered a bricked-up entrance and had decided to investigate what it led to. Rubble was stacked in the corner, and the floor was swept clean. The scent of wolf was stronger here, and Hunter's need to progress quickened his step. Hunter had a lot of questions, but wasn't sure how many he could ask without knowing how much free will he should have under the token's influence. Especially after the ruckus he had caused upstairs. He had calmed down now, rational thought was returning, and he knew he needed to be careful. Perhaps most shifters were more docile on arriving.

Barry ushered Hunter ahead of him. "After you. And no tricks, or the Wey Wolf will judge you poorly."

Hunter stepped through, head ducked, and down a couple of steps to where a stone-walled passageway stretched ahead and downwards, a faint light glowing in the distance. He quickened his pace, noting the stone flagged floor was swept clean of debris, and then passed the first flaming torch on the wall, smokeless and heatless, despite the flickering flames. *A magical flame.* The passageway turned and descended even further, but growing broader and higher, some stones carved with images of wolves. Finally, the way was blocked with a massive door made of bronze, copper, silver, and gold, with the enormous, raised relief of a snarling wolf's head dead centre. Precious gems were laid into the ornate design around the edge, and two huge rubies represented the wolf's eyes.

There was no discernible key or hinges, but the wolf's open mouth had an extended tongue that was far more discoloured than the rest of the relief, as were the sharp tips of the four fangs protruding from the top and bottom of the wolf's jaw. His body knew what to do. Hunter pulled his jacket sleeve up and dragged his forearm under one of the sharpened canines. Blood flowed, and he smeared it onto the tongue. The wolf's eyes glowed blood-red, and with a click, the door swung wide, revealing another passage beyond.

This place was far different. The blocks of stone comprising the walls and floor were huge, the finish was better quality, and there were more flaming torches. Ornate archways marked their route, all carved with reliefs of wolves and forests, and faint voices were ahead. Finally, the ceremonial passage ended at enormous double doors made of dark wood, and this time, his escort stepped ahead of him.

"What's your name?"

"Hunter."

The man smirked. "How apt."

"Better than *Barry*," Hunter snarled.

A flicker of fear passed over Barry's face again, and he pushed the doors wide open. A blaze of candlelight illuminated a small chamber that was again richly carved with images of wolves. Two enormous statues of wolves stood guard inside the entrance. Several passageways led off it, and the sound of voices grew louder. They were shouts—or maybe jeers. Again, Hunter's implanted images filled his mind, and the complex unfolded before him. Several halls, rooms—or perhaps cells—an arena, and a labyrinth. Other rooms remained in shadows, as if hidden from him.

His wolf longed to be free, but Hunter controlled it, taking everything in, memorising it all, and adding to the images he already had. Already he was reevaluating what he thought he knew. This place was ancient. Sustained with blood and combat. But also, guile. Hunter noted that there were no guards. *Not here, at least.*

"You must meet the Wey Wolf," Barry said, appraising Hunter's build. "Then combat will be decided. This way."

Hunter felt a moment's anger that this man—a mere human, not a shifter—should presume to tell him what to do, but then the need to see the Wey Wolf rose up, overriding every other desire. He was led down more passageways until he finally entered what could only be described as a throne room. Several wolf-shifters were in there, some in their wolf, others human, and all turned when he entered, eyes gleaming at his arrival. He barely noticed them as his attention fixed on the figure at the end, dominating the room as he reclined at ease in the huge throne.

The man, or rather shifter, vibrated with power and influence, and was far taller than any normal shifter. That much was obvious, even while sitting. His broad shoulders and bare chest rippled with muscles, his abdomen was flat, and he had long, dark hair that was plaited in sections, framing a middle-aged face. Pleasant looking, but with an edge of brutality. He wore trousers made of some kind of hide, but his feet were bare. Thick, metal torcs dressed his neck and upper arms, but that was the only jewellery he wore. However, Hunter barely noticed any of it. He was transfixed by the shifter's eyes. *The Wey Wolf's eyes*. His eyes smouldered with the intensity of a Super-Alpha, and as soon as Hunter looked into them, he sank to his knees as a rush of desire to please flooded him, overriding rational thought. He fixed his eyes on the ground in obeyance.

"His name is Hunter," Barry said, head down, voice meek.

"Look at me, Hunter," the Wey Wolf demanded. His voice was deep, rough-edged with an accent Hunter couldn't place. "I would see our newest acolyte who has entered my halls. Step closer."

Hunter looked up as the vibrant voice commanded, staring into the storm-grey eyes of the Wey Wolf. Hunter rose to his feet and advanced, unable to resist, finally stopping only a few steps from the throne. The Wey Wolf's eyes churned, ash and amber mixing together as they fixed Hunter with an intensity he had never experienced before. He felt seen. Truly seen. But maybe that was an illusion.

The Wey Wolf's eyes became hooded, his smouldering power veiled. "Interesting. A fighter, certainly. Loyal—on occasions. Stubborn." He sat back. "How did you come here?"

Hunter's mouth was dry, and he moistened his lips. "I found a token."

"Ah. You were summoned."

"My Lord, if I may speak," Barry said, voice faltering. "There is a problem. He had no token to give me."

"Is that so?" The Wey Wolf studied Hunter. "Why not? Those tokens, crafted by my shaman, are not meant to be discarded."

Hunter wanted to confess all, but the cool metal of Briar's amulet strengthened his resolve. "I lost it on the way here. I ran, caught a taxi. I must have dropped it. I was at work, and my pack started to chase me. I panicked."

Another shifter he didn't know stepped forward. "He's from Storm Moon. I recognise him. We have one of their pack already. Hal." Hunter's hopes soared. *Hal was here. Alive*. "He came using a token, too."

"Did he drop his?" the Wey Wolf asked, eyes still on Hunter.

"No." The suspicious attention of the room settled like a weight on Hunter's shoulders. "No one has ever *dropped* a token."

Hunter's natural cockiness reasserted itself, knowing the best form of defence was attack, or maybe it was just his wolf desperate for a fight. He smirked at the unknown shifter, trying to remember if he had ever been at the club. "Maybe it's because I'm from up north. Not soft, like you southern wankers."

The shifter snarled and reached out to punch him, but Hunter had expected it, and he dodged and tackled the shifter to the ground, landing on top of him, ready to throw his first punch. But then others raced in and dragged him off.

The Wey Wolf roared. "Enough! This is not the place to fight. Bring him to me."

Hunter was dragged forward again, and he dropped his gaze. *Do not blow it. Submit.* "I apologise. I don't like to be doubted."

"You may do well here. But know this, Hunter. If I find out you are lying, you will die slowly and painfully, and it will not be honourable."

"Understood, my Lord." Hunter had never called anyone 'my Lord' in his life. He didn't like it, but neither could he stop himself. This damn bewitchment was fucking with his head.

The Wey Wolf continued. "Tonight, you will be given a place in the halls to eat and rest. Tomorrow you will face your first challenge. I must consider it."

"Not tonight?" Hunter stupidly asked, the need to prove himself rearing up.

He laughed. "There will be plenty of challenges to come. Allocate him a place and feed him. I have more acolytes to receive. I feel them getting closer. But you and I will talk again."

This time, another shifter stepped out of the shadows, leaving Barry and the shifter he'd tackled to the ground to retreat. The new shifter was older than him, covered in old scars, his chest bare, but he wore leather guards strapped to his forearms, and loose trousers made of animal hide. With a shock, Hunter realised he was as ancient as the Wey Wolf. In fact, several of the wolf-shifters in here were. They carried the weight of centuries, and he felt their stares on his back as he followed the old shifter.

Out of the Wey Wolf's influence, Hunter felt more like himself, but it was impossible to settle when danger and uncertainty lurked everywhere. He was used to feeling sure of himself, but here, in these labyrinthine passages, everything was different. The scents, the sounds, the obvious age of the place. *How had the Wey Wolf and his ancient warriors been resurrected? Why? And how had this place survived so miraculously intact?* But then he knew the answer to that question. *Magic. The spells of a powerful shaman, perhaps.*

"What time are you from?" he asked the grizzled shifter.

He stopped in the passage and turned to look at Hunter, the light illuminating the numerous scars on his face and arms. "You ask a lot of questions."

"I asked *one*. I'm curious."

"We last walked when Athelstan was King of Wessex, but he was not my Liege Lord."

"Yours would be the Wey Wolf, I'm guessing."

"And now your Lord, too. Do not displease him."

"What's your name?"

"You do not need to know that."

He turned abruptly and marched ahead, finally leading Hunter into a dimly lit and low-ceilinged hall from which the mouthwatering scent of roasting meat emanated. Half a dozen long, wooden tables with benches ran down the hall, and a smokeless fire raged in a central firepit, a huge spit with a pig on it turning slowly. Only a few shifters were in there and they stared at him, eyes hooded, their expression guarded. But Hunter only really saw one of them.

Hal.

His escort gestured to the seats. "Eat, drink. Find a bed in the rooms beyond. Your packmate will help you." He grinned, revealing unexpectedly gleaming white teeth and prominent canines. "Choose your bed well. There aren't many of you yet, but there will be."

He stalked out of the room after that ominous announcement. Hal was seated alone, his back to the wall on an end table, and Hunter immediately headed to his side, keeping his voice low. "Hal, mate. Are you all right?"

Hal smiled, eyes bright with a fervent gleam that immediately worried Hunter. "I'm glad to see you, Hunter. You'll like it here. It's a place of opportunity."

"Is it?" He looked around at the other shifters, and saw what he'd missed when he first entered. They too looked bright-eyed, the wolf within too close to the surface. "An opportunity to do what?"

"Ascend to the Wey Wolf's side—if you prove yourself through challenge."

Hunter was pretty sure how that would work, but he asked anyway. "What kind of challenge?"

"By fighting, of course."

"As a wolf or human?"

"Both." He shrugged. "It's unclear at the moment, but there are tests that we must complete. The details will be revealed as we ascend."

Hunter's wolf was already rising at the thought, but his rational mind rebelled, aided by his amulet. *Ascend? Challenges? Sounds like a damn cult.* "I take it that you entered here using that token? Some bastard planted one in the club, and I found it. How did you find yours?"

"On the street outside the club, on my way home." Hal's gaze darted to the other shifters. "It's how some of us are here. Others—the messengers—come and go."

"Messengers? Interesting." He'd expected as much, but didn't want to tell Hal that. "But you seem okay. You can think for yourself?"

"Of course. Free will is necessary to be able to fight properly."

"And you want to fight."

"It's what I live for." He studied Hunter, eyes questioning. "Can't you feel it, Hunter? The rising energy here. The raw power? If you don't yet, you will."

It struck Hunter that maybe he shouldn't be too honest with Hal. His amulet was giving him some control, but Hal had nothing, as far as Hunter knew. He could betray him. Plus, he suspected he was lying. Hal couldn't possibly have free will, and the Hal he knew certainly did not live to fight. "I met the Wey Wolf. He confused my thoughts, like the token did. I had to get here once I touched it. I couldn't control myself."

"You won't when you fight, either." Hal pulled his t-shirt aside, revealing long gashes already healing that ran down his chest. "It's not to the death, Hunter, but you must prove yourself. You *want* to prove yourself. Plus, the more you do, the more privileges you get."

"What kind of privileges?"

"More food. Better quarters." Hal shrugged. "I arrived yesterday, so I don't know much yet."

Just enough to whet the appetite. "But we will get to leave at some point, right? Some do, as you say. The messengers."

Hal shook his head. "We are token-bound. Like a blood oath. Look at your hand, Hunter." Hunter opened the hand he'd used to pick the token up, and with a shock, saw the image of the fighting wolves shimmering in the centre of his palm. Hal showed him his own. "This says we are bound to the Hall of the Wey Wolf. We do not leave. Ever. And honestly, why would I leave? This place offers all I need."

Thirteen

Morgana had never seen Grey look so serious as he finished relating what had happened in Storm Moon the night before. He had phoned just after eight in the morning, asking to visit early, as he had news to share.

Now, he placed two dull, silvery metallic circles that looked like coins on the kitchen table. "They look harmless, but they're not."

"You don't feel any different after handling them?" she asked him. "You have kept them all night."

"I feel fine. What will you do, Morgana?"

Morgana didn't answer immediately, instead holding her hands over the two tokens. She immediately felt the buzz of ancient magic. "I don't know. I can feel magic, but that's no surprise, seeing as I'm attuned to it. But will it affect me? If it's intended for wolves, in theory I'll be safe."

Grey grunted. "In theory doesn't always work out."

"But you're fine, and I am human."

"What if you pick it up and try to charge out the door?"

"Don't stop me." She smiled wryly, "But don't let Birdie or Odette do the same."

"Where are they?" he asked, glancing around the kitchen again. Like many visitors, he was intrigued by the place.

"In bed. They always rise later than me. Plus, we had a late night. We were trying to find and tweak a Wayfinder."

"Sounds intriguing."

"It was an ambitious idea that I had after remembering we had all sorts of old travelling paraphernalia upstairs. Really old instruments. Magic ones and regular. I was hoping we could use one to find the club. But if you think this contains a map, then maybe we could use this token."

"I take it you didn't manage to make one?"

"Not yet, but we have more concrete ideas than before we started."

"Should you wait for them now?"

Morgana took a breath, making her decision. "No need." She picked up one of the coins, shivering as she felt the tingle of magic in her palm, but fortunately, that was all she experienced. "I'm not sure whether to feel disappointed or not."

"Bloody hell, Morgana," Grey complained. "Shouldn't you have warded it or something first?"

"Not when I want to touch it. Plus, like Hunter, I have my own amulet." She placed her fingers on the large, flat obsidian stone encased in silver that hung around her neck, the stone nestling in the well of her clavicles. "I think Hunter's amulet saved his sanity last night. Just a little, at least. He's brave to have handed this to Jet." She headed to the window and held the coin to the soft grey light of the cloudy morning. "Now, we just need to decide how to unlock its secrets. It must contain a map of sorts. We need to find the key."

"A magical key?"

"A spell. It would be helpful to know how old it is. There are runes on it, which may indicate rune magic of sorts. I think I'll call Harlan. Or..." she hesitated, trying to recall the date when Olivia, the occult hunter, was next due to visit for a check-up on her pregnancy. "I can ask Olivia."

"Olivia?" Grey asked. "Is she all right?"

"She's fine. It's just a regular check-up. You know her?"

"I've met her in the club once or twice." He smirked. "She's in Maggie's pack, with Harlan and Jackson Strange. And that huge unit, the Nephilim."

"Nahum." Morgana huffed, annoyed with herself for not thinking of his abilities. "Yes, of course. Nahum could be of great help. I think they are due this afternoon. In the meantime, I can do some research. Run a few tests. Discuss options with Odette and Birdie. The thing is," she looked across at Grey, "clearly not all shifters need these if they are talking about the club. It sounds as if some can come and go. Like maybe some have free will to leave and others do not. Don't you think?"

"Totally. So, why the distinction?"

"Why indeed. And if some know where it is and can visit it freely—we assume—should we kidnap one?"

"Wow! I never thought I'd hear you suggest that."

"Neither did I."

Grey sighed, doubt written across his face. "I counselled caution, worried we might alert them too soon, before we're ready to act and know how to defeat whatever the shifters might face. To rush in might mean disaster."

"And yet, to wait might risk Hunter and Hal's life."

"I know. Half the security team wanted to grab those," he gestured to the tokens, "and charge in last night. Tommy especially. We could lose half the security team that way, and I don't want to risk Maverick. It could mean the collapse of the pack, which would mean a fight for a new alpha. If we kidnap one of Castor's pack, even with his blessing, and word gets back, we lose any advantage, however small, that we currently have."

Morgana nodded. "Understood. It's good reasoning, but I hate that we know so little. Well, you may as well leave me to it. If I have any more questions, I'll be in touch."

"Thanks." He finished his coffee, and placed his mug in the sink. "I'm going to see Maggie now. She needs to know what's going on. You know she'll want to see those tokens."

"Like a bull at a gate, I'm sure." Morgana knew Maggie only too well. "Tell her there's no point yet, and I'll call her when I have news. Same goes for Maverick. I need time with these."

"We don't have a lot of it."

"I know, but we'll work as quickly as we can."

If they didn't find a way to reveal its secrets, maybe kidnapping a shifter was their only play.

Arlo arrived at Storm Moon early, unable to sleep well after the discovery of the tokens and Hunter's disappearance.

He intended to search the club from top to bottom, even though he knew that Grey had ensured the staff did it the previous night. Jax, his flatmate and a member of the security team, had volunteered to come with him, and he had gratefully accepted. Some people found Jax moody, but Arlo had always got on well with him. As soon as they arrived at the club, they searched the bar on the ground floor again, both wearing gloves that Arlo hoped would give them some level of protection if they accidentally touched a token. They upended chairs, pulled out cushions, and moved tables, but fortunately found no other tokens, or anything else suspicious. Just as they were finishing the search, Arlo's phone rang.

Jax emerged from the underside of a table. "I'll make coffee."

Arlo nodded and answered. Before he could even get beyond his name and make polite greetings, a woman called Lucy, the human wife of a shifter, launched into a confusing babble of distress.

"Slow down!" Arlo instructed. "What's happened?"

As he listened, his heart sank, and after taking down as many details as he could, and giving what he felt were useless reassurances, he ended the call and viciously kicked a chair, sending it sprawling across the floor. "Fuck!"

"Problem?" Jax asked, handing him a mug of strong coffee. "Please don't throw it at me."

"Another missing shifter. Henry Roget's son, Finn. Bloody hell, Jax. He's a teenager!"

Jax rolled his eyes. "She's always worried about him. He'll probably turn up later."

Finn was fifteen years old, and had started to shift a few months earlier. His first shift to his wolf had happened in his sleep, and he'd awoken with a yelp, literally. He had been stuck in his wolf for hours before mastering the shift back to human. As Lucy was human, no one could assume he would become a shifter, as he might not have inherited his father's abilities. However, he had been showing signs of unusual strength, good hearing, and excellent night vision, so they assumed he would likely shift at some point. Both parents had been pleased when it finally happened, and his father had shifted with him. However, even with his parents' support, Finn had worried about his next transformation. Unlike adults, adolescents could not fully control their shifts, which was hazardous, to say the least. After their first shift, they practised extensively to learn to control it, and to then change at will. Some kids picked it up quicker than others. Finn had not. Consequently, Jax was right—his mother, Lucy, always worried about him.

Arlo sipped his coffee, appreciating the shot of caffeine. "I think she's right to worry this time. He didn't come home this morning. He went out with friends last night and had a sleepover."

"Even though everyone was warned yesterday about the current situation?"

"Human friend, apparently. From school. They thought he'd be safe. Except he insisted on walking home this morning."

"So he left his friend's house, but didn't make it home?"

"Sounds like it. Lucy was very upset. She struggled to get out a coherent sentence."

Jax was less than sympathetic. "For fuck's sake. So he's having trouble mastering his shifts, stayed at a human's house, and walked home alone. Talk about fucking idiotic!"

"I thought it, but didn't say it. Apparently, his best mate—the human—helps his mood, and it's been pretty shit recently because of his trouble adjusting to his wolf." Arlo tried to think rationally, but the more he talked it through with Jax, the worse the situation seemed. "He's vulnerable, Jax. Not like Hunter and Hal. He's a kid!" He stared at their club bar, seeing it with fresh eyes. It had always seemed like a sanctuary. Their safe space. And some bastard had come in the night before and planted spelled tokens, and maybe that same person had abducted a child. "I need to tell Maverick. We can't afford to wait. We have to act."

Jax leaned against the bar, brooding. "We don't know where to go. You said Grey was seeing the witches this morning?"

"Yes, he's taken them the tokens. Then he'll meet with Maggie. Hopefully, the witches are working on it already. But it's not enough. Maverick needs to speak to Castor again."

"Castor?" Jax frowned. "What's he got to do with it?"

"Sorry, you must have missed that conversation last night." They had decided to inform the team of Castor's issues, but obviously not all had heard the news. "Castor came to Maverick in confidence. Told him he's having problems in his pack." Arlo summarised the rest. "Maverick said he'd tell only the senior staff initially. He changed his mind last night."

Jax slammed his mug down, sloshing coffee across the bar. "That's not fucking helpful at all, Arlo. The security team should know! We're working blind here. It also suggests that Maverick doesn't trust us."

"It's sensitive, and you know now, so calm down! It means some of Castor's pack—and therefore other wolves—do not need a bloody token, and are willingly involved in whatever this thing is."

"Exactly! I'm not an imbecile. It means there are two layers to this secret bloody club. What's so special about the wolves that know?"

"I have no idea. We know next to nothing about this, and I'm as frustrated as you, so don't take it out on me." He sighed. "Honestly, Jax. There's a reason we keep stuff from some of you sometimes. You go off like a bloody cracker."

Jax fidgeted, a guilty look crossing his face. "I suppose I do. Sometimes."

"There's no *suppose* about it." Arlo liked Jax, but he was exasperating, and he hadn't got time for sulks and egos. "Come on. Let's tell Maverick the latest development."

"I can come with you?"

"Yes! Just keep your damn temper in check."

Grey showed Maggie the photos of the two tokens while he started on his bacon and egg sandwich on white, crusty bread. *No fancy smashed avocado for him.*

They had met in a café that not only offered a range of breakfast options, but excellent coffee, too. Maggie, like him, had opted for a bacon and egg sandwich with lashings of brown sauce. A sight that warmed his heart. He liked her direct manner, profuse swearing, and quick wit. And she was pretty, too. Not in an in-your-face, excessively made-up way like so many women wore now, with pancake foundation and overfilled lips, but understated. Natural. Clear-skinned. Honest. *Yes, that was it. Maggie was searingly honest.*

"Fuck me, Grey," she said, handing his phone back to him. "This is a whole new level of shit. A fucking secret club! Sometimes, I fucking hate this job." She grabbed her sandwich and bit into it with relish.

"Can you get any more 'fucks' in that sentence?"

"Yes. *Fuck you*!"

He sniggered. "Liar. You love this job. It defines you."

"Are you saying there is nothing else to me except my job?"

"Of course not. I presume there are many layers to Maggie Milne." He smirked. "Maybe you do cross-stitch at night while watching *Strictly* or *Love Island*."

She had a mouth full of food, so her response was merely her middle finger, smeared in sauce.

"No? Okay, I know. Detective shows, of course. I bet you work out who-done-it every time."

She swallowed. "Wrong again. That's the day job."

"Forensic crime dramas? Maybe just the radio? The shipping news, perhaps."

"I'm not dead. If you must know, I like house renovation shows. Particularly that big man. The Geordie."

"Like a spot of decorating, do you? Nice."

"As if I ever have the bloody time. It's Saturday morning, and you've just shown me fucking tokens! Magic tokens that steal a shifter's willpower. So now I have to work." She pressed her fingers to her forehead and closed her eyes briefly. "I really wanted to give Stan and Irving the weekend off. We've been so busy."

"Then let me help." He mock-saluted her. "I take direction well. In all kinds of things."

Her eyes danced with amusement. "Really? So helping me find the right taxi sounds like fun?"

"Yes. I need to do something," he confessed. "If we find something concrete to go on, it will lift the pack's mood. I'm worried about them, Maggie. Especially Hunter and Hal. This feels dark."

"Everything in the paranormal world feels dark."

"Not true. Just sometimes." She took another bite of her sandwich as she watched him, assessing his usefulness, perhaps. Or how best to brush him off. He pushed on. "I feel protective of them, and I don't normally. I knew I had to get those tokens out of there last night, and I wasn't sure if Maverick would let me. I honestly felt my balls shrink as I suggested it."

"Sounds like they got bigger to me." She laughed at her joke. "All right. You can help me, and depending on what we find, we'll go from there. For all we know, he gave the wrong address to lead us astray. When do you need to be at Storm Moon again?"

"Later today. Four-ish. Earlier, if possible. I think my humanity offers them a level head right now."

"How is Maverick holding up?"

"Touch and go. He stormed off last night, but then calmed down. He wants to go charging in, so he's frustrated. I take it you haven't heard anything about a mysterious club?"

"No. Or missing shifters."

Then Grey's phone rang, and when he saw Arlo's name, he knew immediately it was bad news.

Fourteen

Hunter had slept on a rough, wooden pallet lined with straw and a coarse blanket, opting to sleep in his human rather than his wolf, although that would have been preferable, as it meant he could wear the protective amulet.

After Hal's ominous words and fervent mood last night, he was determined to wear it at all times, or keep it as close as possible when he fought. Hal didn't want to leave here. It had taken only twenty-four hours for this place and the damn token to bewitch him completely.

The bed was in a dormitory style room with a dozen other beds in it. Only four other shifters were there now though, including Hal. There were other dormitories down the hall, a scattering of shifters in those, too. Hunter was keen to assess how many were imprisoned there—there was no other word for it. He estimated maybe twenty, but was pretty sure there were better quarters elsewhere. As for the messengers, he presumed they went home as they chose. It was all so random and confusing that he didn't really know what to think.

The night before, Hal, normally chatty and relaxed, had not engaged further in conversation. Not surprising, really, as it was late and he'd been fighting, but Hunter suspected it was the effects of the spell that were influencing him more than anything. As for the other shifters, they had all exchanged wary glances with him. A couple were more encouraging, giving him nods of acknowledgement. Hunter forced himself to be patient, adopting their expressions that suggested unhealthy excitement at the prospect of servitude, because that is what it seemed like to Hunter. A willingness to fight for a place at the Wey Wolf's side, and to prove himself when he'd never felt the need to do it before. *Herne's flaming balls.* Plus, Hal had said there was no way out. He was token-bound.

Hunter studied his palm again, the fighting wolves easy to see in the dim light of the dormitory. The figures were silvery in appearance, shimmering with magic, and no matter how much he scrubbed at his palm, the marks wouldn't fade. Fortunately, he knew that the way out was through the twisting halls to the huge metal door carved with wolves. There had to be a way to release it, but perhaps the token magic meant Hunter couldn't cross the boundary. If he found a safe time, when he was alone, he would try to find it again. Right now, however, he needed to pee, and somewhere off this corridor was the water cave that he had visited briefly the night before, a type of bathroom.

Hunter headed to the passageway and found it was empty with no sign of guards, as if they were certain of their captives' compliance. Hunter again pressed his amulet to his skin under his t-shirt, glad that it kept some of his befuddled thinking at bay.

In a few turns of the stone corridor, he smelled fresh, damp air, heard the rush of water, and then the cave spread before him. A glassy black river coursed down its centre, a stone bridge crossing to the far side, where a series of rudimentary toilets—long drops, essentially—were situated. Water flowed over a high rockface creating a natural waterfall, and already a shifter was in it. At the far end of the cave, the river flowed through an iron gate set low in the wall, the thunder of the water reverberating around the cavern as it plunged deep into the earth. London had many underground rivers, and he wondered which this one was. *The Fleet, perhaps. Or the Strand.*

The unknown shifter had exited the waterfall and was already dressing, and Hunter headed to his side. "Can I swim in the river? Is it safe?"

"The current is strong, and it's deep, so I don't advise it. Stick to the waterfall." The shifter didn't look at him while he spoke, focussing on dressing. Hunter noticed fresh bruises and cuts, and the obvious claw marks along his ribs with new scarring.

"How long have you been here?"

"Days? Weeks, perhaps. Time loses all meaning here." He suddenly looked at Hunter, excitement flashing through his eyes. "The only thing that matters is the challenge. The fight. You're new." Hunter nodded. "Then you'll see. Today you will have your first challenge."

"Against another shifter?"

His eyes dropped again. "You'll see."

Maverick met Castor in a nondescript pub halfway between Castor's business, Apollo Pool Hall, and Storm Moon.

Castor looked tired, lines drawn around his eyes. "I hope you have some answers."

"Just more questions, because this has just got a whole lot worse." Maverick was worried about Hunter, but was seething about Finn's disappearance, and worried sick. Finn was vulnerable. He couldn't shift properly, and he certainly wouldn't be able to fight. Not against an adult shifter, anyway. He could easily die. He told Castor the details, gratified that he looked as appalled as Maverick.

"That's underhand."

"I know."

"I wouldn't fight a kid, though, Maverick. Not many adult shifters would. It's too easy."

"But some would. And if they're compelled? They might not have a choice."

"Your guys, Hunter and Hal, they'll look out for him."

"They will if they can, but what if they're kept apart? Or drugged or bewitched? Hunter could barely hold it together last night. And what about your pack? Any shifters missing?"

He nodded. "Two didn't turn up for work last night. I was about to call you this morning, but you beat me to it. They aren't answering their phones, and they're not at home."

Maverick was secretly relieved that Castor's pack had been affected, too. Horrible, yes, but at least he knew Storm Moon wasn't being specifically targeted. "I'm sorry to hear that, but also curious. It seems like some of your pack know more than others, so have they willingly gone, or were they given a token?"

Castor leaned forward, elbows on the table. "Tell me about the tokens again."

Maverick showed him the photos, and explained what Hunter had said, but didn't mention he wore an amulet. He still didn't trust Castor that much. He just said Hunter had reacted quickly before he was too far under its spell, and Castor seemed to accept it.

"Have you seen anything like these in your pool hall?" Maverick asked.

"No. I'd like to search the place, like you, but I can't give away that I know anything." Castor smacked his palm on the table making it shake. "I'm fucking handcuffed. This is ridiculous. I'm the damn alpha!"

"You're making smart decisions, though."

"It doesn't feel like it. It feels like I've made lots of bad ones. Your pack isn't keeping secrets."

Maverick snorted. "I'm sure they're keeping plenty. I can deal with that, as long as they're loyal. But I think most of yours are. The trick is finding out which ones. Are you still suspicious of Hammer?"

"Yes." Castor nodded reluctantly. "He seemed unconcerned about our missing pack members. Plus, there's a couple of regular customers I haven't seen recently. Now, I'm wondering about them, too."

"The ones you overheard the other night in your office. You say you know who they are?"

"Yes, younger, cocky pack members."

Maverick wasn't sure how his next suggestion would be received, so he braced himself. "We need to kidnap one of them."

"You fucking *what*?"

"We need answers."

Castor took his measure for a moment, and then laughed. "You're serious."

"Of course I am."

"How?"

"We use a tranquilliser dart. It worked before. On a therian, of course."

"Sure, because drugging therians is just par for the course. And where will you put my drugged pack member?"

"I was hoping you might have somewhere?"

"I deal with dodgy goods sometimes, Maverick. I am not a human trafficker!"

"Don't you have a lock-up or something?"

"What do you think I am?"

"A fucking crook! You must have a warehouse or somewhere to keep things?"

Castor fell silent and Maverick waited, sipping his pint quietly.

Finally, Castor said, "There is a small warehouse we use. But it's not empty or quiet, so we cannot use it for this."

Meaning it was full of stolen goods probably, and other shifters were there. They could use Storm Moon after closing, but what then? They couldn't keep someone there indefinitely.

Maverick sagged back in his chair. "Damn it."

"All out of dark cellars?"

"Yes." And then he had a thought that really should have struck him sooner. "We could just ask. We're both alphas, and you are *their* alpha. They are sworn to you. You could compel them."

"But it's like I said, without knowing who will support me, I could find myself undermined. Under any other circumstances…"

Maverick's anger that he had bottled up for the last twenty-four hours spilled out, and he no longer wanted to be careful. He wanted to rage. He leaned in, eyes locking on Castor's. "Fuck those thoughts! These are the circumstances to demand loyalty if they want to keep their place in your pack. Because it is *your* pack! Not Hammer's, nor any other deputies you have. Yours. That you earned, and you keep in check. You tell them that you gave them a few hours in which to come clean, and they haven't. So they have a choice. Talk or walk."

Castor's eyes kindled with fire. "Easy for you to say."

"Easy for you to do. We're being too defensive here. Caution is one thing, but getting screwed over is another. Odette mentioned a wolf god in her weird bloody prophecy! I don't know about you, but I will not bend my head to any god. Will you?"

"No."

"Then we need answers, and who better to pick than Hammer? Forget the kids."

"I'd do better with a weaker wolf. But..." He tapped the table, a steady drum of intent. "Tackling Hammer will show I mean business. I need to bare my teeth."

"Yes, you do." Then Maverick had another idea. He still wasn't sure how much he trusted Castor's account of what was happening, but since he was there... "If you let me bring a team—just a small one—I'll join you."

"It could make me look weak."

"Not if I said I needed answers, too. That I demanded information. That we had agreed on a collaboration. Like I said, two alphas are better than one." He lowered his voice. "This bloody *club* is a threat to all of us."

After another long, thoughtful pause, Castor nodded. "All right. Deal."

A loud bang and a puff of smoke emitted from the token in the middle of the pentagram, but it remained utterly unscathed, and

Morgana swore. "By the Goddess! That's another bloody spell that won't work."

Birdie tutted. "My dear, if it was this easy, where would the fun be?"

"Fun?" Honestly, Birdie was infuriating sometimes. "Hunter is missing! Spellbound by this damn thing. And Hal. And now a young boy, too! There's nothing fun about this."

Birdie looked contrite. "I meant fun in that it's a challenge. Of course the rest of it isn't fun. Poor Hunter. I have a very soft spot for him. All of them, actually. However, this is an opportunity to learn as well as unlock its secrets. It's a clever spell, layered and complex, and obviously cast by someone with great power. Someone from many years ago."

"A shaman," Odette said from her place outside the circle, her gaze fixed on a distant horizon as she gripped the second token. "Not a witch."

They were in the tower spell room, a bright fire crackling in the hearth to warm the room while they worked. Grimoires, manuscripts, and other books were spread across the floor for reference. They had all been working for hours, and Morgana was tired and hungry, but at Odette's insight, she cheered up.

"You've seen something."

"A feeling only. Of a hand reaching forward across time. Old. Powerful. Grasping."

Odette closed her eyes and Birdie and Morgana fell silent, Morgana fearful of moving in case she disturbed Odette's concentration. Her strange prophecy—if that was even the word—from the day before, had left them all chilled with the prospect of what might come. The battle hunger, the old one that would rise… Had risen, in fact, by the sound of it.

Odette nodded to herself, hand gripping the token. "There are so many passages. So many rooms and smokeless flames. And the scent of fear is strong. But also exhilaration." She opened her eyes again, a shudder running through her slight frame. "It's underground."

Birdie clasped Odette's shoulders as she faced her. "Well done! That's good. Anything else?"

"I felt a presence, but whether it was the wolf god or whoever crafted this token, I'm not sure."

"You said 'shaman,'" Morgana reminded her cousin. "What made you say that?"

"An insight. I just know. This token was made over a millennia ago. I know that, too."

"Norse, perhaps?" Birdie suggested.

"No. It's rooted here, in England. In this place of ancient kings."

"Olivia is due here, any minute now," Morgana said, opening the circle of protection she had used to seal the pentagram that she worked within. "I'll show her that token, if you've finished with it. You can keep the other one, try a few more spells. We'll be no longer than an hour."

Odette handed her the token, rubbing her palm afterwards. "Of course. It's odd. I can feel it on my skin, but I was probably holding it too tightly. It's nothing." She shrugged it off.

Morgana left them to it, walking quickly along the winding corridors of Moonfell and down the back stairs to the kitchen, just in time to hear the long tolling of the front doorbell that sounded like a gong. It reverberated around her, and Morgana sniggered. Odette had spelled it to sound like the old Rank Films intro, so that any visitor was announced with great pomposity.

Olivia and Nahum stood at the threshold, both looking worried and hopeful all at the same time. Olivia was an attractive woman in her late thirties, always stylish, even when dressed in hiking boots and khakis. Nahum towered over her. They were a striking couple.

"Look at you, two!" Morgana said, hugging them both. "You look so well. So happy!"

"We'll be happier after this examination," Olivia said, patting her slightly rounded stomach, her pregnancy finally beginning to show.

"Follow me. It will be fine."

"What's with the doorbell?" Nahum asked. "I felt quite impressive."

"Just Odette being silly." She smiled. "And you are!"

Morgana's consultation rooms were part of the main house, but had a separate entrance. Just an office, examination room, and a bathroom, but all were as dramatically decorated as the rest of the house. One of the many places Morgana retreated to if the house felt too full of people during seasonal celebrations.

They settled in her office, and Morgana focussed purely on Olivia and the baby. She still didn't know what would happen long-term with the Nephilim child. Nahum had warned that the baby might not survive to adulthood, as none of them ever had millennia ago. She refused to accept that. So far, the pregnancy was proceeding well, and the couple were clearly very happy. She reassured them, and pregnancy dealt with, she produced the token.

"I want to get your opinion on this, but please don't touch it, Olivia, just in case."

"It's spelled?"

"And then some." She outlined their current dilemma.

Nahum had no qualms about handling it. "*Welcome Brother.* Nice."

"I forgot you could understand all languages," Morgana said, eyes on the token. "Intriguing, isn't it? The shifters can see the wolves moving, apparently. Fighting in the centre. It's attuned to their shifter power. Odette has had some fleeting insights. She says it was crafted by a shaman, and that it was made a millennia ago."

"Silver, certainly," Olivia said as she leaned forward to examine it. Nahum placed it on his palm, turning it back and forth.

"Yes, silver holds spells well."

"Anglo-Saxon, I'd say."

"Really?" Morgana looked at her, surprised. "You can tell so quickly?"

"I'm an occult hunter, so I need a wide range of knowledge in many areas. I studied Art History at university, with a few extras on the side and since. Yes, this is Anglo-Saxon. I can tell from the way it's made."

Morgana sat back in her chair, digesting the information. "Interesting. That matches with what Odette said. I presume that it was spelled at the same time. A shaman would fit within that time frame."

"Powerful leaders and kings would have been advised by shamans and Druids. Even through the Medieval period and onwards," Olivia said. "That's essentially what JD was. An advisor to Queen Elizabeth I. Her 'magician.'"

Nahum nodded. "It was the same in our time. This wolf god would have had advisors and soldiers and lackeys. *If* he was a god."

"You doubt it?" Morgana asked.

"He could have been a powerful shifter who *wanted* to be a god, or was elevated to a godlike status by magic. I wonder what caused his downfall."

"If we could find that out, we can do it again."

"He's clearly been sleeping—if that's the right word," Olivia said, thoughtful. "A state of suspended animation, from which someone somehow reanimated him. I'll speak to Harlan, see if he can tell us anything useful."

"Unless he's not an old wolf god at all," Nahum suggested, handing the token back to Morgana. "What if a shifter stumbled upon an old temple and absorbed some ancient magic? He could have used a ritual, or blood magic, and reinvented himself."

Morgana blinked, shocked at his suggestion. "I don't think any of us have even considered that. You're right. That could absolutely have happened. It's an opportunistic grab for power."

Nahum shrugged. "It probably won't change how you stop him, or rescue the captured shifters, but it would still be good to find out. If you need help, I can be part of the team." He smiled. "I'm pretty useful."

Morgana had hoped he'd offer, but didn't want to presume. "Thank you. I'll update Maverick with our news and let him know."

Fifteen

"I'm coming today," Domino said to Maverick, "so don't even try to stop me."

"Of course I won't. You're my head of security, for a start."

"If we get an address, we move straight away, yes?"

"Within reason."

Domino was furious, worried, and tired. Since Hunter's disappearance, and now Finn's, she was desperate to find the club and rescue their pack members. Anything could happen to them in captivity. *Anything.*

They were in Maverick's flat with Arlo and Vlad, preparing their strategy, and they hadn't got long. They were due to meet Castor at the Apollo Pool Hall within two hours.

Domino glared at him. "What does 'within reason,' mean?"

"It means that if we find out it's a fortress, we need to consider our approach." Maverick's eyes burned into hers. "We don't wish to die or be bewitched, either."

She dropped her eyes to the floor and took a breath. "No. Of course not."

"I'm as worried as you, but we must keep a clear head, especially with what Morgana has told us." The witch had updated them with their news and theories. "Plus, I've had Lucy calling me all afternoon in a mad panic, so I don't need any more of that."

"Who are we taking?" Vlad asked. "Things might get ugly at Apollo. They have before."

Maverick reeled a list off. "Tommy, Monroe, Jax, and Cecile. And me and Domino." Maverick looked at Arlo and Vlad. "I need you two here."

"Here?" Arlo gritted his teeth, jaw clenching as he obviously sought to control his frustration. "But we'll be back by the time we open."

"Not necessarily. We have no idea how this will play out. The club needs protection, and the staff need senior figures present. That's you two. Grey will be here, too. Don't worry. I'm not charging into an unknown club without you. Just the pool hall."

Domino nodded, ignoring Vlad and Arlo's frustration. "Good suggestions. I like that we're not taking Xavier. He can stay here and guard the club with the others. It will be under-staffed, though."

Arlo huffed. "Fran and Mads will be annoyed."

"Mads knows that we need the club properly protected," Vlad said, unconcerned. "So will Fran. They'll need to be extra vigilant on the doors today."

"You've shared that man's image?" Domino asked Arlo, knowing he'd been busy all morning.

"Yes, I texted it out to everyone."

"He'd be an idiot to come back," Vlad said.

"Not if he's an arrogant prick," Maverick pointed out. "It strikes me that they are all arrogant. They think they have the upper hand."

Domino laughed, but there was no mirth in it. "They have, for now. We're still scrambling to catch up."

"But we will," Maverick reassured her. "We've already learned a lot more thanks to Hunter, but Nahum raised a good point. This might be a modern-day shifter who's simply absorbed old magic."

"It doesn't change the way we fight it," Vlad said.

"It might. When we go in, I want the witches there, too. Or at least one of them. We need to counter the shaman's magic in that token. I would imagine the source—the temple—would have more of it." Maverick raked his hand through his thick, dirty blond hair. "Damn it. This is not something I would have envisaged happening. A damn resurrected temple! It's madness."

"You know," Domino said, swinging her legs as she sat on the barstool at the kitchen counter, "the humans could be compelled, too. Why would they do all this otherwise?"

Arlo nodded. "Good point. Unless they were promised rewards of some kind."

"Or threatened," Vlad said.

So many scenarios, and so much they still needed to find out.

Domino's phone rang and she took the call, leaving the others in brooding silence. "Grey. Please tell me you have good news." She listened, aware that the others were watching her intently as Grey rattled off information and a plan that exasperated her. "I don't think that's a good idea—" but he had already gone. "Fuck it! The cab dropped Hunter off at the Manor House Tube Station. That's as much as we have. No address."

"That's better than nothing," Arlo pointed out.

"But it's a huge area. He either covered his tracks deliberately, or couldn't help himself. Probably the latter."

"What," Maverick asked, clearly annoyed, "is Grey doing that is 'not a good idea?'"

"He's going there with Maggie to investigate."

"Fucking fuck!" Maverick exploded, slapping the countertop. "That's stupid."

"Maggie's idea, apparently, and they promised to be careful. Grey is not a fool, Maverick, nor Maggie. If we fail to get any info out of Hammer, we'll need to do that anyway." Domino jumped off the stool, eager to get moving. Fear for their friends' and the pack's safety—especially Hunter's—driving her anxiety. "I'm going to assemble the team. Time to rumble."

Maggie exited the Tube station to a busy road surrounded by urban sprawl, Finsbury Park lying across the main road.

"Right, where first?" Grey asked. "It's a big place. There's the park, houses, shops, and the bloody wetlands are behind us."

"I know. And a whole bunch of warehouses, too." The Harringay Warehouse District was close by, a mixed live and work zone where most of the old warehouses had been repurposed. "I think we should look there. Lots of big buildings that could easily accommodate a club."

"But it's underground," Grey reminded her. "That's what Odette said."

"The entrance could still be there. I think it's very likely."

"They're wolves. They like space."

"If it's underground, it doesn't matter."

Grey pulled his jacket around his shoulders to ward off the chilly April wind. "Fine. We'll start there."

"Thanks for coming," she said, as they walked together. "I know you wanted to be at Storm Moon."

"I'll get there not long after it opens, hopefully. I didn't want you doing this alone, though, and you had that stubborn look in your eye." Fortunately, he looked amused rather than annoyed.

"I can't just sit around and do nothing. It's my job! If some bloody shifter god is establishing territory in my city, I need to stop him."

"*We* need to stop him."

"Exactly. I am fully aware I need Storm Moon's help." She was also fully aware that Maverick was heading to the Apollo Pool Hall, and she didn't like that idea one bit. "I'm surprised at Maverick. Castor is untrustworthy."

"He knows. We all do. But he's genuinely worried. This whole thing is just weird." Grey stopped on the pavement, causing Maggie to stop, too. "A shifter who doesn't respect borders."

"What?" she asked, confused.

"The fact that he doesn't respect borders. He—they—are trampling all over them. Family units. Pack territories." He picked up the pace again. "Interesting."

"Maybe he's too powerful to care." She took stock of the surroundings again as they entered the warehouse complex. "We better keep our wits about us. Just in case. There could be guards everywhere if the whole area has been claimed by him. Can you recognise a shifter now?"

Grey shrugged, head wagging. "Mostly. You?"

"Usually. They have a way, don't they?"

"When you know what you're looking for."

Maggie always thought of it as a presence. It wasn't just their build; it was the look in their eyes, too. The energy they gave off. "If you see one, stay cool."

"I was born cool."

Maggie laughed. There were worse ways to spend a Saturday afternoon than with Grey, hunting for dodgy shifters.

Sixteen

Hunter spent the morning training.

The labyrinthine passages of the Hall of the Wey Wolf contained a long room with all manner of weapons. Spears, swords, daggers, a variety of chains spelled with magic whose purpose he couldn't discern, and punching bags made of leather. Everything was centuries old, and while some of the weapons were beautifully crafted, most were plain. A dozen or so shifters were already there, sparring and training, in groups or alone. They all acknowledged his arrival, a couple appearing friendlier than others. They were assessing him, as he was assessing them. Wondering how well he fought. He was used to it. It was something all shifters did, but this situation just enhanced that.

Hunter had no idea how to use swords or spears. He fought with his fists, claws, or teeth. However, it was clear some of the other shifters could, especially the original guards who were also practicing. The ancient shifters who had resurrected with their king. They were assessing them all, and making sure, no doubt, there wasn't too much interaction between them. Hunter was confused by the whole thing, not sure whether he should be trying to bond with the token-bound or keep his distance. The entire atmosphere felt odd, and he felt out of step. *The amulet's doing, perhaps.*

Plus, his lack of skills worried him, but even worse was the room beyond the training area. It was a big, square pit surrounded by seating, like a gladiatorial arena. Beyond that was the entrance to a dark passageway that he believed was the labyrinth—or so the token's implanted memories told him—and he wondered what awaited him inside. *Was there a Minotaur at the centre?* That wouldn't surprise him in the slightest.

Then Hal entered the room, eyes darting with anticipation, and he joined Hunter, lifting a sword from the wall next to them. "Good to see you here, Hunter. Want to spar?"

"You can use a sword?"

"I can now. Can't you feel it?" He frowned at Hunter. "This place gives us those skills. The token, too."

"You still have yours?"

"No, but it imprints memories. As does the sword. Pick one up."

With horror, Hunter realised the amulet may be preserving his judgement, but it was blocking things he needed to know. *Unless...* He reached for a sword, the hilt cool but comfortable in his grip, and a thrill of knowledge like an electric shock exploded skills into him. Moves, counter attacks, and stances. Blood pounded through his veins, and he was desperate to test his abilities.

"Why?" He stared at Hal, confused. "Surely this gives us unfair advantages in a challenge."

"Not when we all have that knowledge. The Wey Wolf demands a spectacle. Besides, sometimes you do not fight others. Or you fight as a wolf. I experienced that yesterday." Hal stripped his t-shirt off but left his jeans on, showing the scars from the fight the previous day.

"Did you win?"

"I did. I forced the other wolf into submission. But we need to practice. Today there will be many challenges, and we'll watch some of them."

By now the scent of blood and sweat that hung around the halls, along with whatever strong magic had been cast there, had awakened Hunter's fighting instincts that were never far from the surface anyway. He took his t-shirt off too, slipping his amulet into his pocket, and once it was no longer touching his skin, he felt the urge to prove himself grow stronger. Within seconds he and Hal were sparring, moving quickly in their corner of the room on nimble feet. Muscle memory flared, and after a few false starts, Hunter found he could fight with confidence. But it was odd, as if another body inhabited his own. The more he fought, the stronger that other self seemed. When they finally finished, both sweating from the exertion, Hunter was sure of his instincts. A shadow warrior moved with him. *Another consequence of being token-bound.*

Casting another wary glance around the hall, he asked, "Do you feel your normal self here, Hal?"

Hal grinned. "Better! I can fight with a sword now."

"But other than that?"

"I feel this is where I'm meant to be. Amongst warriors. Part of the Wey Wolf's pack." His eyes kindled with shifter power again. "The best pack to belong to. Soon, none will stand in our way. Glory will be ours, Hunter." He slapped Hunter hard on the shoulder, hunger for success blazing from his every pore.

Hunter wasn't certain he should ask his next question, but he had to be sure. "You don't care about Storm Moon, then?"

"Yesterday's news. Soon, no other packs will exist. All will stand beneath the greatest alpha of all. The Wey Wolf." Hal frowned and leaned close, voice low. "Surely, you know that? These challenges are to prepare us for the fight that will come."

Shit. Hunter shrugged, trying to appear as nonchalant as possible. "I'm still getting used to the place. Of course, you're right. I'm being slow. But there's not enough of us here."

"This is just the start, Hunter." Hal grinned broadly again, his expression fervent. "*We are the start.*"

Hunter had no idea how to respond to that, but fortunately, the sound of loud voices distracted them both. "What's going on?" he asked Hal.

"The audience, of course."

Edging to the door, Hunter pulled it ajar and saw the seats around the fighting pit filling up. He had little idea of the time in the sunless place, but had imagined a fight would be at night. *Surely, it couldn't be night already.* As he shut the door and turned his attention back to the training room, he saw a couple of shifters he knew. Shifters from the North London Pack.

"Hal, you recognise them?"

"Sure, but I don't know them. Castor's shifters, originally. Ours now. We're all on the same team here, Hunter."

"But we still fight each other."

"Challenge, to prepare us for the fight ahead." Hal frowned. "Honestly Hunter, you're being really slow with this."

Mustering enthusiasm he didn't feel, he just smiled. "I get it now. We are of the Wey Wolf. One pack."

"Exactly. And those out there? Watching. They too have their place. They watch now, but they will also face challenges. I'm glad that you're here, Hunter. You're a good fighter. I cannot wait for my next challenge."

Hunter had always believed himself to be smart, but Hal was right. He had been slow to see this, and that must be because the amulet was blocking that blind loyalty to the Wey Wolf.

He spent a few moments watching the other shifters in the room, impressed at the speed and skill on display, especially the old shifters. The ancient ones, as he called them. They were more brutal. Sweat, testosterone, blood, all mixed and heightened his shifter energy. His wolf longed to break free, and his natural aggression simmered. He didn't care who he fought, or what with, he just wanted to fight regardless. He was inhabited by a shadow warrior, and it was taking root. Blocking reason. That was also why he knew this place so well. He had the shadow warrior's memories. *Was that also why he understood them? Why they all spoke the same language? Or perhaps that was magic, too.*

A guard strode through the training room, summoning everyone's attention. "Time for your first challenge." He pointed to one of the shifters who Hunter had presumed to be a lone wolf from the way he carried himself. "You first, the rest in the stands."

He nodded, throwing his shoulders back, his powerful muscles rippling. "Who do I fight?"

The guard smirked. "Yourself."

Morgana was on her way back to the tower when she received a text from Odette telling her to join them in the India room—a vastly underwhelming name for such a treasure trove of a room.

It had taken much longer to search it the previous evening than they had expected. The deep red walls were lined with multitudes of shelves and storage cabinets, some of them glass fronted. They contained sculptures made of bronze, clay, porcelain, and silver, fragments of pottery, miniatures, stacks of postcards, jewelled rings and bracelets, unusual daggers with ornate hilts, piles of silks, embroidered gloves and scarves, as well as books, maps, and scrolls. It was bewildering. A treasure trove of ancient cultures, and a window into another time. Of course, there was also an array of instruments. Cartographers' tools such as compasses, sextants, astrolabes, telescopes, and hourglasses, all of which Morgana found fascinating and baffling. Unfortunately, none of them were magical, and too tired to continue—and her head full of images of exotic travel—they had gone to bed, temporarily defeated, as she had admitted to Grey that morning.

After his visit, her thoughts had been consumed with the tokens, but it seemed Odette and Birdie had resumed the search for a magical Wayfinder. She stepped onto the second-floor landing, greeted by shadows cast by ornate lamps, shafts of fleeting sunshine, and the scent of incense. It was rare in Moonfell to find any overhead lights switched on. They all found them too glaring and utterly lacking in romance. Using a ceiling light was akin to sitting in a dentist's waiting room, and there was an unspoken rule that they would never be switched on unless absolutely necessary. This would soon be the floor her bedroom was on, and the thought utterly delighted her.

"Not long now," she muttered to the walls, patting them as she passed. One last portion of decorating, and she would be done.

She found Odette and Birdie leaning over the huge wooden desk in the centre of a faded Persian rug. "Have you had success with the token?" she asked them, heading to their side.

"Unfortunately not." Birdie lifted a tarnished bronze disc the size of a side plate that contained three concentric rings. Silver, rose gold, and copper were inlaid into the design, making it an object of great beauty. "We gave up in a fit of pique and returned here after you left. We found this."

"Ooh! That looks interesting." Morgana took it from her hands, finding it unexpectedly heavy. "Where was it?"

Odette pointed to an ebony trunk richly embellished with carvings in the corner of the room, the lid lifted open on brass hinges. It was surrounded with fantastical objects. "In there, along with the other objects we have stacked around it."

"Magical?"

Odette's lips twitched with a smile. "Looks like it. Compasses spelled to find precious metals and jewels. An armillary sphere that is moving ever so slowly. Plus an astrolabe that has the weirdest markings on it. Those are just a fraction of them. But the one you're holding looks promising for our needs."

Morgana's attention returned to the flat disc, noting it had moon phases etched on the middle ring. "Moon phases. Intriguing. Cardinal points on the inner ring. Strange. You would think they would be on the outermost one. How is it used?"

"We're not entirely sure at this stage. Moon phases and cardinal points are all well and good, but it has a small direction pointer, so something must cause that to move somehow."

"Don't forget the back," Birdie said, examining the tokens again.

"I'm getting there." Odette rolled her eyes. "You just focus on your job! Look at the outer ring, Morgana. That's the most important. Can you see the markings on that?"

She'd been focussing on a flat, indented area within the inner ring, but switched her gaze to the outer ring, noting odd markings etched into it. Struggling to see them clearly, she took it to the window for extra light. "They are animals. Wolves, birds, bears…is that a boar?"

"And a stag, plus another couple we haven't quite worked out yet." Odette's eyes blazed with excitement. "Now the back."

The back plate was made of silver with inlaid geometrical bronze shapes. In the centre was etched in bold cursive: *To track all manner of shifters*.

Morgana took a sharp breath. "A shifter tracker! How fantastic." Then she frowned. "Why would our ancestors have needed this?"

"Perhaps they were hunters of rogue shifters. Or bounty hunters. Or they just liked collecting curious objects." Her arm swept outwards to encompass the room. "Our family are magpies. This room, and in fact the entire house, is evidence of the fact. We collect all sorts of things and have trouble letting go. This place is like a museum. Admittedly, a very comfortable one."

"I must admit, when I thought we'd find something of use, I didn't expect *this*. How does it work?" Morgana turned it over again, trying to discern the other engraved images. "This one's a chimera. Look at all the different body parts. That's why it looks so odd. That one is a Djinn."

"A Djinn is not a shifter."

"Not in the strictest sense, but it can change shape." One image was perplexing Morgana. "A bat? Are there bat-shifters?"

Birdie snorted. "Vampires. They change shape, too. I encountered one once, many years ago. I was in my twenties."

Morgana couldn't believe her ears. "You encountered a *vampire*?"

"Encounter is perhaps the wrong word." Birdie looked vibrant with health, despite her years. "It was hardly a stroll in the park. I staked it through the heart. It was quite a tussle, but I wasn't alone, of course."

"You actually staked a vampire! Why don't we know about this?" Odette asked.

"I try to forget. It was horrible. They are such vicious creatures." She brushed it away casually, and once again, Morgana was struck by how little she knew of her grandmother's past, and she filed it carefully away for future discussion. "Anyway, my point is that they shift. They can be bats, wolves, mist, shadows...even moths have been reported. There are others, and not just animals or insects. Therefore, I suspect the bat means vampire. It is its most commonly associated shifter animal."

"Okay, so we have a very useful tool that can track all manner of beings that shift. There's one final symbol that's odd, though. The infinity sign." She showed it to Odette, who nodded.

"We think it stands for God or Goddess. Infinite knowledge. Infinite life, perhaps."

"And that's because," Birdie put in, "there are numerous shifter gods, too."

"It covers the whole range, then," Morgana said, handling the Wayfinder with more reverence. "What an amazing object. Just imagine what else is stored around the house that we haven't found yet."

"One thing at a time. Pop it on the table, please," Birdie instructed.

Morgana placed it down. "Have you uncovered anything else about the token?"

"No, but I thought we should try something. That flat area in the middle of the disc is too large for this token, but we should drop it in anyway, don't you think?"

Odette tucked an errant curl behind her ear. "We must try, but we need to move the needle out of the way, or hand, or whatever you call it."

"It looks like a blade to me," Morgana said as Odette lifted it free of it's fitting. "A stiletto. Isn't that what they're called? Shouldn't there be two, or even three of them?"

"We have no idea what it should look like," Birdie said, carefully placing the token in the area. "Right. Let's see what happens now."

But when Odette fitted the stiletto pointer back in position, absolutely nothing happened at all. "Bollocks. We're missing something."

Birdie's phone started ringing, and she picked it up, distracted. "Hello? Harlan! How lovely to hear from you." She listened and nodded. "Of course. I'll send them now." She ended the call. "He wants photos of the tokens. Let's hope he has some fresh ideas."

Seventeen

Maverick had been warned that the Apollo Pool Hall would be open when they arrived, as Castor wanted to ensure that everything looked normal to his pack.

Unlike the previous time they had visited, there wasn't a bouncer on the door, and Maverick presumed it was because it was late afternoon. Even so, the place was reasonably busy, the hum of conversation and the clinking of pool balls a pleasing accompaniment to the Saturday afternoon football on the TV screens fixed to the walls. It was a bastion of testosterone, with only a few women in attendance.

Maverick entered without fanfare, his attention on the room as he took in the mixed groups of shifters, humans, and witches. A few of Castor's pack were spread across the floor as expected, but there was no sign of Hammer, the lean, scar-faced pack second. The atmosphere seemed relaxed—for now. Castor was seated at the bar talking to Barney, their grizzled bartender, but as soon as he saw Maverick, he called him over.

Maverick turned to his team. Tommy and Monroe, equally large, loomed over him, and Jax, Cecile, and Domino had spread out to either side. Voice low, he said, "Stay close to the door, and stay sharp." He doubted very much that this was a trap, but old habits with Castor were hard to break.

He crossed to Castor's side. "It seems settled here. Where's Hammer?"

"In my office, organising shifts."

"Seems a domesticated task for him."

Castor smirked. "He's surprisingly good at it. Barney, get Maverick his drink of choice."

Maverick shook his head. "Later, thanks."

Danny, one of Castor's men, was playing pool, but he straightened up, glaring at him. "What's Nancy-boy doing 'ere?"

"He has a meeting with me," Castor shot back. "As such, this place is closing for a short while. You," he pointed at his various customers, "need to leave. Your games will be waiting for you, as will your drinks."

A chorus of groans and complaints started up, and Maverick noted some very worried looks passing between his pack members. He estimated there were a dozen, at most.

Danny frowned. "Closing? Now?"

"Now." Castor raised his voice. "Are you all deaf? *Out now*! My staff will stay."

"Where's the rest of your pack?" Maverick asked, watching as the customers exited vocally.

"Not due until later. Word will get around quickly, and these are the witnesses. I trust most of them."

"Including Danny?"

"I think so."

"And the ones you overheard? Are they here?"

With a discreet nod, Castor indicated a man in his early twenties, lean of build, with light brown hair. "The young kid is called Will. The other one, Ben, is standing at the next pool table, with blond hair. They work together a lot. I want your team to watch them, and if they try to run, stop them."

"And Hammer?"

"We'll call him out now. We do this here, at the back of the hall. Just questions."

Maverick looked to the rear of the hall, beyond the pool tables, seeing the cluster of tables and chairs situated by another huge TV screen mounted on the wall. "If he resists?"

"We stay flexible." Castor looked grim, but determined. "Danny, shut the doors. We're having a meeting."

"Boss?"

"Just do it."

Maverick called Domino over and updated her, leaving her to organise the others. Danny locked the doors as the final customer hurriedly left, glaring at the Storm Moon Pack with ill-disguised hostility. They all ignored him.

Hammer must have seen the activity, because he exited the office. "It's the middle of the afternoon! What's going on?" Then he saw Maverick and sneered. "Nancy-boy is back for a beating. And he's brought more Nancy-boys. And the ladies, too. Party time, then."

"Shut it," Castor said, earning a sharp-eyed stare from Hammer. "We need to chat. Now. Park your arse on this." He dragged a chair from a grouping around a small table and set it in the centre of the seating area. "I have questions."

"For me?" He looked nervous, but belligerence lurked behind his words. "What's going on? And why do we need *them*?" He shot Maverick a vicious look.

"Sit, and you'll find out. The rest of you, sit behind him. Be quiet and listen." Castor swelled in stature as he spoke, his alpha magnetism gilding him with an aura of power, and although it looked like a couple of his pack might argue, within seconds they submissively sat on hastily grabbed chairs. Except for Hammer. "I said sit."

Unexpectedly, he squared up to Castor. "I'd rather stand."

"Your alpha commands that you sit. Do it." Castor took one step towards him, and even Maverick, with his own alpha-power, had to exert himself against the power he wielded.

For one breathless moment, it seemed Hammer would withstand the order, but then his knees gave way and he sat heavily on the chair, staring up at Castor with a glazed expression. The room was tight with tension. Maverick's team remained standing, Jax positioned by the rear emergency exit.

"You," Castor began, "are concealing something from me, and I want to know what it is."

Hammer blinked. "Nothing. You're wrong."

"Then why have you been re-arranging your shifts? Avoiding me? Your eyes slide away from meeting mine. You're the pack second, except you have been avoiding your duties."

"I have had other things to attend to."

"Like the club I am not supposed to know about?"

Maverick was watching Hammer intently, but at those words he felt the energy in the room shift. He looked beyond Hammer to the shifters behind him, and saw Will, Ben, and two others flinch as confusion spread across the others. He exchanged a quick glance with Domino and knew she had seen it, too. *What was happening?*

Hammer ground out between clenched teeth, "There is no club."

"You think that you can lie to me? Your alpha? There *is* a club. A secret, fighting club. A club for challenges that you stupidly thought you could hide." Castor's hand shot out with lightning reflexes, pulling Hammer out of his chair so that he was upright and they were on even eye level. "Admit it, you lying bastard. Why lie to your alpha?"

Hammer's guarded expression suddenly changed, and gleeful pleasure spread across his face as his eyes kindled with aggression. "Because there is no place for you!" he roared, thrusting Castor backwards, hands on his chest. "The Wey Wolf commands me now."

Castor's grip held firm, and he picked Hammer up and slammed him against the wall. "Who is this fucking Wey Wolf, and where do I find him?"

"That is not for you to know." And then Hammer did what should not have been possible. His hands flashed out, changing into a wolf's paws, claws long as he slashed Castor's body.

That was the trigger.

Maverick charged in with his team as another four shifters turned on their pack, and a fight erupted.

"I'm worried," Arlo said to Vlad. "I think this is a bad idea."

"What? Maverick helping Castor?"

"Yes. He's going to question Hammer, but I think it's too soon."

"You didn't say that earlier."

"Because we need answers."

Vlad sighed. "You're talking in riddles."

"But it feels wrong." He patted his chest. "In here."

John, their regular doorman, was with them. "I'm worried sick about Finn. He's too young for whatever this is. If he had been one of mine, I'd tear the city apart." He fell into silent brooding, which only added to Arlo's worry.

They were chatting around the staff table in the corner of the bar, eating a plate of dumplings the kitchen staff had prepared. It was an hour before opening, and Storm Moon was ready for customers. The place had been searched from top to bottom, and no other tokens had been discovered. That had brought some relief, but it could still happen again. Another unknown man could enter their bar to plant tokens, and another shifter could disappear. The security team had been briefed on the man responsible, but everyone was uneasy, especially because of Finn's abduction. Although John was with them, and the bar staff were chatting together in the staff room, the other shifters were in the security room downstairs, no doubt brooding, too.

A loud banging on the club's front door had them all on their feet.

"Let me," John said.

Too worried to sit, Vlad and Arlo followed, but found only Harlan Beckett, the American occult collector outside.

He grinned rakishly at them. "A reception committee. I know you're not open yet, but I knew you'd be here, and well, Maggie told me about what's going on. And Olivia, actually. I'm here to help."

"Good," John said. "The more the merrier."

They ushered him inside, and while John locked up again, they returned to the table.

"You had us worried," Arlo confessed. "Irrational, I know. I had visons of someone throwing a fistful of tokens at us."

"Jumpy, but warranted, all things considered." Harlan slid into the booth, placing his leather messenger bag next to him. "I've been studying those tokens. They're different."

Vlad sat opposite him. "No, they're not. They have the same markings."

"Ah, my friend. That is where you are wrong. Any chance of a drink?" He asked as he extracted his phone.

"Bourbon?" Arlo asked, knowing his preferences.

"Beer. Holy shit, Arlo. It's only late afternoon!"

Arlo laughed as he headed to the bar and grabbed four beers from the fridge, returning to his seat at the same time as John.

Vlad pursued his questioning. "The differences? They looked the same to us."

"That's because you were looking only at the front and back. The edge is where you'll see the difference." Harlan pulled a pound coin from his pocket and handed it to Arlo. "See? A regular coin is thick enough to leave marks on."

Arlo frowned. "Only just."

"And yet, here we are." Harlan handed Arlo his phone. "I got in touch with the Moonfell ladies. Man, I love them. They sent me more photos. Can you see the marks?"

Arlo enlarged the image of the token's edge as Vlad leaned in. "They're just tiny lines."

"They're *runes,* and they spell names. The witches agree."

"What kind of names?" John asked, sipping his beer.

"Anglo-Saxon names. Dunstan and Leofric."

Astonished, John said, "That's really old. Like, what, a thousand years?"

"And then some. That's how old these tokens are. Olivia knew that immediately."

Arlo felt like an idiot. "Which means what? The names, I mean."

"They are assigned to individuals."

"The tokens?"

"Yes." He tapped the screen, looking at the three shifters like a teacher looked at a child. "This token is assigned to Dunstan." He swiped. "This one to Leofric."

Arlo looked to Vlad, hoping he was confused as him. "I still don't see the relevance. What does it matter? Hunter raced out of here possessed by whatever knowledge it imparted. A map, we think. A way to get to this challenge club."

"Sure. But what map? From whose mind? Who put it there?"

"A spell."

"Created from *who*?"

"Fuck me, Harlan! If we knew that—"

Vlad put a hand on Arlo's arm to stop him. "You said *from* who, not *by* who."

"Yeah, I did." Harlan leaned back. "Why put a name on a token unless it has relevance? Because this is Dunstan's token, and this is Leofric's. I think they contain the essence of them. And now perhaps so does Hunter, and the other shifter who has been affected by these."

"Hal," Vlad said. "And now Finn, we presume. One of our youngest shifters."

Harlan's eyes widened in surprise. "Shit. I hadn't heard that."

Arlo's attention was still on Harlan's suggestion. "Hold on. You're saying the tokens are imprinted with an ancient shifter's memories?"

"I'm suggesting it's a possibility."

"But London looks nothing like it would have then. It would have been nothing more than a big village. If this club is in north London, then it could well have just been fields then. And not necessarily underground, either, although I know that's what Odette has said."

"It's underground now because that's how things work," Harlan said patiently. "Years pass, cities get built on cities. And yes, it might well have been in the countryside then. However, if it's intact enough for people to be in it, then it was probably underground all along."

"Then how does an ancient shifter's memories of an old structure know where to direct shifters now? In a massively changed city?"

"I presume that it works more like a GPS location. Coordinates. Not a street-by-street how to get there."

John shrugged, impressed. "That sounds logical."

"I suppose it does," Arlo conceded. A chill ran through him. "So, Hunter and Hal might have other memories that belonged to those shifters. You said it could contain their essence. Do you mean their soul?"

"Hey, I'm just offering possibilities based on the fact there are names on those tokens. If we find another one with another name, then that will support that." He paused, thoughtful. "Just how possessed was he? Hunter, I mean."

"Could barely control himself, according to Jet," Vlad told him. "She said he struggled to hand the token over."

Arlo still had questions. "So, according to Odette, a shaman crafted these tokens and put *essences* into them. From dead shifters?"

Harlan shrugged. "A shaman crafted some kind of spell into them, and I'm just floating the essence idea. The witches are struggling to uncover any kind of map locked within it. This is another angle to try. Say I'm right, and for all we know, this possession—or compulsion--is fleeting. It could stop once they get to the place. Of course, if it doesn't..."

He trailed off, and Arlo didn't like the implications of his idea at all.

Eighteen

Domino leapt into action as the Apollo Pool Hall descended into chaos.

She tackled Will, the closest shifter to her, as he attacked his own pack member, his face rippling with an inhuman snarl. "Restrain them!" she shouted. "We need answers."

But that was easier said than done. Will and Ben and two other shifters were fighting viciously with the other pack members who had been taken completely unawares by the sudden turn of events. As Domino and two others wrestled Will to the floor, her team members tried to restrain the others. Cecile and Monroe subdued one quickly, but then clothes tore as some of the traitors shifted to their wolves. It was turning into a bloodbath. The traitors were risking everything to maim, kill, and escape.

Will snapped at Domino, teeth sinking into her upper arm as he pinned her to the ground with brute force. Danny, who was fighting him with her, punched him to try and loosen his grip, but Will's face was already more wolf than human. And then Tommy weighed in, punching him so strongly that his head snapped to the side and thudded against the floor. He fell limp, and from the crack of shattered bone and pool of blood, Domino knew he was dead. Unfortunately, his body was still pinning her down, and the skin and muscle in her upper arm was badly torn as his teeth were wrenched away.

Tommy and Danny were immediately pulled into other fights, and Domino twisted furiously, using her good arm to push Will off and slide out from under his weight. Her changed position meant she saw Maverick and Hammer fighting ferociously in their wolves, clothes torn to shreds around them. Castor, barely conscious, lay on the floor, in a pool of blood flowing from the huge, raking wounds that ran down his ribs.

She winced as she dragged herself upright to help Maverick, legs still trapped, noting that Tommy was already shifting to help his alpha, but then Ben barrelled into him, knocking him to the floor, and Jax piled on top to restrain him. Monroe and Cecile were still engaged in furious fights with the other two traitorous shifters, all assisted by Castor's loyal pack members, but it was getting uglier by the second.

Racing across the floor, shotgun cocked, was Barney, the grizzled barman. For one horrible second, Domino didn't know whose side he was on, and still trapped, she was powerless to stop him. He strode up to Hammer, whose snarling snout was mere inches away from Maverick's throat, pressed the gun to his exposed side, and pulled the trigger. Blood splattered everywhere, killing Hammer instantly. The report was so loud and unexpected that the fighting momentarily stopped.

Barney swung around and aimed at Ben, who was straddled over one of his pack, Monroe's huge arm pinned around his throat as he tried to drag him off. "I'll use it again, Ben," Barney warned him, staring him down, "so back off. All of you."

For a moment, Domino thought Ben had seen sense, but then he leapt forward, breaking free of Monroe's grip, and went for

Barney who fired at him without hesitation. Domino was caught by stray shot, but it didn't stop the other two traitorous wolves who immediately started fighting again as Barney reloaded the gun. It was as if they were beyond reason, and one was halfway to the rear door of the building, clearly trying to escape. Finally pushing Will off, she dragged herself to her feet, intent on helping her team, but the aggressors were now vastly outnumbered and had been pinned to the ground by the mixed packs.

Maverick shifted back to human. He was bleeding heavily from the many wounds inflicted by Hammer, but he seemed not to notice them as he stood upright, eyes glimmering like molten gold as his alpha-power magnified. He strode across the room so that he was standing over the traitors, who still struggled to break free. "I command you to stand down now. Your will is subject to mine."

Finally, they fell limp against the ground, submissive, but fury poured out of them.

Maverick addressed Barney. He was blood-spattered, but his gun was still cocked, aim steady, ready to shoot. "Have you got rope or chains?"

He nodded, finally lowering the gun. "Back of the bar. I'll go get them. I'll get the medical kit, too."

A heavy, shocked silence had fallen over the room, a tableau of horror and blood laid out before them, but Domino edged to Castor's side, taking in the extent of his wounds. He was unconscious, but his chest rose and fell with uneven breaths, and she turned to the others. "He's still alive. We need to take him to a doctor, or a healer. Danny," she addressed the shifter she knew, "who do you use?"

His eyes flickered across Castor's prostrate body. "Barney or Ben, and Ben's dead now. We sometimes use a local witch, but haven't for a long time. We manage."

"Castor will need more than bandages," Domino said. She looked up at Maverick. "Why isn't he shifting to his wolf?" It was normally an automatic thing to do when faced with such grave injuries.

He shook his head. "I don't know. We'll see if Barney can patch him up, and we go from there. And I suppose you'd better call Maggie."

Hunter settled on a bench surrounding the fighting pit, the amulet tucked in his pocket rather than around his neck. Questions vied for prominence in his mind, the strongest being, who was the shadow warrior that lurked within him, and how much control did Hunter have over him?

The long benches that comprised the seating area were made of wood and stacked in tiers, so that everyone could see. He did a quick headcount, and after adding on a couple of guards and the Wey Wolf himself, reckoned there were close to thirty shifters present. The benches could hold many more. He studied faces, committing them to memory. He recognised three from Castor's pack, but knew there could be others he didn't know. Then there were also lone wolves, lots of them, obvious from the way they held themselves. Half a dozen ancient guards stood by, with old-fashioned haircuts and strange clothes. Plus, there were others who looked like fathers and sons. And not one single woman.

There was also one human who remained alone, sitting on his own on the very top tier. He looked like the man who had escorted him. Barry. *A brother, perhaps.* He must have detected Hunter's stare, because he looked at him, a flicker of fear in his eyes before turning away. *Why was he here?*

A couple of shifters emerged from a dark doorway, almost invisible in the staging beneath the lowest tier, dragging out an unusual mirror, well over the height of most men. Its surface was dull, like pewter, and as they maneuvered it to the centre of the space, a rumble of voices rang out around the tiers. Hunter ignored the object for now as Hal settled beside him, eyes intent on the pit. Instead, Hunter focussed on the room. He noted the solid stone walls, well-constructed out of huge blocks of stone, an ornate relief running under the ceiling showing all manner of wolves. Fighting, hunting, families, cubs, and again and again the Wey Wolf, striding amongst them all. A wave of dizziness rolled over him as other memories intruded. Flashing images of battles, of long tables in a smoky hall, of dark, tangled forests. He took a deep breath and shook them off. There was no doubt about it. This place had been the central gathering point for a pack. A big on e. *But who had woken the Wey Wolf, and how?*

Before he could think about it further, there was another flurry of activity below, and another half a dozen shifters were admitted to the pit, quickly clambering up onto the tiers to find seats. With horror, Hunter recognised Finn. He elbowed Hal. "It's Finn! What the fuck is he doing here? He's a kid."

Hal's eyes narrowed with confusion, and then he nodded, his expression clearing. "He is young, but that's good. He'll pick things up quickly. We can teach him."

"He's a child!"

"Hunter, this is the Wey Wolf's way. It's fine." Hal frowned at him, perplexed, and Hunter realised he was in danger of giving himself away.

"Of course. We'll teach him." He smiled, forcing himself to relax. "Let's hope we see more of our pack soon."

"Exactly. And now the Wey Wolf comes." Hal turned away, as the sound of voices carrying to them.

With great fanfare the Wey Wolf entered, an entourage of guards surrounding him. He was brimming with power and energy, his chest bare and gleaming with oils, a cloak of supple hide edged in fur flowing from his shoulders. His stormy eyes glittered as he surveyed them all. They stood as one, Hunter feeling the compulsion to both impress him and to fall at his knees, should he command it. Memories again flooded through him of battles fought, blood spilled, the snarl of combat, and the spoils of victory. Blood surged in his veins, and his wolf rose.

The Wey Wolf walked to an enormous chair in the middle tier, his alpha authority surging around the spectators. He extended his arms to his pack, all eyes drawn to him. "Welcome, all! New members have joined us, and our pack is growing. Soon we will be able to challenge those who resist joining us." Huge cheers greeted his words, and Hunter joined in, knowing he had to. "We grow stronger in challenge, and none will be able to resist our might. Hours of spectacle now await us." He gestured down to the pit. "Let us begin."

As the shifter stepped out, a hush fell. He was a big man, solid with muscle, and he strode across the space without fear until he stood in front of the mirror. The flat pewter surface shimmered like water, and without hesitation, the shifter stepped into it and out the other side. But he wasn't alone. Another stepped out with him. A shifter that looked very different, and who dressed in the old-fashioned manner of the guards.

Hunter leaned forward, blinking as if to clear his vision. But he hadn't imagined it. The shifter had walked through the mirror, and now two shifters stood where one had been. Instantly, Hunter knew who the other man was.

The shadow shifter that lurked inside them all.

Nineteen

"Found it!" Morgana said, extracting the slender pointer shaped like a stiletto blade. "It was wedged in the bottom."

She straightened up, hair tumbling back over her shoulders as she righted herself after being virtually upside down in the ebony chest. All of its contents were now on the floor, a pleasant scent of wood and old incense ballooning around her, and she decided they needed to make room in another cabinet. She couldn't possibly pile these things back in the chest. They need to be seen and examined, and more importantly, used.

"Well done!" Birdie said, attention on the token she was holding. "I'm not sure it will make the Wayfinder work, though. Not if Harlan is right."

"It might not need the token now." She handed the pointer to Odette, who was sitting at the table, poised ready to fit it. "Although, it must surely need activating somehow."

"We need to test it on a shifter," Odette suggested as Morgana joined her coven. "Moonfell is ringed with protection. It's probably blocking all signs of anything."

"Finding spells work," Birdie pointed out.

"Perhaps this is more sensitive."

Morgana groaned and leaned her chin in her hand, elbow on the table. "I hadn't considered that. I'm so drained by it all."

Birdie lowered the token. "We can't afford to delay. Wolves are at risk."

"I know. I'm not giving up." She rubbed her temple. "It's just all so confusing. Do you really think that the essence—or even soul—of a shifter is in those tokens?"

Birdie's lips settled into a thin line. "It's certainly possible. There are spells that can capture souls and put them in objects. Cruel, dark spells that would probably require a blood sacrifice. It is such a small object to use though, isn't it? If I was going to do such a thing, I would want the object to have weight. Significance." She studied her granddaughters. "You know what I mean? Like a sculpture. Or a book."

"Or a painting, like in *Dorian Grey*," Odette said as she finished fixing the pointer in place.

"Exactly. Tokens are so insubstantial and easily lost." Like Morgana, she settled her elbows on the table and her chin in her hands. "Or I'd use a bottle, like the Genie was trapped in."

"You're so devious," Morgana said dryly, a sly glance to Odette. "And not very reassuring."

"What about memories?" Odette asked, her focus elsewhere. "Could they be trapped?"

"I would imagine that would be even harder!" Morgana said, appalled. "They are a part of who we are."

"But at the moment of death, perhaps?" Odette placed her hand on Morgana's arm as if to reassure her. "I'm sorry, I know it's a weird question, but I'm just trying to work out how a token can affect the shifters so much. We're lucky that Harlan spotted names around the edge…it's as if they were hidden."

Morgana nodded. "Hidden is a good word. Their names could have been put on the face of the token. That would have been easier."

"Which means," Odette said, voice rising with excitement, "the tokens are handmade. Poured into a mould, perhaps, but then the names were etched individually."

"Of course," Birdie said, frowning. "What are you driving at?"

"What if more than just silver is in the tokens? Maybe a drop of blood? Or something else from the individual. Ground hair. Or skin."

"Like a poppet?" Morgana asked.

"Exactly. A token not just with the name of an individual, but containing a tiny fragment of him. That would certainly make it more possible to imbue them with the individual's qualities. I hesitate to say *soul*."

"It would certainly make it more personal," Birdie agreed.

Odette's expression became distant again. "I sense the shaman's hand in it all. He's a shadowy presence who manipulated everything. I'm sure he made these. I just can't discern a purpose—beyond giving directions of course."

Morgana tried to recall all the information they knew so far. "Let's be logical and talk it through again. I feel we have been bombarded with information, and my head's reeling. For a start, Hunter could barely speak to Jet. He was just able to give her his token, said he knew where *it* was, but couldn't tell her, and then he said not to stop him."

"And we presume that 'it' means the club," Odette said.

"Yes. Domino and Hunter found Jake, and he told them that someone had resurrected a god who needed blood sacrifices. Blood that was given during a challenge. Yes?"

Birdie nodded. "Sounds right."

"Odette's prophecy—her insight—also talks of the wolf god and his ancient throne. That he will rise and reclaim his prize of old. Territory, perhaps? Or status," Morgana continued. "Both corroborate the other, and a wolf god needs a base. The club."

"Or temple," Birdie put in, "if we consider the faint image behind the fighting wolves. Far more likely for a god's base."

Morgana nodded. "Agreed. But not all need a token to gain admission, because it seems that some come and go. Doesn't that mean some go willingly?"

"Unless," Odette said, turning the token over in her hands, "once imprinted or possessed, the effects can be modified?"

Birdie rapped sharply on the table, the crack summoning her granddaughters' attention. Her eyes were burning with excitement. "Why would any god care who gives them a sacrifice? They just want to be worshipped. They generally don't give a crap. This one does." She rapped again, like a judge with a gavel. "This one wants shifters affected by the tokens, and these tokens have names on them. And they only affect shifters. No one else. This isn't just about a challenge. That's why some of Castor's pack are being secretive. They don't want an alpha involved. They're too strong. Another alpha doesn't want that kind of challenge, thank you very much!" She paused dramatically. "Which means, he's recruiting to make a new pack!"

"That makes horrible sense, Birdie," Morgana admitted. "Not just a shifter god. He's the alpha of a pack. A very old pack."

"Exactly. And these tokens contain the memories, or the essence or whatever the hell we call it, of his pack. He's bringing them back. One by one."

Panic rolled through Morgana. "What about Hunter and Hal and all the others? What of their soul? Their own memories?"

"Perhaps that is part of the challenge. To determine which shifter survives. The victor keeps the body."

Morgana shuddered. "By the great Goddess. If you're right, that's horrific!"

Birdie clenched her small fists, power and anger radiating from her. "I *am* right. I know it. I can feel it. And what do we have here?"

Odette drew a sharp intake of breath. "A token that hasn't been used."

"Exactly. It's not a map. We can't extract directions from it. Whatever essence was put in there, is still there! It hasn't been *implanted* in anyone. We need to pull out a shifter. We need to drag answers from it. And we have to do it today! Before Hunter and Hal are lost forever." Birdie stood so quickly that her chair crashed to the ground. "We need spells. Now!"

Grey pushed through the door of the Apollo Pool Hall before Maggie, keen to ensure it was safe before she entered.

"All quiet now?" he asked Cecile, who had let him in. She looked composed, but her clothes were torn, and long claw marks down her arms showed how bad the fight had been. "Shit. You're injured."

"We're all injured. I have more than these, I can assure you," she said, her French accent always stronger when she was angry. "These bastards are strong. Crazy." She pointed at her head. "They have no reason!" She nodded to Maggie who stepped in behind Grey, locking the door again. "Good to see you, Maggie. I warn you—it's a mess. A big, bloody mess."

"Anyone dead?"

"Three. All Castor's pack." She led them to the back of the room where the shifters gathered around the dead bodies. "Tommy killed one. Barney killed two with a shotgun. He tipped the fight in our favour."

"And saved my life," Maverick added as he ended his conversation with a shifter Grey didn't know and joined them. "Hammer was insanely strong. Far stronger than I expected."

"Because of magic?" Maggie asked.

"I think so."

"Maybe," Cecile suggested, "those damn tokens helped them."

Grey barely took in what they were saying, too side-tracked by Maverick's injuries. He only wore ripped jeans, so his chest was bare, and he was covered in bruises, plus a mix of deep and shallow claws marks. His skin was torn in places, flaps of flesh still actively bleeding. "Fuck. You're a mess, Maverick."

"I'll survive." He was grim-faced, and there was no joy over the victory. "It was brutal. Maggie, I'm sorry. I didn't intend for any of this to happen."

Maggie studied the injured and the dead behind him, especially the shifter who stood at Maverick's side, waiting silently. Finally, she looked at Maverick. "I'm sorry, too. I know if you'd expected this, you'd have brought a bigger team along. Only six of you?"

"And Castor's pack. This is Danny." He introduced Grey and Maggie. "Temporary alpha and new pack second."

"Until Castor chooses otherwise, at least." Danny shook their hands.

Grey took stock of his injuries, too. More bruises, deep cuts, and scratches. "Your pack betrayed you?"

"Five of them. Bastards. I'm glad three are dead." He flashed a nervous glance at Maggie. "Sorry, but I am. Castor is almost dead because of Hammer."

"What happened to him?" Grey asked, watching Domino and two unknown men work on Castor's injuries.

"Hammer did the impossible," Maverick said. "He partially shifted to wolf. Not full wolf," he reiterated. "*Part*. His hands turned to huge wolf paws, and his claws ripped into Castor before he even knew what was happening. He threw him against the wall, then pounded him into the ground before I could intervene."

"He needs a doctor." Maggie said, watching the others work on him.

"He's stable. I want him to go to Moonfell instead. Morgana will help."

"But I don't know her," Danny protested, sounding as if he was continuing a previous argument. "And I have no fucking idea what I'll tell the rest of the pack."

"We'll work something out," Maverick assured him.

"You can trust Morgana," Cecile said, adding weight to Maverick's argument. "She saved my cousin's life."

"What about them?" Maggie asked, staring at two shifters bound in chains and ropes.

Their clothes were torn, but their eyes, like their expressions, were oddly blank. Other shifters were grouped around them, a mix of Castor's and Maverick's pack, and Grey was relieved they were getting on okay. Comrades bonded over a bloody fight.

Maverick sighed. "Those we need to question. I commanded them to obey me as soon as we overpowered them, but then they just seemed to shut down. They haven't uttered a word."

"We're supposed to be reopening this place," Danny added. "More of our pack will be turning up soon."

Maggie snorted, already reaching for her phone. "Open? Not fucking likely. I'm about to get my team in. Nothing else will happen here today."

Grey saw how all this would look. "You need to get in touch with your pack immediately, Danny. If word gets out about Maverick being here, they might think the Storm Moon Pack is behind this. We do not want retribution."

"Fuck!" Maverick rubbed his face with bloodied hands. "I didn't even consider that. We need to warn Arlo."

"I'll do it," Cecile said, heading to a quiet corner.

Maverick turned to Danny. "Who can you trust in your pack now?"

"Good question. I'm pretty certain a couple of my good mates are unaffected—Crowley and Rafe. I'm just baffled by the rumours of this club. I swear, I haven't heard a thing." He shook his head. "All packs have small rivalries, but this is something else. Anyway, I'll ask them to get the pack to meet at our warehouse." He flitted shifty eyes at Maggie. "Another base."

"Don't worry," she shot back. "I'm not interested in your dodgy deals right now. What about Barney? He saved you, so I guess he's clean. Does the pack trust him?"

"I reckon. He's been here forever. He and Hammer weren't friends, though. They never got on. It would be good to speak to him properly later. See if he noticed anything odd over the last few days."

Grey felt uneasy. "If you gather the rest of the pack together, and there are more traitors, another fight might break out. You could lose more trustworthy members. It might not be wise."

"But we have to say something to them," Danny insisted. "We can't ignore what's happening. Not now. We must address it, or rumours will spread, and it will become even more of a bloody nightmare."

"Then get your mates to go prepared with other weapons. In fact," Grey hesitated, knowing how this would sound. "There's something I need to tell you. Have you spoken to Arlo, Maverick?"

"Not since the fight. I've not had time. I've been bringing Danny and his team up to speed."

Maggie grunted as she walked away, phone in hand. "I'll leave this to you, Grey. I need to call my team in."

"Harlan turned up at the bar—a friend of ours," Grey explained to Danny. "He has a theory about the tokens, and it might explain why those guys," he nodded towards the imprisoned and dead shifters, "were abnormally strong."

"Wait," Maverick stopped him. "I want everyone to hear this. Danny?"

Danny nodded in agreement, and Maverick summoned the other shifters, including Cecile, who had finished her phone call. Only Barney, who was working on Castor's injuries, didn't join them.

Grey waited until he had their full attention, relieved that Maverick was allowing Castor's team some agency, and prepared himself for their response. "Harlan found names on the tokens, running along the edge. Long story short, we think they're possessed by dead shifters. Saxon ones."

Tommy reacted first. The big man looked feral. He was covered in blood spatter and human tissue, and also what looked like pellet wounds. "Fucking *possessed*? How?"

"Magic that is yet to be determined, but we're working on it. Or rather, the witches are. It's in hand." Grey didn't need to elaborate on their fears for their own affected pack members. It was written on everyone's faces. He allowed a moment for everyone to digest the information, a buzz of incredulity humming around the group. "I think this fight has confirmed what we suspect. As for the ability to only partially shift their body into a wolf, that must be part of the token's magic. We need to tell the witches that, too."

"What about you?" Jax asked. "Did you and Maggie find any sign of the club?"

"No. Not a trace. But we always knew that was a long shot." He took in their resigned faces. "At least we're farther along than we were. We're making headway."

Maverick gave a barely perceptible nod. "Slowly."

"We know more than we did." Grey took stock of the room. The shattered chairs and tables, the pools of blood and splatter of flesh. The stink of cordite. "You can't question the traitors here. Maggie's team will be here soon. And you all need to step up," he eyed the injured shifters one by one, "to verify that what happened this afternoon is true, and to hear what the traitors say. Maverick certainly does not need accusations that his pack is responsible."

"Of course not," Danny said immediately. "That won't happen. We know we'd be dead without your help. As for where we question them, there's a storeroom next to the kitchen we could use. Or we use Castor's office. That's a decent size."

"Castor's office," Maverick said. "It's closer. We'll move them now. I want two of you watching them at all times, understood?" He included both teams, and they nodded. "Good, but we wait to interrogate them. I want Castor to be stable first, and moved out of the way. After we question them, our pack will meet at Moonfell. I think Danny and Castor should be there, too."

One of Castor's pack members stepped forward, lip curling in disdain. "If we get answers, we don't need witches, or this Moonfell place. We'll just go in and get our shifters back."

"Has this fight taught you nothing?" Maverick asked, eyes blazing. "We need a strategy! Without one we die, or submit mindlessly to a wolf god. Is that what you want?"

The shifter's eyes flickered with doubt. "No, but..."

"Then stop being a fucking idiot."

Danny nodded, gathering himself to face his pack. "Maverick is right, Thorne. We need a plan. We move together or not at all." He didn't look as if he was ready to be alpha. That needed to change.

"I'll call Moonfell." Grey turned away to make the arrangements, aware that the next twenty-four hours were critical. If they didn't find the temple soon, they might lose their pack members forever.

Twenty

Hunter watched the fight with grim fascination, taking in the brutal menace of the two shifters, surprised to find that there were a series of three different challenges—wrestling, sword fighting, and finally, a fight between their wolves.

The lone wolf-shifter had won the first fight but lost the sword challenge, almost losing his left arm during the battle. His opponent had pulled back, a wicked gleam to his eyes, knowing he'd just bested the modern shifter. Finally they fought as wolves, each snapping and snarling at the other, tearing at each other's limbs as they rolled around. It was clear what they were trying to do, because he would have done it, too. The wolf who had his jaws around the other's throat would be the victor. One wrong move, and whoever got the best position could rip his opponent's throat out. It was a quick fight, fur went flying, and when the old shifter finally got the better of the modern one, the other submitted.

The watching crowd grew quiet, and someone Hunter hadn't seen before stepped out of the shadows from under the lowest tier of seats. Dressed in a long cloak, a deep hood covering his head, he strode forward, and with a guttural command that Hunter didn't understand, both wolves rolled apart, then shifted back to human. The old shifter smiled in triumph, but the lone wolf was impassive, eyes veiled, curiously blank of expression. Almost as if preparing himself for something.

The newcomer threw his hood back, revealing a shaved head covered in tattoos, and when he brushed his cloak back from his shoulders, he revealed bare arms also covered in dark, swirling marks. He turned around, tattooed face upturned as he surveyed the crowd, hands outstretched as if to say, *there, it is done*, and Hunter felt his gaze cross him like an icy wind. For a moment, it seemed he paused on him, before swiftly moving on. Again, a memory flashed through him. An image of a dark room, a firepit, and tattooed hands making strange signs over a pot of bubbling metals. The vision was then replaced with the man's pale grey eyes, merciless as they stared into his own.

Hunter blinked, and the vision vanished, leaving him knowing that the man was the shaman. Blōdbana, Binder of Spirits. A shiver passed through Hunter that he tried not to show.

Blōdbana turned to the lone wolf, making a swift gesture with his right thumb across the man's face. Instantly, a thick black mark appeared, diagonally from the right temple to lower left jaw. Then Blōdbana bowed to the Wey Wolf.

Their alpha stood, looking—to Hunter, at least—as if he'd grown younger. He addressed the crowd. "One more has been chosen to join our pack. Where one becomes two, now must they reconcile." He gestured to the shaman.

The mirror was carried to the centre of the pit again. With another flurry of symbols drawn in the air by the shaman that Hunter couldn't fathom, the defeated man stepped through the mirror, the victor behind him. Only one emerged on the other side again. It looked like the lone wolf, because he was dressed in his clothes, but his blank expression had gone, and so had the black mark on his face. His features had subtly shifted, and Hunter knew without a shadow of a doubt that now the shadow warrior had taken prominence. In fact, as far as he knew, the other shifter was dead. With a roaring cheer, the crowd rose to their feet, and the shifter joined the benches below where the Wey Wolf sat. *The chosen pack*, Hunter deduced. *The victors of the shadow warrior battle.*

Hunter took advantage of the excited murmur of conversation, and leaned closer to Hal. "Is that what you witnessed yesterday?"

He nodded, eyes gleaming. "Four fights."

"Did the shadow warrior always win?"

"No. The strongest wins, that is the way of the challenge."

A wave of relief washed through Hunter, but it quickly vanished. "How long do we train before we face him?"

"You mean yourself," Hal said, confusion wrinkling his brow. "It's your own warrior you face. No one else's."

"That's what I meant. Sorry." He could curse himself for his stupidity. *But did Hal really not know?*

"Another day or so. The shaman decides who is ready. That is why I need to train again. The fight yesterday was part of my preparation."

"Of course. But..." Hunter paused, wondering how to phrase his next question. "Sorry, Hal, I'm struggling to understand the way of the Wey Wolf. To be the best warrior I can be, to serve him to the best of my ability, I need to know why it matters that we train, if we just face ourselves anyway?"

Hal smiled. "Because in fighting our self, our inner wolf, we become stronger. Our inner self may be stronger than we know.

It carries the weight of our ancestors, don't you see? If we don't prove we are superior, the other must come forth. But it's still us."

Hunter felt his opinion swaying, and he gripped his amulet again, hand in his pocket, trying to keep a clear head in this madness. *Was it true? Were they really just fighting themselves? Or were they possessed? All of them fed lies and magic that masked the true horror of what was happening here.* Then he felt an icy breeze on him again, and he quickly released the amulet, schooled his features, and turned around. The shaman was looking up at him. Hunter lowered his eyes reverently, emptying his mind of anything except the need to fight.

When the feeling passed, he looked up. The shaman had gone, and the next shifter was ready to fight. But then he felt other eyes on him, and looking around, he saw the human, the one who looked like Barry, sitting on the top stand. The second their eyes met, Hunter saw his fear and desperation, and a flicker of hope, and knew he was the answer to all of this.

He needed an ally, and that man might just be it.

A full hour had passed at the Apollo Pool Hall before Maverick could start questioning the captured shifters.

It offered his own team—and himself—some respite after the fight. Maggie's crew had arrived, and it included a small woman in excellently tailored clothes who Maverick remembered was Layla Gould, the doctor and Forensic Pathologist who worked at The Retreat.

He didn't interfere with their work, instead making sure that Castor was situated comfortably in the room behind the bar where Barney said he'd watch over him. Barney faced the door with the loaded shotgun, a whiskey at his elbow, eyes hooded but alert.

Maverick asked him, "You don't trust the pack?"

"I trust Danny. As for the rest, we'll see."

Maverick dragged a spare stool over to face Barney and sat down, knowing he might be able to give him much needed answers. "Did you suspect that something was wrong with Hammer?"

"Something has always been wrong with that bastard. I don't know why Castor ever picked him as his pack second. He was loyal to Castor only as long as it suited him."

"But he never vied to be alpha?"

"Nah. Too much responsibility. Too many eyes on him. Pack second suited him. He had fans, though, like those bastards still tied up."

"And Ben and Will? The ones that are dead?"

Barney shuffled in his seat. "I thought they were loyal to Castor. I admit, I'm surprised. You say it's this token business?"

Maverick had already described the situation to him. "Yes. I'm pretty sure they didn't have a choice. You observe everyone here, I'm sure. Being behind the bar gives you the perfect spot to watch and listen. Did you suspect anything was wrong? The slightest thing?"

"I thought there was another deal going on." He shrugged. "There are always deals here. Castor encouraged the entrepreneurial spirit, as long as he had his cut." Barney's lips wrinkled with disdain. "I didn't know he'd gone to you, though."

"He needed an outsider. Someone he could trust, after he heard whispers of a secret club." Maverick smiled at his discomfort. "Turned out, he was right to be suspicious. He didn't want to challenge them until he knew more, and his instincts were sound. If it wasn't for my pack, you, Danny, Castor, and the others might well be dead by now."

He tapped his shotgun. "I had this. Saved *your* life."

"True, thank you." Maverick liked to think he'd have got the better of Hammer, but he wasn't so sure. "But you'd have been taken down by the others without us. It was a team effort. You'll get a lot of questions from the pack about you killing Hammer."

"I'll handle it." Barney grunted. "It was no 'ardship to kill that bastard. Especially after what he did to Castor." His eyes drifted to where Castor lay on blankets on the floor, wrapped in bandages. Blood was already seeping through the dressings.

"Nevertheless, I appreciate it. As for Castor, he needs proper attention. He's not in his wolf, and his wounds are still bleeding."

"Like Danny says, we don't know your witch."

"Look at him." Maverick leaned forward, his voice urgent. "Right now, I don't know if he'll survive the night. He might not even be the alpha anymore. Wolves—as you know—can be brutal. Your pack is in disarray and needs strong leadership. Danny has stepped in, but he hasn't earned that position. Not according to pack rules. What if someone challenges him? Or takes advantage of Castor in this state, and kills him and you? Plus, more could have been affected by this damn club. Have you heard any mention of it?"

"Nothing. But they wouldn't talk about that in front of me. I'm just a human."

Maverick tried another tack. "You said you thought there was another deal going on. Who was involved?"

"Hammer, obviously. The two you have tied up. And the ones who haven't come into work. Maybe Gunnar and Graves. I told Danny already who I have doubts about."

"Good. How many shifters are missing from your pack now?"

"Eight."

"*Eight?*" Maverick didn't realise there were that many. "Shit. And you have, what, forty-five in your pack in all?" He had talked to Castor about it only the day before.

"Yep. Big pack."

"It might not be, anymore. Reconsider, please. Take Castor to Moonfell. You'll be safe there. Leave Danny to organise everything else."

Before Barney could answer, the sound of raised, angry voices had Maverick on his feet. Then the door flew open, and another shifter stood on the threshold. He was Maverick's height, with sandy brown hair cut short and a wiry build. A scar ran from his lip to ear, and his eyes burned with fury.

Maverick's wolf rose. "Stand down, Wolf."

"Get the fuck out of my way. I want to see Castor."

Barney shot to his feet, shotgun levelled at the newcomer. "Back off, Axel. One step closer and I'll blow you away."

Danny appeared behind him, and threw his arm around the newcomer's throat, trying to pull him backwards. "I don't know how the hell you heard what happened, but back off, right now."

Axel resisted Danny's attempt to remove him, throwing him off with determined strength, and instead squared up to Maverick. "A wounded alpha is no alpha at all. Why the fuck are you protecting him? Or *him?*" he added, eyes burning with hatred as he glared at Maverick.

Danny, glowering with fury, leaped forward again, but Maverick acted first, punching Axel so hard that it drove him to his knees. At that point, Danny wrestled him to the floor, ably assisted by Jax, who came running at the sound of the commotion.

"I am not responsible for this," Maverick told him, "so I suggest you shut up and listen to what really happened." Maverick turned to Barney as the other two dragged Axel away. "Do you trust Axel? Is he part of this?"

"He's a dick, but I don't think he's involved."

"Okay." Maverick nodded, determined to ascertain that for himself. "After seeing his behaviour, though, are you sure you want to stay?"

Defeat flashed across Barney's face. "Fine. I get it. Tell me where to go."

Twenty-One

Morgana volunteered to organise rooms for Castor and Barney, and to prepare to examine Castor's wounds. As the healer of their coven, it was her job anyway.

When she ended the call with Maverick, she left Birdie and Odette searching for spells in the library, and headed to the still room off the kitchen, the place where they kept all of their supplies. Dried herbs, potions, salves, balms, and tinctures, as well as homemade candles, dressing supplies, and other useful things. She had assembled the ingredients she thought would be most helpful, based on her experience with Xavier, and had finished clearing the kitchen table to examine Castor on—a seemingly odd choice, but it was huge with good lighting—when the booming gong of the front door announced their arrival. She hurried down the hall, wondering how she was going to get the barely conscious man down the corridor. A feather spell, perhaps, to make him temporarily light in weight. But when she opened the door, she smiled in relief.

Three men stood outside, and one of them was Monroe, supporting a man who looked half dead. *Castor Pollux*. An older, grey-haired man stood on the other side of him, helping to supporting his weight.

She beamed at him. "Monroe. I didn't expect to see you. Come on in. I'll examine him in the kitchen."

Monroe grinned at her as he entered, creating a warm glow that lifted Morgana's mood. "Barney needed help. I volunteered."

"Thank you." She led the way, her attention immediately focussed on the injured man. "Castor, I presume, and Barney?"

Barney grunted at her, but his eyes roved everywhere, suspicion radiating from every pore.

Monroe rolled his eyes. "Yes, this is Barney. He didn't want to come here, but when some thug called Axel threatened Castor, he saw sense."

It took only moments for them to lay Castor on the table, huge towels spread beneath him, and Morgana immediately started to take off the dressings that were already soaked with blood. She talked while she worked. "You made the right decision, Barney. I appreciate that you don't know us, but it's safe here." She glanced up at him, but his attention was on her hands. "These dressings are good. But," she peeled back the final dressing and winced, "his injuries are awful. I can see his rib bones. Some are cracked. It's a miracle his lungs weren't punctured."

"Or his guts ripped out," Monroe added. "Can you heal him?"

"Yes, but it will take time." Castor groaned, eyes fluttering open as she eased the blood-hardened dressing off. She placed a hand on his brow, feeling his energy levels. "Any head injuries?"

Monroe shrugged. "We don't think so, but he landed heavily on the floor. Hammer threw him aside. It's hard to say, if I'm honest. The whole place erupted into utter chaos. I wasn't paying attention to Castor specifically." He met Morgana's eyes, his own dark and velvety, soft and welcoming when he teased her, but hard now with recent memories. "They were stronger than we expected. The effect of the tokens, we think."

"You fought two shifters in one body."

"It certainly felt like it."

She moved to the top of the table, looking down the length of Castor's body, and placed her hands on either side of his head. She had never met him before. He was tall, like most shifters, with lean, sculpted muscles. He was in his late thirties, she estimated, and very fit. And he was covered in old scars. Morgana wasn't like Odette. She couldn't read people as easily, but she knew this man could be brutal. Could see it in the lines of his face. She wasn't sure she would like him, but she'd heal him anyway. And Barney? Well, he was a wizened old warhorse, and had seen his own share of fights, too. He was clearly loyal to Castor, and she wondered what their story was. Barney was old enough to be his father. *Something to consider another time.*

For now, Morgana focussed on Castor's head, probing for injuries with her magic. She gently felt the back of his head, and immediately discovered a huge lump and a mix of fresh and dried blood, hard to see because of his thick, dark hair. No wonder he was unconscious; that, and the pain of his other injuries. She needed other strategies. Gemstones to balance his energies, plus spells to ease the contusion.

"This will take a while," she finally said, looking up at the other two. "I'll place poultices on his bodily wounds, but then I must work on his head."

"Let me help," Barney said immediately. "Prepare the poultices for me, I'll apply them. I need to do something."

"All right. Thank you. You made a good job of the bandages." She turned to the two large bowls on the counter behind her, one full of a thick, sticky substance made of balms and carefully prepared oils, the other full of warm, fragrant water filled with herbs. "First, clean his injuries with the herb water, then we apply the poultice. I've already soaked some gauze in the herbal paste. You can separate out the layers and apply them to all of his wounds. I'll work on his head primarily." Barney sniffed the bowls, and his countenance settled, brow less furrowed. "And tea, I think. A herbal remedy that will help you, Barney."

"I don't need 'erbs." And then he hesitated, asking, "What kinda 'erbs?"

"Just chamomile, rosemary, lemon balm... To calm and heal." Her lips twisted with amusement. "No cannabis."

"Sounds terrible, but all right. I'll follow it with a whiskey."

"I'll make the tea, then," Monroe insisted, winking at Morgana.

While Barney cleaned Castor's wounds, Morgana consulted her grimoire and found a few spells to treat Castor's head injury. "It's probably why he's not shifting," she murmured, half to herself, as she worked. She looked over to Monroe. "You won't be there, then, when Maverick questions the two captured shifters?"

"No. Shame, but I decided I'd rather see you. And someone needed to help Barney, so..." He shrugged. "I'll go back there once we've taken Castor upstairs and settled him in."

"Well, I'm very happy you came. I owe you a meal."

"You don't owe me anything. However, I would love another meal. We'll go out again."

"Or I'll cook. I'm organising a small kitchen next to my new bedroom on the second floor. Not as grand as this of course. Something more intimate."

He grinned. "A suite of rooms?"

"Sort of."

"I'm glad I get to see them. I'll bring wine."

Date organised, she was about to turn back to her books again, when another thought struck her. "Your captured shifters. What will you do if they don't talk?"

Barney interrupted them. "Beat the shit out of them, knowing our pack."

"Which won't help them talk," she said, not surprised at all by his response. Shifters tended to use violence over diplomacy.

Monroe finished making the tea and placed a mug of the calming brew close to where Barney worked on Castor. "Your drink. It will do you good. Trust me." He passed a mug to Morgana, then sipped his own, settling against the counter, eyes on hers. "No, more violence won't help. Actually, I don't expect them to talk. They retreated once we tied them up. Their faces were blank. Eyes dead. Like their brains have shut up shop."

"Or they're biding their time," Barney said, still methodically treating Castor's injuries. "Waiting for a chance to strike."

"They'll wait a long time, then. Those chains aren't coming off," Monroe said. "Which means we then have to decide what to do with them."

"We'll find a place." Barney straightened up, hands at the small of his back. "Will they recover from this *possession*?"

Both looked at Morgana. "I'm confident we can heal them. Somehow…" *Drag the spirit kicking and screaming from them, perhaps. Or an exorcism.* "But perhaps while we have two afflicted shifters, you should get Odette to see them. She may find out much more than you will."

"Who's Odette?" Barney asked suspiciously.

"My cousin. She reads people, and other things." She deliberately left it vague, but cocked her head at Monroe. "I'm surprised Maverick didn't suggest using her."

"It's not just our choice. Their pack is not like ours, and I'm not sure they would welcome such a thing. I think that's why Maverick hasn't called her over there yet."

"If you want answers, take her with you. It will give us some much-needed insight, too. I obviously haven't discussed it with her, but I know she will go."

Monroe hesitated, and then nodded. "Fair enough, but won't that slow you down?"

"Birdie is fired up and working quickly, and I'll join her soon. In fact," she looked at Castor's prostate body. Healing him would take time, and Monroe should leave. "I'll use a spell to take him upstairs. We can manage without you. Odette is in the library, so I suggest you get her now."

Monroe drained his cup, crossed the room, and pulled her to him. Then he leaned in and kissed her, leaving her breathless. "Until next time, then."

Twenty-Two

Harlan lay on Maverick's luxurious sofa, eyes closed, the steady drumming of the rain a pleasing backdrop to his wandering thoughts.

While talking to the shifters in the bar, they had opened the doors and it started to fill up, the noise levels steadily rising, and he had asked Arlo where he could go for some quiet. This whole situation was swirling around in his head, and he needed space to think. He had expected to be shown to one of the offices behind the bar, but instead Arlo had let him into Maverick's flat.

It was blissfully quiet there, and warm from the heating that banished the April chill. With only one lamp turned on, he stretched on the sofa and sank into a meditative calm. He often thought better this way. He wasn't sleeping, but instead hovered on the edge of consciousness, his thoughts ebbing and flowing and making connections that sometimes his fully conscious mind wouldn't.

He mulled over the tokens, convinced he was right about the names and what that implied. Unfortunately, that raised other questions. Both Jake and Odette had referred to a god, and yet that didn't make sense to him. Gods liked to be worshipped. They were all-powerful beings that couldn't be contained. And yet this supposed god was recruiting wolf-shifters. In addition,

Odette had sensed a shaman's touch behind all this. Gods did not need shamans, either. Tribal leaders needed shamans. They needed their magic and cunning. Which meant that this wolf god rising on his ancient throne was nothing more than an alpha who had somehow found a way to preserve himself over hundreds of years. *No doubt with the aid of his shaman.*

Hammer had called him the Wey Wolf. *Interesting.* They had found that out when Cecile phoned Arlo and updated him on their situation.

Perhaps he had been defeated in battle, badly wounded possibly, and had retreated to his hall to heal and it had gone wrong somehow. Or maybe faced with defeat, he had retreated, sealed his hall off with his closest pack members, and had been spelled to sleep for a millennia, like some weird aberration of Sleeping Beauty. Along with the shaman, too. Or maybe the alpha had been ambushed and put under a spell by an enemy. *But who would do that?* Surely you'd just kill him and his pack. That's what Harlan would do. That's what anyone with any sense would do. So, he circled back to it being a willing choice. Without knowing the specific timeframe, it was hard to guess what might have triggered it. Invasion, perhaps. It might have been intended to only last for a short time, and it was an accident that a millennia had passed.

Anyway, somehow it had happened, and now he had awoken. His hall—not a temple—lay underground. It would have been sealed. Odette had experienced fleeting glimpses of flickering torchlight. *Had someone deliberately searched for it, or stumbled across it? Were they human or shifter? If it was an accidental find, surely that would be a human. Plus, humans had to be involved to plant the damn tokens.*

And then there were the missing shifters, but clearly not all were missing. Some knew about the club, yet didn't succumb. Or maybe they did, and yet possessed some quality that had made the shaman, if he was still around, release the hold the tokens seemed to give. Hammer certainly didn't want Castor knowing, because an alpha was bigger competition. Yet Hammer had been strong enough to injure his own alpha, almost killing him. And that's because he had the strength of *two* shifters. The other shifter, whose essence was in the token—and who was clearly much more present than Harlan had initially thought.

He sat up, his torpor slipping off him. Maverick was going to question the affected shifters. *What if they weren't as dormant as they seemed? What if they could slip out of the shifters as easily as they had slipped in? But surely they would have done that already, during the fight?*

Nevertheless, he reached for his phone and called Maggie, knowing she would still be at the pool hall. He stood as he did so, heading to the elaborate tapestry on the wall that was marked with all of the shifter safehouses, the paranormal figures, the borders, and the rivalries. He shivered. Suddenly, the distant past felt very close indeed.

Domino wasn't sure it was a good idea to question the captured shifters with Maggie's team still outside.

Layla Gould had gone, taking the dead bodies with her, but a small team remained. They had interviewed the survivors, and were now going through the dead men's belongings, trying to find anything that could help find the location of the club, especially their phones. They were in the main room, leaving Castor's office to the shifters. They had lowered the blinds and pushed the desk aside, and the two shifters were still bound in chains, still curiously devoid of expression. She had discovered that their names were Russo and Lockhart.

Domino and Tommy accompanied Maverick, Danny, Thorne, and Axel. The others remained outside, the room too small to accommodate them all. Domino didn't like Axel. He eyed her dismissively, and treated Danny with disdain, too, but after his outburst earlier, it was deemed safer to include him in the proceedings than not. He'd calmed down considerably, but he still bristled with resentment that the Storm Moon Pack were there. As for how he'd known what was happening, it seemed one of the customers who had been thrown out had contacted him with news of Storm Moon's arrival, and he'd presumed the worst after bursting through the front door. That had been sealed again, and the blinds at the front remained lowered, concealing the destruction within. As for Axel's knowledge of a club or the Wey Wolf, the name Hammer had yelled, he had denied knowing anything.

"They're your shifters," Maverick said to Danny, getting things started. "I suggest you question them. I'll jump in with questions as I have them, if that's okay?"

Danny nodded. "Sure. Russo!" He nodded to Axel, who stood by Russo, and he lifted his head which had been slumped onto his chest. His face remained slack. "Russo, you hear me? Tell me about the Wey Wolf." Russo remained impassive, and Axel cuffed him sharply about the head. Other than one slow blink, he didn't move a muscle.

Danny persisted for the next few minutes, moving from Russo to Lockhart. Questioning, shouting, and cajoling, but nothing stirred them. Axel, acting as the enforcer, struck them harder each time. Domino caught Tommy's eyes, and he shook his head almost imperceptibly.

This wasn't working.

She edged to Maverick's side, and while the interrogation continued, she lowered her voice. "Maverick, perhaps it's time to use your alpha influence."

Still focussed on their prisoners, he shook his head. "It's like they're not even there. I don't think we're going to find out a damn thing, but I'll try. If I'm honest, Harlan's concerns are now magnifying my own."

"You think there's another shifter in there, waiting to come out?"

"Don't you?"

"Honestly, I don't know what to think." She watched their captives again, wondering what was really going on behind their passive expressions. "I'm scared for Hunter. And Hal and Finn, of course," she added hurriedly.

"But you care for Hunter, right? It's different."

"Yes, and like an idiot, I've been holding back." She finally looked at Maverick, glad to be confessing her feelings. "I was worried about my job, how it would look. Now I feel like I missed my chance."

Maverick's eyes glowed with inner fire again. "You haven't. I'll get him back. I'll get them all back. Can you check where Monroe is? Odette might be the solution here. Bring her up to speed, please."

Domino left them to it, rejoining the others in the main hall. Cecile was talking to Jax, leaning against the wall, but she called Domino over. "Getting anything from them?"

"Not a damn thing. What about Maggie and Grey?"

"They're looking at Hammer's phone, but of course it's locked. They're trying to crack the password to get in. He might have numbers they can trace."

Jax shrugged. "They're getting his phone records anyway. And Will and Ben's."

Domino nodded, pleased. "Have they tried his fingerprints? Thumb print?"

"Yep, no deal," Cecile informed her.

Even so, Domino was pleased they had avenues to follow. "I'm actually hoping that Monroe is nearly here with Odette."

"Just a few minutes away, last we heard."

"Good. I can't see us making any progress without her." She glanced to the front door that was still sealed. The room was darker now, and a few lights had been put on over the green baize of the pool tables. The back of the room, however, was starkly lit, the puddles of blood and bodily matter ghoulish under the full lights. A small team of three were taking photos, but Domino knew it wouldn't be investigated as rigorously as a regular murder case. Paranormal deaths were treated very differently, especially in circumstances like this. "I'll have a word with Grey."

Leaving Jax and Cecile talking, she joined Grey and Maggie, who had set up at the counter of the bar, perched on barstools.

"Out already?" Grey asked, surprised.

"Waiting for Odette. Those two aren't telling us anything. I don't even know if they can. Have you found anything?"

"A crumpled receipt in his pocket. Woohoo!" Maggie waved it, voice dripping with sarcasm. "Bank cards in his wallet, a few notes and change. And his bloody locked phone, of course."

Domino picked up the well-worn jacket on the counter. "Hammer's, I presume?"

Grey nodded. "We found it in the office. Will and Ben's belongings, the other dead shifters, are there." He pointed to a bundle of clothing in plastic bags.

"No tokens in their pockets, I suppose?"

"No." Maggie sighed. "I'm not sure whether I'm annoyed or relieved. How's your arm?"

Domino flexed it as she looked at the thick bandage. "It's sore, but better than it was. Barney bound it well. I should have been quicker. Will caught me unawares." She was still annoyed with herself. "Then I was pinned down by his dead body and I couldn't move. It was a bloody disaster."

"You survived, that's all that matters," Grey said.

Suddenly, a loud banging resonated on the front door, and she heard Monroe shout, "It's just me with Odette."

"Excellent. I'll get them." Domino let them in, moving aside to allow them to shake the rain off their jackets while she locked the door. "Thanks for coming, Odette. I know you were busy." She turned to Monroe. "All okay with Castor?"

"Morgana is doing her thing, ably assisted by Barney. That's as much as I know."

Odette was dressed in jeans, a jumper, and boots, with a large waterproof jacket over the top. Her curls were damp, and she ran her hands through them. "I'm glad to help, and I'm hoping to get some real insight into what's going on." Her gaze took in the room, and she waved at Grey and Maggie. "Where are they? The shifters, I mean."

"The office. Do you need a drink first?"

"No. Let's get on with it."

"Need me?" Monroe asked.

Domino shook her head. "Not yet, but stay close, just in case." And then another thought struck her. They had planned on being back at Storm Moon by now. The bar would be open, and they were low on security staff. "No, change of plan. Head back to Storm Moon, and take Cecile and Jax. I don't want them vulnerable."

He frowned. "You think there'll be trouble?"

"I don't trust some members of this pack. Axel came storming in here, threatening to kill Castor, and accusing Maverick of killing the others. He might not be the only one who caught wind of what happened here this afternoon."

"Sure thing. Any messages for the others?"

"No, just to stay wary."

Leaving Monroe to talk to Cecile and Jax, she led Odette to the office, updating her with the latest news, and warned her what to expect. When she opened the door, it was to find the situation unchanged, except for the tension, which seemed to have ratchetted up.

"This the witch?" Axel asked, sneering. "Doesn't look like much use."

"Shut your fucking mouth," Tommy growled out.

Odette ignored Axel as if he'd never even spoken, but gave Tommy a beaming smile as she crossed to Maverick's side. "How are you, Mav?"

"Frustrated. We can't get a word out of them. Thanks for coming." He introduced her to Danny and Thorne, pointedly ignoring Axel. "They have eight missing shifters, three dead, and these two seem bewitched. Anything you can find out would be brilliant."

All business, Odette took her jacket off, threw it over the closest chair, and dragged it to the shifters. She didn't speak, instead studying both of them. Frowning, she settled in front of Russo. He was the smaller of the two men, and like all of them was covered in blood, bruises, and scratches. A sheen of sweat marked his brow and upper lip, and his eyes remained glazed.

"His name?" she asked.

"Russo," Danny told her, exchanging a worried glance with Thorne. "What are you planning to do?"

"Try to wake him. Or his shadow. I feel a presence much closer to the surface than with the other." She finally looked at Axel, who hovered behind Russo, ready to strike again, no doubt. "Move out of the way. I don't want you near him."

He stared her down. "I don't think so. I'm staying put."

Odette flicked her fingers at him and he flew backwards, slamming into the wall with a resounding thwack. "There's a good boy. Stay back until I say so."

Everyone was taken by surprise, including Domino. She didn't know that Odette could do such a thing. Axel strained against his magical bonds, but Danny stepped forward, a low growl in his throat.

Maverick's arm shot out to stop him. "Wait, and watch."

Twenty-Three

After the first trials ended, Hunter sat silently as the watching crowd dispersed, heading to the dining hall. The scent of food drifted down the passageways, and from what Hal told him, it was common that everyone would gather and celebrate—combatants, guards, and the messengers. And the Wey Wolf, of course, presiding over everything. A ritual from out of the Dark Ages.

Once again, Hunter's head swam with memories that weren't his own, and gripping the amulet, he forced them back. It was as if Briar whispered soothing words in his ear, telling him to stay calm and focussed. The feeling was enhanced when his feet hit the ground, as if her earth magic welled around him. However, the longer he stayed here, the stronger his shadow warrior became. The other that dwelled within him. His thoughts became more insistent. *The urge to draw blood. The desire to bow low before the Wey Wolf.*

Knowing that he had barely any time to spare, as he was expected in the hall, he hurried down the passage that led to the river cave. Many of the shifters were heading there to wash after their trials or practice, so he used it as cover for his own activities—finding the human. His scent already marked him out, and Hunter had watched him leave, noting the route he took. What he was proposing was risky. If the man betrayed him, then they would search Hunter, take his amulet, and might even kill him. He could face combat with his shadow warrior, and if he lost, he would lose himself forever. He'd already made himself different by not having the token.

But he needed answers.

Halfway down the passage that led to the water cave, he saw the man turn to the left, an area that remained shadowy in Hunter's mind. He slowed his pace, waited until there was space between him and the other shifters, and ducked into the passage. He had barely gone a dozen steps when he spotted a door partially open on the right, and the scent of the human grew stronger. He checked behind him to make sure no one followed, and then darted to the open doorway. The man stood against the far wall of the room, watching him. Hunter froze, but the stranger beckoned him forward.

Heart pounding, Hunter studied the basic bedroom and stepped inside, pushing the door a little more closed behind him.

"You're taking a risk, shifter," the man said, fear etched across his face.

"So are you. How did you know I would follow? And who are you?"

"I'm Dean. I knew because you are the shifter who lost his token."

"You know about that? Does everyone?"

"The guards. The Wey Wolf. And the shaman, of course. My brother told me."

"You're Barry's brother?" Dean nodded. "I thought I saw a resemblance."

He studied him. "You are not like the others."

"Not yet, but I need answers. I need to get out. If I head to the door—"

"You won't make it. The shaman has spelled it. Only a few can leave."

"But you're still here. Why?"

"Insurance. To keep my brothers behaving."

"Brothers? Barry and how many others?"

"There are just the three of us. Barry, Andy, and me. You must have seen Andy at the house. I know Barry brought you here."

Hunter recalled the other man who had intervened in the hallway. "I remember him. Were you in the throne room?" Hunter was sure he'd have seen him.

"No, I'm not allowed there, but Barry saw me afterwards. As soon as we found this place, I knew it was bad news, but we were drawn onwards, and Andy was gripped by it as soon as we saw that door."

"You discovered this place during your renovations?"

"Yes. Two months ago." He swallowed. "The door, the big one with the wolf on it, was closed, but a section to the side of it had collapsed. The whole passage was a mess. We should have just let it be."

"But you got inside, and found what?" Hunter asked, needing him to hurry. "Was the place like this? Was the Wey Wolf awake?"

"No, it was a tomb, but we made the mistake of waking the shaman."

Hunter had so many questions, he wasn't sure where to begin. "A tomb? You mean there's a tomb in here? With coffins?"

"Stone coffins. The Wey Wolf and his guards were inside—although we didn't actually know what they were at the time. A dozen in all. All wrapped in shrouds. It was the fucking creepiest thing I've ever seen." He jerked his head to the right. "Further down that corridor. This place is huge. We spent hours exploring it. Discussing how much money we might make with this discovery. We thought the place was empty, until we found the tombs." He shuddered again. "They must have sealed themselves in. I still don't know why."

"Tell me about the shaman."

"We found him in another place, covered in a shroud, too. He was surrounded by weird symbols." Dean paused, and his lips tightened again. When he spoke, his voice was almost a whisper. "He's the biggest danger. He is terrifying."

Hunter edged towards Dean. "How did he wake? How did any of this start happening? Anything you can tell me might help me defeat him." Hunter glanced behind him again. "I haven't got long."

"The shaman is too powerful. So is the Wey Wolf, and if I'm honest," the man took a breath, fighting to keep calm, "I'm not sure Andy wants it to be over. He's enjoying this. He's gripped by the Wey Wolf and the shaman, as much as any shifter. Now you need to go, before you're missed."

"Not yet. I need answers. If the shaman is the key, then that's who I must kill."

"No. There is more than him to consider now. The shadow warriors are stronger than you realise, and with every new pack member, the Wey Wolf grows in strength."

Hunter stepped back, ear to the door, hearing the softest noise outside, and lifted his finger to his lips. Shifter senses on full alert he listened, poised to act, but all he heard was silence, and the pounding of his heart.

"You need to go." The man had crossed to his side. "You'll be missed before long. Stop asking questions. I see you talking to your friend. I don't know how you still have some control, free will, but you need to hide it better."

"I need to get out."

"You need to keep your head down. Losing the token, however you did it, has roused suspicions. It's only the fact that the Wey Wolf is so damn arrogant and sure of himself that he doesn't worry about *anomalies*."

Hunter's wolf that always simmered close to the surface reared up again, as frustration at his current situation bubbled over. "Don't you want to get out?"

Dean stepped back, the scent of his fear strong. "Of course, but I don't want to die, either."

"Okay. I get it. I'll be more careful. Does the shaman watch me?"

"Yes, and the guards, but they're all busy right now with the shadow warriors. Don't give them reason to act. Now go!"

Confused, Hunter asked, "But don't you have other family? Isn't someone missing you? Work?"

"No. That's why I'm here and not the others. Now go."

Hunter took a breath, trying to calm his agitation. Dean was right. He was taking too long. "Can we meet later, then? I have more questions." It hadn't escaped Hunter's attention that Dean hadn't answered his questions with any great detail. Was that because he couldn't or wouldn't?

"After combat tonight, in the water cave. Late."

And with that, he swiftly pushed Hunter out the door.

Arlo couldn't settle himself to anything at Storm Moon, too worried about what was going on at the Apollo Pool Hall.

The bar was busy, but the club was still closed, as it was too early to open there. However, that night's band had already arrived, and they were bringing in their equipment through the stage door. The staff that organised the sound and lighting were already downstairs setting up, as were the bar staff.

He felt redundant. Useless. Three pack members were trapped in some damn club, and he was just sitting there, while Maverick and the team interrogated shifters. He had been sitting in the corner booth, brooding with Vlad and debating whether to join Harlan upstairs, when John raced inside from the front door. He crossed the room with long strides, not caring that the customers were shooting him curious glances.

Vlad and Arlo immediately stood, and Arlo asked, "What now?"

"The North London Pack have just arrived. They pulled a van around the rear. I'm pretty sure they haven't come to party. Not in a good way, at least."

"How many?" Arlo asked, already heading to the stairs that led down to the club.

"Half a dozen easily."

"Tell the bar staff to keep serving, and send Mads down. If they try to get in the front, lock the door." Mads had been on the door with John.

As John hurried away, Arlo raced down the stairs after Vlad, who had already bounded ahead of him. He mentally ran through the security team presently on site. Fran, Rory, and Xavier were all downstairs, but that was it. Mads would join them, but even with Vlad and Arlo, they were understaffed. There were human staff down there, as well as the band, but they couldn't get involved. And there was Jet.

He pounded into the club, hearing raised voices from the rear door. Vlad was still ahead of him, already ripping his *Storm Moon Staff* t-shirt over his head in preparation to shift. Arlo did the same, not caring right now what the human staff thought. Two startled figures on the stage watched them, alarmed. A man called out, "I think there's a problem out back…"

"Stay inside," Arlo yelled, "and *do not* call the police!"

Jet emerged from the dressing room at the rear of the stage and jumped down to speak to Arlo. "How can I help?"

"You know where the shotgun is kept in the security office? The locked cupboard?"

"Yes. And I know where the key is."

"Good. Get the gun, and meet us down here. And keep everyone out of our way."

Arlo had no intention of shooting anyone, but he certainly hoped the gun would serve as a deterrent. Vlad had already thrown the emergency door open, and Arlo followed him outside, horrified to see at least ten shifters gathered on the steps and in the unloading zone. All wielded weapons—metal bars, mainly—clearly intent on doing a lot of damage to property, as well as shifters.

Fran was nose to nose with a man, on the verge of shifting herself. "Get back now before I rip your fucking throat out!"

"You haven't got it in you." The man leered over her. "Female shifters are only good for one thing, and it isn't fighting."

Before anyone could intervene—not even Rory, who stood next to her—Fran lashed out. She might be a woman, but she worked out, and was packed with muscle. She was fast, too. She knocked the shifter flat with a single, powerful punch, and then laid into the one behind him.

Before Arlo had a chance to even try to calm the situation, they were all fighting.

Twenty-Four

Morgana joined Birdie in the library once Castor was resting in his room on the second floor, Barney settled in a chair next to him.

It had taken longer to work her healing magic than she had anticipated, because of Castor's head injury. Barney had watched her every move, as if she might try to kill him rather than heal him, but he was a useful helper, and once they were done, she'd told him to use the shower to wash the blood and guts off himself.

She updated Birdie, and asked, "What about you? Any useful spells?"

Birdie straightened up, pushing her reading glasses onto her head. "I think we need to use this one." She jabbed her finger at the page. "It's a variation of what we used to expel the Fallen Angel from Olivia. I have other options, of course, but this one strikes me as being the best."

Morgana scanned the spell. "I see. It's object-based rather than personal. In theory, this should be easier."

Birdie tucked an errant strand of hair back into her messy bun. "In theory. But you know, I have had another idea. It sounds a bit mad…"

Birdie hadn't become High Priestess of Moonfell on a whim. She had been chosen, like Morgana, who would be the next High

Priestess after Birdie. They were both considered by the house as the most powerful witches of their generation. "Unconventional, no doubt," Morgana said, "but probably brilliant."

Birdie smiled, a hint of smugness in her expression. "I think so."

"Go on, then."

"What if we try to move the essence of the shifter in the token directly to the Wayfinder?"

"Okay, but the token has the shifter's blood or hair—we think. The Wayfinder doesn't."

"But it's like the Genie in the bottle, or Dorian Grey's painting. Once we have him, we can put him anywhere, in theory."

Morgana nodded. "That has merit. You think if we put it in the Wayfinder, it will give us the location of this temple, or hall?"

"I think it's possible. From what Hunter told Jet, which was admittedly brief, he said he knew where it was. This shifter," she tapped the token, "wants to go home. It might trigger the mechanism."

"Wow. That is actually a genius idea. We might even be able to put it in a compass."

"But the Wayfinder has magic already. I feel it will bond better. That's the idea, anyway." Birdie sighed. "It might not work, in which case we would have to question the shifter himself."

"The spirit shifter?" Morgana asked, with healthy scepticism. "Like an interview?"

"Isn't that exactly what Maverick and Odette are doing now?"

"I suppose it is."

"I suspect they will resist the interrogation, in which case we must provide an alternative. Let us head to the tower room and make it happen."

Maverick watched Russo's features ripple under Odette's scrutiny, as if he was recoiling from her. Or rather, the shifter within was.

Odette had painted strange symbols on Russo's face with her fingers, and they had shimmered before vanishing. She then painted them around his wrists, and after examining his palms, painted them there, too. After that, she had been locked in silent battle with him for almost ten minutes, his hands clasped within her own, and she had leaned in, maintaining eye contact, too. A strange force seemed to be surrounding them, growing ever more palpable. His own pack watched patiently, used to Odette's odd ways, but Danny and Thorne shuffled at the wait, and shot Maverick doubtful glances. His commanding stare silenced them. As for Axel, he was still stuck against the wall behind him, furious at his inability to move or speak.

The silence was suddenly shattered when Odette said, "I have found him, the shifter within, but I fear that if I draw him out, it might kill Russo." She didn't move, her eyes still on Russo, his hands still clasped tight.

"Why?" Maverick asked, crouching next to her.

"Because he is firmly embedded in him. Imprinted onto his mind. I suspect he's been directing him for days. Maybe weeks."

Danny intervened. "I don't believe it. Russo has seemed like his normal self."

"Nevertheless, he's in there. Ordwulf is his name."

"Ordwulf?" Domino asked. "Another old name."

"As old as the shifter's spirit."

Danny had a whispered conversation with Thorne, and then asked, "Can you ignore him and talk to Russo? If he can tell us where the others are, it's worth the risk."

"I don't know if I can," Odette said with a slight shake of her head. "After the fight, whatever free will Russo might have had seems to have been brought under Ordwulf's control. If I can make him speak, then I might be able to work out more. I might be able to discern lies from truth. But Ordwulf is sharp. Watchful. I have seen glimpses of the hall again, a vast, sprawling complex, and again, that guiding force. The shaman."

"But Russo is okay?" Thorne asked, seeking reassurance.

"No." Her blunt response shocked the room. "Ordwulf stares at me even now, wondering how strong I am. It will be better to question Ordwulf, but you need to decide quickly whether you want me to, because I cannot hold him close much longer."

Maverick stared at Danny. "There is much more at risk than just Russo. Your whole pack. Our shifters. The whole structure of wolf-shifter society in London, and maybe further. We don't know what this Wey Wolf and his shaman can do."

Danny nodded. "Do it."

Odette began immediately. "Ordwulf, I see you now. You have buried yourself in Russo, yet you cannot escape me. I command you to reveal yourself to all here."

Russo's chest heaved in and out as if he was struggling for air, and his dull gaze cleared. Unexpectedly, Russo's eyes changed colour, from hazel brown to bright blue, and it was so disconcerting that Maverick almost stepped back in shock.

Russo's voice was deep when he spoke, rasping as if unused for a long time, his lips contorted with effort. "Leave me be, witch. I am not yours to command."

"Yes, you are. We have questions for you. What do you want of Russo?"

"This body. It will be mine, eventually."

"Why not now? What's stopping you?"

"Let me go." He ground the words out as if it was hard to speak, not answering her question.

"No. Why can you not claim Russo's body now?"

"There is work to be done. I am tasked by Blōdbana."

"Who is that?" Odette asked, leaning forward. Russo tried to pull away, but Odette had a firm grip of his hand, and the swell of her magic increased. "I see. He is the shaman. What does he want you to do?"

"To recruit the willing, and subjugate the rest. We will form the biggest pack. All will submit or die." His head shot around, locking eyes with Maverick.

Maverick recoiled, suddenly knowing what Odette meant. The spirit wolf was there, distinct from Russo, and he felt ancient, his presence emanating with vicious intent. Maverick took advantage of it, kindling his own wolf and exerting his alpha dominance. "Tell me where the Wey Wolf's hall is. I want to meet this shifter."

"You will see him when it is time. For now, you are not welcome."

"Because I'm an alpha. He fears me, just like you do."

"We fear no one."

But Maverick saw a flicker of doubt, and he leaned closer, his face inches from Russo's. "Liar. Tell me where the hall is, and fight like a proper shifter. Not a coward who skulks around in others. Hiding."

"The Wey Wolf will make you pay for that."

"No. This is not your world, Ordwulf. Your days are gone, and you should be dust. If the Wey Wolf thinks he is so strong, I demand he fights me."

A sneer started on Russo's lips, and then suddenly everything changed. The bright blue eyes of Ordwulf turned a stormy grey, and Odette yelled, "Get back!"

Harlan's peaceful evening of restful contemplation was shattered when he heard the screech of brakes, and shouts erupted from the carpark at the rear of Storm Moon.

He shot off the sofa, the auction's catalogue landing in a heap on the floor, and his phone slid under the coffee table as he raced to the window at the rear. Below, men were streaming out of a large, battered blue transit van, and he could just about see Fran and Rory at the back of the club.

It could only be the North London Pack, based on what he knew had happened to Castor. *Unless, of course, these were possessed shifters, intent on recruiting more.* That thought was even more terrifying. Harlan looked around for weapons, but unlike in his own flat, there wasn't a baseball bat leaning against the bedroom wall, or even a golf club to grab from the set he'd bought after some ill-advised lessons a few years before. Golf would always be a boring sport, no matter how many lessons he had.

But he did have a Taser in his messenger bag, a useful way to defend himself after the encounter with a demon that made shifters change to their wolves without control. He grabbed the Taser and raced down the stairs, emerging onto the carpark and a scene of carnage. A full brawl was underway, and the Storm

Moon shifters were outnumbered. Some shifters were in their wolves, others fought as human, and the North London Pack were swinging metal poles around, smashing wolves, the rear doors, and whatever stood in their way.

But no one had spotted Harlan, and even better, a discarded metal pole lay on the ground. He aimed his Taser at the closest enemy shifter, a man at the bottom of the steps who was about to strike a wolf at his feet with his weapon. Harlan had a good aim, and hit him in the chest, earning an outraged scream before the man hit the ground with a thump. He immediately took aim at the next shifter and shot again, and he crumpled too, collapsing in a spasm of twitching. At this point, everyone had spotted him, and having no time to reload, he grabbed the metal pole.

A shifter raced up the stairs towards him, horribly quick as he bounded up several steps at a time, but Harlan was already crouching, making himself a smaller target. He swung the pole out low, cracking the shifter's legs, which brought him down in a heap. He followed it up with another almighty crack on his arm. He knew from long experience that you couldn't hesitate with a shifter. They were too quick, so it was all or nothing. Then, to add another distraction, he swung the pole at the van and smashed the side mirror and window. At the same time, the loud report of a shot echoed around the carpark, and every single shifter froze.

Jet stood at the emergency exit door, shotgun trained on the closest enemy shifter—a huge wolf with its hackles up. With a steady voice, she said, "Calm the fuck down, or I'll shoot one of you next."

Harlan took the opportunity to reload his double Taser, and when the shifter at his feet moved, he shot him, and then pointed it at another. "Me, too. I have a Taser, and I'll use it again."

Vlad shifted back to human, covered in blood, and strode to Jet's side, as if to protect her, but his wolf was close to the surface, and he was simmering with rage. "You heard them. Back off. We have a common enemy now."

A scowling, bearded man, covered in blood, squared up to Vlad. "Your alpha almost killed ours."

"No, he didn't. *Hammer* did. Have you heard of a phone? Don't you talk to each other? Call Danny, he'll tell you everything."

By now, the panting, injured wolves had withdrawn into their respective packs. The bearded man snarled. "Hammer would never do that."

"Well, he did. In fact, call Barney. He'll confirm it. What?" Vlad asked, scowling as the man hesitated. "Scared of the truth? Barney is the one who killed Hammer, defending Castor."

Another shifter, a hulking man with no neck, laughed. "That's bullshit."

"No, it's really not. Go on, ask him."

Harlan maintained his position halfway down the steps leading to the bay outside the stage door. He still had the metal pole in one hand, and the Taser in the other. All of Storm Moon's wolves, other than Vlad, were still in their wolf. He recognised Arlo, Fran, and Xavier. The other two he was unsure of, but they were all injured, and blood dripped from their jaws, showing how much they'd hurt the others.

The bearded man, one of the only shifters not to have been in his wolf, reached into his back pocket and pulled out his phone. "If you're lying, this fight is not over."

Vlad didn't respond, and instead they all waited, rage simmering, violence ready to erupt at a second's notice. Fortunately, the conversation was short, and the shifter listened with increasing incredulity.

"And Castor?" he finally asked. He nodded slowly, ending the call. He dropped his weapon on the ground, the clang of metal on concrete echoing around the area. "Seems you're right. So who's this fucking Wey Wolf?"

Twenty-Five

Domino had mere seconds to react after Odette's warning.

Something swelled out of Russo, striking at Maverick like a cobra, and bypassing Odette completely. Maverick was too close, and although she knew Maverick had excellent reflexes, her instincts kicked in. Fearing for his life, Domino threw herself at Maverick, knocking him backwards and onto the floor into a crunching heap.

They rolled in a tangle of limbs, and she righted herself in time to see Tommy try to pull Odette back. However, Odette had warded herself off, locked in a circle of protection with something that looked like darting black smoke. Danny and Thorne had backed into the wall next to Axel.

Having secured Maverick's safety, Domino was now terrified for Odette, but Odette looked victorious. She was ensconced in a second circle of protection, one that sealed her from whatever she had brought forth. She no longer held Russo's hand, and her voice purred with excitement. "Here you are, Blōdbana. I can even see your face. Your tattoos, your runes that bind. The blood sacrifices you made. Tell this to your master. We will find you. There is nowhere to hide in your hall."

Russo shot to his feet, puppet-like with jerking limbs, mouth contorting to speak. Strange tattoos bloomed under his skin, and with horror, Domino realised the shaman was trying to take over Russo's body, not Ordwulf. He stood so quickly that he knocked Lockhart, the other shifter who was tied up next to him, onto the floor.

Again, Odette was equal to it. She thrust her hand out, sending Lockhart flying across the floor so he was well out of the way. The strange symbols she had painted on Russo flared with a silvery glow, and she shouted, "Shifter and shaman of ages past, your time in this vessel cannot last. By my will and sacred light, I cast you back to your rightful site!"

Russo shook from his head to his toes, his lips peeled back and his jaw wide, but the strange tattoos that threatened to manifest more clearly instantly vanished. Within seconds, Russo collapsed on the floor with a heavy thump. Odette didn't bother to examine him; instead, she raced over to Lockhart.

"Will the shaman try to come for him, too?" Domino asked, rising to her feet with Maverick.

Odette painted the strange symbols on his face again, just liked she had with Russo, and finally said, "I don't think so. He exerted a lot of effort to do that. Lockhart should be safe for now."

"And the shifter in him?" Maverick asked.

"Still there."

"What about Russo?" Danny called over. He crouched next to his pack member, lifted his eyelids, and felt for his pulse. "He's alive, but unconscious."

Odette joined him, completing her silent appraisal. "I think he's gone. The other shifter, that is. Unless he's buried so far back I can't find him. Probably best to keep him bound for now." She stood slowly, rolling her shoulders, her pale face even paler than usual. With a flick of her fingers, she released Axel. "Aren't you pleased you stood back now?"

Axel growled, a low rumble in the back of throat. "If you ever do that to me again—"

"Shut it!" Danny instructed him. "You saw what happened. This is not something we can tackle alone."

And then the door flew open, and Grey stood at the threshold, rigid with fury. "Storm Moon has been attacked." He pointed a finger at Axel. "*You* did that!"

Domino knew that Monroe and the others would not have arrived in time, but Maverick beat her to the question. "Are they okay?"

"There are injuries. Lots of them, but no deaths. Same for your guys," Grey said, addressing Danny. "However, it seems that, for now, we have a truce."

Hunter returned to the dining hall with a small group of shifters, returning from the water cave after having a brief wash.

His hair was still damp, and no one was looking at him suspiciously as he sought out Hal. It was more crowded than the previous night, but large areas of tables remained empty. The smokeless fire still burned in the centre of the hall, and the scent of roasting meats emanated from the chicken and pork turning on spits. Dean watched over them, another job the man had to fulfil, alongside another couple of shifters.

Grateful he hadn't been missed, Hunter debated whether he should sit next to anyone else, and then worried he would give himself away, decided against it. And then he remembered Finn, the young shifter who had arrived earlier. With relief he saw him with Hal, and hurried to join them.

The hall was now dressed for the feast. Platters of meat and bread were placed in the middle of the tables, as well as wooden plates and cutlery. Jugs of wine, beer, and water were readily available, too. Another reason, no doubt, that some shifters could still pass out of the hall. It would take several people to keep this place filled with supplies. *But what funded it? Who paid?*

Realising he was starving, he decided to consider those questions later, loaded up a plate with food, and sat next to Finn and Hal, finding they were talking about the next bout of fights. Finn's eyes were bright, too bright, as he listened to Hal, but he turned to Hunter and said, "I hear you're fighting next, Hunter?"

"I think I am. I welcome it. You know me, Finn," Hunter smiled. "I always love a good fight. But how are you? I think you're one of the youngest here."

"I'm all right." He nodded several times as if to convince himself. "I'm just not as strong as the others."

"Yet," Hal put in, wiping chicken juices off his chin with the back of his hand. "You will train first. The Wey Wolf wants the strongest shifters."

"Yes, but..." Finn hesitated, blinking as if to clear his thoughts, a trace of embarrassment in his voice. "I'm still having trouble shifting. Those fights today. I couldn't do that."

Hunter tried to reassure him. "You're young, and when you first start shifting, it's always hard. I struggled for a while, but then it all clicked into place." Actually, that wasn't strictly true. Hunter had shifted early and mastered it quickly, but everyone was different. "It will happen. You're a shifter. It's in your blood. The fact you're here is proof of it."

Hal nodded in agreement. "Absolutely. This is a training ground for warriors, Finn, and the Wey Wolf is the strongest alpha. Better than Maverick, and especially Castor! It's an enormous honour. Together we will all be part of the greatest pack the world has seen in a long time."

Hunter realised as he watched Hal, that even in the last few hours, he'd changed. His expression appeared harder, his attitude more entrenched, and his sense of humour seemed to be vanishing under this fervent urge to be in the Wey Wolf's pack.

Finn played with his food, but Hunter kept eating, half watching the teen. The poor kid looked scared under those fervently bright eyes. "Hey Finn, I presume you had a token this morning? Or was it last night?"

He looked startled, and his long fringe flopped across his face as his head jerked up. "Yes, this morning. I was on my way back from my friend's house, and someone jostled me. The next thing I knew, I had a token in my hand, and I had to get here. I took the Tube."

He was targeted. It wasn't an accident, like it had been for Hunter. Some bastard had selected a young kid. Did they think he would be more compliant? But like Finn himself said, he was nowhere near as strong as the adult shifters. Was it meant to divide the Storm Moon Pack? Ignite fear and doubt in Maverick's abilities? Whatever it meant, Finn was vulnerable.

"I met the Wey Wolf," Finn continued. "I think I prefer Maverick."

Hal froze, staring at him. "How can you think that?"

Hunter leapt in. "He's young and confused, that's all. The Wey Wolf is better than Maverick, Finn. Don't worry, you'll see it in time." He flashed a look of warning to Hal. "He'll learn."

Hal's lips twisted in disdain. "Learn quickly, Finn. There's no room for that talk here." He stood, troubled, and Hunter didn't like his expression one bit. "We're fighting soon, Hunter, so don't linger, or eat too much. You don't want it to slow you down."

"Just finishing up and I'll be there."

Finn was staring at his plate again, and Hunter knew something was wrong. Finn was filled with too much doubt. His fervent, glazed look from earlier had vanished, and only a troubled boy was left in its place.

Hunter casually said, "Don't worry about Hal. He means well. He wants you to succeed, like I do. To be part of the pack. But, I'm just wondering, can you feel the inner warrior? Your wolf struggling to become stronger? It's sort of..." *Shit, how to phrase this?* "Like your wolf ancestor is helping you to develop. This hall helps to do that, you know. Bring him out. It's who some of the shifters fought earlier."

Finn stared at him, obviously confused. "The mirror thing? That was their wolf ancestor?"

"Yes." Hunter wanted to shout *no* and incite a riot, but he just smiled. "He helps us."

"I thought I felt him earlier, but he's gone now."

"He'll be back, I'm sure." Hunter pushed his plate away. "Why don't you come with me, Finn? We'll help each other train."

As Finn nodded his agreement and finished his meal, Hunter was debating something else. Finn seemed to have too much free will. He questioned more than Hunter, which was both a relief but also terrifying. Finn's safety might be in danger. But the biggest question was why, and Hunter suspected it was to do with Finn's wolf. He hadn't mastered his shifts, and he couldn't summon his wolf at will. Did that mean that the shadow warrior couldn't take hold, and that Hunter had another ally?

Or did that just make Finn more vulnerable to being consumed by another wolf-shifter completely? In which case, Hunter couldn't trust him at all.

Twenty-Six

Morgana idly spun the pointer on the Wayfinder again, watching it whirl around the disc, skimming over the indented circle in the centre, and wondering what their next course of action should be.

They had been in the tower room for over an hour, trying to extract the spirit of the wolf-shifter from the token and move it to the Wayfinder, but so far, all their efforts had failed. Frustratingly, they had also heard from Grey, who had informed them that they didn't find any phone numbers on Hammer's phone that could provide a clue to locating the mysterious club. All of Hammer's calls had been to other pack members. They were at a dead-end.

Birdie was sitting on the floor, cross-legged in the centre of the pentagram, face creased in thought. She flicked the token between her fingers, as perplexed as Morgana.

"Birdie, I think we should fit the token in the centre of the Wayfinder and try to combine their effects."

"An interesting suggestion, but if we can't get the little blighter out, it's pointless."

She suppressed a smile. Only Birdie would call a troublesome spirit a 'little blighter.' "You have a point, but perhaps we should change tack with that, too. So far we're trying to drag it out. What if we lure it out?"

Birdie tapped her pursed lips with her index finger. "Interesting suggestion. I presume you mean with blood. Shifter blood."

"Exactly. Whoever crafted that thing—the shaman, we presume—made it highly sensitive to shifters, and only shifters. We can't risk it touching one, but blood might tempt it."

"We have Castor, so access is easy."

"Exactly." Morgana considered her idea, trying to refine how it would work. "We could smear his blood on the token and on the Wayfinder."

"And then slap them together!" Birdie struggled to her feet, not quite as agile as she had once been.

"Sort of." She shrugged, uncertain. "Something like that. It has got to be worth trying. So far, everything else has failed. Storm Moon and Castor's pack are clashing, or were, but how long will that truce last? They're volatile."

"So is Maverick when his back is against the wall."

"True, but we don't need this escalating. You prepare what you think will work, and I'll go and get some blood. We can use Castor's bloody bandages, and I need to check on him, anyway."

Morgana hurried to Castor's room with a few supplies, and to her surprise found him sitting up, fully awake, talking to Barney. "Oh! Thank the Goddess! I thought you'd be unconscious, or in your wolf."

Castor may have been awake, but he looked exhausted and pale, pain etched across his face, his cheekbones looking impossible sharp in the low light cast by the bedside lamp. He reminded her of a cobra, ready to strike. He narrowed his sharp-eyed gaze at her, taking her in from her head to her feet, a look that made Morgana bristle with indignation. But then he focussed on her face. "I gather you saved my life. Thank you."

"I wouldn't put it quite like that. Barney did an excellent job of stopping the blood flow. My poultice helped, and I eased your head injury, of course. If I can be honest, though," she stepped closer to the bed, taking in Barney's sour expression, "you still look half dead. You should sleep now, not talk."

"Exactly what I said," Barney added, shooting Castor an impatient look.

"I can't stay here, not with the pack at risk." Castor made as if to get out of bed, and immediately fell back, wincing with pain.

Morgana tutted. "And yet, you can't move. Castor, your body needs to heal, but you can help them in other ways."

"How?"

"I'd like some blood, please." She ran through their plan. "It might not work, of course, but we're running out of options."

"And they need to get in that hall."

"*We* do. If there's a shaman in there, shifters will need magic—our magic—to battle him."

He smiled. "This really isn't your fight."

"It most certainly is. Storm Moon are our friends. We fight together."

Castor extended his arms, covered in scratches and bruises. "Take what you need. If it works, will the old shifter trapped in that token come for me?"

"No. It won't have a chance to. Besides," she added unable to resist teasing him, "he'll take one look at you and change his mind."

"Bloody charming."

Barney just sniggered.

She placed the bowl she'd brought with her on the bedside table. "I'll just use some of your bloodied dressings, that's all."

"No. Take fresh. It will be more potent."

"Blood is blood, Castor."

"I've got alpha blood, Morgana. Take it. Soak the damn token in it, and draw that fucker out."

"So be it. And then you must shift to your wolf and sleep. You'll heal quicker, you know that."

He was already struggling to stay awake, eyes flickering with the effort of staying open, so she worked quickly, making a small incision in his arm and collecting his blood in the bowl. When she finished, because he was already naked except for the sheets that covered him, he shifted to his wolf.

"You need sleep too, Barney."

But Barney was on his feet. "I want to watch you."

"Don't trust us?"

"I'm interested."

"As long as you keep out of our way."

When they returned to the tower room, Birdie had rearranged the space in the centre of the pentagram. "Morgana, I have crafted a spell that... Oh!" she spotted Barney. "A visitor?"

"Barney wants to watch us. He's the Bar Manager at the Apollo Pool Hall, wielder of the shotgun."

"Ah! Welcome, Barney. Are you sure you want to watch?"

He folded his arms across his chest. "Never surer."

"Then take a seat," she gestured to one, "and do not interfere!"

"Even to save you?"

Birdie threw her head back and laughed. "Oh, you're fun. I can assure you that we will not need saving." Birdie clapped her hands, playing to the audience of one, and the candle flames flared into life.

Morgana edged next to her, lowering her voice. "Please do not turn us into performing monkeys."

"Oh, hush. A little fun never hurt anyone."

Making sure that Barney was in his seat, she said, "You were about to tell me about a spell."

"Yes. I have amended one. I will command the spirit to direct us to his home, but the Wayfinder must be soaked in blood."

"I took enough from Castor. He was a willing participant, and as he pointed out, he's an alpha with more potent blood."

Birdie nodded. "Good. So hopefully we can direct the spirit into the Wayfinder, and then trap it there. That will be tricky."

"I don't think so. The Wayfinder is already magical. It has been designed to find shifters. Besides, the damn spirit doesn't want to leave the token...why will it leave the Wayfinder once it's in there?"

"We have to assume anything will happen," Birdie said. "I also have a spell that will seal it in."

"But we might have to consider another problem," Morgana said. "What if the Wayfinder won't function because the spirit is in it? Why point elsewhere?"

Birdie patted her arm to give reassurance. "Because my spell will make it. We can debate this 'til the bees come home, but we've wasted enough time. If it doesn't work, then we reconsider. I'll raise the circle, you work on the Wayfinder."

The protective circle was a way to keep the spirit trapped. It added risk to them, of course, but there was no other way. Morgana nodded, knowing that the fear of damaging their only lead was making her doubt herself. She smeared blood into the indented circle in the Wayfinder, then dropped the token in position, fighting wolves face down, compass rose facing up instead, hoping it didn't trigger before she was finished. Happy the token was in place, she secured the pointers in position and proceeded to quickly smear Castor's blood over the whole Wayfinder, rubbing it into the engravings and inlaid metals, and along the pointers, hoping they wouldn't send them astray by leading them down to Castor's bedroom. She was banking on the fact that the shifter's spirit would be stronger.

Then she prepared to activate the token. "Ready?"

However, before she could do anything, the token started to tremble, rattling against the Wayfinder. "Birdie! It's already moving. The blood around it must be enough." She stood over it for a moment more, making sure it wasn't an anomaly. "It's moving even more."

"Good. Stand by me, Morgana."

Morgana hurried to her side, hoping their distance from the Wayfinder would be safe enough as Birdie raised her voice and uttered her commands. "*Spirit of wolf, bound in this token, break your bonds, by blood your prison broken. By my will, take new abode, In the blood-soaked vessel, your power bestowed.*"

The token continued to shake and judder more violently, threatening to dislodge the pointers over the top of it.

Birdie gripped Morgana's hand. "Say it with me!"

Together they cast the spell again, repeating it over and over, commanding the spirit to break free. The power in the circle built, and Birdie added to their spell, commanding the four elements to assist them, drawing power from the room and magic of Moonfell.

Suddenly, a figure ripped free of the token. It was hard to make out its features, as the shifter's shade was as insubstantial as mist, but Morgana could just about discern the face of a surprisingly young shifter, eyes burning with a golden light, before it morphed into his wolf. It flickered in between the two, one form sliding into the other, almost warring with itself, and unexpectedly, Morgana felt sorry for the man who had died so young.

But then other concerns crowded out her regret. She had hoped the spirit would slide easily from the token to the Wayfinder, but for some reason, it resisted. She felt Birdie's stance change as she prepared another spell to force the spirit into the Wayfinder, but she had barely uttered half a dozen words when a second spirit emerged from the token, and Morgana almost stumbled backwards in shock.

The shimmering vision of a shaven-headed man appeared, covered in tattoos, and the ferocity of his stare was like a punch to her gut. She knew immediately who it was, and she threw up a hand to protect herself and Birdie, sending a pulse of power back to him.

"Birdie, you focus on the shifter, I will manage the shaman."

She drowned out Birdie's spell with her own, but the shaman, for all of his intensity, had little power here. She suspected it was a show of strength to control the shifter, not to attack her or Birdie. Although maybe it was to see them, too. To know what he faced.

Morgana cast a banishing spell, careful to use it only on the shaman, and within seconds, his spirit vanished again. She rejoined Birdie, but the wolf-shifter's resistance had weakened, and it poured into the Wayfinder. For a few seconds, the pointers spun so quickly that Morgana feared they could fly out of position, but then they settled to a slow turn, as did the token placed in the centre.

Both witches fell silent, edging closer to the Wayfinder that was placed on the small table in the centre of the pentagram. The two pointers moved independently, one settling quickly on to the image of the wolf. The other kept moving, at a slightly different speed to the token beneath it.

"The house's magic, perhaps," Morgana suggested, "just like we thought."

"Perhaps. Or maybe he's just stubborn. I'll release the protection circle, you carry it to the window."

The Wayfinder felt warm beneath Morgana's fingers, perhaps warmed by the shifter's energy that had ignited its new vessel. She carried it to the window that overlooked the back of the house, facing north, the direction they believed the hall to be. The pointer still spun slowly, the token idly turning, too. *Was one feeding off the other?* Again, she felt the strange connection to the lost shifter, feeling not his need to take control, but his loss. His loneliness.

She adjusted the spell they had discussed, infusing it with love and a soft yearning. "*Wandering shifter without a home, lost in shadows, forced to roam. Reveal the haven your spirit seeks, find the alpha whose howl now speaks. Severed from kin in darkest night, yearning for pack with all your might, the sanctuary your heart desires, waits where your chieftain's call inspires.*"

Birdie caught her eye and smiled as she joined her. "Nicely done, Morgana."

Morgana didn't answer, her focus back on the pointer. Within a few moments, the compass pointer settled, as did the token beneath, and both pointed north.

Twenty-Seven

Arlo knew the best way to soothe an agitated pack—two agitated packs, in fact—was through food and beer.

Too exhausted by the fight to worry about what his bar staff and the visiting band might think, he had led the two packs to one of the private lounges to the side of the main floor. The packs remained wary of each other, but were too interested in current events to let that stand in their way, and they settled in together, questions flying.

After phoning Maverick and Grey, he left Vlad to keep an eye on things, then headed to the bar to order beers. He found Harlan and Jet already on stools and propped against the counter, talking to the clearly intrigued bar staff of three, two men and one woman, including Miles, the tattooed young man with the mohawk.

"Guys," he said addressing the bartenders, "will one of you do me a favour? Take a crate of beer to them, please. And someone order some food from the kitchen. Whatever they have that's quick and easy. Fries, dumplings, anything. Just keep them happy for now."

The young woman, Sunita, grabbed a crate and headed to the lounge without hesitation. For some reason, Arlo had assumed they would be reluctant to head in there, but instead they seemed desperate to know more. The other young man, Eddie, headed for the stairs leading to the ground floor.

"We were just saying," Jet said, catching Arlo's eye, "that a local gang had the wrong idea about this place, but that it's okay now."

"Yeah," Harlan drawled, a smirk hovering on his lips. "Annie Oakley to the rescue."

"Says Taser-man! And who the hell is Annie Oakley?"

He rolled his eyes. "The youth of today! She was an American sharpshooter in the Wild West. It's a compliment."

"Oh." Jet looked mollified. "Thanks."

Miles slid Arlo a beer, not hiding his amusement as he looked between the three of them. "So, which one of you is going to come clean about the shifters running this place?"

Arlo nearly spat his beer out. "The *what*?"

"You heard me. You should do, as the only shifter here. You have excellent hearing, after all."

Harlan roared with laughter, and Arlo shot him a look that was supposed to shut him up, but only made him laugh louder. "Arlo, give it up! You've been made. And clearly, our friend Miles here doesn't give a shit."

"Nope, I don't. In fact, it makes this place way more interesting. Even more so if you let me in on the secret—properly."

Jet didn't look surprised. "I always wondered if you knew. You just take every odd thing that happens here in your stride. Anyone else know?"

"Sunita and Eddie. When you guys started tearing your shirts off as you ran through the door, it raised questions." He wiped the bar down, looking smug. "It was too much fun not to share what I knew. Plus Vik and Caitlin."

Vikram worked in the upstairs bar mainly, and Caitlin was kitchen staff.

Arlo considered denying it, but after Harlan and Jet's response, he had no choice. "Fine, so you know. Are you about to walk out? Are they?"

"Arlo, wild horses wouldn't drag them or me out of here. This is the coolest place to work, and now even more so."

"What about the other non-shifter staff? Do they suspect?"

"They remain blissfully ignorant, and will stay that way."

Arlo rubbed his face, and then wished he hadn't. His eye was swelling after he'd sustained a punch, and it was sore. "How did you find out?"

"I've met shifters before, and I am aware of the paranormal world. I know the signs. You bunch are all classic shifters." He winked at Jet. "Those shoulders. That intense stare." He feigned waving a fan. "Scorching."

Jet and Harlan laughed, but Arlo scowled. "Fuck off. All of you."

"Seriously, though," Miles said, smile vanishing, "what was that about? Something to do with those funny tokens you had us searching for? That man who tried to pass one off as change?"

Arlo really needed to not underestimate his human staff. They noticed way more than he thought they would. "Kind of. The other guys—shifters—in there," he nodded towards the small lounge, "are part of the North London Pack, and their alpha is severely injured. They thought we were responsible, but we weren't. He'll survive, but their pack is not like ours. Whether he's still the alpha after all this is another matter."

"But that's not the half of it," Jet said. "Shifters are being kidnapped for some hidden club. We need to find it. With luck, we'll work together now."

Miles nodded thoughtfully. "I assume Hunter and Hal's disappearance is part of that?"

"Yes," Arlo confirmed. "And Finn's, as of this morning. He's just a kid, far too young for this crap."

"I wish I knew something, but I don't."

"That's okay, Miles. It's not your fight. But it's good to have things out in the open."

"I'll be back there if you need me." Miles tactfully withdrew to the small room behind the bar, taking Sunita with him, who had just returned with an empty crate. She stared at Arlo with wide eyes, like a rabbit caught in the glow of a wolf's stare.

Arlo gave her a slow smile. "We'll chat another time, okay?"

"Yes," she squeaked out, as she hurried after Miles.

Harlan sniggered. "Got yourself a fan there, Arlo. Gotta admit, I did not expect this to happen this afternoon. I should have known better."

"Thanks, both of you," Arlo said, raising his beer bottle in a toast. "You turned the tide in our favour."

"But what now?" Jet asked.

"Well, I've already spoken to Grey and Maverick. They have no concrete leads, but they're heading back here. It seems Odette was able to draw the shifter's spirit out, and he confirms what we suspected. The Wey Wolf—as Hammer called him—is seeking to make his own pack. Some shifters have obviously been possessed, but they appear to have a balance between their own will and the spirit shifter's will—until the spirit decides otherwise." He shuddered. "It's horrible. Their aim is to recruit, and they have been at it for a while. Many shifters are already trapped in the hall, but a shaman is behind it all. Everyone involved is heading back here now. The Apollo Pool Hall is sealed off by the police. Maggie is coming here, too." He looked over to the lounge, imagining the discussion that would take place next. "We'll meet in there. That room is marked *Private* tonight. No one else uses it. Now," he sighed, summoning his energy, "I need to phone Morgana and Birdie." If the witches had failed, he had no idea what they would do next.

"Let me," Harlan said, grabbing his phone off the counter.

But before he could do any more, the door to the club flew open, and Birdie and Morgana raced towards them. For a second, Arlo wasn't sure if it was good or bad news. *Please let Castor still be alive*.

He stood up, heart pounding. "What's happened?"

Morgana flourished a round, metal object. "We can find the hall. Now we just need a plan."

Maverick studied the mix of shifters and humans in the private lounge from his seat in the corner where he had retreated to think. It was an interesting collection of people with whom to storm an ancient hall that belonged to a Wey Wolf.

Their voices were loud in vigorous discussion, the packs mixing together fluidly. Strategies were discussed and abandoned, and the testosterone level was building in the confined space. Most of Storm Moon's security team were present. Monroe had arrived with Cecile and Jax, too late for the earlier fight, but keen to make up for it later. Grey and Maggie were there, too, as were the two unconscious shifters. They had no choice but to bring them along with the group. The witches had placed them in a protective circle in the corner of the room, bound in magic designed to block them—or rather, the shifters lurking within them—from the discussions they were having. They were planning their attack, and they certainly didn't want their enemy gaining an advantage.

The nature of that attack was still undecided. Obviously, once they found the hall they would fight their way in, but after that? It sounded simplistic to suggest that they fight every shifter they might meet. They needed to save those who were possessed, so injuring them badly was not an option. Besides, if they fought as fiercely as they had in the pool hall, it would take two of their own shifters to fight one of theirs. Plus, they had no idea how many shifters there were in there, or more importantly, how strong the mysterious Wey Wolf was.

The other issue was how far Storm Moon could trust Castor's pack. Maverick wanted to think they could work together as they were now, but how long would that really last? And also, how many of the North London Pack should they take? Fortunately, Danny and Thorne seemed to believe only those present should go—which unfortunately included Axel. No one else in their pack could be trusted, at least at such short notice, and Maverick agreed. Maverick certainly wasn't taking anyone outside of his own security team. They were trained to fight, and although other shifters could too, Maverick refused to put them in that position. And again, there was the issue of trust.

So essentially, the shifters in the room were the team they had, and no one else. Plus, of course, the shifters currently manning the doors, now that the club was open. Knowing they needed as big a team as possible, that meant waiting until after midnight to attack. That would give them around 25 or 30 shifters in total. It felt like enough.

He hoped it was enough.

Maverick could also count on Grey, Harlan, and Maggie, plus the Moonfell witches, of course. They were sitting together, heads close and expressions serious, and Arlo and Vlad were with them. The witches' involvement was crucial if they were to deal with the shaman and the spirit shifters. Maverick had just decided to join them, when Danny sat down next to him.

"How's your pack?" Maverick asked him. "Have they accepted you as temporary alpha?"

"For now." Danny rolled his neck as if to reduce tension. "A few aren't happy, but they were shouted down, so we have unity for tonight, at least."

"And Axel?"

Danny smirked. "Odette shook him up badly. He's surprisingly quiet right now. It won't last, of course, because he's seething with resentment too, but for now I'm taking that as a win." He glanced over to the witches. "We still don't have a location though, right?"

"No, not until we're on the move, but the Wayfinder is maintaining that north is the direction, even when Morgana tested it again outside, so we trust that it's working. It should keep adjusting as we get closer."

"We leave from here, then?"

"Yes, if that's okay? You can't go back to the pool hall. Unless, of course, you want to meet outside there?" He suddenly realised they might not want to wait around at Storm Moon for hours. "That will be fine."

"Actually, we're all starving, so we were thinking of heading out for a curry in the village, and then coming back here in a few hours. Your team is welcome to join us."

"Food, of course." If Maverick hadn't been so preoccupied, he'd have realised how hungry he was. "That's a great suggestion. Ask Domino to organise our team. We still need to cover security here, but whoever we can spare and wants to go with you, can. I'll stay here. I need to talk to the witches. I suggest that we make sure we're all back by eleven-thirty at the latest. We'll make our final plans then, and share any updates. This room is ours for the night, and your team has a free pass on the door. There's a good band on too, so you may as well enjoy it."

Danny held his hand out, and Maverick shook it. "Thanks, Maverick. That will be brilliant. If I didn't say so earlier, I really appreciate your help this afternoon."

"I'd say it's my pleasure, but it really wasn't—if you know what I mean." Maverick was still aching after his bruising encounter with Hammer, and several shifters were still covered in dried blood. "And perhaps remind your team about the staff shower upstairs. We have plenty of towels. It wouldn't do to scare the locals."

Danny laughed and walked away, and reflecting on what a weird day this was, Maverick joined the witches.

Twenty-Eight

The training room filled up quickly as Hunter entered with Finn. It seemed the Wey Wolf was keen to have more fights that evening, and Hunter knew he'd be called imminently.

The atmosphere seemed even more highly charged than it had been earlier, so Hunter trained hard, refusing to touch the amulet in his jeans' pocket, and focussing on letting the spirit shifter within him grow stronger. He had to prove himself, and he could not afford to make mistakes now. The more he fought, the more his wolf rose, and the stronger the strange presence within him became. He not only sparred with Finn and Hal, but with other shifters too, sizing up their strengths and weaknesses.

It was all starting to feel very real now, far more so than just as a spectator earlier. He fought with his fists, as a wolf, and with the swords, which were deadly. One wrong move could result in death, if not serious injury. He was glad to see Finn trying to use them, but hated the way he looked so vulnerable. *Surely no one would make him fight?*

The sparring became more violent too, and soon Hunter had bloodied hands from bare knuckle fights, and a sore jaw. The more the wolves fought, the greater the stakes became, even though it was supposedly practice. Unfortunately, the more often he was hit, the more he felt that he needed to strike back.

And then a hush fell as the shaman entered. *Blōdbana*.

His pale grey eyes were even more unnerving up close. His tattoos, more blue than black, covered much of his face and upper body. They were strange, occult symbols that Hunter didn't recognise, apart from a few runes. His cloak was so long it swept the floor, and his thick leather boots were laced partway up his calf, over rough linen trousers. He only wore a type of leather waistcoat over his chest, and he was as sinewy with muscle as the shifters. Blōdbana's power was palpable, and it seemed he intimidated everyone.

Blōdbana prowled the room, studying each shifter's face, staring at them as if he could read their every thought. Hunter let his mind quiet, and his shadow warrior surface. The shaman stepped in front of him, and Hunter suddenly had the impression that he was the one he'd come for in the first place. That studying the others had been a ruse. His piercing eyes looked into Hunter's, and he felt stripped. Hollow. His shadow warrior responded.

But so did he.

Hunter did not like to be examined like an insect, or judged by a non-shifter. His wolf and his natural aggression flared, and he knew his eyes kindled with golden light. The shadow warrior responded. Hunter, eyes locked with Blōdbana's, saw a flash of recognition in his eyes. One old warrior talking to an ancient shaman. Hunter's own thoughts slammed away, replaced instead with memories of an ancient blood rite, the stink of smoke, and pain of a mark burned into his palm.

The fighting wolves from the token.

And then it was over. The shaman stepped back, his lips twisting with a grimace. "You," he said, staring at Hunter, "and you." He whipped around, pointing to Hal. "Your wolves will fight."

Hal met Hunter's eyes with grim satisfaction.

Grey was relieved that Harlan and Maggie would be joining their raid—if that was even the right word. It was reassuring to have other humans on his side that couldn't be possessed by some random spirit-shifter when they finally found the hall later. *When*, of course, was a hopeful word, but he had faith in the witches—although right now they were making it clear that they had a different objective to the shifters.

They were still in the private lounge, the rhythmic thumping of music dull in there compared to the main hall, and the remnants of food brought down from the kitchen were still on the low table they were gathered around. The lounge was mostly empty, as many shifters had gone for a curry, fuelling up for later. Only Maverick remained, along with some of their team, who were ensuring the club ran smoothly over the next few hours.

Grey snagged the last chip from the plate, and asked, "You're proposing that you focus on finding the shaman?"

Morgana nodded. "Yes. He is the root of everything. His magic made the tokens, and we think he controls the spirits, even now." She turned to Maverick. "You saw what happened this afternoon with Odette, and Birdie and I had a similar experience. He had little strength to attack us, but there's no doubt that won't be the case in person."

"I think," Odette said, "that perhaps his first appearance with us must have taxed him. It's good to know that he has limitations."

Maverick sighed. "I just wish we knew how he has preserved himself and the Wey Wolf all this time. We're going in blind. Unless they're spirits, too."

Harlan frowned. "Interesting suggestion, but unlikely."

"Which means their bodies have survived somehow."

Birdie shrugged. "Magic. Spelled coffins, rituals, maybe rune magic, or all of them. There will be a central place where that will have been achieved, I'm sure." She paused, thoughtful. "Potentially the whole place is protected by magic. We might have trouble getting in."

"Perhaps. There's a limit to how much we can know," Grey pointed out, "before we get there. Once we're in, we'll have to adapt."

"I'm more curious," Odette said, "as to why they preserved themselves in the first place. I really hope we find that out, too."

"You didn't see that?" Maggie asked.

"No, but I saw glimpses of the hall again. It's big. I fear we'll have a lot of ground to cover—and who knows what else before we even get in there."

"We need an advantage," Harlan said. "Something they won't expect. Something spirit-shifters can't influence. No offence, Maverick, but you'll all be vulnerable. We have no idea how many tokens are still active, and we're walking into token central."

Harlan had voiced what Grey was thinking, and no doubt what the others thought, too.

Maverick sighed and kicked his feet up onto the table as he reclined against the sofa's back. "I can't deny that. What do you suggest?"

"Not what. *Who*. Nahum, the Nephilim. He's deadly. We'd be idiots not to ask for his help, and I know he will gladly accompany us. Right, Maggie?"

"Fuck yes." Her eyes lit up with excitement. "That's a brilliant suggestion. The Nephilim's capacity for causing bloodshed and mayhem is even greater than yours, Maverick."

Morgana nodded. "I saw him today, so he's aware of what's happening. At that point, though, we had no idea where to go."

Maverick frowned. "Have I met him?"

Harlan laughed. "You'd remember if you had, but you met Gabe, his brother. And you, Grey."

"We did?" Grey asked. "When?"

"When you first met me. I was with a big guy with dark hair, and a woman with long, fair hair. Very sassy. That's Shadow. I've mentioned them before, I'm sure. Nahum is Gabe's brother. He can fly, and he's very useful with a sword and throwing daggers, and plenty of other weapons besides. There's another guy I'd suggest using, Lucien, but he's in France right now so he can't help us."

"What's so special about him?" Grey asked, wondering if Harlan had access to some kind of secret army.

He exchanged an amused glance with Maggie, and she answered instead. "He's a super-soldier, essentially. He was enhanced alchemically, which means his skin can become metallic, amongst other things. It's a long, complicated story."

Grey just stared at her, wondering how many other secrets she had tucked away. "Well, you can share more about that one over drinks."

She responded with a cheeky grin.

Maverick sighed. "Fine, ask him. I'd like to tip the odds in our favour anyway, just in case Castor's pack turns on us."

"You really think they will?" Birdie asked, breaking away from a quiet talk with Morgana.

"It's possible." He narrowed his eyes. "What are you two plotting?"

"I was suggesting that we three," Birdie gestured to her coven, "leave now to find the hall. It could take us a while, and I'm pretty sure you don't want a bunch of shifters trailing after us and getting impatient. It means we can observe the place for a while, too. See who goes in and comes out."

Grey nodded in approval. "That's a good suggestion. Harlan, Maggie, and I should go, too. We'll keep you informed, Maverick."

Maverick frowned, looking as if he would object, but then nodded. "Yes, that makes sense, actually. That way we waste less time later. You're not involving Stan or Irving, Maggie?"

He was referring to the detective sergeants on Maggie's team. She shook her head. "I'm actually wary of taking too many people in. Things will be confusing enough. Unless…" She stopped, gazing into the distance as she obviously considered her options. "I think I'll keep them outside, with cameras. They can take photos of who's coming and going. That way, we make sure we account for everyone, just in case people escape." She shrugged. "Things may not go the way we want tonight."

"Excellent." Grey nodded, relieved. "That sounds like a great plan. Let's do it."

Twenty-Nine

Maggie knew that finding the Wey Wolf's lair wouldn't be easy, but even so, this was getting tiresome.

The six of them were crammed into the witches' old Range Rover. Odette was driving, and Morgana was in the passenger seat, which left the rest of them squished together in the back. It might have been a big car, but not big enough for four on the back seat, which meant it was illegal. The good news was that she was close to Grey. Like hip to hip, knee to knee, so that was nice. It was also a good job that Birdie was so small.

"Damn it," Morgana said to Odette. "Stop now! It's right. Turn around."

"For fuck's sake," Maggie huffed. "Are you sure that fucking thing works?"

"Yes! It's not a state-of-the-art GPS, you know."

"Maggie," Grey warned, voice low and soothing, as if she were a toddler. "Try and show some patience. We are a lot closer than we were."

Harlan, squashed against the other door, smirked and gave an exaggerated sigh. "Maggie, Maggie, Maggie..."

"Fuck you, fuck you, fuck you."

"Do not," Birdie warned, stuck between them, "make me spell you both to silence."

Maggie gave Harlan the silent finger instead.

"Left!" Morgana instructed. "I think we're getting closer. The pointer is swinging less wildly."

Everyone immediately craned to see out of the windows.

"Where are we?" Birdie asked.

"Finsbury Park," Harlan answered. "The park is up ahead."

"Right," Morgana shouted, more excited now.

Odette slowed down, cruising down a suburban street full of Victorian houses. At the end of the road was a junction, but before she reached it, Morgana said, "I think that's it. That house."

"The Wey Wolf lives *here*?" Harlan asked, incredulous. "That doesn't sound right at all. Are you sure?"

Morgana twisted around in the seat, showing them the Wayfinder. The pointer was aimed directly at a house with a huge skip outside it. A ground floor light was on, but that was all.

"Okay," Maggie said, thinking quickly. "Drive on, past the junction, and circle round. Then stop much further down the road. We do not want to be spotted. Keep an eye on the Wayfinder, Morgana. Make sure it's not a false reading."

Within a few minutes, Odette had circled as instructed, and they pulled up much further down the road.

"No, it's definitely that one," Morgana confirmed. "The pointer is not budging now, and while we were driving around, it kept adjusting."

Maggie studied the quiet suburban road. "This is not what I was expecting, but if you're right, Odette, and it's underground, then that house must be the way in. It's right about now that I wish I had a shifter's nose."

"We're not far from the park," Harlan said. "It's old, you know. Established over one hundred years ago. Before that, it used to belong to bishops or something like that, which potentially means it's never been built on."

"I get it," Grey said, nodding. "No digging for foundations. A big, underground structure could well be there. I suggest that me and Maggie head out for a stroll, and just saunter past it. What do you think?"

"Excellent idea."

Maggie followed Grey as he exited the car, pulling her coat around her. The April night was chilly, and although the rain had stopped, the clouds were still heavy overhead. Grey's hands were in his pockets, but he extended his elbow towards her, and she hooked her arm through his as they strolled down the road. Lights were on in the houses, and cars were on the road and driveways, but there was little pedestrian traffic.

"I wonder," she said, as they drew level with it, "if we can get behind it somehow."

"Not unless you want to hop over garden fences."

The house might be undergoing renovation, but it didn't look as if they had got very far. The skip was full of rubble, as was the small front garden, and the paint on the trim was still worn. "They must have found something during the renovation," she reasoned.

The sound of a door slamming had them quickening their pace. A man exited the building with a bin bag and threw it into the already crowded skip, then paused at the end of the drive, lit a cigarette, and inhaled deeply, but Maggie didn't dare risk looking over her shoulder for long. They turned at the end of the road, and halted behind a privet hedge, clipped high enough to hide them. Grey waited a beat, and then looked around the corner.

"Still there, still smoking. He doesn't look worried, though. I doubt we've been spotted."

"Damn it. I wish the bin was at the end of the drive. We could search it."

"Forget that. It's too tricky."

"Let's pretend we're lost," Maggie suggested. "Ask him for directions to the park."

"Why? Will your shifter detector be back online then? Unless you're planning on showing him your ID."

"Of course I'm bloody not." She stared down the road, noting the other houses that sat at a right angle to the one they were investigating. "You know, hopping over fences might not be such a bad idea. Or," she added, having a much better one, "Nahum could fly over them."

"Which is bloody pointless if it's all underground. I'm pretty sure that man at the end of the drive is human," Grey said, edging back for her to see him.

He was right. He didn't have the build or the presence of a shifter, but someone else was approaching who did. A couple of tall men, long-limbed and sharp-eyed, and she pulled back, ceding her place to Grey, and bringing her fingers to her lips. She mouthed, "*Shifters.*"

He waited a beat before checking. "I agree. Let's see what the others think, and if they agree, we'll call everyone in."

Hunter's fight with Hal was short but brutal, and he knew it wasn't Hal he was fighting at all.

But then again, he was sure he wasn't fully himself while fighting, either.

Other insistent thoughts kept entering his head, urging him on and suggesting new ways to attack, and all the while he was aware of the Wey Wolf's intense stare, and that of his chosen pack that already gathered below him. He needed to impress. To win. To earn his place.

To dominate.

Hal was a good fighter, but he was younger than Hunter, and Hunter had been brought up running wild in Cumbria. Their old pack was physical, and they fought often. Those fights had been hard, especially when he had challenged their old alpha. A fight that had almost killed him. He had learned from that experience, and when he saw his chance, he attacked savagely, pinning Hal down, jaws around his throat. With one move, he could end him.

But that wasn't the point of this fight. He had earned his win. *And*, Hunter reminded himself forcefully, as his shadow shifter exacerbated his bloodlust, *Hal was his friend*. Hal yelped in submission, and Hunter edged back, blood dripping from his jaws. He might not have ripped his throat out, but they had bitten each other, seeking out tender spots as they sought to dominate and incapacitate.

The shaman stepped between them, and Hunter shifted at the same time as Hal, both glaring at each other, eyes molten as blood poured down their limbs. Hal was furious at losing, and resentment blazed from every pore. It seemed he had expected to win, and the loss stung.

The Wey Wolf roared his approval, and the watching crowd followed suit. Hunter turned to him and bowed, suddenly eager to please his alpha. Again, his shadow warrior fought for dominance, inflicting his need to impress and subjugate himself at the same time, and without his amulet, Hunter was vulnerable. The hall felt like home. The pack that waited for him would be his family.

When he stood upright again, the shaman stood before him, his pale grey eyes boring into his, but Hunter refused to show deference. He was a wolf-shifter. Superior to humans in every way, including shamans. Hunter assessed the man's build and level of threat, wondering if his tattoos offered protection. Blōdbana certainly didn't show fear. But Hunter also realised that Blōdbana was searching for Hunter's shadow warrior, and *he* thought very differently about the shaman. Hunter felt his deference, and something else...

Before he could follow those thoughts, the Wey Wolf interrupted them. "Enough, Blōdbana." Hunter tore his gaze away, back to the alpha. Everyone around him faded to insignificance. "You have both fought well. With more trials, you will be ready to face your ancestor. Now," he waved a heavily muscled arm to the guards, "bring on the next."

As the audience roared their approval and stamped their feet against the wooden flooring of the tiers, Hunter walked to the training area, accepting the applause that was his due, and passing the next two combatants. He needed quiet to consider his shadow warrior's behaviour with the shaman, and for that he needed his amulet.

Hal was hot on his heels, still seething, and Hunter tried to placate him. "You fought well."

"Not as well as I should have." He grabbed a towel and wrapped it around his waist. "I want to be in this pack, Hunter."

"You will be. The Wey Wolf wants all of us. It didn't matter today whether I won or lost. You said it yourself yesterday. This is all a spectacle. Entertainment, as well as training. It is our shadow self we need to master."

"To learn from," Hal said, a flare of suspicion in his expression again.

Surer of himself now, Hunter stepped closer, lowering his voice. "*And* master. We are better than our ancestors. More evolved. Stronger. Yes, we can learn some things from them, but we are superior in every way." Hunter saw Hal's doubt, and then a flicker of acknowledgement, and pressed home his message. "We are the dominant force here. We were chosen. Token-bound or not, this is *our* place now. Our time. Our bodies. Our brains. *Our wolves*."

As he said it, he started to believe it. Hunter's place was in the Hall of the Wey Wolf. Its ancient magic and challenges promised a return to his visceral roots. Recognising that he was losing himself, he fumbled for his jeans, needing to find his amulet. However, when he reached into his pocket, it was empty.

Panic flooded through him, and he fought to subdue it as he checked the other pockets.

"Something wrong?" Hal asked him.

"I think," a deep, heavily-accented voice said, making Hunter spin around, "that he is missing an amulet." Blōdbana had entered so silently and quickly that neither Hunter nor Hal had detected his approach. He had no scent; he was like a void. The silver amulet dangled from his fingers, but his pale grey eyes bore into Hunter's. "You dare to bring another's magic to the Wey Wolf's court."

Hunter brazened it out. "I was wearing it when I was summoned, that's all. It's nothing. Just a gift to symbolise my wolf."

"Nothing?" Blōdbana stepped closer, and his strange emptiness made Hunter feel like he was falling into a pit. "Yet, it is filled with magic. Worse, no matter how hard I search, I struggle to see your wolf ancestor."

"He's here, I can assure you of that. I like to test myself before needing him."

"Is that so? Then perhaps we can devise another test for you later. You won't need this anymore." He placed the amulet in his pocket, and after another, long searching look, walked away.

Thirty

"Once they arrive," Harlan said, staring out of the car window at the house where another three shifters had just entered, "we need to act quickly. We can't have a bunch of shifters congregating around like a church meeting. It will give the whole thing away."

"I'm sure we will," Odette reasoned. "And we'll need to leave shifters on the door, too."

Morgana nodded in agreement. "To stop others from entering. Although, we could cast some protection." She grimaced. "That would take too long, though."

"A small spell is better than nothing," Nahum said, looking hopeful.

The Nephilim had arrived an hour earlier after flying around the area, and had joined them in the car. Grey and Maggie had also returned after their walk, cramming in the rear to discuss their hurried plans. Now that Maggie had the address, they had been able to confirm who owned the building, finding that it belonged to three brothers. None of them had police records, and basic background checks gave them nothing to worry about, except how they had become involved in the whole thing in the first place.

The witches had veiled the Range Rover in a spell that made passersby look the other way, as if they weren't there. It didn't stop Harlan from wanting to duck his head down every time someone passed them. Eventually, Grey and Maggie left again, waiting around the corner on the next street for the packs to arrive. It was late now, after midnight, and yet another shifter approached from the other direction.

"Fight night," Birdie murmured, half to herself.

"What?" Harlan studied her profile.

She kept her eyes on the house. "Fight night. All those shifters arriving, and no one is leaving. With luck, they might all be drunk or fighting each other when we get inside."

"Or spoiling for a fight with us. I don't like that idea."

Nahum grinned. "Sounds fun to me."

"Just don't kill our guys," Harlan reminded him. He knew how hard Nephilim fought.

"Only if they're trying to kill me. I take it the Wey Wolf is fair game?"

"I reckon. I presume he'll be easy to identify."

"And you're staying with the witches, once we get in?" Nahum asked.

"Yep. We're trying to find magic central. We figure there must be a place where the tokens were made, and the bodies were preserved."

Morgana nodded in agreement. "Finding that could help break the spell the others are under, because the shadow warriors are controlled somehow, I'm sure of it."

Harlan's phone buzzed with an incoming message. "The shifters have arrived, and Maverick is leading the way in. We will incapacitate whoever is on the door, and go from there. Time to roll."

Maverick strode down the garden path, past the skip, and rapped on the front door, Arlo and Domino immediately behind him.

He was eager to act after waiting impatiently for Storm Moon to close. The last thing they needed was another shifter possessed by a token spirit, but the evening had passed uneventfully, and even better, the two packs had tolerated each other well, all eager to find the club and rescue their pack members.

Now, a few shifters were gathered behind him, a mix of his own and Castor's pack, while the others waited at the end of the drive to watch for newcomers. The scent of wolf-shifters was strong, so he knew they were in the right place, but he wasn't expecting a very average human to answer the door. He had assumed that an aggressive shifter acting as a bouncer would greet them, so although he was poised to act quickly, Maverick hesitated. This had to be one of the brothers who owned the house.

The man looked him up and down, and then at the shifters behind him. "Newcomers. Have you got tokens?" He looked puzzled. "Or were you invited? In which case, where is your messenger?"

Maverick inhaled, scenting only humans in the hall with faint traces of shifter left behind. "I'm invited. Move aside." He pushed the man backwards so that he stumbled over his own feet in the hallway, and immediately Domino darted left, and Arlo right. Danny and Thorne followed them, intent on searching the house, but Tommy shadowed Maverick. Maverick leaned over the man. "Tell me how to get in the club."

"But someone should be with you," the man insisted, words tumbling from his mouth in a breathless rush. "Or the token."

"Fuck the token." Maverick gripped the man's wrists as it looked like he was going for his pockets, then spun the man around, deftly pinning his arms behind him instead. Tommy took over, securing him firmly.

"Maverick." Domino stood at the end of the hall, another man caught between her and Danny. "There's no one else here. The kitchen is behind us."

"No one upstairs, either," Arlo confirmed, coming downstairs from the upper level with Thorne. "Or in the front rooms. The house is empty. Looks like a couple of bedrooms are in use, but it's a bloody mess. However," he pointed beyond Maverick to the door in the hallway, "we haven't been through there yet."

The hall was a shell, desperately in need of plaster and paint, and it smelled of cigarette smoke with an undercurrent of dampness, but there was a door in the hallway that no one had entered. Maverick opened it carefully, wary of attack, but found only a dark landing and steps leading down. The scent of stale air and shifters was strong. *That must be the way.*

Maverick addressed Tommy, nodding at their captive. "Take him to the kitchen with the other one. What's it like in there, Dom?"

"A mess, but it looks like it's where they spend their time. There's a TV, a small sofa, a half-modernised kitchen. No sign of tokens, not that I've looked too closely, though."

Maverick studied the two men who had barely said a word. The smaller man looked worried, the other belligerent. He spoke now, looking at Maverick with ill-disguised contempt. "You don't know who you're messing with. Coming here will be the end for you."

Maverick wanted to question him, to know why two humans were guarding a wolf-shifter club, but knew he couldn't linger. Instead, he addressed Domino and Danny. "Try to get some sense out of them—how they're here. How they're involved. And where the other brother is. Arlo and Thorne, check the cellar—and be careful!" Then he stepped to the front door and called Cecile, who was partway down the drive. "Call the others over, and bring Russo and Lockhart in, too." They'd no choice but to bring the two spirit-possessed shifters with them. "There are no shifters in the house. I want four left on the door, and the rest inside."

"And if others arrive?"

"Tell them the club is closed."

The witches hurried down the drive with Grey, Harlan, Maggie, and Nahum. They couldn't delay. If other shifters arrived and called for help, they could be fighting on two fronts.

"Birdie, can you cast a spell on the house to hide the entrance or something? Just to buy us time if anyone else arrives."

"It will be temporary," she advised him. "Because then we're coming with you, and we haven't got time to do anything elaborate."

"A delay is great."

They had discussed a few scenarios earlier, and he turned to Maggie, Grey, and Harlan as the witches started their spell on the driveway. "There are two humans in the kitchen."

Maggie interrupted him. "The brothers?"

"I presume so. We're missing one. Check them for tokens, and then search the kitchen. We might need one to get in."

"Well, you're not touching it," Grey warned.

"I might not need to." He waved them ahead of him, finding Arlo waiting at the door in the hall with Thorne.

Arlo's eyes burned with excitement, a molten gold as his wolf rose. "There's a hole in the wall down there, and a passageway beyond it. It leads down, and it's long, but we didn't risk going far alone."

"It's the right place," Thorne confirmed, as excited as Arlo. "The scent of shifters is strong, Maverick. Ready to check it out?"

Maverick paused, head cocked as he listened. Apart from the voices in the kitchen, the house was otherwise silent. The whole thing was weird. Unexpected. He savoured the moment of calm, knowing it would all end soon, and unsure of how things would unfold. Then the other shifters arrived behind him, testosterone and energy building.

Although the urge to rush onwards was strong, Maverick hesitated. "Is there any clue as to what we might find at the other end?"

"Not that we saw," Arlo said. "The passage was long and sloped downward, and we explored only the start of it, but it's old, Mav. Really old."

"I don't like it. Why leave only two humans up here? Why no shifters? And why involve humans at all?"

"It's their house," Thorne reasoned. "Maybe they're compelled somehow. Your witch talked about a shaman."

Nahum, who he had met briefly on the street before entering, had been standing close by, listening. Now he joined them. "It's possible that there's probably some sort of test before you enter.

Possibly," he stressed. "Temples can be like that. I've experienced it, and it wasn't fun. That's probably why there are only humans here. Plus, if for some reason the police were to come, well, they own it. It makes everything plausible. Less suspicious."

Maverick still didn't like or understand it, but doubted he would until this was all over. However, more information would be useful. "Wait here. I won't be long."

Maverick returned to the kitchen, where the shifters were questioning the brothers. Maggie sidled up to him. "These are Barry and Andy. We're missing Dean. Barry is the easiest target. Andy is a belligerent wanker."

He nodded, happy to know who to pressure. "Are there any tokens here?"

"None that we've found so far. As you can see, they bought this place to renovate it. A joint venture. They have some building experience. I would imagine that finding the shifter hall has derailed things." Maggie watched the group gathered around the brothers. "We've barely had time to ask anything."

Domino leaned against the counter, watching the men who were now sitting in kitchen chairs, flanked by Harlan and Tommy. Danny stood over them, his stance threatening. "Where are the tokens?"

"What tokens?" The belligerent man, Andy, scowled. "I have no idea what you're talking about."

Danny frowned. "Your brother has already mentioned them, you idiot. They're the way into the club."

"In fact," Domino said, voice rising as she recognised him, "you were the man leaving them in Storm Moon. We caught you on CCTV." She started forward as if she'd attack him, and he flinched backwards. "It's because of you that our pack members are in this mess, you bastard!"

"I had no choice!" Andy looked at the floor, as if he couldn't bear her stare. "And I don't keep the tokens."

"He's right." Barry, the smaller man, looked scared now. "Blōdbana keeps them all. What are you doing here? I don't understand how you know—"

"Never you mind." Tommy cut him off, leaning over him, and he cowered back.

Grey straightened up from where he'd been checking a cupboard, and looked across to Maverick. "No tokens yet."

Maverick called over his shoulder. "Cecile!" In seconds, she was behind him. "Take over for Harlan. Harlan, help Grey and Maggie search the rest of the place, just in case Andy and Barry are lying. We might need a token to get in, but make it quick. We've found the entrance downstairs, a long passageway, so we'll investigate it."

"And these two?" Domino asked.

"Keep questioning them. Leave two shifters watching them when you're done. May as well keep Russo and Lockhart in here with them. Do we at least know how they found the damn place?"

Danny answered. "Barry said they were cleaning out the cellar for storage when they knocked a section of plaster off. They found a bricked-up doorway beyond and thought it was extra cellar space. Seems they found more than they bargained for. But that's as much as we know."

Leaving them to continue questioning the men, Maverick returned to Arlo, Nahum, and Thorne. The hall and the room beyond was packed with shifters now, all eager to explore, all jostling for position. He squared up to them. "We take this carefully.

Slowly. I want to rush in just as much as you, but I don't want to be bound to the Wey Wolf, and I'm pretty sure you don't want to be, either. Understand?" He trusted his own pack to listen to him, but not Castor's. Already he felt some eyeing him impatiently, especially Axel. Ultimately, what they did was up to them, but he did not want them compromising his pack. "Arlo, Thorne, lead the way."

"Wait," Nahum said. "Let me go first."

"Worried about tokens again?" Maverick asked.

"If I were you, I would be." He lifted his head to address the others, especially Arlo and Thorne who had started down the steps. "You all should."

Maggie and Harlan were right. He did have a presence. Ancient magic rolled off him, and his tattoos, arcane and occult, visible on his bare arms in his t-shirt and fatigues, enhanced that feeling. Plus, the sword at his side reinforced how dangerous he could be.

"Fine. Thorne, let him pass." Maverick bridled against being protected, but Nahum was right. He didn't want any of them to be spellbound before they'd even started. "And let's keep the noise down."

At the bottom of the steps was a cellar, and the rough doorway Arlo had described was knocked through the wall. Beyond it, a step down, was a passageway. Again he inhaled, scenting damp, shifters, and old magic.

Odette was suddenly at his side, and he swore.

"For fuck's sake, Odette. You're like a damn ninja assassin."

"You feel him?" She ignored his outburst. "Blōdbana, the shaman." She stretched her fingers out like a cat using its whiskers. "He's strong. You must be careful." She looked over her shoulder at the gathered shifters. "All of you."

"Well," Nahum said, "I doubt the tunnel is booby-trapped, seeing as that's where the shifters go."

"Wait!" Domino pushed through from behind, Barry in tow. "Barry has agreed to lead us. His brother is less forthcoming, but you've had enough of all this, right, Barry?"

He nodded. "I'm sick of it. Sick of them." He stared at Maverick, lips set in a grim line. "My other brother is trapped in there. Will you end this?"

"All of it." Maverick studied him, trying to decide how useful he may be. "Do you know the layout?"

"Some of it. Most of it, actually. But it won't be easy. The Wey Wolf is intimidating, and Blōdbana... Creepy."

"You communicate with them?"

"Not at first. We didn't understand a thing. But then the shaman did something." Sweat beaded Barry's brow. "He stole our voices. Just for a few hours. It was terrifying. Then they came back."

"A type of language spell," Odette said. "You're lucky he didn't take your tongues. He must have known he would need you."

Maverick was so shocked that he lost his own voice for a second. "Okay. That's disgusting, so let's move on. How many shifters are in there? Or humans? Anyone."

"Up to fifty, I estimate. Old guards and new shifters. More tonight, because of the fights."

"When will it end?"

"Tonight? It could go on until dawn."

Domino interrupted. "The whole place has been going for a couple of months, after Barry and his brothers woke the shifters."

"Accidentally," Barry added hurriedly. "Worst day of my life."

"Then you can make up for your error tonight," Maverick said. "But if you betray us..."

"I won't, but I must save my brother."

Maverick nodded. "Who's with Andy, Dom?"

"Xavier, with one of Castor's pack. Morgana is finishing the spell with Birdie."

"Then let's go."

The packs were as restless as Maverick as they rushed down the passageway. Maverick barely took any of it in, only noting the stronger scents of shifters, and beneath it, blood. Barry told them what had happened as he walked, eager to talk now, as if confessing his sins. He described finding the hall and entering through a broken wall that was now sealed and protected with magic. Their discovery sounded chaotic, but exciting, and Maverick could imagine the thrill of entering a hidden hall of ancients. They had expected to find gold, jewellery, or a hoard, but instead had found something very different. Unfortunately, Barry was talking quickly, gabbling, missing out details that Maverick would dearly love to know if they'd had the time.

"What about the room the Wey Wolf was in?" Odette asked him. "And the shaman. We need to find it."

"I can take you there."

Maverick exchanged a worried look with Odette. He didn't trust Barry, or his newfound wish to help them, but Odette wasn't a fool. Maverick hurried onwards, not even questioning the smokeless torches that illuminated their passage. The shifters had fallen into an unnatural silence, cowed perhaps by the increasing grandeur of the stonework around them. The carvings. The sense of import. Maverick found himself slowing down, appreciating his surroundings, until a huge door with a wolf's head on it suddenly blocked their way.

"Wow," Nahum murmured. "That's impressive. Bronze, gold, silver. It makes a statement, right?"

"And it's imbued with magic," Odette added.

Maverick felt an overwhelming need to genuflect before it, but sheer willpower kept him upright.

"Blood," Barry said. "On the canines and the tongue. That's how you enter. But it will only work if you're token-bound or a messenger, which are virtually the same thing."

"What's beyond it?" Danny asked. He had forced his way to the front to be at Maverick's side, and Maverick accepted it. This was a joint venture, and it kept the North London Pack appeased.

"A complex of rooms, passageways, the arena, and the labyrinth, but I barely entered that," Barry told them. "There's also a throne room, which is where the Wey Wolf greets newcomers. However, pretty much everyone will be in the arena tonight. This door is sealed with magic from the inside, so no one can leave unless you are a messenger. They're confident they are safe. That's why we are the only ones at the door upstairs."

"So how the fuck do we get in?" Axel said with a growl, leading the rumblings of discontent.

"I can't do it," Barry said, shuffling from one foot to another. "I'm not a shifter, or token-bound."

"Unfortunately," Vlad added, looming behind him, "Grey hasn't found any tokens. He's behind us, with the others. I don't think using Russo or Lockhart is a good idea, either."

"No, agreed." Maverick glowered at Barry. "You brought us down here knowing there is no way in?" *Was this a trap? Were shifters attacking from behind them? Was the passage booby-trapped after all?* Seething with impatience, Maverick lifted him off the floor, hands at his throat and shoved him against the wall. "If this is a trap, I will kill you first."

"It's not." Barry's voice squeaked. "I thought you'd have a way to get in."

"You must be able to enter. You must have means! You guard the damn place!"

"No, we don't! I can only get in when the token-bound arrive."

"I have a way," Odette said, the Wayfinder in her hands. "We have a ghost shifter trapped in this Wayfinder. He led us here, and he might get us through that door. Maverick, put him down. Vlad, let my coven through, please."

Maverick reluctantly dropped Barry to the ground, and within a few moments, Morgana and Birdie wriggled their way through the mass of shifters to Odette's side, and Grey, Harlan, and Maggie followed in their wake. The whole place felt claustrophobic and hot. Odette had a hurried consultation with her coven, and there was a lot of nodding and muttering.

Harlan was busy taking photos on his phone. "This place is phenomenal. This passage is ceremonial, meant to instil fear and awe. And this doorway. Wow."

"It's pissing me off," Tommy grumbled from the crowd. "I told you I should bring dynamite."

"And risk bringing the roof down?" Vlad said, voice low with menace. "I don't fucking think so."

"Odette," Arlo said, leaning close to the witches, "we need a way in before they turn on each other."

Morgana whirled around to face Maverick. "Blood, just as Barry said. We want yours on the canines, and then smear it on the wolf's tongue."

"And then what?" He rolled his sleeve up, exposing his forearm.

"We put the shifter in it—sort of. Everyone, stand back." She looked apologetic, eyes furtive. "We're not sure how this may go."

Maverick pierced his skin with the sharp tip of one silver-tipped canine. A flood of memories and experiences washed over him in seconds before vanishing again, brief but intense. A sense of drumming, firelight, tattoos, animal skins, and combat that was heady and uncertain. He took a breath to settle himself, then smeared his blood as instructed before stepping back to leave several paces between them and the door. Birdie sketched a quick half circle of runes on the ground before the door using her fingers, and they shimmered with a silvery light, sealing the three witches inside. Then, using a strangely sibilant language that Maverick felt he should know but didn't, they cast a spell.

A spectre rose from the Wayfinder, and a gasp ran across the shifters as a misty male figure manifested and hovered in the air. Unfortunately, all they saw was his back, and Maverick barely had time to take in the old-fashioned trousers and large tattoo spread across the man's muscular shoulders before he plunged into the wolf's head relief on the door.

A white light flashed around it, illuminating the raised surfaces, before homing in on Maverick's blood. There the light settled, as if the ghost was trying to soak in all of Maverick's essence. The witch's chanting increased, as if wrestling with it to stay put, and Maverick had a horrible vision of it escaping and barrelling into him.

But then the door swung wide open, revealing an elaborately decorated stone passage beyond, and his immediate elation shattered as the semicircle of runes was broken. The ghost streaked out of the door and hurtled into the Hall of the Wey Wolf, and the witches chased after him.

Thirty-One

Over the course of the evening, Hunter watched the fights in the arena, his emotions warring within him. He was increasingly absorbed in their outcome, but also increasingly paranoid as to what Blōdbana knew, and what he had planned.

However, as the night progressed, he found that he cared less and less about potential consequences. More shifters arrived, bets were laid, and the hum of excitement grew. Even Finn, seated a couple of rows below him, seemed absorbed by the spectacle. The fights became bloodier, the stakes seemed higher, and the injuries more brutal as bloodlust took hold. But still, no one was maimed beyond what they could heal in their wolf. Mostly.

Hunter had fought again, this time battling a shifter he thought was in Castor's pack. They fought with fists, which soon descended into kicks, and then they wrestled and punched as they rolled across the ground. His thoughts became increasingly cloudy, his shadow warrior seeking dominance. Then, with horrible clarity, he realised the other shifter would kill him if given half a chance, and he caught the sneer of Blōdbana watching from the side, half under the lower tier. A glint of silver hung from his belt, taunting him with his amulet. This wasn't a fair fight. It wasn't meant to be. But seeing the amulet and all that it represented meant that finally sense kicked in, and Hunter submitted very clearly. The other shifter had to withdraw.

Hunter dragged himself to his feet, every muscle aching, and covered in grazes and cuts. Blood poured into his eye from a cut above it, and he wiped it away, vision swimming. He had only hours left before he submitted to his shadow warrior. He knew it. He could feel it encroaching on his reason.

Then, just as he thought that it couldn't get any worse, he heard the next fighters called as he limped out of the arena. He thought he was hearing things until he saw them. Finn had been summoned to the arena, and he was fighting Hal. Hal shouldered past Hunter as if he didn't recognise him, chest bare, waiting on the sidelines as the crowd settled, but Finn's eyes flickered towards Hunter with ill-concealed fear.

Hunter caught his arm as he passed. "What type of fight?"

"As a wolf. I can't shift properly, Hunter." His voice was low and full of panic. "What am I supposed to do?"

"Submit as soon as you can."

"But if I can't shift?"

"You're young. They'll understand."

"They won't. Hal will kill me."

"Hal knows you."

"Does he?" They both looked over at him, and Hunter knew it wasn't Hal there anymore.

Hunter had no intention of letting Finn die. He would intervene if he had to, although fuck knows what would happen to either of them if he did. However, the guards were watching, and Hunter forced himself to calm down, even though the shadow warrior lurked closer and closer to the surface.

If the young wolf can't shift, he's better off dead.

Where the hell had that thought come from?

"Don't be scared, be angry. You're a wolf. Let him out. He is you, and he's stronger than you know."

"But I can feel the other one. You know…"

"Focus on *your* wolf."

Finn nodded as the guards hustled him away. He was tall, but nowhere near as muscular as Hal, and Hunter knew this was also Blōdbana's doing. This was Hunter's test, just as much as Hal and Finn's.

But what of Finn's shadow warrior? With a weak wolf on display—if there at all, would Finn stand a chance? Would the shadow warrior force his wolf out and take over?

Hunter settled at the side to watch.

Domino raced down the stone passage, close behind Nahum and Maverick, dragging Barry along with her. The warrior ghost had vanished, and the witches had no idea where to.

The rest of the two packs followed, all silent, but not nearly as quiet as Domino hoped. To her ears, their feet sounded like thunder. But they had worse things to worry about.

Two guards stood in what Barry had told them was a throne room, leaning casually against the wall as they talked. It was obvious they weren't modern shifters from the clothes they wore, and their relaxed attitude soon vanished as the door opened. *At least*, Domino thought fleetingly, *they hadn't heard their approach*.

Nahum beat Maverick to them. He killed the guards with his sword when they were both mid-attack, blood splattering across the throne. He shrugged. "We don't need guides, right?"

Harlan wasn't kidding about his speed or ruthlessness.

"I guess not, seeing as we have Barry," Maverick said. "But questioning them would have been useful."

"They'd have told you nothing. Where now?" Nahum asked Barry, sword to his throat. "And be quiet, or these will be the last words you utter."

Barry stuttered out a response. "The passages lead to all sorts of rooms, but the dormitories are down to the left, and the arena is at the far end, close to the dining hall. All the main passages lead there. The labyrinth is beyond the arena."

"Have you been in the labyrinth?"

"Barely." Barry shuffled, clearly nervous. "I didn't like it."

"And the place you found their bodies?" Morgana asked.

"Off the passage that leads to the water cave."

"What about where he makes the tokens? That's probably where we should go."

"It's close by it."

"Listen!" Vlad intervened, and in the silence that followed, they heard cheers and roars in the distance. "The arena, I presume?"

"Yes. The only other place they're likely to linger now is the dining hall, or the water cave where they wash up after fighting. We may find a few shifters walking back along the corridors, but it's unlikely. My brother is probably in the arena."

"Are they likely to fight us?" Domino asked, thinking really of Hunter. "The token-bound, I mean?"

"Probably, yes. I don't know how it works, but the token seems to possess them. All they want to do is join the Wey Wolf's pack. It's some kind of magic the shaman uses. They forget who they are." Barry looked guilty. "I see it in their eyes. It's horrible.

Honestly, you have to believe me, we had no idea what we were letting loose when we found this place. And there's something else you should know." He hesitated as he stared at the shifters. "Eventually, they use this mirror that splits them into two. They fight the warrior inside themselves. The one that loses is gone forever. They call it the ancestor within. It's not, though. It's really the Wey Wolf's old pack."

Domino's heart skipped a beat. "How long until they fight the shadow warrior?"

"Usually at least a few days. They fight each other in different ways first. In wolves, or human combat. They lead hunts into the labyrinth, too. Not all exit, according to Dean."

This was a house of horrors.

Maverick whirled around to speak to Danny. "Take your pack to the right, clear the rooms as you go. If you find stray shifters, lock them in if possible. We'll head left. Remember, we're here to save all the shifters, not just our own. If they're distracted by the fights in the arena, leave them alone. We're buying time for the witches to release them with a spell. That just means that hopefully we'll only have the guards, Blōdbana, and the Wey Wolf to fight." He then turned to Arlo. "Take our team to the left and do the same."

"Wait!" Barry held up his hand to stop them. "There's something else you should know. If you see the arena, a few of you might be able to join the crowd and watch the fights, if you keep a low profile. Lots of shifters don't know the others. That's a weakness we've noticed. Plus, they can't see each other's token-bound warrior either, from what Dean has observed. But the seats below the Wey Wolf are filled with his pack. The guards, the old ones, are loyal to him. Plus, the new pack is growing, and they are loyal to him, too."

Maverick waved the waiting packs on. "Be careful. I'll follow soon."

Domino glared at Maverick as they vanished. "I am not babysitting Barry."

"No, you are not. You are joining them," he nodded to the witches and the humans, "with Barry. You need to help them find that room, and Barry's brother, Dean. That is our priority if we are to break this damn spell."

"It sounds," Grey said, "as if it's too late for some." He squeezed Domino's shoulder in an effort to reassure her. "At least our pack members have been here days only."

She nodded, but it didn't really help calm her. She turned back to Maverick, trying to rein in her anger. "They're witches! They don't need me."

"I want a shifter with them. Please, Domino." His stare intensified, as if to drive home his will, but then suddenly softened. "I'll find Hunter. I promise."

Not wanting to have a full-on pissy fit, but seething with resentment, she nodded. "Fine, I'll do it."

Maverick flashed her a brief smile. "Thanks. Nahum, you're with them, please."

"And you, Maverick?" she asked.

"I'm going to find the Wey Wolf. If necessary, I'll challenge him."

"Where now?" Morgana asked Barry, worry making her tone clipped.

This hall and its seemingly endless passageways was oppressive with the weight of centuries pressing down around them. She loved history. Part of her wanted to explore, but the more cautious part wanted to leave now and never look back. Magic was soaked into the fabric of the stone, just like in Moonfell, but whereas Moonfell was as familiar and warm as a cocoon, this place was chilling. Plus, Monroe was out there somewhere, potentially fighting for his life, but she certainly didn't need those concerns clouding her judgement.

"We need to skirt around the arena," Barry said, leading them off the main passageways. "The guards will be positioned around it, and we don't want to be caught."

Harlan flourished his Taser. "I've come equipped, Grey and Maggie have shotguns, and Nahum, well, is Nahum. I'm sure we're all equal to it."

"I'm very happy not to run into anyone, thanks," Birdie said. "I'll save my energy for Blōdbana."

"You know," Harlan said, as they made another turn, "we should take a moment to just appreciate this amazing place. We are in a genuine Anglo-Saxon hall. Intact! Magical."

"And fucking deadly," Maggie added scathingly. "With a sociopathic alpha and his henchman shaman. I'll appreciate it once they're dead."

Morgana appreciated their banter as it alleviated some of her anxiety. The deeper Barry led them into the complex, the quieter it became, and the sounds of shouting shifters receded. But the magic grew stronger as they reached the area where Barry believed Blōdbana performed his rituals. He had described the place to them. An unusual room with stone tombs, strange marks that sounded like runes, and a kind of altar. Everything appeared darker, and it wasn't because of the lack of lighting. Menace surrounded them, and shadows crept closer. Morgana fought the urge to turn back, and even Nahum gripped his sword tighter.

"I don't get scared easily," Grey admitted, "but I am feeling very creeped out right now."

Harlan jerked and fired his Taser, and it missed Nahum by a whisker. "Shit. Sorry!"

"What the fuck?" Nahum said, rounding on him. "Have I pissed you off?"

"I thought I saw something behind you."

"It's nothing, you jumpy idiot."

Unfortunately, everyone was twitchy and trigger happy, and Morgana quickly cast a spell to calm everyone down. "It's just magic that's designed to deter people. We're reaching Blōdbana's private areas. He's protecting them."

"I think you're right. We're close now," Barry said, "but it feels different." He hesitated as he came to a junction in the passage. "I'm sure it's to the right, but my thoughts feel woolly."

"More magic," Nahum said. "I can feel it. It grows thicker here. Like a veil."

"Stop." Odette's voice was so urgent it sent tingles up Morgana's spine. "He knows we're here."

"Blōdbana? How?" Birdie asked. Then she rolled her eyes. "That damn ghost."

"Perhaps." Distracted, Odette leaned against the wall, hands pressed into the stone, her eyes suddenly vacant. "He's coming. I feel him. Or something is..." She stood upright, facing the way they'd come. "You go. I'll wait and slow him down."

"I don't bloody think so," Birdie said belligerently. "We stick together, and block him from entering his own rooms. Barry, can he get in another way? Another route, perhaps?"

Barry shrugged. "I don't think so, but it has been a few weeks since I've been here, of course."

"Fingers crossed, then. Let's get a bloody move on."

Morgana was relieved she didn't have to continue without her coven, but she needed to remove the veiling spell. She countered it with a spell to clear thoughts, sending a wave of spring-filled fresh breezes, rosemary, and sage along the corridors to banish the gloom, and the gentle breeze tickled her neck. With renewed vigour, Barry continued onwards. Within another few turns of the passage, and some additional spellcasting, the corridor ended at an ornate door blazing with a large sigil in the centre, and one around the chunky iron lock.

"I take it," Maggie said, keeping a wary distance, "that it didn't look like this when you found it?"

Barry shook his head. "No, not at all. The whole place was in darkness, including the door. We just opened it. We actually marked our way with chalk because we were worried that we'd get lost. I can see a few faint traces of it, but most of it is gone. This place was the last area we found. We spent hours exploring the hall. I felt like Indiana Jones."

"I know that feeling," Harlan murmured.

Odette hung back with Domino, distracted by Blōdbana's approach, but Morgana and Birdie examined the sigils, Harlan and Nahum at either side, while Grey and Maggie continued to question Barry.

"I recognise some of these, but not all," Morgana admitted to Birdie. "That's the trouble with sigils. If you can combine several, it's hard to know what the originator has used."

"They're elaborate, as if he's making a statement," Birdie said, by far more experienced with rune magic than Morgana. "Can you differentiate them, Nahum?"

Nahum could read and speak any language, a gift from their Fallen Angel fathers, but even he shook his head. "Like you say, too many combinations to be sure. I think they are all variations of protection."

"It certainly feels like it," Morgana agreed.

"Reminds me of the damn sigils on that demon-summoning witch's door," Harlan said, swinging around to look at Grey. "Remember that?"

"Like I could forget. There'd better not be demons here."

Nahum shook his head. "No, not demons."

Morgana knew she had to act quickly. Time was not on their side. "They're not strong sigils, even though they're complex. They're designed to keep shifters and humans out. Not witches. Maybe that's the point, Birdie. They're meant to impress, more than anything."

"Good point. I have a counter-spell we can use. We just need to be wary, in case there are other measures inside. The other good thing is that we are familiar with Blōdbana's magic now."

"Not as familiar as I'd like to be," Morgana said, eyebrow arched with annoyance.

It had an arcane, raw feel to it. Unsophisticated, in general, and blunt. There was no finesse, and Morgana wasn't sure if that was just Blōdbana's way, or if it came from the time in which he had lived. The tokens were undoubtedly more sophisticated, but as far as the sigils on the door went, he would surely enter the room regularly, so they were made to be undone.

Logically, if this was her spell, she would choose the easiest way to reverse it. It seemed Birdie thought so, too. After a hurried discussion, Birdie picked the one most likely to work and cast it, intending to unravel the sigils and the magic within them. After several small variations, it worked. The sigils' fiery outline vanished and dissolved, leaving the door and lock unblemished.

"Allow me," Nahum said, opening the door.

Thirty-Two

Hunter sighed with relief as Finn successfully shifted, but it was short lived. His wolf was far smaller than Hal's.

Submit now, Hunter urged him. Head on paws, nose down, submissive. *Just do it.* No self-respecting wolf would pounce on a juvenile.

Instead, Finn faced him, and a shimmer seemed to pass over his body. Hunter blinked, thinking he was seeing things. The wolves faced each other, trying to stare each other down, and Hunter thought Finn had lost his common sense. Then, without waiting a beat, they both pounced, tumbling end over end in a snarl of teeth and claws.

And that's when Hunter knew it wasn't Finn. It was the shadow warrior who had found dominance in the face of Finn's weakness, and neither wolf was intending to submit. Hal wanted a place in the pack, and would kill for it. The shadow warrior wanted out.

Hunter studied the Wey Wolf, hoping he would halt the fight, but instead he leaned in eagerly, as did the rest of the watching crowd, as if the bloodlust had got the better of everyone. The roars of the shifters increased, and the thumping of feet on the wooden tiers intensified.

Two guards stood between Hunter and the arena, but right now he didn't care. He'd take them both out to save his pack members. Fortunately, he was alone in the training area. His opponent had left, and no one else was there yet. He was about to slip out of his jeans to shift and intervene, when something caught his eye. A strange, flitting shape entered the arena, skirting under the lowest tier where Blōdbana watched the fight, giving Hunter fleeting glances of grim satisfaction.

What appeared to be a ghost settled in front of the shaman. The figure of a man.

Blōdbana's eyes widened with shock, and a grimace set his lips into a thin, hard line. He marched out of the arena, summoning half a dozen guards to follow him. Hunter had no idea why, but he saw his chance. Knowing the time for caution had gone, he shifted, ripped the Achilles tendon out of one distracted guard, darted past the other, and joined the fight.

Arlo raced down the silent passageways, in constant communication with his pack as they cleared rooms and advanced. Most had shifted to their wolves, but he understood them anyway. The tilt of the head, the flicking of their ears, the low, throaty rumble, the yips and snarls. If anything, their eerie surroundings enhanced their communication. The whole place was soaked in shifter magic. Stone carvings, reliefs, the earthy scent of wolf, and the presence of the Wey Wolf drew them on. As did the shouts up ahead that were getting steadily louder.

Arlo felt like he'd stumbled back in time, and so did Monroe, who was, like Arlo, still in human form.

"This is just plain fucking weird," Monroe growled. "This entire place has been down here for centuries. It's creepy as fuck. And why are there so many rooms? Most of them are unused."

"I guess he had a big pack once, and is no doubt planning one again." They checked another room, then rapidly moved on. "The Wey Wolf isn't overwhelming you? Because his presence is like a hammer on my brain."

"It just makes me want to smash his face in. I fucking hate feeling like this. That constant dominance. That's why I like Maverick so much."

Arlo nodded, knowing exactly what Monroe meant. "What are we going to do when we reach the arena? Just watch? Try to subdue other shifters?" Arlo's frustration grew. "This is nuts. I feel I'm entering a fight muzzled."

"I'm hoping that inspiration strikes. Perhaps we can pick the guards off one by one."

Just as Arlo was thinking they would reach the arena without incident—which, in his head, was like some kind of gladiatorial pit—he heard footsteps, and in seconds, several old guards appeared ahead of them. It was obvious that they were the Wey Wolf's original team. Like the two they had encountered in the throne room, everything about them was old-fashioned. Their hair, their clothes, their manner of tattoos, and that scent of age. Must, dust, stone, and blood. But some things didn't change, and like all aggressive wolf-shifters, their eyes were molten gold.

Vlad, Tommy, and Jax were ahead of them, and without a second's hesitation, they attacked the guards, covering the distance with a burst of speed that took even Arlo by surprise. The guards hesitated for the briefest seconds, probably surprised by the sheer number of them, and then advanced. Some wielded swords, others shifted into their wolf. They met brutally in the middle of the passage, and the rest of the pack dived in to assist, fur flying. Fran, Cecile, Rory, John, and Mads. They aimed for wrists and arms, and swords clattered to the ground to even the fight.

Howls erupted, horribly loud in the confined area. It was the last thing they needed. Noises echoed from the other passages, and then more shouts. *Castor's pack.*

"We cannot be trapped here," Arlo said. "All these passages are interconnected. We have to get to the arena. Try to block their way out, or we'll be overwhelmed." He whistled, then shouted, "Fran, Cecile, Rory! With us."

Monroe was already ahead of him, taking side passageways and countering dead ends, always following the noise and the ever-increasing scent of wolves. And food.

"The dining hall," Arlo said, sniffing. "We're getting close."

Maverick had followed his pack at first, and then separated from them, crisscrossing with Castor's pack who were clearing one side of the complex. Stealth and solitude served him well, and without distractions he found the arena quickly.

It was bigger than he expected, housed within a room that was also part cave. The corridors sloped down to reach it, allowing the roof to be high. Acoustics magnified the shouts. There were no other obvious escape routes, except for a rounded archway on the far side of the space that led to a dark passageway. *Was this the labyrinth Barry had mentioned?*

Maverick endeavoured to be as nonchalant as possible as he climbed the wooden steps to the upper tier of the arena. He spotted Danny and Thorne ascending in other areas, but his sharp ears detected sounds of fighting from the direction they had come from, and he hoped both packs would be okay. The arena lay at the far end of the whole complex, but he still hadn't found the water cave yet, which must be close.

All other thoughts vanished though as Maverick reached the fourth tier and looked down. Horrified, he saw Finn and Hal enter the arena. *What the hell was Finn doing there? Surely, they wouldn't make him fight a grown shifter. He was just a child.*

Maverick's wolf rose, an instinctive need to protect his pack, especially the young, but he forced it down, trying to be rational. Finn was facing Hal. One of his own pack. *How affected could Hal be already?* Trying to subdue his increasing discomfort, he focussed on the rest of the arena and the shifters spread over the seating. There were more than they had brought with them, but nowhere near enough to fill this place. The Wey Wolf had grand plans. *Speaking of which…*

In seconds, he saw the alpha. It could only be him. A huge man, muscled and bare-chested, looking every inch a bully, sat in the middle tier on an imposing chair, surrounded by guards and acolytes. His attention was solely on the impending fight, a cruel, amused glint in his eye, despite the almost affable smile on his face. An alpha who might appear more approachable now, but he wouldn't be when his pack was established. Then his true brutality would come to the fore. Even at this distance, Maverick could feel his aggression. His need to dominate. He'd like to say he was a relic, but that would be a lie.

Remembering what Barry had told him, he studied the row below. Over a dozen shifters sat at ease, confident in their position. Some were scarred, while others bore marks of recent injuries already healing. All were modern men. *But how many were actually the mysterious shadow warriors?*

So far, no one had taken the slightest notice of Maverick. He saw a few others from Castor's pack find spots in the tiers. *Where the hell was his own pack?*

A flurry of activity below made him focus on Finn and Hal, and without fanfare, both cast aside their clothes and shifted. He was initially relieved that Finn had achieved it, and then horrified as they tackled each other in a brutal clash. *Was that really Finn?* He might be fighting as fiercely as Hal, but he was no match for him in size.

And then Hunter raced into the pit with a blood curdling howl that mixed with the piercing scream of a man in horrifying pain. Another wolf raced after him, and then another, and suddenly shifters were on their feet in the stands.

The Wey Wolf roared with fury. For a second, everyone stopped, and silence fell at the magnitude of his power.

Danny caught Maverick's eye, and he nodded to the pit, mouthing *"Yours?"*

Maverick nodded. Danny's gaze panned across the arena, making a cutting motion to his throat with his thumb, and Castor's pack started swinging punches in the crowd. Fights erupted everywhere.

The Wey Wolf rose to his feet, outraged. His pack scrambled, and Maverick took that moment to leap across the tiers, treading on anyone who stood in his way. When he was close enough, he dived onto the Wey Wolf.

Arlo and the pack burst out of a narrow passage back onto a main one, stumbling right into the middle of a group of shifters exiting a large doorway.

From the scent of roasted meat alone, Arlo knew it was the Great Hall, and he glimpsed long tables and a central fire in the room beyond. He smashed into the shifters like a bulldozer, and Monroe followed up. The men stumbled backwards, but not far. Regaining their balance, a couple charged, while another couple shifted.

Monroe picked up a large wooden bench made for seating and hurled it at them. Fran flew past him and landed on the chest of a shifter who had feinted to the left to attack Arlo. She had come in fast, low, and unseen. He landed on the floor with a thud, his head striking the stone slabs.

Arlo pulled one of the doors closed. "Fran! Leave it. We'll lock them in."

In the scrambled seconds they had, they locked the doors using a huge, iron lock.

"That won't hold them long," Monroe said.

"Long enough."

The noise of their encounter was so loud, it had almost drowned out the arena.

Almost.

As Arlo turned, following Cecile and Rory, he noted that the corridor widened, the floor sloped downwards, and numerous doors were on either side. But it was the large archway at the end that captured his attention, and the back and underside of the tiered seating beyond it.

They had found the arena.

But something was wrong. Very wrong. The sound of fighting as they stepped inside the vaulted space was too intense for a single match. It sounded as if everyone was fighting, not just a few in the arena itself.

"Is this normal?" Arlo asked Monroe.

"How the hell should I know? My Saturday nights don't involve secret fight clubs. Well, unless the job requires it, of course."

And then a shifter in his human form tumbled from the tier above and landed at Arlo's feet, covered in blood. He staggered to right himself, wiped the blood from his eye, and stared at Arlo in confusion. Then he raced back up the stairs, no doubt to finish his fight.

"What the fuck?" Arlo raced after him, emerged onto the lowest level, and saw brawling across every tier.

He took a few seconds to take it all in, trying to spot his own pack members. He saw plenty of Castor's pack though, and they were all fighting. It was even worse in the pit, which was filled with lots of wolves and guards. Blood was splattered across the sandy floor, and in the middle of it all, Hunter was trying to protect a smaller wolf and clearly failing, because Finn—it was pretty obvious who he was—was like a rabid dog. Hal was fighting several wolves who stood between them. And then he saw Maverick brawling with a huge shifter on the middle tiers.

He rejoined Monroe, who in the seconds he'd been gone had found the rest of the pack. They gathered together, many of them covered in blood. Some were limping, but all were alive.

"They're all fighting," Arlo said with disbelief. "Every single one of them. Maverick is attacking someone who must be the Wey Wolf, but I've seen Hunter in the pit, and something is very wrong with Finn."

Arlo suspected that access to the central pit was easy from where they were. Huge struts supported the benches above, a mix of stone and wood together to create a warren of spaces beneath.

He led the pack under them. "This way. I don't care how we get them out, but we'll make it work. We have to."

Thirty-Three

A shiver ran over Grey's skin as he entered the room that Barry said was Blōdbana's space.

To his eyes it was an occult chamber of horrors. Part ossuary, part crypt. Stone shelving lined one long wall filled with stacks of skulls—human and wolf—leg bones, arm bones, rib cages, and pelvic bones. Stone tombs filled other deep recesses, and a dozen were lined up in the centre of the room. All were carved with various images too numerous for Grey to get a fix on now. However, the tomb that really caught his eye was an enormous one in the middle of the room, the rearing wolf rising out of the stone as if it would leap to life and tear him limb from limb.

"Wow!" Nahum exhaled with a whistle. "I guess that is the tomb of the Wey Wolf himself."

"And bones," Grey exclaimed, scanning the room. "I didn't expect this."

Morgana paused at the threshold, throwing out her arms to stop the others. "Wait. Just let us feel for spells."

Harlan nodded. "Traps. I get it."

"Remind you of anything?" Nahum asked him.

"The Mithraic cave in France—although, no bones in that one."

"Plenty of cells though, right?"

"Yep. An absolute nightmare with a bloody great minotaur in it."

"You two are full of surprises," Grey said. When this mess had been dealt with, he fully intended to sit down with both of them for a long chat about their exploits.

Maggie snorted. "I'm just glad you didn't find it in England."

Harlan gave her a sly grin. "Lucky you have this one, then."

"I think we're clear," Morgana said, striding into the room with renewed confidence. "But be careful of what you touch. I'm sure you can see the runes and sigils. I'm not entirely sure of their purpose yet."

"If they even have one," Birdie said. "Some of them might be names. Epitaphs, perhaps."

Grey noted that Odette followed more cautiously, and she shut the door behind them as soon as Domino entered. "Can you still feel him, Odette?"

She nodded, her dark eyes seeming hooded from the light cast by the smokeless torches that burned in this room, as they did all across the hall. "He's getting closer, but I can't tell his route."

"Is that because his magic is everywhere?" Domino asked. "Surely, it's his power that keeps these torches burning."

"Yes, he's everywhere here. Just like we are at Moonfell. And he's stronger in this room, more than anywhere else." Odette called over to Birdie. "We should seal this entrance. Buy us some time."

Domino started stripping. "I'm shifting to my wolf. My senses will be more acute that way. Any objections?"

"Shift away," Grey said.

"I'm going to check what's through there," Nahum said, pointing to a door set in the far wall, while Birdie joined Odette.

"I like to know my exits—or another way for our shaman friend to enter. Barry, why don't you join me?"

Barry had shuffled in quietly, but his eyes darted around the place in a way that unnerved Grey. However, Barry didn't object to Nahum's suggestion. "There are rooms back there. A type of smithy, if I recall."

"A smithy?" Morgana was standing next to the central tomb, fingers hovering above the stonework in a way that Grey had grown to recognise. She was feeling for more magic. "That could be what we're looking for."

"And why are we looking for a smithy, of all things?" Maggie asked, progressing clockwise around the room.

Grey accompanied her, shotgun cocked. She didn't need his protection, but it made him feel better.

"Somehow," Morgana said, "the shaman preserved their bodies and brought them back to life. That alone is intriguing. More importantly, he found a way to store the spirits of the pack in those tokens."

"The spirits that are now in the modern-day shifters," Harlan said. He was examining the bones, his torch shining into dark spaces and panning over the walls. "Neat trick."

"Exactly. We think he treated the silver tokens like we would make a poppet. We assumed he would have used blood and hair, maybe skin cells. That would have been millennia ago, we presume."

"Lovely," Maggie said with grimace. "I thought you all were good witches."

"We only do such things if the occasion warrants it," Morgana answered, suitably mysterious. "We think he made each token with an individual's body matter. Then he trapped their spirit there, too. It's a working theory, subject to change."

"What about bones?" Harlan asked. "Would they be effective if you ground them up? Let's face it—he has enough to choose from."

"That's an excellent point." Morgana strode to Barry and Nahum's side. "I'll come with you two. The rest of you, please see what else you can find in here. I feel there are secrets we have yet to uncover."

"Slow down!" Maggie instructed, her face creased in confusion. "What happens then? If you find how he made the tokens, I mean."

"Hopefully, it will give us greater insight into how to break the spell, and free the shifters from their possession. If not, then we must attempt a gigantic exorcism, but seeing as Odette could see no way to do that earlier, it doesn't bode well now."

"This is a shitshow," Maggie muttered to Grey as the three vanished into the rooms beyond, and Domino followed.

"I agree, but we saw the aftermath of what happened earlier. I have no better ideas, do you?"

"No. But I think if the modern-day shifters are challenged, either by magic or physical attack, then the old spirits will take over their hosts—for want of a better word—anyway."

Grey shook his head, unconvinced. "So why don't they just do that from the start?"

"Because this is some sick game!"

"No, I disagree. It's exactly what the shifters say it is. It's a challenge. The Wey Wolf wants the strongest warriors, right?"

Harlan joined them, overhearing their conversation. "Yes. They train the shifters and see who comes out on top. Today, when they were threatened at Castor's place, it upended that. It was too soon. Or maybe Castor's pack had already decided where their loyalties lay. It sure as hell wasn't with him." Harlan gave a wry grin. "I guess that's the thing with possession. There are no guarantees. In that sense, it is a shitshow."

Grey was getting a headache trying to wrestle with the varied permutations of it all. "I'm sick of trying to second guess how this could go. Why don't we check these tombs while Birdie and Odette complete their spell?"

The two witches were still by the door they'd used to enter, light flashing from their palms as they cast their spell. It was horribly quiet, and Grey had no idea what was going on in the rest of the complex. Half of him wished he'd have gone with the pack, because he was eager to see the whole place, but he also knew that being around fighting wolves was dangerous, even when they were your friends. Being amongst a pack of vicious wolves he didn't know, would be suicide. Perhaps he'd have time to explore afterwards, if he survived. He was intending to, but something about this place manifested dread. He felt as if a trap was about to be sprung.

It was as if Maggie had read his mind. "Do you trust Barry?"

"Don't you?"

"No. He's a little too helpful." She rolled her sleeves up. "But then again, I distrust everyone until they prove otherwise. I generally find it a very helpful stance to take."

"Should we be doing something, then?" Harlan asked. "Like questioning him? Warning Nahum and Morgana? I mean, what do you think he'll do?"

"I don't know." Maggie called over to the witches, who had just finished their spell. "Odette. Do you feel anything unusual from Barry?"

"Honestly, I'm feeling bombarded by lots of things right now. Blōdbana's magic, shifters and their energy, the sheer age of this place… I tried to mute it with a protection spell, but that made me feel vulnerable." She pushed her fingers through her thick, curly hair. "I need to get a grip."

"Don't say it like that," Birdie said. "You're sensitive at the best of times. Just roll with it. Use it now to see what you can pick up from this room. Like you said, you're feeling Blōdbana strongly. It may help us. As for Barry…"

"Forget it." Maggie waved her arms airily. "I'm just a cynic. A jaded copper who has seen more than is healthy. Let's add to that by peering into an old tomb, shall we? Are we thinking these will all be empty?"

Grey shrugged. "I guess so, if they're all walking these halls."

But when they pushed the first stone lid off, after a great deal of grunting, they were met with bones and bits of skin.

"Holy shit!" Maggie straightened up, eyeballing everyone aggressively. "That's gross."

Grey shrugged apologetically. "We'd better check the rest."

"And we," Birdie to Odette, "had better tackle these runes."

But before anyone could do anything else, there was a resounding crash, and the entire doorway shook.

Blōdbana had arrived.

"Quick!" Maggie yelled. "Get the tomb tops off. Perhaps we can stake him or something."

Grey was pretty sure he could fall very heavily for Maggie from that statement alone. "He's not a vampire, darling."

"But his body is here..."

"It can't be here, if he's out there...he's reanimated!"

"Let's burn his clothes or belongings, then. We must be able to do something while the witches keep him out."

Birdie and Odette were already mounting their defence.

"Can't hurt to try," Harlan said. "Let's make it quick."

Hunter was fighting a losing battle. He'd raced to Finn's side in the centre of the fighting pit, but trying to get between him and Hal was nightmarish. Both seemed intent on killing the other, and now him.

Fortunately, within seconds of him arriving in the pit after maiming the guard, other fights broke out in the stands. He couldn't work out why, but it proved fortuitous. Suddenly, another half a dozen shifters were in the pit with them, plus guards, and they all started fighting, which at least distracted Finn and Hal

.

Although maybe *fortunately* was the wrong word. Now they were fighting on all fronts, and in the chaos of the moment, his sense of self was slipping further and further away. Instinct conquered reason, and all he wanted to do was fight. And then when Finn attacked Hunter, leaping over another shifter who came between them, he lost it.

Damn pup taking a shot at him. Hunter snarled and leaped, his powerful haunches bunching and springing beneath him, jaws wide, ready to take Finn down.

Until something crunched into him, rolling him away until he struck the side of the pit, almost knocking himself senseless. A huge wolf loomed over him, and clarity flooded through him.

Arlo had arrived.

Thirty-Four

Morgana quickly realised that the other connected rooms weren't where Blōdbana slept. There was no bed, for a start. These were his work rooms that he'd tacked on to the crypt.

It seemed an odd choice to her, but maybe he was heavily involved with the rites accorded to their dead. The rooms beyond the crypt also contained bones, but this time of various animals such as birds, deer, and small mammals, as well as feathers and objects that looked like dried skins and furs. There were also bolts of scented linen, all strangely well-preserved. *Magic.* Nahum had quickly ascertained that there were no other exits.

They found the smithy, easily identifiable because of the firepit in the centre of the room, over which was suspended a tripod and cauldron. A stone bench ran down one side of the room, covered with paraphernalia.

"The token moulds are here," Nahum said, calling her over. "I can see the fighting wolves and the compass rose. There are quite a few of them."

Morgana examined one of them, all casually strewn across the bench as if they had been used recently. "There's so many of them."

"He wants a lot of spirit shifters. Makes sense to craft several at once."

Barry sniffed, nose wrinkling. "What are those jars?"

Morgana's gaze shifted to the shelves lining the wall above them, filled with hundreds of clay pots. She reached up and lifted one down. It was small, a vial more than a jar, stoppered with tarred leather, and she shook it, hearing the faint rattle of small things. "I suspect these are the remains of warriors, ready to be added to the metal, as we thought." Detecting no magic directly on them, she eased the lid off and shook them out on her palm. "I think Harlan is right. I am guessing this is ground bone, and there's hair, and I think..." she lifted her hand closer. "Part of a tooth. By the gods. There are so many pots."

"Enough for a small army," Nahum suggested.

Domino shifted back to her naked human shape, earning a startled look from Barry. Ignoring him, she picked up another vial. "Runes are scratched on the bottom."

Nahum, valiantly not staring at her admirable physique, picked up another, while Morgana examined her own. "It's a name," he said confidently.

"So he could keep track of who was who." Morgana nodded with relief. "Something else we were right about, then."

"Surely," Domino suggested, "there's far too much matter in these pots to use in the tiny tokens."

"For spares, I suspect," Morgana mused. It's what she would do.

Nahum turned back to the fire. "The embers are still warm. He's either using the fire for other means, or he's still making them."

"In which case, where are they?"

Barry walked to the far end of the bench where a stack of wooden boxes were stored, and lifted a lid. "They're in here." He took one out for them to see, and Domino stepped back.

"Thanks, Barry," Nahum said, noting Domino's discomfort. He crossed to his side and took it from him. "There aren't many in this box. Twenty or so, perhaps." He checked the next one. "There are more in here. Forty or fifty."

"We did bring the two we have, didn't we?" Domino asked Morgana.

She patted her pocket. "I have them, but there shouldn't be any spirits trapped in these anymore." Morgana studied the room again, this time noting the crucible Blōdbana used to melt the metal, which prompted another question. "Where is the metal he used?"

"Maybe it's all gone."

"I doubt it. He will have extra, surely. Jewellery to melt down, perhaps. Torcs and bracelets. Or even just raw silver or other metals." She shook her head. "That doesn't matter right now. What we really need to know is if those tokens are inactive. You know, already used on someone. If they are, that works in our favour."

"But there's no way of knowing, is there?" Domino asked. "Unless you can tell. You have two tokens. One active and one not. Can you see the difference?"

"I couldn't. They're both inactive, now, remember. We extracted the spirit for the Wayfinder."

Nahum smiled and beckoned them over. "Blōdbana marked the boxes, and he didn't pick runes. He chose Latin. From what Olivia told me, Latin replaced runes sometime after the seventh century. Especially for Christians. I suspect that Blōdbana and this pack were pagan, but Blōdbana strikes me as an educated man. Clever."

"Really?" Morgana hurried to his side. "Where do you see it?"

"Branded onto the box. This one says *complete*. The one with more tokens inside. Probably ones that have been used already."

"On our shifters," Domino said, starting to shiver in the chilly air. "The bastard."

Nahum shrugged out of his jacket and handed it to her. "You're cold. Wear this."

"Thank you."

"So, what now?" Barry asked. "How do we stop him?"

"More importantly," Nahum asked, settling against the counter, arms folded, "how did you wake him and the Wey Wolf? Knowing that could help us. You said that this place was cold and dusty when you found it. What happened?"

Morgana had been so focussed on finding the tokens and working out how to deactivate them, or summon the spirits back to them, that she had forgotten that important question. "Excellent point. And where was Blōdbana? Was he in one of those tombs out there?"

"Actually," Barry shuffled nervously, eyes everywhere except on his companions, "he was—"

And then he stopped abruptly and clutched his throat. He started hacking, as if he'd swallowed something. "He was—" Barry's eye's bulged and his face flushed.

"Bollocks!" Morgana leaped at him, magic flaring at her fingertips as she cast the quickest protection spell she could think of. "He's spellbound. Get Odette and Birdie!"

Nahum vanished, and Morgana grasped Barry's head, staring into his eyes. All she saw was panic. Her spell hadn't worked.

Domino grabbed his shoulders from behind, trying to pull him upright. "What do you mean, spellbound?"

"He knows a secret that he cannot tell. Fuckity fucking fuck! How did I miss this?"

"Because Blōdbana is a clever bastard."

Morgana focussed on casting a spell again. One designed to give him free will, but even as she was casting it, she knew it wouldn't work. Blōdbana's spell was too strong. "He'll choke to death before I can free him from this."

"So save him!" Domino looked at her in desperation. "How do we save the others otherwise?"

"If Odette can help, then she can read him."

"No she can't." Nahum was back at her side. "Blōdbana is attacking the door, and she has her hands full."

"Then I have only one choice." Morgana spelled him to sleep, and Barry's eyes instantly closed. She released her hold on his head, and it dropped to his chest. She helped Domino ease him to the floor. "We're screwed."

Maggie was determined not to die in a tomb like a cornered rat, but after finding that the majority of the tombs were empty, they were fresh out of ideas.

"Open the damn door and let that fucker in," she demanded, forgetting her own gun in her haste. "Grey can shoot him!"

"Really?" He looked at her, appalled. "Let a shaman in? Have you seen what he's doing to that door?" He looked over to Harlan. "Why do people think this shotgun is a magical cannon?"

"You wield it very efficiently."

"Look at the damn door! It's solid wood and it's bulging!"

Maggie didn't want to look at the door for that very reason. The very thick wooden door was pushing in like someone had stuck their hand in dough. Wood didn't do that naturally. And the noise was colossal. As if a gigantic fist was beating it. Birdie and Odette stood a short distance away from it, shoulder to shoulder, reinforcing their protection spell with arcane chanting. They were keeping him out for now, but it wouldn't last long.

Harlan pulled his Taser out, and Grey aimed his shotgun, but despite her earlier command to Grey, she knew a shotgun wouldn't stop the shaman. But they did have a Nephilim.

Nahum had already darted in once, and then ran back for the others, but as he came racing in again, Domino and Morgana with him, she called over to him. "Can you stop him?"

"Not from this side of the door, Maggie! I'm not a ghost Nephilim!"

Harlan snorted. "You did ask for that!"

"Oh, fuck off!" Morgana appeared stricken with worry, and Maggie looked to the door behind them. "Where's Barry?"

"Unconscious," Morgana said. "I spelled him to sleep."

"Why?"

"Because he was spellbound. He was trying to tell me something and couldn't. He was going to choke to death otherwise."

Maggie looked victoriously at Grey. "I fucking knew we couldn't trust him!"

"Gold stars to you, madam. Doesn't really help us now, does it?"

She gave him the finger, then stepped in front of Morgana to stop her from joining her coven. She knew a clue when she heard one. "What was he trying to tell you?"

"We asked him how he'd woken Blōdbana. We presumed he was in one of these tombs, but we still have no idea how the brothers woke him—or any of them, actually. We don't know the trigger. I was focussed on the tokens. Nahum made a good point. Knowing how they woke them could help us stop them."

"It sounded to me," Domino said, interrupting, "as if he was about to say that Blōdbana wasn't in here. Remember? He looked really nervous, shuffled around, and then said, *Actually...*and that was it. He almost choked to death."

"He's led us down the garden path!" Maggie declared, furious. "That devious bastard."

"Actually," Nahum pointed out, shouting to be heard above the colossal banging on the door, "he led us where we wanted to go. We wanted to find the tokens."

"But he could have offered us that information," she argued.

Morgana was obviously distracted, wanting to help her coven. "We wanted the tokens, and now we have them. We just have to figure out how to use them—if we can keep the shaman out."

It was very hard to think because of the noise and the fear of attack, but it suddenly struck Maggie that this was the point. "Even if you do stop our shifters from being possessed, it doesn't get rid of Blōdbana or the Wey Wolf and his guards. This is a distraction." She turned to Domino. "You have the best nose here. Can you smell him? Or anyone out there. You'd be able to, right?"

"Sure. Wolves have an excellent sense of smell." She shrugged out of Nahum's jacket, shifted to her wolf, and padded to the door that continued to bulge with every blow. Within seconds she shifted to human again, shouting to be heard. "There's no one out there."

Odette and Birdie stopped their chanting, and Birdie said, "Are you sure?"

"Absolutely. I can't scent or hear anything, other than the banging."

Birdie faced Odette. "I thought you could feel him."

"I can—everywhere!"

Maggie was furious and exasperated. "Fuck it! He's trapping us here because there is somewhere else we should be. Open the door!" She marched over to it, tugging on the handle. "Open it!"

"Are you insane?" Grey asked.

They were all looking at her as if she'd gone mad. Not surprising, really; the door was bulging alarmingly behind her.

All except for Domino. "She's right. No one is there. Open it." She directed this at the witches, who had sealed it.

Nahum withdrew his sword, waiting poised at the door. "Do it. I'm ready."

Birdie took a breath. "If you're sure."

In moments, she released their earlier spell, and Maggie opened the door. The corridor outside was empty, and the banging stopped instantly, leaving a shocking silence in its wake. She should have felt victorious, but instead she was even angrier. "I fucking knew it! So where to now?"

Harlan grinned. "What's the one place that Barry mentioned that we know nothing about?"

Grey considered his question for a moment, and then grinned, too. "The labyrinth. He skirted around it."

"Of course!" Maggie addressed Odette. "You feel Blōdbana everywhere because he *is* everywhere. Like you said. His magic is soaked in the stone here as much as yours is in Moonfell. He's like a spider in his web. The labyrinth is its centre—power-wise if not geographically. It must be where they found his body, because I'm pretty sure none of these tombs are his." She snapped her fingers, ordering her troops. "Grab those tokens and anything else you think we need. He thinks he's outsmarted us. I am very happy to prove him wrong."

"No." Morgana shook her head and squared her shoulders as if preparing for a fight. It made Maggie twitchy. "There are two aspects at play here. The shadow warriors that are stuck in modern-day shifters' bodies, and Blōdbana, who has masterminded everything. Two things, two teams. You want to take Blōdbana out. Destroy him. You're right to do that. I need to stay here. This place is where he made the tokens."

"You want us to split up?" Maggie hated that idea.

"Yes. What if this psychic attack is to distract us? What if he's been listening through Barry all along?"

"No, I doubt that," Grey said.

"We can't assume anything. Banishing those spirits is my job. I'll do it alone."

"No." Odette shook her head, curls bouncing. "Blōdbana is overwhelming me. I fear if I push on that he will weaken me. Here, I can help you. Plus, I'm sensitive to the shadow warriors. We'll work something out. But that means you are going on alone, Birdie. Well, without your coven, obviously."

Birdie, vivacious, worldly, and always unpredictable, just winked. "I'm the High Priestess of Moonfell, and more than a match for this dusty old shaman. Good luck, Granddaughters. Maggie," she faced her with an imperious stare. "Lead the way."

Thirty-Five

Maverick felt as if he were fighting a tank.

The Wey Wolf was packed with muscle, and had a serious mean streak. *That was fine. So did Maverick*. But he was concerned less about fighting, or even winning. Maverick merely wanted to distract him.

The stands had erupted into chaos, and props to Castor's pack for that. In mere seconds, they had provoked enough shifters to cause a brawl. Now, the arena was filled with howls, shouts, and taunts. The tiers thumped and creaked beneath them, and several shifters had already fallen. The pit was also full, and out of the corner of his eye, Maverick spotted his own pack, who had finally arrived.

All Maverick wanted to do was stop the Wey Wolf from marshalling his pack and guards into some sort of order. Chaos was suiting him right then. And he wanted to keep the Wey Wolf human, too. Taunts worked better that way.

"You're a man out of his time," Maverick said, ducking to miss the Wey Wolf's mighty fist. "You may as well give it up now."

"I would sooner embrace death than yield. I submit to no one." He crunched into Maverick, tackling him to the floor of the wooden tier with a resounding thwack that reverberated through

Maverick's entire body. His head sang with the impact. "I will send you to the Shadow Realm before me."

His archaic phrasing only emphasised the oddity of Maverick's opponent. Blōdbana's language spell might enable them to understand each other, but it also reinforced how different his thinking was to his own. *The Shadow Realm.* The place where his spirit would go after death. Where the shadow warriors had come from. Dim lights shone across the elaborately engraved torcs on the Wey Wolf's arms, and a heavy pendant draped around his neck. They made shadows on his stubbled jaw, and played across his blunt cheekbones, darkening the thick eyebrows that topped his intense stare. For a second, Maverick's head swam as he fought the alpha's power. He carried some of the Shadow Realm with him. He had seen death and conquered it. He didn't fear death now, and that scared Maverick.

The Wey Wolf lifted his fist, ready to pound Maverick's face in, and it served to jolt Maverick back to the present, just as another guard fell from a height and landed next to them. With an almighty, shuddering crack, the wooden floor splintered, and they all tumbled through it. Maverick struck planks and beams, bouncing down until he hit the ground hard enough that it sent the air out of his lungs with a whoosh.

For a second he just lay there, grateful the Wey Wolf also seemed stunned. Maverick rolled to his side, ready to lever himself upright, and then squinted, thinking he was seeing things. Through the support beams, he caught a glimpse of running legs, and realised it was Domino's team racing along the outskirts of the arena towards the labyrinth.

He knew he couldn't let the Wey Wolf spot that, so dragging himself to a standing position, he attacked again.

Domino tried to ignore the overpowering scent of wolves and the fury of howls, snarls, and shouts that resounded in the passages around the arena.

Instead, she focussed on finding the shaman. It didn't take long to find the arena. The noise drew them there, and the corridors that led to it were empty. She was in her wolf again, and Grey was carrying her clothes in his pack. Domino's keen sense of smell picked up the shaman's scent. He was a human, and was distinct from the scent of Barry and another human she presumed must be his brother.

Barry had said the labyrinth was beyond the arena, so they headed straight there, following Blōdbana's scent to the dark doorway at the back of the hall. At the entrance she shifted to her human, easing back so the others could run in after her.

"He's down here," she said, stepping further inside. This corridor was hewn out of rock, smooth in some places, coarse in others. It was broad, though, with a high roof. "I have no idea how much of a labyrinth this is, but I should be able to follow his scent. Other scents are here as well, but not as fresh as his."

Grey looked doubtful. "But can we trust his scent? He lives with a wolfpack. Surely, he's learned to disguise it. Lay false trails, perhaps?"

"Delaying is not helping us," Maggie said, clearly impatient.

"Dying is not helpful, either," Nahum pointed out dryly. "Caution is better."

"And a spell." Birdie was always so quick with her simple answers. "By the Goddess, sure and true, cast a light to lead us through. Labyrinthine halls and twisting paths, bring us to the shaman's past."

In seconds, a bobbing blue light manifested ahead, Domino shifted to her wolf, and they steadily progressed.

Morgana and Odette worked quickly once the others had left, building the fire up in the smithy and gathering all the tokens.

"We need to melt all the tokens down," Morgana said to Odette. "Make that fire as hot as possible."

"You think it will release the spirits?"

"With our help."

Odette's eyes were clouded with confusion, and Morgana knew she was still battling to think clearly because of Blōdbana. "But the spirits who are already in the shifters are not here to release. How do we deal with them?"

Morgana pointed to the clay pots. "The essence of hundreds of them are there. Hair, skin, bones, teeth, and nails, and those are still in the tokens, even though their spirits aren't. We have to send them to their rest. Ultimately, these are just spirits, Odette. They have been misused. Mistreated." She gathered the tokens first, and then started pulling down the pots from the shelves. "When we pulled the spirit from the token to put into the Wayfinder, I saw him." She paused, saddened by the memory. "He was so young, Odette. As young as my son. It broke my heart to see him. He died young, and I don't know if it was an accident or through a fight, but he looked lost." She quickened her pace, anxious to help all of them. "We are assuming they are malevolent, but what if they're just young warriors wanting their place in the world again?"

"You might be right. When I was at the Apollo Pool Hall, I saw the two spirits locked in the shifters. They were so angry, but Blōdbana was there, too." The fire was blazing now, and Odette swung the cauldron over the flames, using the tripod to heat the metal. "He's behind it all, or maybe he masterminded it with the Wey Wolf, but I still don't know why."

"Maybe when we liberate some spirits, we will find out. Right." She held the box of tokens that hadn't yet been bound to another shifter. "Let's melt these first. Can you start an invocation to release them?"

"Of course. Do it." Odette swung the hot cauldron in front of her.

Before she could doubt her own actions, Morgana upended the box into the cauldron. Within moments, the tokens started to melt, bubbling against the hot metal of the cauldron, and Odette started her spell.

In the dark, cave-like room of the smithy, with firelight leaping, Morgana felt as if she were slipping back in time. Two witches gathered over a cauldron. She shook it off and upended the second box, then swung the cauldron over the fire.

Odette's chanting increased, her tone commanding and pleading as she saw fit. Morgana then gathered a handful of pots, tearing off their seals and emptying the contents in, too. Then she threw the door of the chamber open so they could see into the main tomb, allowing Odette's voice to carry through there.

Morgana then pulled out the herbs she had brought with her, intended to cleanse, and added those to the cauldron, using a different spell to weave with Odette's. Power was building, and she felt a loosening, as if things long bound were slowly unravelling.

But she still had to add all of the pots. Quickly.

Harlan was used to halls like this one. He'd become familiar with such places over his years as an occult hunter.

The shadowed passages, sharp turns, and dark hollows gave him a respectable fear, and a healthy head for directions. But normally they were deserted, and he wasn't being pursued by the howls of fighting wolves; plus, these passageways offered several different routes, at the end of which bloomed bright lights. Suddenly, despite his previous self-assurance, he was lost in Blōdbana's ever-increasing magic.

"False trails," Birdie whispered, halting at a junction.

Harlan played his torch down a passageway, but it only illuminated a short distance before the darkness swallowed it. "Illusions?"

"I think so. He's trying to distract us."

"Lead us to our deaths, more like," Grey said, as the scent of decaying flesh ballooned from the passage to the right.

Domino whined and pawed the ground, indicated the direction they should take, but Birdie's bobbing blue light circled lazily. Nahum stepped forward, sword outstretched, ready to follow Domino's directions. "This way leads down and around. Birdie, it would be great to get some confirmation."

She nodded, arms raised. "With sacred steps we journey deep, through memories the ages keep. By this spell our way is shown, the shaman's truth shall now be known. As I say it, reveal to me."

The bobbing blue light flared and spun, sharp rays banishing the darkness, and then it glided onwards as Domino had suggested.

But the further they progressed, the odder things became. Strange whispers carried to them on honeyed breezes, along with snatches of song that had Harlan almost hypnotised until Birdie intervened.

"I'm turned upside down," Maggie whispered, gripping Grey's arm. "No wonder it's called a labyrinth."

"But we're cutting through his illusions," Birdie said, voice ringing as clear as a bell around them, and Harlan's thoughts emerged from the fog.

Suddenly, as they turned a corner, the construction of the walls changed. A squared off entrance with a thick stone lintel and doorposts carved in runes and spirals marked the entrance to a passage made of layers of stone and flint.

Harlan's heart pounded with excitement and recognition. "Holy shit. It's a burial chamber, like you'd find under a barrow." Harlan shone his torch light over the inscription, but knew Nahum could read it just as well in the dark. "What does it say, Nahum?"

"Here lies Blōdbana, guardian of ancient wisdom, speaker to spirits who have passed through the veil. Tread softly stranger, for Wyrd awaits you." He huffed. "Liv will kill me for not being here."

Domino whined again, and then shifted to her human. "What the fuck is going on?"

"We've found Blōdbana's tomb," Birdie said, sending her witch-light bobbing ahead down the passageway, "and I think his tomb's entrance was spelled so that whoever crossed it would wake him. The brothers did it, and they didn't even realise." She placed her hands on the stone entrance. "I feel remnants of it. He might have even prepared it himself before death." Her brow creased with confusion. "Or some type of induced stasis."

"They weren't led astray by the illusions?" Maggie asked.

"There weren't any until he awoke." Birdie gathered herself together. "Are we ready?"

"No! What might we find?" Domino hissed. "This is seriously creepy."

Harlan shrugged. "Grave goods, gifts for his next life, the place where his body was laid to rest. Maybe acolytes. And him, I presume. No point dawdling."

"Did you notice the direction we've travelled?" Grey asked. "I think we're under the arena."

"Like I said," Maggie reminded him. "He's the puppet master. That's why Odette can feel him everywhere. His magic fuels this place. And wolves are at each other's throats up there. Let's get on with it."

Birdie turned to Domino. "Can you find your way out again?"

"Yes, absolutely. Why?"

"Because you need to tell your pack to leave. Things are going to get ugly."

"But what about you?"

"There are enough of us." Birdie gripped her hand. "Go and stay safe."

Nahum led the way, gripping his sword, as Domino shifted to her wolf again and ran back to the arena.

Harlan didn't know what to expect, and was pretty sure his Taser would be useless, though he gripped it anyway. But as the last person crossed the threshold, a stone door snapped down, sealing them inside.

Arlo saw reason return to Hunter's eyes as he crunched against the lowest tier in the pit, and relief rolled through him. But all around him, chaos reigned.

Shifters and guards were fighting in their wolf and human form, and their aggression showed no sign of abating. Storm Moon and the North London Pack were making sure it didn't. They goaded, taunted, and provoked with verbal and physical means. Tommy, in particular, was a whirlwind of madness.

Arlo knew that as the pack second, he had more power than many shifters, and he sought Finn out, intending to bring him to reason. Monroe, Vlad, and Cecile had herded him away from the fighting, trying to protect him from injury, but they were finding it hard. He snapped and snarled at them, trying to attack, thwarted all the time. Finally, Monroe cuffed him, sending him rolling across the ground, and then sat on him, one huge paw planted firmly on Finn's head. They did well to keep their patience with him.

While Hunter indicated he was going to find Hal, Arlo stood over Finn, locking eyes with him. His power swelled as he stared Finn down, and the youngster, unable to move, had to submit to his stare as Arlo tried to find the young shifter within.

But Finn fought him, eyes burning with resentment, and with horror, Arlo realised he couldn't see the Finn he knew in there at all.

Thirty-Six

"Ignore the damn door!" Grey shouted to the others as their exit was sealed, and urged them onwards. "We don't want to get out until we've killed him, anyway."

"But I would like to get out at some point," Maggie snapped, "and not die in the process."

The passageway, however, was short, and the chamber at the end beckoned. Grey caught a glimpse of low, flickering light in a circular room, but that was all, because something picked him up and slammed him against the wall. Whatever it was caught most of the others unaware too, and Grey slid to the floor, every inch of him aching, sure he had broken some ribs.

Nahum's response was startlingly quick. His wings burst out of his shoulders, filling the narrow passage, and almost crushing the others behind him. Birdie, however, had thrown up a protection spell, and it glowed before her like a shield.

Harlan yelled, "Nahum, for fuck's sake, you're going to suffocate me!"

He immediately tucked the wings behind him, but they stayed on display, a majestic vision that was hard to look away from. Birdie, however, was marching resolutely ahead, her strident voice casting a spell in a language Grey didn't understand. Rune shapes fizzed from her fingers as she sent them cascading down the hall ahead of her, and Nahum followed like an avenging angel.

Grey felt horribly out of his depth. He struggled to his feet, pulling Maggie up next to him. "Harlan, mate, you, okay?"

"Winded." He heaved himself to his feet. "Caught by Nahum. The gigantic idiot."

They hurried after the others, Grey anxious to see what lay ahead. "I guess you're used to that? Nahum, I mean."

"Sure. I see them and their wings all the time. He's very useful. Has his own magic."

"He's a fucking killing machine is what he is," Maggie said, bulldozing ahead of him.

But they had only progressed a few more steps when light sizzled around them, bleeding out of the walls, and stabbing at them like bolts of lightning.

"Down!" Grey yelled, pulling Maggie to the floor with him. Harlan fell on top of them.

For several horrible moments, Grey was convinced the entire structure was about to crash down on their heads, or failing that, they'd get fried, but Birdie's voice resonated as if she had a microphone, and everything stopped.

"I have a feeling," Grey said, forcing himself upright again, "that we should have stayed with Morgana and Odette."

"Or taken our chances with the shifters," Harlan said. "With Domino."

Nahum and Birdie were ahead of them, and they were anxious to catch up, but they had barely made any progress when several shapes manifested ahead of them. *Spirit shifters.* A mix of wolves and humans barrelled towards them. Grey blasted them with his shotgun, salt spraying everywhere. Maggie followed suit and the ghosts vanished, leaving the way clear.

"This bastard," Harlan said, "is really pissing me off."

Within only a few steps they found themselves at the threshold of a circular room. It was dimly lit with lanterns filled with candles and smokeless, flickering torches mounted on the wall. In the centre Blōdbana raged, magic crackling out of his hands as if he wielded a storm. He hurled lightning bolts and fire at Birdie, who blocked them and threw them right back at him. They were both caught together in some sort of protective bubble that Nahum prowled around like a caged tiger.

"I can't get close to him," he raged, huge wings expanding and taking up a lot of space in the chamber. "As soon as we walked in, he struck at Birdie, and she locked them inside that *thing*. How the hell do we help her?"

Grey watched, transfixed. It was the first time he had seen Blōdbana after hearing so much about him, and he wasn't what he'd expected. He had thought the shaman would look like Gandalf, but instead his head was shaved, and he was fit and muscular, despite his middle-aged appearance. Plus, he was covered in faded blue tattoos. His bone and feather necklace rattled against his bare chest, and his eyes were startlingly pale. Almost white. As if he knew Grey was staring, he spared him a cunning glance, arm shooting out to cast a spell at him, but Birdie's magic blocked him. She thumped her carved staff into the ground, and it seemed to draw the shaman's magic like a magnet.

"Harlan," Nahum yelled, darting forward and jabbing ineffectually with his sword at the protection bubble. "How can we help?"

"I'm thinking!"

Grey wanted to just shoot the shaman, but was worried the salt would undermine Birdie's magic, rather than help. He certainly couldn't ask her; she was far too preoccupied.

"What do you suggest?" Grey asked, watching Harlan study the room.

"This is his grave. The centre of his power. Stacked slate and stone, just like a burial mound, and it has alcoves filled with offerings and grave goods. Objects he held dear. Things to help his journey to the afterlife." Harlan picked up a curiously carved sculpture and smashed it on the ground. "Let's destroy everything." He picked up a bowl filled with tiny animal bones and threw it on the floor, then ground it to powder under his boot. "This is his power centre, and he didn't think we'd get in. He didn't expect to encounter a kick-ass Birdie either, or he might have opted to meet us somewhere else." He looked at them all. "Get on with it!"

"This," Grey said, using the butt of his shotgun to crush a collection of jars, "feels sacrilegious."

"On the contrary! It feels bloody marvellous," Maggie said, swinging into action.

On the other side of the chamber, Nahum started breaking objects too, using his wings as well as his hands to sweep items to the ground.

They succeeded in distracting Blōdbana. He raged as much at them as Birdie, but despite the scale of their destruction, he didn't seem to be weakening. *Although*, Grey noted, *he seemed scared of Nahum*. He only noticed that because Grey found it hard to take his eyes off the powerful shaman. His oddness and sheer antiquity—plus, his magic—were hypnotic.

Harlan summoned their attention again. "There are seals on the floor. Sigils. Destroy those, too."

"I need more power," Birdie shouted, as Grey was swapping out salt shells for real ones. She danced in the centre as she fought, almost glowing with her own magic, but it was obvious that they were at a stalemate. "The longer this continues, the more he'll wear me down."

Grey blasted the seal, and stone and dust billowed around them. The shaman staggered, a secondary shudder shook the entire place, and dust rained down.

"Yes! More of that!" Birdie shouted, casting some kind of spell that seemed to momentarily freeze Blōdbana in place.

"Birdie, can you use Nahum?" Grey asked as Maggie fired at another seal.

"Use him how?"

The chamber shook again, rattling loose tiny stones. *Shit.*

"Nahum unnerves him. I can see it. Anywhere Nahum is, he tries to scoot out of the way."

"And," Harlan pointed out, "he has Fallen Angel magic. Use it, Birdie."

Nahum nodded. "Yes, use me! How?"

Birdie's hair was wild now, looking like the archetypal witch of old. "I need to get you in my circle, but only if you're happy that I use your power."

"Do it!"

"*No!*" Blōdbana launched wave after wave of attacks at Birdie, a battering ram of howls and spirits of fire, but rather than respond, she strengthened her own protection to fend him off.

There were another half a dozen seals set into the floor around the centre of the room. A long, flat slab with a crack down the middle was dead centre, suggesting that Blōdbana might have been buried beneath it.

"We destroy two seals at the same time," Grey suggested. "That will weaken him even more."

"Three!" Harlan said, holding a large rock in his hands as a weapon, and standing over a seal.

"Good. Three. He will weaken *a lot*. Birdie, can you let Nahum in somehow?"

She nodded, fielding off another attack from Blōdbana by blocking him with her staff. "Yes, but Nahum, do not hesitate."

"Maggie?" Grey glanced over to her to see her standing over another seal.

"I'm ready."

"Now!"

They fired simultaneously, and Harlan smashed the rock like a demented man. Blōdbana staggered back, outraged, but also clearly weakened. Birdie froze him in place, dropped the shield, and Nahum stepped inside. In seconds, the shield was back up, and she gripped Nahum's hand.

All of a sudden, pure, white light exploded out of both of them.

Morgana was surrounded by the remains of hundreds of cracked pots that were shattered on the floor of the smithy. The cauldron bubbled and blazed with an unearthly green light, filled with all the tokens she could find, and the contents of every single pot.

Odette was close to tears. "I feel them all, Morgana. All of their pain and suffering. Their sadness. Their confusion."

"Confused? Why?"

"They don't know why they're here." Their eyes locked over the cauldron. "They didn't all want this. The promise of another life."

"Can you tell how they died?"

"Not yet. But if we liberate them..."

Morgana nodded. So far, the spirits whirled in the cauldron's interior, still bound by the magic that the shaman had used to trap them in the tokens, or their parts that had been sealed in the pots. Tiny essences of a life lived.

She gripped Odette's hands. "Let's begin, then."

They had already decided on their spell. In the end, it was something simple. An exorcism of sorts, the language crafted to suit the age of the spirits. It should—they hoped—work not only on the spirits bound in the tokens, but also for those already bound to shifters.

Together, they chanted, "Shifter spirits young and old, out of time, weak and bold. Beholden to the Wey Wolf, but released at death, trapped by a shaman, denied your rest. Leave us now, the Shadow Realm is your fate, where the Hall of the Ancestors awaits. As we will it, so mote it be."

The cauldron bubbled and the steam swirled, magnifying with every word. By the time they had finished the spell, Morgana could see the spirits rising, their fluid forms whirling in the vortex of air. A strange feeling of peace flowed over them, and the scent of meadow grass and summer was strong.

Odette gripped her fingers. "Again. There are more."

Morgana nodded and redoubled her efforts, the invite now a command. As their intent intensified, thunder cracked, and the cauldron bubbled over.

Maverick was running on sheer anger and adrenalin, but knew that would not sustain him for much longer.

The Wey Wolf was a beast, and Maverick was stretched to the limit fighting him. They were both in their wolf now, but fortunately, he wasn't alone anymore. Danny and Thorne had joined in, and then Tommy and Mads had piled in too, also drawing more shifters into the fight who sought to protect the Wey Wolf.

And then Domino's howl cut through everything. It was haunting and plaintive, an electrifying call to her pack that sent shivers down Maverick's spine. When she repeated it again and again, he knew what it meant. *It was time to withdraw.*

He abandoned the fight, raced into the centre of the pit, and repeated her howl. The call to action was picked up by his pack and Danny, but the other pack members weren't disengaging. Arlo howled his frustration, and he saw Monroe sitting on Finn. Hunter was fighting Hal. Not a full fight, though. A darting, jabbing attack, meant to frustrate but not kill.

Then an enormous crack that sounded like thunder rumbled overhead, and the entire arena shook. Wolves threw back their heads and howled, while some just fell to the ground, twitching.

What the fuck was happening?

Finn had been thrashing under Monroe's hefty paws, but then he fell still, and a murky shape seemed to float out of his body. *The spirit shifter.* As he looked around, he saw that Finn wasn't the only one affected.

Indistinct figures floated out of the affected shifters, shuddering as if to shake off something unpleasant, and were replaced by shimmering wolves that bounded away and vanished into thin air.

The witches had succeeded.

But the Wey Wolf wasn't giving up yet. He pounded into the centre of the pit as if he would plough straight through Maverick, but he shifted before he reached him, instead standing in his human form.

He lifted his head and roared his displeasure, and the stands shook again. "No! This is your Shadow Realm. This is your afterlife. I am your alpha. I command that you fight with me!"

Maverick was just gearing himself up for another fight, when a man darted out from under the tiers carrying a beam of wood. Maverick knew it was the third brother from his appearance and scent. He kept behind the shifters, dodging through them like he'd practised it for hours, and with an almighty swing, smashed the Wey Wolf across the head.

The huge man collapsed, senseless, on the ground, and Maverick pounced, ripping the Wey Wolf's throat out, the blood hot and sweet in his mouth. His remaining guards scattered, and the wolves hunted them down one by one.

All around them confused shifters shook themselves as if waking from a dream. Maverick howled, signalling his pack to leave. Hal was wobbling on his feet, but Hunter supported him, nudging him along. Domino, however, pounded into the pit, and shifted to her human.

"Maverick! Birdie and the others are beneath us."

He shifted, too. "Which others?"

"Harlan, Grey, Maggie, Birdie, and Nahum. They are fighting Blōdbana. Well, I think they are. Birdie sent me to warn you."

"Can you find them again?"

"Of course."

"Then take me there. I'm not leaving without them." Arlo was rounding up the pack, and he shouted over to him. "Arlo, find Morgana and Odette and get them out of here. I'll follow as soon as I can."

"What the absolute fuckery is going on?" Maggie bellowed, almost blinded by the light. "Am I dead?"

"I would hope to all the gods that exist that you would be a damn sight quieter if you were," Harlan complained.

"Shush!" Grey roared. "Birdie and Nahum are—"

But his words died on his lips, and Maggie blinked rapidly, trying to see what was happening. When she could, she realised why Grey's words had failed him.

Birdie and Nahum were surrounded by a blinding white glow. Nahum looked incandescent, his wings a cascade of magnificent, shimmering light. Birdie directed it at Blōdbana like a surgeon wielding a scalpel. It cut through him, shattering his Earthly body, which just seemed to dissolve into nothingness, and freeing his spirit.

For a second, the shocked look on his spirit-face was comical. His eyes and mouth were wide open, his skin as unblemished as the day he was born. And then he just disappeared.

The chamber plunged into darkness, as every single candle and flaming torch extinguished. Well, apart from the rapidly fading white light still emanating from Nahum.

"What the hell did you do?" Maggie asked, almost breathless, as if she'd just run a marathon.

"I used Fallen Angel magic," Birdie said, a slight swagger to her walk. "Time to go. I have no idea how much of his magic sustains this place. I do not wish this to be my burial chamber."

Maggie was only too happy to oblige, and she raced down the passage and then horrified, stopped dead at the sealed door.

"Stand aside," Birdie commanded. She aimed her staff at the door and uttered a spell that blasted it away. "Blimey, Nahum. You've left me juiced up and raring to go."

"Go where?" Grey asked, amused, as he pushed Maggie out the door ahead of him.

"Anywhere." She patted Nahum's cheek affectionately.

"Happy to oblige, ma'am. I, meanwhile, feel like I've had my insides sucked out. And not in a good way."

Harlan, however, paused at the entrance, looking back to the chamber with a wistful expression. "I really want to explore this whole place more. This is...amazing."

"If the place survives," Maggie said, "I promise I'll let you in."

"*You* promise? Why you?"

"I'm the fucking police! My rules."

Maggie didn't want to say *if* they survived. It seemed doom-laden, but she had no idea what they might face back in the arena.

But as they reached it, they only met more darkness, and her heart sank. Birdie sent a dozen witch-lights out, and they illuminated two pairs of wolf eyes racing towards them. *Maverick and Domino.*

"You made it!" Maverick said, shifting to his human. "And Birdie and Nahum are glowing."

"Angel magic," Maggie said dryly. She felt more like her normal self out of the labyrinth. "Are we evacuating?"

"Of course. We found the other brother, and Arlo has gone to find Morgana and Odette."

"And the possessed shifters?" Birdie asked, tone urgent.

"Not spirit-bound, but as to how they are, it remains to be seen."

"Good," Maggie said. "Let's get the fuck out of here."

Thirty-Seven

Hunter had never been so glad to be back in Storm Moon, or to feel like his normal self now that the shadow warrior had been exorcised.

Or to see Domino again. She had kissed him with an enthusiasm that promised much more later, and even now, she watched him as she circulated Storm Moon's bar, checking on the pack, desire burning steadily at the back of her eyes.

After the Wey Wolf's death, they had evacuated the hall quickly, and now most of those involved were at Storm Moon, celebrating success and dealing with their injuries. Even Danny's team and rescued pack members were there. They certainly couldn't return to the Apollo Pool Hall, as it was still a crime scene, and the lure of free alcohol and the chance to party was enough encouragement to lure them south of the river again. Consequently, the bar was packed, conversations flowing as the shifters exchanged news of their possession and how it happened. Most had been far more severely affected than Hunter, and they sat together, still haunted by their experience. That included Hal and Finn, who were being questioned by Arlo, Odette, and Birdie in the corner of the bar. Every now and then Hal shot Hunter a look of confusion mixed with apology. They had come close to killing each other that night.

"You look miles away, mate," Tommy said, leaning forward across the table. They were sitting with Vlad, Monroe, and Morgana, clustered in a booth with drinks in hand. "Are you sure you're all right?"

Hunter forced a laugh. "Not really. My brain feels scrambled. I spent the last two days battling some ancient shadow warrior in my head. If it hadn't been for my amulet, I'd look as bad as Hal. And now I've lost it." He studied Morgana, who seemed even more reserved than usual. "Thank you for the help. I owe you."

"No, you don't. It was my pleasure—my job—to free you. I did it for everyone. Doing something like that is not for an exchange."

Monroe kissed her cheek and pulled her to his side, arm around her shoulders, and she blushed with pleasure. "You're amazing, and very humble."

It was the first obvious sign they were together, that Hunter had seen at least.

"But it was so sad." Her fingers played with her glass. "Especially for Odette, who could feel the spirits far more strongly than I could."

"Well, it was really bloody weird," Tommy said, "seeing them all floating up in that arena. Gave me the shivers."

Vlad snorted. "I don't believe *anything* makes you shiver. You were like a berserker in there!" Vlad looked invigorated by the events, at ease in the corner of the booth.

Tommy grinned. "I like to give Maverick his money's worth. Poor old Maggie is going to have a lot to process after this."

Hunter hadn't really taken notice of much at all as they evacuated, but as his equilibrium returned, he had a lot of questions.

"Do we know how it all started? Or what happened to the ones that were part of the new pack?"

Vlad shook his head. "There's a lot we still don't know. We think most of the guards were killed, but in the confusion of the lights going out and the endless tremors after Blōdbana's death, it's hard to say. I definitely saw a few shifters just leg it down the street once we got out. I have no idea where they went." He sipped his whiskey, studying Hunter over the rim. "Do you think they'll cause problems?"

"No, but some of them are fully the shadow warriors now." He described the mirror challenge. "It was like a horror show. If I'd have lost to my shadow warrior, I'd be gone. Dead. He was strong. Do you think Blōdbana enhanced them somehow?"

"I'm pretty sure," Morgana said, "that having another spirit inside you is just overwhelming anyway, plus he would have been fighting for survival, too. As for how it all started," she said, referring to his earlier question, "the brothers triggered Blōdbana's arrival when they stepped inside his ancient tomb, under the arena. As for why he set up the whole thing, we have no idea. Odette caught glimpses of an ancient battle. We think that the Wey Wolf and his pack were facing certain death, and that Blōdbana saw a way to protect them with magic. To return when it was safer for them. Maybe they were threatened by a king or another huge pack? Maybe a terrible disease was wiping out shifters?" She huffed. "It's frustrating, but hopefully further research will answer some questions. Whether they intended to be asleep—if that's even the right word—for quite so long, though, is something else. I take it you don't know anything from your spirit warrior?"

"No. I caught glimpses of his memories, but they were fleeting."

"But how did the Wey Wolf have his proper body and not look like a walking corpse?" Tommy asked. "Or his guards? Magic?"

"Layers of it," Morgana answered. "I found well-preserved linens that I suspect the bodies were wrapped in, and of course their spirits were preserved, too. When Blōdbana was woken by the brothers, I suspect he set the rest in motion. When Maggie gives us the all-clear, we'll go back to the hall and see if we can get any more insights. She just wants to make sure the place is stable first. And clean up the bodies, of course."

Hunter glanced around the room. "Where is Maggie?"

"At the hall, with her sergeants. Grey and Harlan are still there." She laughed. "Harlan is in his element. Maggie tried to send him away, but he was having none of it. Nahum is with them, too."

"And Maverick?" Hunter realised he hadn't seen his alpha for a while.

"In his flat," Vlad said. "With Danny."

"You are going to let Castor recover first, right?" Maverick asked Danny. "Challenging him now would be cruel."

"I'm not sure I will challenge him," Danny said, with a note of impatience. "The pack is in disarray right now. Maybe keeping the stability of Castor as alpha will be a good thing."

They were seated at Maverick's kitchen counter. A bottle of rum was between them, and both had hefty measures. Maverick wanted peace after all of the chaos. A chance to gather himself after a brutal fight that left every part of him aching. He had cuts, bruises, a sore hip that made him limp, and the simmering rage that came from sustained fighting. Plus, he could still taste the Wey Wolf's blood in his mouth, and although his wolf had been in control, he still lurked close beneath the surface. He hadn't killed another wolf in a very long time, and didn't like how it made him feel. He also felt as if something from the Wey Wolf's brutal hall had slipped under his skin. The challenge, perhaps, which was why he was confronting Danny now.

Maverick took a breath, knowing that Castor's pack and whatever happened next was not his problem. And yet, he felt it was. "He tried to do the right thing, you know. Another alpha might have exacerbated the whole thing."

"I know."

"But this is not my business. I only want you to be fair."

"Plus, better the devil you know, right?" Danny smiled and sipped his drink.

"I know you now. There are worse options. Like Axel."

"That won't happen. In fact, that would be a disaster."

"We're in agreement there."

"I'll see Castor tomorrow, after checking with the witches, of course. He and Barney need to know what happened. I'll go alone, of course. Then I can take them both home." Danny nodded at Maverick's tapestry. "May I?"

"Sure."

Maverick walked over with him to stand in front of it. "I bought it at the auction. I wondered if anything from that had started this whole thing. It seems not. Now, however, I want to know more about our past. The shifter dynasties."

"Dynasties? I hadn't considered we'd have those, but after tonight, I see your point."

"Look at all those safehouses." The gold thread shimmered in the light. "All across Europe. It makes me think our connections were stronger back then. That maybe our society was more sophisticated than we know. I want to know more."

Morgana had documents from the auction that she would share with him, plus his brother was in Italy, and they were on good terms now. Harlan would help him, too, he was sure of it.

"You're already making plans," Danny said, amused.

"Yes, when the dust settles. I can't let it drop now. I've been caught up in too many things lately that have made me question our past, and tonight's events have just added to that. I'll certainly return to investigate that hall. I want to know more about the Wey Wolf."

"I admit, tonight was intriguing, but I like the present too much to go rattling about in the past. It's not my way, or our pack's."

"I don't know. Castor might be more interested than you think."

"He has too many secrets of his own to go hunting for new ones."

Secrets. Maverick hadn't considered their history in those terms. *Were there secrets? Or was it just stuff that had been forgotten?* The word fired his curiosity even more.

Now he wanted to know all of it.

"Maggie," Harlan remonstrated. "I'm not touching a goddamn thing!"

"You better bloody not be, my American friend, or I'll have your bollocks for breakfast."

"You're obsessed with balls. You can leave mine out of it, thank you very much."

They were standing at the threshold of the arena that was now lit with huge arc lights that had been dragged down the corridor all the way from the house. They lit up the passageways, the tomb chamber, the high-carved roof, and the half a dozen police officers and a SOCO team who scurried below it, but fortunately, the sprawl of dead bodies was hidden from view in the centre of the pit. Only Blōdbana's tomb, Harlan's favourite part of the entire complex, was untouched—for now.

"At least," Harlan observed, hoping another sudden shudder wouldn't manifest, "there's no dust coming from the roof anymore."

"We'll get a specialist in here tomorrow. Make sure it is safe, especially Blōdbana's burial site, and then the real investigation can begin. We need to know how this started. Make sure it's not connected to anything else. Barry says not, but I don't trust him or his brothers. Maybe Stan can get more sense out of them."

Stan was in the house with another constable interviewing the brothers to get a timeline of events and work out the logistics. The shifters who had been trapped in the hall could tell them some of it, but the brothers would know about the delivery of food, recruitment, and the token network.

"I especially don't like," Maggie continued, "the fact that all of this happened under my very nose! It's infuriating."

"You can't have eyes everywhere all at once. Plus, you only have a team of three."

"What about The Retreat?" she asked, turning and leading them back up the corridor to the entrance. "They should have eyes on everything, and no one noticed a bloody thing! I shall be speaking to Jackson about this tomorrow."

Poor Jackson. He was the Deputy Head of the Paranormal Division, based under Hyde Park in the winding passages of The Retreat. He was good friends with Maggie, and technically her superior, not that such ceremony would stop her from bawling him out.

"They were careful, Maggie. They went after lone shifters first, and then sneakily set about the rest. It's lucky Storm Moon was across the river, or the club and the pack would have been caught up in it much sooner. You will let me back in here in a couple of days, right? With Liv? She'd love this."

"Yes, fine. Then I guess we need to decide if we make a public announcement. About the site, of course, not the fucking shaman and his bloody great Wey Wolf. I think we should keep it under wraps for as long as possible. *Shit.* I need some fresh air."

They fell into silence as they trudged up the final passageway, through the house, and out onto the road. Several unmarked police cars and vans were lined up along the street, and Grey was in one of them with Irving, the other DS in Maggie's team, going through the photos they had taken of shifters that evening. Maggie would not be able to keep all of this a secret as long as she wanted to. Neighbours were nosy, and asked a lot of questions.

Maggie leaned against the back of a plain black van, looking as exhausted as Harlan felt, and he wondered whether he should just go home. He was shattered, and the fresh air wasn't waking him up. He felt like he could sleep for a week. And then a large black Mercedes sedan pulled past the van and parked across the street.

Maggie groaned. "That better not be the damn higher-ups. I can do without that shit right now."

A woman with long, ebony hair and a slender figure crossed the road. She was dressed entirely in black. A skirt reaching her mid-thigh revealed shapely legs, paired with a leather jacket and knee-length leather boots that had Harlan's mouth falling open. He closed it quickly and straightened up.

"Maggie Milne," she said by way of a greeting. The woman held her hand out, and Maggie warily shook it. "I am Calixta Darkholme, the Raven Queen. I was in the area when I saw that you had some trouble. I thought I would take the opportunity to introduce myself."

Harlan stuck his hand out, recovering quicker than Maggie. "Harlan Beckett. Collector for The Orphic Guild. Pleasure to meet you."

"Did you say *Raven Queen*?" Maggie asked, voice shrewish.

"I did. I'm new to London, but won't be staying long. Business in Europe keeps me busy. However, having often heard about you, I couldn't resist this opportunity to meet you."

"Are you spying on me?"

"Of course not." Calixta looked amused. "I fly at night, and noticed you were having some shifter issues. I didn't interfere, of course. Wolf-shifter business is not ours. Neither would you appreciate it. However, here I am, saying hello. Just in case I'm back again."

Calixta was taking very little notice of Harlan, but nevertheless he cleared his throat, repeating Maggie's question. "Raven Queen? How does that work?"

"Our clans are undergoing a restructuring period. I am the rightful leader of the bird clans."

Harlan thrust his business card at her. "I deal with all manner of occult interests. Please keep my card."

"Of course." She slid it into her pocket. "But I doubt I'll need it. As I said, I'm leaving London, but just wanted to meet you. Who knows. I might be back."

With another enigmatic smile, she walked away. Maggie and Harlan watched as she slid back into the passenger seat and the car drove away, leaving them both gobsmacked.

Maggie just glared at Harlan. "Don't say a bloody word."

Harlan sniggered. Another player was in town. A very hot one. *Excellent.*

Thank you for reading *Wolfshot*. Please make an author happy and leave a review here.

There will be more Storm Moon Shifters to come, but the next book I'll write will be the second book in the Moonfell Witches series.

Newsletter

If you enjoyed this book and would like to read more of my stories, please visit my website at tjgreenauthor.com. You will get two free short stories, *Excalibur Rises* and *Jack's Encounter,* and will also receive free character sheets for all of the main White Haven witches.

By staying on my mailing list, you'll receive free excerpts of my new books, as well as short stories, news of giveaways, and a chance to join my launch team. I'll also be sharing information about other books in this genre you might enjoy.

Ream

I have started my own subscription service called Happenstance Book Club. I know what you're thinking! What is Ream? It's a bit like Patreon, which you may be more familiar with, and it allows you to support me and read my books before anyone else.

There is a monthly fee for this, and a few different tiers, so you can choose what tier suits you best. All tiers come with plenty of other bonuses, including merchandise, but the one thing common to all is that you can read my latest books while I'm writing them, in rough draft form. I will post a few chapters each week, and you can read them at your leisure, as well as comment in them. You can also choose to be a follower for free.

You can discuss my books, chat about spoilers, and be part of a community on Ream. I will also post polls, character art, rituals and spells, share the background to the myths and legends in my books, and some of my earlier books are available to read there for f ree.

Interested? Head to:
https://reamstories.com/happenstancebookclub

Happenstance Book Shop

I also now have a fabulous online shop called Happenstance Books and Merch, where you can buy eBooks, audiobooks, hardbacks, and paperbacks, many bundled up at great prices, as well as fabulous merchandise. I know that you'll love it! Check it out here: https://happenstancebookshop.com/

Substack

I'm also on Substack, and my page is called Where the Witches Gather. I'd love to see you there. Substack has a wonderful community of witchy writing and seasonal celebrations. You can find me here: https://wherethewitchesgather.substack.com/

YouTube

If you love audiobooks, you can listen to mine for free on YouTube, as I have uploaded all of my audiobooks there. Please subscribe if you do. Thank you. https://www.youtube.com/@tjgreenauthor

Read on for a list of my other books.

Author's Note

Thank you for reading *Wolfshot*. I really love the Storm Moon characters and setting, and am really looking forward to diving further into shifter myths and legends, and the whole background to shifter society. I don't know where it will take me, but I'm sure it will be fun. I couldn't resist involving Nahum either.

The shifter society is large, so it felt natural to include a bird-shifter tease at the end. I love the idea of a royal clan, hence the Raven Queen. If you've read my Rise of the King series, you'll know that Brenna is a bird-shifter, so that idea has its roots there.

I was intending to keep the Moonfell witches more separate, but they're so entwined with the shifters, it just feels natural to keep their stories together. I adore Moonfell, and can't wait to write the next book in their series. That's next on my writing list. There's something about diving into the past that sets my creative juices flowing. Hopefully there will be many more books in both of these series.

Future plans include writing the fourteenth book in the White Haven Witches series, and I'm still ruminating on a Hunters book, but no firm decisions made as to that yet.

If you love merch, you will be pleased to know that I have added some Storm Moon and Moonfell merch to my shop, Happenstance Books and Merch.

Thanks again to Fiona Jayde Media for my awesome cover, and thanks to Kyla Stein at Missed Period Editing for applying your fabulous editing skills.

Thanks also to my beta readers—Terri and my mother. I'm glad you enjoyed it; your feedback, as always, is very helpful! Thanks also to Jase, my fabulously helpful other half. You do so much to support me, and I am immensely grateful for you.

Finally, thank you to my launch team, who give valuable feedback on typos and are happy to review upon release. It's lovely to hear from them—you know who you are! You're amazing! I also love hearing from all of my readers, so I welcome you to get in touch using tjgreenauthor@tjgreenauthor.com email.

I encourage you to follow my Facebook page, T J Green. I post there reasonably frequently. In addition, I have a Facebook group called TJ's Inner Circle. It's a fab little group where I run giveaways and post teasers, so come and join us.

About the Author

I was born in England, in the Black Country, but moved to New Zealand in 2006. I lived near Wellington with my partner, Jase, and my cats, Sacha and Leia. However, in April 2022 we moved again! Yes, I like making my life complicated... I'm now living in the Algarve in Portugal, and loving the fabulous weather and people. When I'm not busy writing I read lots, indulge in gardening and shopping, and I love yoga.

Confession time! I'm a Star Trek geek—old and new—and love urban fantasy and detective shows. Secret passion—Columbo! Favourite Star Trek film is the *Wrath of Khan*, the original! Other top films—*Predator*, the original, and *Aliens*.

In a previous life I was a singer in a band, and used to do some acting with a theatre company. For more on me, check out a couple of my blog posts. I'm an old grunge queen, so you can read about my love of that on my blog: https://tjgreenauthor.com/about-a-girl-and-what-chris-cornell-means-to-me/. For more random news, read: https://tjgreenauthor.com/read-self-publi shed-blog-tour-things-you-probably-dont-know-about-me/

Why magic and mystery?

I've always loved the weird, the wonderful, and the inexplicable. Favourite stories are those of magic and mystery, set on the edges of the known, particularly tales of folklore, faerie, and legend—all the narratives that try to explain our reality.

The King Arthur stories are fascinating because they sit between reality and myth. They encompass real life concerns, but also cross boundaries with the world of faerie—or the Other, as I call it. There are green knights, witches, wizards, and dragons, and that's what I find particularly fascinating. They're stories that have intrigued people for generations, and like many others, I'm adding my own interpretation.

I love witches and magic, hence my second series set in beautiful Cornwall. There are witches, missing grimoires, supernatural threats, and ghosts, and as the series progresses, weirder stuff happens. The first spinoff, White Haven Hunters, allows me to indulge my love of alchemy, as well as other myths and legends. Think Indiana Jones meets Supernatural!

Have a poke around in my blog posts, and you'll find all sorts of posts about my other series and my characters.

If you'd like to follow me on social media, you'll find me here:

- facebook.com/tjgreenauthor/
- pinterest.pt/tjgreenauthor/
- tiktok.com/@tjgreenauthor
- youtube.com/@tjgreenauthor
- goodreads.com/author/show/15099365.T_J_Green
- instagram.com/tjgreenauthor/
- bookbub.com/authors/tj-green
- https://reamstories.com/happenstancebookclub

Other Books by T J Green

Rise of the King Series
A Young Adult series about a teen called Tom who's summoned to wake King Arthur. It's a fun adventure about King Arthur in the Otherworld.
Call of the King #1
The Silver Tower #2
The Cursed Sword #3

White Haven Witches Series
Witches, secrets, myth and folklore, set on the Cornish coast.
Buried Magic #1
Magic Unbound #2
Magic Unleashed #3
All Hallows' Magic #4
Undying Magic #5
Crossroads Magic #6
Crown of Magic #7
Vengeful Magic #8
Chaos Magic #9

Stormcrossed Magic #10
Wyrd Magic #11
Midwinter Magic #12
Sacred Magic #13

White Haven Hunters

The action-packed spin-off featuring Shadow and the Nephilim.

Spirit of the Fallen #1
Shadow's Edge #2
Dark Star #3
Hunter's Dawn #4
Midnight Fire #5
Immortal Dusk #6
Brotherhood of the Fallen #7

Storm Moon Shifters

Paranormal Mysteries set around the wolf shifter pack, Storm Moon.

Storm Moon Rising #1
Dark Heart #2
Wolfshot #3

Moonfell Witches

This series features the mysterious and magical witches who live in Moonfell, the sprawling Gothic mansion in London. They first appeared in Storm Moon Rising, Storm Moon Shifters Book 1, and then in Immortal Dusk, White Haven Hunters Book 6, and features characters from both series. However, this series can be read as a standalone.

If you love witches and magic, you will love the Moonfell Witches.

The First Yule: Novella

Triple Moon: Honey Gold and Wild

Printed in Great Britain
by Amazon